Someone To Come Home To

Zanne Sweeney

ISBN: 0692246584
ISBN-13: 9780692246580

DEDICATION

After reading this book you will understand why I gratefully dedicate this romantic adventure to Firefighters and Smoke Jumpers.

To my family, thank you for understanding when I'm 'in the zone'! I will return to Wife/Mom mode soon! No, really I will :) just let me finish this chapter – lol.

To Mom and Lori, I very much appreciate everything you have done and continue to do to help me make my dream come true. Hugs!

To my Ladies of The Lake, I love that we read the 'spicy' parts out loud, even though I pretend I don't. Cheers!

To my friends who continue to support and encourage me, I love you guys, thank you!

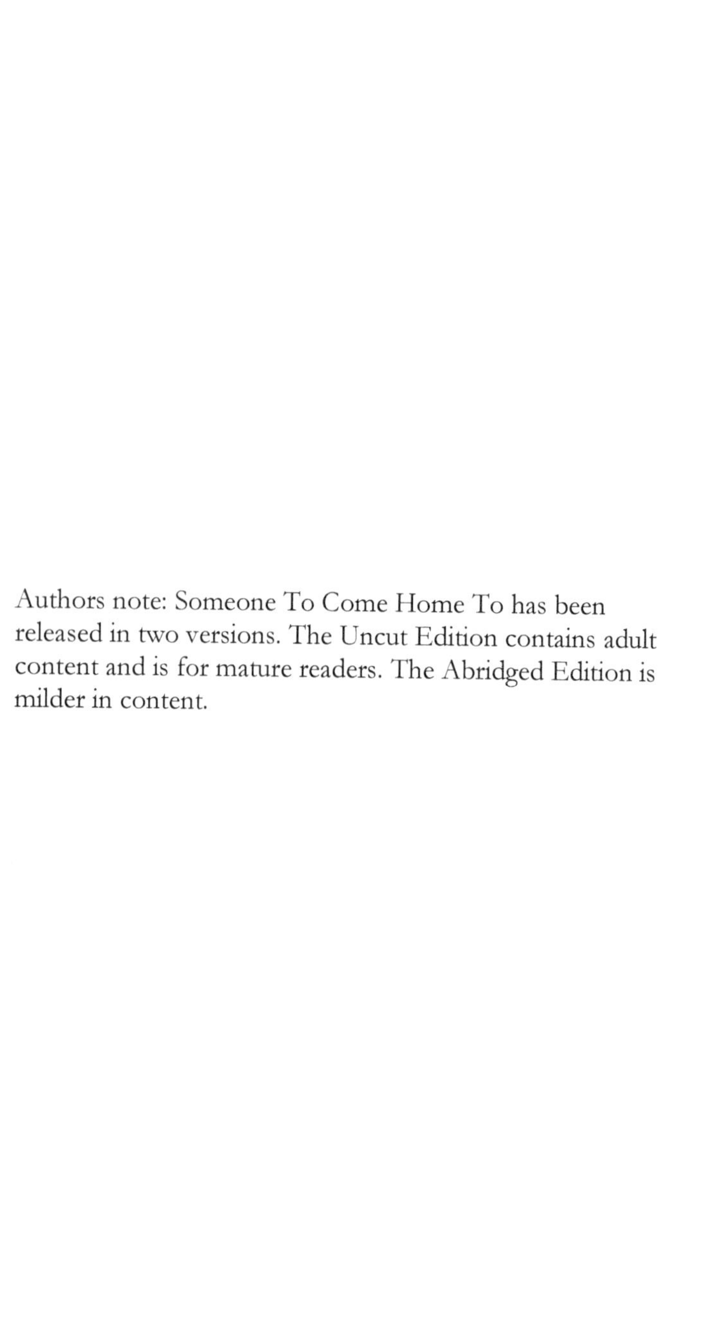

Authors note: Someone To Come Home To has been released in two versions. The Uncut Edition contains adult content and is for mature readers. The Abridged Edition is milder in content.

ACKNOWLEDGMENTS

Heather Sowalla

Editor

Windy Hills Editing Services

Nada Orlic

Book Cover

Prologue

Karen Sue Murphy quietly watched out the passenger side window, as she got closer to her house and the shambles of her marriage. Her backyard neighbor, who she worked with at Madison Junior School, had kindly picked her up from the service station where Karen Sue had dropped her car after work. Her neighbor had kept up a steady stream of conversation throughout the ride that Karen Sue tried to follow, but the closer they got to home the more depressed she became. She shut her eyes trying to will away the sadness that threatened to overwhelm her. Her life was seriously a mess.

She loved her home and she was doing everything in her power to hold on to it. Her wonderful parents had given it to her, free and clear, as a wedding gift. They were currently enjoying their golden years in an over 50 community in Florida. With no snow to shovel and golf almost every day her parents were blissfully happy. They weren't fully retired either. Karen Sue's dad was a retired detective and he continued to work on a part-time basis as a corporate consultant. Karen Sue's mom worked three days a week in the schools as a reading specialist.

Receiving the house had been a wonderful surprise for her and her husband Ray. It had also been a little unnerving knowing she wasn't going to be seeing her parents on a daily basis, but back then she had Ray. Their generosity had alleviated the stress of buying a home of their own for the two newlyweds who were on a shoe - string budget.

When they had first married, Ray had always helped around the home. It had been their home regardless of who's name was on the deed, or in this case not on it. They'd done everything together, raking in the fall, weeding in the summer. After finishing the yard work they would kick back on their patio, drinking cold beers, enjoying the satisfied feeling that comes with seeing the results of a day's hard work.

Now the house was in bad need of repair, the lawn was a mess and the patio, where they had once enjoyed a multitude of warm evenings on, was overgrown with weeds.

Two years ago, out of the blue, Ray had asked her to add his name to the houses ownership deed. Karen Sue had been surprised with his request. It wasn't like she lorded the sole ownership over his head or anything. She told him no and gently explained that it was the one stipulation her parents had demanded of her when they had transferred the deed into her name. Her parents loved Ray but the house was to remain in her name. Karen Sue didn't understand why it would matter to Ray; however it obviously had, because that had been the precursor to the beginning of the end for them as a happy couple.

A few months later he suggested, rather adamantly, that they needed to upgrade the house so it would maintain its market value. Ray was a financial whiz so Karen Sue, knowing this was his area of expertise, agreed. He convinced her the only way to foot the bill for all the needed repairs was to take out a mortgage and so Karen Sue did. The bank only gave her half the money Ray had wanted. Karen Sue however was silently relieved that their house was not fully mortgaged.

Ray had promised to be in charge of all the upgrades; a new roof, new air-conditioning unit, add a front porch, upgrade the bathroom, and the kitchen, but no improvements were ever made. He also promised he would take care of repaying the new mortgage that was in Karen Sue's name. She remembered how trusting, how naive she'd been. At first she thought Ray had been too busy at work and had not had time to arrange for the work to be done. It wasn't until three months later when Karen Sue saw the unpaid mortgage bills hidden under a pile of papers on Ray's desk that she realized there was something wrong.

Karen Sue and Ray's had been high school sweethearts and better still, best friends. He had been her first kiss, her first love, and her first sexual anything. They continued their fairy tale romance through college and were married the day after they graduated. She had a degree in art education and a minor in sociology. Ray graduated with honors with a dual degree in economics and the new field of Computer Science.

Ray was a true geek when it came to computers. Karen Sue had been so proud and amazed at the ingenious and creative ways he used his knowledge with computers to keep his accounting firm vanguard. The only reason Ray was never geek-ti-fide in his classmate's eyes was that he was also a fantastic baseball player. Ray used to joke that baseball was a game of numbers and he loved numbers so the game fit him. Karen Sue had been so head over heels for her brilliant, baseball playing man she just hung on for the ride enjoying every second of it.

They were a popular couple especially in college. Everyone wanted to be friends with the computer genius that could throw a 96-mile an hour fastball. Karen Sue was not as outgoing as Ray, but popular in her own unassuming way. She was considered to be pretty with a cute All-American demeanor. She had a great figure, although she never flaunted it like the other girls with tops that were to tight or skimpy skirts. Karen Sue was shy, but Ray had always kept her in the center of everything he was involved with, so no one ever knew. At parties she was often the friend holding the hair back for a barfing Barbie, as she so aptly named them. She tutored athletes, helping them to maintain their grades keeping them eligible to play their sport. She was renowned for hosting the best parties, complete with fun games that she'd make up or revamp from current TV shows. Once she had hosted a 'Survivor' party that had the entire baseball team running around campus in grass skirts. Everything Karen Sue was happy doing all that she did as long as she wasn't the center of attention.

Along with spending much of her time with her geeky, sexy boyfriend, tutoring and hosting parties Karen Sue still found time for her true passion, which was art, especially sketching. She discovered that she could make extra cash with her God given talent. She would sit for hours at street fairs, sketching people's faces sometimes paid up to $50.00 a sketch. Ray would often find her long after his game had ended immersed in one of her drawings.

After they had married life seemed perfect, Karen Sue had a job teaching art in the local school district and Ray had opened his own accounting firm that used on line tax returns for simple files. Life was good. Weeks were busy and weekends were fun, with couple time, dinner with friends, working on the house, doing laundry, food shopping, and of course relaxing in front of the TV.

Then everything started to change. It began with the missing second mortgage money, and then an extremely large credit card cash withdrawal that Ray claimed was a mistake, and finally the monthly bills that began to accumulate. Ray always had excuses though, and of course Karen Sue believed every word he said.

Socially, the Saturday night dinner dates with friends had stopped. Karen Sue couldn't help but notice that Ray had begun to spend more time at work. It unnerved her that he was always making sketchy phone calls at odd hours, claiming they were work related. Not only did he not contribute to the daily chores around the house, but his financial contributions to their household had declined as well. Things were falling apart but the worst had been how Ray changed. He was moody and unapproachable, often closing her out of their bedroom or staying out late at night with no explanation of where he had been. Her first thought was that he had a mistress, but that didn't explain the money problems. Karen Sue begged him to let her in, to tell her what was wrong, but he firmly pushed her further and further away.

After a good six months of downhill, which consisted of no money ever being deposited in their joint account, no bills being paid, the fact that they rarely even spoke anymore except to argue, and of course they had had no physical contact of any kind, Karen Sue decided she needed to confide in someone, and that someone was her dad, the ex-detective.

It took Gary Bruce, Karen's father only two days to discover what was causing his son-in-law of two years to act the way he was. After calling up north to some of his still active police brothers, Gary Bruce was told that his son-in-law was gambling. It was even rumored that he was in financial trouble with the mob, but that couldn't be confirmed. Gary Bruce sadly told his daughter what he had uncovered.

Armed with this information Karen Sue confronted Ray and after a verbal knock down drag out of a fight he finally confessed that he had a gambling problem and that his company had gone belly-up. He regretfully informed her that he owed a ton of money everywhere. The money she had obtained from mortgaging their home had been squandered. He explained that he had had 'a sure thing' that would have gotten him out of debt, but he'd lost it all, every penny and because of that he was in even more trouble. He then asked her to sell the house to help him start to pay back some of the debt he had acquired. The amount he owed was so mindboggling that Karen Sue realized that selling the house wouldn't begin to dig him out.

Six months ago he had given her two thousand dollars in cash to put towards bills. She remembered how he had been so excited to give her the money, like her old Ray would have been. He surprised her with another thousand the next month and then two thousand more the next month. Karen Sue didn't question his windfall and she gladly accepted the money putting it towards the endless pile of bills. Unfortunately the past three months he had not given her any more money and his mood had become eerily pensive.

Karen Sue begged him to go to rehab but he refused. He told her he needed to square his debt. He asked her to go live with her parents, while he resolved this mess and she, of course, adamantly refused. Ray then confided in her that he was working on something big, something that would erase all his debt, but it had finally become too much for her to bear. Karen Sue tried to get Ray to tell her what was going on but he politely and cryptically told her the less she knew the better. All he said was 'he was working on a way out.'

"Out from what?" She had asked frustrated.

As her young life imploded around her Karen Sue took control of what she could. She had been lied to too many times. The gambling addiction had consumed her sweet Ray, leaving behind a sad shell of the charismatic man she had fallen in love with in high school.

The final blow to Karen Sue's façade of resilience had been when she filed for divorce and Ray refused to contest it. He said it was for the best, and that hurt more than Karen Sue could ever imagine. They became captives in their home in an ugly stalemate. Ray's lawyers had told him not to leave the house until the divorce was settled. Karen Sue was told she needed to stay there as well.

So after 4 years of marriage, two of them great, two of them awful, Karen Sue, at the tender age of twenty-six, was fighting off debt collectors and awaiting for her divorce to finalize, to the only man she had ever cared about.

Chapter 1

With a fake smile and a hopefully cheery voice Karen Sue thanked her neighbor for the ride home. She opened the rickety gate that separated their backyards and the familiar squeak of the rusty hinges brought forth bittersweet memories.

Years ago she and her best friend Katrina had practically worn the hinges off that white, little gate as they ran from one house to the other seeking better snacks or newer toys. The memories still stung even though an entire decade had passed. Katrina and her family had moved to Ohio, leaving Karen Sue to bravely face her freshman year in high school without her best friend of 13 years.

Not too long ago Karen Sue had been filled with pride and contentment when she came home to her cozy house. Now as she crossed her weed choked lawn, a small frown tended her lips as she noted that the grass, well dandelions now, needed to be cut again.

Wearily she walked down her short driveway towards the front of her house to get the mail. She sighed somberly knowing there would be bills with 'Urgent' red stamps marring the white envelopes. As much as she had been denying it she knew she was going to have to sell her beloved home to dig out from the havoc Ray had created to her once good credit. She knew she could get a good price for her house that would pay off her bills and leave her enough money to restart, if…if Rays lawyers didn't try to claim any of it.

Three young boys that Karen Sue taught at school peddled past her driveway on their bikes, waving shyly to their beautiful art teacher. Karen Sue smiled and waved back as she juggled her computer case and purse to free a hand. A large black sedan parked in front of her house with the motor running drew her attention from the boys. She could see someone sitting in the driver's seat and he appeared to be talking on a cell. Her eyes caught his when he glanced up to his rearview mirror. Karen Sue figured the man was being responsible and had pulled over to talk on the phone, she wished more people did that.

She gathered the mail from the mailbox that she had painted flowers on just three years early, when life was good. Now when she opened the brightly painted box she was stung with how drastically her life had changed. Turning back she walked up the driveway and let herself into the house through the side kitchen door. Placing the mail down on the dull Formica counter without looking at it, she settled her computer bag and oversized purse on the nearby kitchen table. Coming home was never a good thing anymore. Karen Sue pulled her arms out of her lightweight coat and hung it on the wooden hook behind the door; it was then that she heard voices, angry voices coming from the adjoining room.

Curious and slightly alarmed she headed towards the swinging door that separated the kitchen and living room. She heard Ray say. "Leave her out of this, she doesn't know anything."

As she extended her arms to push open the door she heard three sounds, like wet snowballs hitting a wall, followed by an anguished low grunt. Without warning the door slammed back inwards forcing Karen Sue's arms back against her body. Ray fell through the swinging door his back colliding heavily with her chest. The force that had propelled Ray through the door caused them to both to keel over backwards. She landed painfully on the kitchen floor with Ray sprawled on top of her. Their prone bodies acting as a door stop holding the swinging door wide open. The jarring Karen Sue's body took knocked the breath from her and she fought for air. The moment became surreal as Karen Sue noticed many things at once.

Two men were in her living room; a smaller man in a dark business suit holding a gun, and standing next to him was a larger man in dress pants, a collared shirt with gold chains surrounding his beefy neck. It was clear that the smaller man had just fired the gun, although she hadn't seen it. Realizing that a man she didn't know, held a gun in her living room and the gun had been fired, Karen Sue vainly struggled to push up on her elbows hoping Ray would move. Gasping for breath she peered over Ray's shoulder wondering why he wasn't getting up. It was then she noticed Ray's shirt was blooming with crimson wet circles, two in his chest and one in his shoulder.

Karen Sue tried to maneuver out from underneath his heavyweight but the floor was slippery. Rivers of blood seeping onto her body ran off her pooling onto the floor below them. A copper smell permeated her senses as she tried to suck in air. Her face was wet and she panicked realizing it was Ray's blood that was splattered on her skin and soaking her clothes.

Ray was not moving, at all, his deadweight hampering her ability to regain her lost breath. She heard the smaller man say, 'shit" as he looked at her. His head tilted to one side, as if he was in thought. Karen Sue watched him hand the gun to the larger man who was also looking at her. Her mind was slush, she couldn't think, her survival instinct was urging her to get out from underneath Ray and run. She frantically pushed against the kitchen floor but the blood coating the floor had her hands slipping frantically, like Fred Flintstone's feet when he started his car. The front door burst open, momentarily halting Karen Sue's attempts to escape. A large, muscle-bound younger man dressed in a black tee shirt and dress pants appeared. His eyes darted over to Karen Sue and Ray, surveying the scene he had walked in on.

He then looked to the man in the suit and said; "Boss, we gotta go, scanner says cops are on their way." Karen Sue was silently praying, 'Go, please, go.'

"How the fuck are they on their way?" The smarmy thin man questioned.

"Don't know but I think a neighbor called in a suspicious vehicle."

Karen Sue was listening to this conversation as if she was watching a TV show that she was staring in. Her shocked, small body clenched tightly to Ray as if he could somehow help her. A gooey blob of wetness slid down her cheek jolting Karen Sue back into reality. Ray had been shot and he was currently pinning her down and three men, one wielding a gun were in her living room getting ready to do God knows what. Bile caught in her throat as she swiped what she knew was a bloody piece of her husband from her face causing her to whimper in distress.

The older man took the gun back from the gold- chained gorilla like man and handed it to the new guy. “Kill her,” he said. He then turned and walked out the front door. The gorilla remained behind guarding her front door. Karen Sue knew she was the ‘her’ that was about to be killed.

Try as she might she couldn’t lift Ray off of her and the blood had caused the linoleum underneath them to become so slippery she couldn’t even scoot backwards. She could hear sirens in the distance, but she knew there was no way they would get to her in time. Her mind slipped into a hyper focused state and her body trembled with terror. Her random thoughts were crazed as she thought about the many times she had watched horror movies and had laughed at the victims who had stood shocked and unmoving just before they were slaughtered. The muscle-bound man approached her; his large frame blocked her sight from the gorilla standing at the door.

She feebly lifted one arm palms out stopping gesture and garbled out, a lame “please, don’t...” The killer raised the gun, aiming it at her and Ray. She noticed his hands were not shaking in the least and she knew that only a monster could kill someone without emotion. She had a moment of bravado and decided if this bastard was going to kill her then she was going to be looking him in the face when he did it. She saw his mouth move without speaking and she thought he mouthed the words. “Play dead,” then he squeezed the trigger. Her last conscious thought was that the bullets silently firing from this gun sounded like the blow darts the natives would use in the old Tarzan movies. Karen Sue’s head hit the floor with a hard thump, her arm slipped limply to the blood coated linoleum as her eyes rolled up into her head. A welcoming blackness engulfed her.

Chapter 2 Colt

Colt AKA Petey caught movement in the rearview mirror as he sat in the car pretending to talk on his cell. His body tightened apprehensively. A young woman had just walked down the driveway and was pulling mail from the box. He had seen her picture before and recognized her as the pretty little spouse of the guy inside, Ray, whom his boss was currently paying a visit too. Petey was outside because he was the lookout, but he was thrown because he had been watching for her car. Mr. Pallone and Big Tony and been in the house longer than he expected, so he knew whatever was happening inside was not good. Colt's brain ran through his options as he watched the young woman wave to three young boys on their bikes, who were showing off for her by riding without their hands on their handlebars.

Colt, AKA Petey was also undercover DEA. He'd been under for two years now, slowly climbing his way up the trusted list of Mr. Vincent Pallone's crime family. It was a huge syndicate with major drug connections. They also had a stronghold on all gambling operations in the area and they dabbled in human trafficking. Colt was a few months away from having enough inside information to put the crime boss away for a long time and he could not afford any slipups now. He cursed himself that he had not been prepared for the wife to come home by any other means than her car.

'Petey' had done some heavy-handed things to prove himself to Pallone, and he countered his guilt by reminding himself that the men he had messed up were criminals themselves. Colts breath hitched as he watched the young woman head towards her house and realized, without a shadow of doubt that shit was about to hit the fan if he didn't do something quickly. He didn't want an innocent person to get hurt and he knew from reading the wiretap summaries that this woman was a true innocent. Colt also knew his partners were not going to be able to intervene fast enough. They were currently sitting in a van two blocks away, keeping their fingers crossed as they listened in to whatever was going down inside the house. Today they had hoped that Pallone would incriminate himself and that the man Ray, who's house they had wire tapped without his knowledge, but with a court order, would agree to testify against him and go into witness protection. Unfortunately Ray's unsuspecting spouse was getting ready to walk in on whatever conversation was taking place and that would put her on Pallone's radar.

The story was that Ray had pulled some real ingenious computer crap on Pallone. The man knew some heavy secrets and was holding something significantly big over Pallone. Gino, one of Pallone's lackeys, who was a blabbermouth once he started drinking, told Petey that this guy Ray had to have balls the size of coconuts. Gino had heard that Ray was blackmailing Pallone to bargain out from a hefty debt he had incurred. Gino told Petey that Pallone, who would normally just kill a man for making threats like that, couldn't just whack the guy because there was evidently a large sum of money missing from Pallone's books and this guy Ray, who was a computer genius, had hidden the money online in an account. He was using that to barter for his and his wife's life, plus free him from his debt to Pallone.

Colt knew he had to move fast. He tapped the preloaded number on the burner cell he had hidden in his ankle and allowed it to ring once before he hung up. He then called 9-1-1 and anonymously reported a domestic disturbance at the address they were at. Colt bolted from the car and ran his ass off towards the house, hoping to interfere quick enough to save the oblivious wife from becoming a victim.

As Colt burst through the front door his stomach pitched as he saw the young woman pinned under a lifeless bloody man. She wasn't crying or screaming and Colt recognized she was in shock. Little whimpers were coming from her throat and for some strange reason he wished he could comfort her. Petey focused on his boss, quickly informing the two men they needed to leave, that the police were coming. Pallone's face turned ugly, his brows furrowed and then he calmly took the gun that Big Tony was holding and thrust it into his hands telling him to kill her, nodding at Karen Sue.

Colt knew there was no way he could kill an innocent person, but if he didn't do something Big Tony would just finish her off and there was no way he could allow that to happen. He couldn't just take Tony out because that would blow his cover and his chance to bring down Pallone. Colt approached the blond haired woman purposely positioning his own large body to block her from Tony's line of sight. He made sure he was close enough and he prayed she would read his lips. Then he pumped two bullets into the already dead man's shoulder watching as the new blood spray pelted the young woman's pale face. He watched her head fall back hard against the floor and her arms go limp. She passed out and Colt thanked God because now it looked like had killed her.

Petey turned quickly from the two seemingly lifeless bodies and hustled Big Tony out of the house and down the steps to the still idling car. As their car turned the corner at the end of the block, Colt saw flashing lights turn onto the street behind them. He knew that the guy Ray was history and that he had just saved the woman's life. He was confident his aim had been true and he had only shot the dead man. Colt breathed easier knowing his team would be on the scene promptly, suppressing any news of the incident and whisking the girl away so Pallone would remain unsuspecting. Fact was, Colt thought, this could help him move into that trusted circle that Pallone surrounded himself with.

Chapter 3 Karen Sue

"I think this is Gary Bruce's daughter," someone whispered behind her. Karen Sue tried to open her eyes but only one would cooperate and barely at that. She moaned as burning pain seared through her right shoulder. Two blue uniformed cops hunched over her. One was baby faced and being a teacher she recognized the signs of someone getting ready to puke. Sure enough the young cop stood up, turned and ran to her sink emptying his stomach.

She thought the veteran cop looked familiar. He must have worked with her Dad.

"Hey kid, remember me?" He said.

Karen Sue looked at him and nodded numbly. She was having trouble breathing and as the nightmare of what had just happened skidded back into her brain she realized Ray's unresponsive body was still on top of her pinning her to the wet floor.

Errant sounds were coming out of her mouth that was strangled and unintelligible. She tried to push Ray off of her chest but the sharp pain in her one shoulder caused her to become light-headed and moan.

"Hold on, I know you're hurt, medical is on its way. Let me help you." The cop rolled Ray off her body and the plopping sound he made as his weight hit the floor made Karen Sue's stomach churn. She rolled on to her side, her shoulder screaming in protest and vomited where she lay.

EMS arrived and Karen Sue was promptly attended to. A female officer was at her side gently talking her through everything that was happening around her. It had the desired calming effect and Karen Sue hung to the lifeline the officer had thrown her. She told Karen Sue that her shoulder had a bullet lodged in it but it was close to the surface because it had passed through the man's body first so it hadn't gone in far.

"My husband, Ray." Karen Sue wheezed out after hearing her describe him as 'the man.' The female officer nodded, "Your husband." She acknowledged.

They were, of course, treating her for shock. EMS swiftly had her strapped to a gurney and she was wheeled briskly through her living room. She looked back towards Ray and saw the finality of her life, as she knew it lying bloody and lifeless. Karen Sue began to cry.

As she was taken down the front steps, her vision slightly distorted by the avalanche of her unchecked tears, she saw that outside her house was organized chaos. Her neighbors were watching and whispering from behind the police tape surrounding her property. Cops were everywhere and news vans were starting to set up along the curb. A helicopter was even hovering above. She saw the teenager next door capturing all the action on his iPhone. Karen Sue closed her eyes and the female officer gently pulled the sheet over Karen Sue's face hoping to protect her from prying eyes.

The EMT's wheeled Karen Sue into the Emergency Room and a young attending physician promptly directed them towards a curtained room. Her new entourage consisting of the female officer, the veteran officer, that knew her dad, and the baby faced rookie who had barfed in her kitchen. They tried to follow her gurney but the doctor stopped the group, only allowing the female officer inside the small room. With the help of a nurse the doctor stuck a syringe into Karen Sues shoulder, close to where the bullet lay numbing the wound area. Karen Sue yelped in pain as she glared at the doctor who continued to work his triage magic. He then deftly pried the small, bent bullet out of her shoulder, sealing it in the small baggie the female officer had produced. The thickly accented doctor had been talking to Karen Sue nonstop, but she had no idea what he'd been saying as he cleaned and dressed her wound. The nurse handed him another syringe and the nurse told her that it was an antibiotic. She then handed him a third syringe, which the doctor administered immediately and before Karen Sue could ask what that one was for she fell asleep.

Groggily fighting to open her eyes Karen Sue hissed at the fiery pain in her shoulder. She tried to wet her lips but her tongue was thick and dry. She heard voices before she saw them. The first thing she noticed was a nurse taking her vitals and speaking with the female officer who she remembered from her house. Karen Sue groaned and the officer came to the side of the bed and the nurse acknowledged her back to the land of consciousness with a kind smile.

"How you feeling, honey?"

Karen Sue fought to hold her eyes open and stared first at the nurse then at the officer. The nurse continued talking. "Dr. Singa took a bullet out of your shoulder, do you remember that? He'll be in shortly. To check on you."

Karen Sue nodded and croaked out, "Water." The nurse pressed a button on the side of her bed to elevate her head enough for her to drink and then she lifted a pink plastic cup with a straw and told her to sip slowly. Karen Sue sucked hard, welcoming the cool wetness into her parched throat. The nurse pulled the straw from her mouth and Karen Sue frowned at her. She put the straw back into her mouth. "You can't drink too fast okay?" Karen Sue nodded as she monitored her sips on her own and the nurse relaxed.

The officer, whose nameplate read Zucco, cleared her throat to get her attention. "Ma'am, I know you have been through a lot, but there are detectives here that need to speak with you now."

Police officer Zucco left her bedside and returned with two men dressed in jackets and ties. Karen Sue followed officer Zucco's movement and when she opened the curtain Karen Sue saw there was a uniformed officer standing guard outside her room. The horror of what had happened seeped into her still drug hazed mind and Karen Sue fought the hysteria threatening to overtake her sanity.

Her mind kept flashing back to Ray flying through the swinging door as blood sprayed from his wounds. Her white kitchen wall turned instantly into a sickening mural of modern art. She tried to put her hands over her face but the one shoulder hurt too much and she cried out in pain dropping it to her side and only using her left hand to press against her eyes. She heard the nurse say she was going to get the doctor and then heard her shuffle away.

A small hand touched Karen Sue's good shoulder. "Ma'am? I know this is hard but the sooner we talk to you the sooner we can catch the guy who did this." She looked up and Officer Zucco gave her an understanding smile. The two detectives were still standing a couple feet away from her bed affording her the moments she needed to pull herself together. Their kid glove approach surprised her at first until she took a better look at one of the detectives and realized she'd seen him before; he'd worked with her dad.

"I know you." Karen Sue said so softly she had both detectives leaning towards her bed so they could hear her.

"I was friends with your dad on the force. I called him. He and your Mom will be here as soon as they catch a flight. I'm Detective Randal and this is Detective Pat."

Karen Sue nodded and tears spilled down her face at the mention of her parents. Officer Zucco handed her a tissue that Karen Sue used to sop up the droplets sliding down her cheeks and to wipe her nose. She then crunched the tissue into a ball and held it tightly in her fist.

"Mrs. Murphy can you tell us what happened?" Detective Pat asked her.

Karen Sue scooted her behind upwards into the bed trying to get a higher perch. Officer Zucco took the control from the side of the bed. "Would you like to sit up a little more Mrs. Murphy?"

Karen Sue nodded a yes. Officer Zucco pressed the button and Karen Sue's upper body slowly started to rise up. When her bed ceased to move Karen Sue thanked her and took a deep breath hoping to settle her nerves so she could tell them what she had seen.

"I came home from school and I heard voices in the living room. Before I could open the door..." Karen Sue gulped down the bile that was threatening to come up. "Ray... Ray came through the door. He fell...on top of me. He was bleeding. I think... I'm pretty sure... I don't know... I'm pretty sure he was dead." Karen Sue finished off her last statement so softly that she again had the two detectives leaning towards her.

"Did you see who shot him?" Detective Randal asked.

"I didn't see him get shot. I saw a man holding the gun pointing like he had just... I didn't hear any loud shots, just soft pops."

"So you are on the floor?" Detective Pat said. Prompting her back to the scene.

"Yes, Ray was on top of me. There was so much blood. He's dead isn't he?" Karen Sue's voice cracked and her eyes glazed over as she remembered how heavy Ray's lifeless body felt on top of hers.

Detective Pat looked sorrowfully at her and nodded his head. "Yes ma'am. We are sorry for your loss."

Karen Sue blew out a breath and sniffed in more tears. She knew he was dead but for some reason she needed it verbally confirmed.

"Ray was on top of me. I looked up and the one man had the gun pointed at Ray. Then he handed the gun to another man." Karen Sue sighed and shut her eyes trying to wipe out the image. "A third man came in and told them they needed to go. I couldn't move. I was watching but nothing made sense, I couldn't think...The one man, the smaller one, took the gun from the man he had just given it to and he handed it to the man that had just come in. He told him to kill me." Karen Sue started to shake and tears again filled her vision.

Her curtain moved again and Dr. Singa came through. He shot the detectives a nasty glare. "She just had a bullet removed. I will not let you upset her. Everyone out." The doctor was waving his arms towards the opening.

"Doc, she just saw her husband get killed we need to find out who did it."

"An hour or two won't make a bit of difference. Wait until we move her to her own room. This is an Emergency room. There are other patients in here."

"Can you move her now? This is important."

The doc looked at his clipboard and came over to Karen Sue's bed making the detectives back up so their backsides were pressing into the curtained wall. He then wrote something down on his board and looked down into Karen Sue's face.

"I can make them leave." He said gently as he peered down at her.

Karen Sue smiled up at the doctor recognizing that he was championing her. "It's okay." She said. "I want to get it over with."

"Okay, if you're sure. I'm going to move you to a room. The other families think we have a big movie star in here with all the extra security." He chuckled lightly.

Karen Sue thanked him and he told the detectives they needed to leave while they made her ready to transfer her to a floor room. Detective Pat grumbled and turned to leave. Detective Randal stepped towards Karen Sue and hesitated before speaking.

“Mrs. Murphy I can’t imagine how difficult this is for you. We’re going to meet you in your room. We need to talk to you, it’s important to our investigation. You know this. You’re the daughter of a cop.”

“I know.” Karen Sue acknowledged. “I want to help.”

“Okay we’ll see you when you are settled.” He gave her arm a little fatherly pat and left her cubicle leaving behind Officer Zucco.

As Detective Randal left a male orderly came in followed by the nurse. They tucked Karen Sue into her bed and readied her monitors putting the one between her feet at the foot of her bed. They wheeled her out of the Emergency area; Officer Zucco followed loyally alongside the mobile bed.

She was pushed down a hallway and into an elevator; the nurse pressed the button for floor 3, riding in silence until the elevator dinged and the doors opened. The orderly wheeled her onto the brightly lit corridor and to the end of the hall to a large private room, complete with a small refrigerator and a couch.

"I can't afford this room." Karen Sue squeaked.

Officer Zucco patted her bedside rail. "Mrs. Murphy you won't be paying for this room. The DA told the hospital to make sure you were comfortable and secure."

"Secure?"

"I'm sorry, we need you secure. You're a witness."

Karen Sue nodded. The orderly positioned her bed and locked the wheels in place before leaving. The nurse set up the monitors and then said good-bye leaving Karen Sue alone with Officer Zucco.

"This is bad isn't it?" Karen Sue murmured.

Officer Zucco paused before speaking. "It's big Mrs. Murphy. I'm not supposed to talk to you about it, but it's big."

A knock sounded outside of her opened door and Karen Sue turned her head to see the two detectives standing outside of her room.

"Can we come in?"

Karen Sue nodded and the two detectives entered coming to stand on either side of her bed.

Officer Zucco melted into the background again.

They looked at Officer Zucco. “Thanks Danni.”

Karen Sue gave Officer Zucco a question when they referred to her as Danni. Officer Zucco smiled. “D. A. N. N. I. My parents were huge Grease fans.”

Karen Sue smiled knowingly. “Ahhh, I like that movie too.”

“Okay Mrs. Murphy can we continue?” Detective Pat had a pen at the ready. Karen Sue nodded.

“You said you saw the one man pointing the gun at your husband. Can you describe him?”

Karen Sue took a deep breath and closed her eyes briefly; conjuring up the horrible images that she knew would never leave her mind.

“The one man...”

Detective interrupted. “Which man? The one with the gun?”

“Yes, the man with the gun. He was small, the smallest of all three. He had slicked back gray hair. His face had wrinkles. He was older than the other two. He was dressed like he was a businessman. He had on a long black dress coat.”

“Would you recognize him?”

"Yes."

"Did you see him pull the trigger?"

"No, Ray knocked me over and when I looked up he was pointing the gun like he'd just pulled the trigger."

"Okay, so the smaller man handed the other man the gun. Then what happened?"

There was commotion in the hallway outside of her room prompting Karen Sue to look towards the door. Her heart slammed into her chest when she saw the man that had shot her charge through the doorway. Karen Sue muffled a scream into her hand before clenching the bed sheets to her chest as if they could protect her. A woman dressed in a business suit, carrying a briefcase and two other intimidating men quickly walked in behind him.

The two detectives at her bedside reached for their weapons as they pivoted towards the intruders. Karen Sue's heart was beating so fast it was painful. Officer Zucco had jumped from her chair in the corner and had strategically placed her body between Karen Sue and the hulking male that was now striding towards her.

Karen Sue couldn't take her eyes off the giant of a man that was staring daggers at her. One of his muscled arms was held immobile against his chest in a sling.

"What the fuck!" Detective Randal said as he placed his back to her bed and assumed a protective stance.

Karen Sue tried to make herself as small as possible. Black spots swam before her eyes. He was back to kill her.

"Relax, everyone relax." Karen Sue heard the woman with the brief case bark out aggressively, effectively commanding the people in the room to pause.

The large intimidating man stopped in his tracks. His dark eyes swept up and down Karen Sue's shaking form in the bed.

"You were hit? Shit!"

Karen Sue paused in disbelief. Had she heard him correctly? She stopped quaking as the icy fear that had been racing through her veins dissolved and was replaced with red-hot anger.

"Yea that happens when someone shoots at you!" She snapped back.

The man pushed his hand not hampered with the sling through his thick dark hair.

"Shit!" He said again. He tried to step

towards her bed but Officer Zucco refused to remove herself from his path.

"Officer, stand down." The woman with the brief case said sternly. Officer Zucco looked to Detective Randal and when he nodded Officer Zucco hesitantly moved to the side. The detectives holstered their guns.

"What's going on Barrett?" Detective Randal asked the woman, who was undoubtedly in charge.

"This is Colt Andrews." The woman said pointing at the gunman. "He's undercover DEA. He's been embedded with Pallone for two years. These other two gentlemen are US Marshall Mann and Jim Sargent the DEA coordinator in charge of Colts undercover operation."

The older of the two new men that had entered her room looked towards the detectives. "Guys we hate to pull jurisdiction crap here, but we need you guys to clear the room now. We got this."

Detective Pat started to spit out expletives under his breath and Detective Randal looked to DA Barrett for an explanation.

"Guys this is big, bigger than you can imagine. I know you have a murder to solve but we all know who did it and we need to nail him for not only that but for other things. We need him in jail.

Between what Colt here knows and with what Mrs. Murphy saw and heard we can do that now."

Karen Sue sucked in a sharp breath. The guy that shot me is a good guy? He was still scary as shit looking. Detective Randal patted Karen Sue's arm and moved away from the top of the bed stopping to whisper something in US Marshall Mann's ear. Marshall Mann nodded and they shook hands. Officer Zucco nodded a good-bye to Karen Sue and then she and Detective Pat followed Detective Randal out the door.

Colt now had a clear path to Karen Sue. He looked feral. He stepped quickly to the bedside and looked down at her. His size blocked her view of the others in the room. All of sudden she felt vulnerable, afraid. She wished Officer Zucco hadn't had to leave.

"Tell me you saw him pull the trigger?" Colt snarled at her.

Karen Sue slid towards the side of the bed Colt was not hovering over. The man was huge and frightening. He wore the same clothes that he'd had on in her house except he had on a scrub top exposing his thick arms. Karen Sue could see dried blood near his neck that ran underneath the scrub. His one arm was bound to his broad chest with a blue sling and that hand was clenched in a fist close to his chest.

Karen Sue shook her head back and forth slowly. "No, I didn't see him pull the trigger. I only saw him pointing it at Ray."

"Damn it! Are you sure?"

Karen Sue looked at Colt in disbelief. She may have let her husband kick her around a bit but she was not going to take any crap from this Neanderthal. She had had enough of this shit. Her no-good husband had been killed, she'd been shot, she was in pain and four people she didn't know were crowding her hospital room. Her self-preservation instincts kicked in and she snapped.

"Maybe I was too busy being slammed into the floor by my dead husband's body!" She yelled as she returned Colts lethal glare.

An eerie hush fell over the people in the room. Karen Sue was breathing hard, like she had just finished a run. Colt had straightened up after her outburst giving her a little room now. He was staring at her as if seeing her for the first time. The DA, US Marshall Mann and DEA agent Sargent were looking back and forth between Colt and Karen Sue like they were watching a Ping-Pong match, waiting for what would come next.

Colt's shoulders sagged slightly and he sucked in a deep breath as his eyes took inventory of the small woman who was visibly shaking with anger that he had incited. He realized all that heat was aimed at him. He was an ass. He had shot her, he hadn't meant to and it had saved her life, regardless, bottom line, he had shot her, and now he was yelling at her. Her short blond hair was coated in dried, rust colored blood. The short sticky strands jetted out from her head in different directions. Her bangs lay plastered to her forehead above her light brown eyebrows and he noticed that she had one small strand of hair colored royal blue. On someone else it would have looked Goth, but on her it looked artsy. The blue in her hair only served to highlight her eyes and Colt was uncharacteristically drawn into them. They were a mesmerizing azure blue, almost sapphire, with small gray flecks. Colt felt a stirring when he looked at her eyes that he hadn't felt in a long time. The quaking woman had a small, lightly freckled nose and full pink lips that were currently pressed tightly together. Her skin looked like it would be soft to touch and Colt fisted his hand to stop from reaching out to test his theory. She was unbelievably cute and her fiery little outburst only added to her allure. He mentally kicked himself. She had just lost her husband and now he was seriously checking her out. He'd been under cover too long.

When he had seen her in the house he was so caught up in how to save her life that he hadn't noticed what she looked like. Well, he had; she had looked like a frightened doe that was in a hunters gun sights. He remembered she hadn't screamed or even begged except for a hushed 'please.'

Karen Sue clamped her lips tightly together as she struggled to reign in her emotions. She watched the big man, as he looked her over from head to toe. She noticed his eyes had darkened when he looked at her bandaged shoulder. He appeared younger now than when she'd seen him in her house. His dark brown hair wasn't slicked back as it had been and soft strands fell across his furrowed brow. He had an angular face with a tan toughened complexion. His expressive lips were stretched tightly over white teeth. Long, thick, dark eyelashes showcased piercing blue gray eyes that were similar in color to the West Point Cadets uniforms. He was big everywhere. The arm not hidden in the sling boasted a huge forearm connecting to a seriously muscled upper arm. His arms were so thick that they were snuggly encircled by the short sleeve of the scrub shirt. On most men the sleeve would have hung loosely around their arms, but not on him.

Colt finally found his voice. Speaking to her in a soft deep tone that conveyed his regret. "I tried not to hit you. I was aiming for your husband's shoulder. I thought you saw what I had mouthed to you?"

Karen Sue settled back into her pillow with voicing a loud "humph." “Well, you missed.” She said haughtily.

DEA Sargent coughed gently from behind Colts massive shoulders. “Well, he didn’t. His bullet went through your husband’s shoulder and into yours. It was a smart idea and he probably saved your life.”

“You played dead so well I thought you understood what I wanted. I thought you were okay.” Colt said quietly.

Karen Sue looked thoughtfully at the man who just a few hours earlier had shot her. He had also obviously saved her life. She was so confused. Her head started to pound with the beginnings of a migraine. Tears rimmed her eyes again. God she was so tired of crying, she never cried and today she’d probably shed more tears than she had in her entire life. Karen Sue again noticed Colt's arm in a sling.

“What happened to you? Did the police shoot you?” She asked him softly. Colt recognized the unspoken truce she had just called between them.

Colt chuckled giving her an ever so small smile, “I wish it had been the cops.”

Karen Sue became even more confused if

that was possible. She wiped her eyes and took in a long heavy breath; her eyes looked up to Colt pleading for answers.

"I don't understand what's going on here. Can you tell me what happened? What was Ray involved in? Why was he shot? If the police didn't shoot you then who did? Please tell me." Karen Sue's voice trailed off as she finished speaking. Her eyes never left Colt's face. She knew he had the answers she needed.

Colt looked over to the woman who Karen Sue realized was known by everyone in the room except herself. The woman nodded to Colt and then stepped to the foot of her bed.

"Mrs. Murphy I'm DA Barrett and I have been assigned to your case, at least for now. Colt here, like I said earlier, has been undercover for a couple years. He has been trying to get close to a man named Victor Pallone who is the head of a major crime family."

Karen Sue nodded, acknowledging that she understood everything so far. The other two men moved to stand behind DA Barrett, content for the moment to hang in the background. Colt took over the explanation.

"I wasn't privy to everything, but I learned a few things. Your husband was into the mob for some big money."

DA Barrett interrupted. "Did you know anything about that?"

Colt interjected before Karen Sue could answer. "Does she need a lawyer?" The DA looked at Colt and she was pissed. Karen Sue looked at him gratefully.

"No." DA Barrett said heatedly. "Her house has been bugged for months. We know she isn't involved."

"Then why did you ask?" Colt snarled back at her.

"I have to cover all my bases Colt you know that!"

"My house has been bugged! Holy Shit!" Karen Sue felt like she was living in one of her crime drama shows.

"Your house and landline." DA Barrett answered.

"Oh God, this is so not good." Karen Sue said out loud. "Well, to answer your question, no I did not know he was into the mob for money but I knew he had a gambling problem and needed money. My Dad is an ex-cop and he checked him out when things started to get...get difficult. Ray tried to get me to give him rights to my house; I think he wanted to use it for collateral. He had already run all our credit cards to the max. I've been trying to pay them off." Karen Sue paused and then she looked as if something had slammed into her chest forcing her upright.

"Oh God, if I had let him sell the house would he still be alive?" The anguish in her voice tore at Colt and he felt a twist like tug in his gut hearing that this little woman had been paying off her husband's debt.

"Mrs. Murphy he was into Pallone for way more than what your house was worth, no offense. The thing is, from what I understand he was slowly paying off his debt by working for Pallone. He was a computer accountant guy right?"

"Yes, Ray was a genius with computers."

"Yea that's what I heard. So evidently he was moving money for Pallone and I guess, at first, it was okay because he managed to get himself and you off of the red list."

"What's a red list?"

Colt looked uncomfortable and looked to the others in the room.

Agent Sargent looked at Karen Sue and in as calm a voice as possible told her.

"Pallone has a list he calls the 'red' list. It's a list of people he has a problem. He has his enforcers hurt them physically and in some cases kill."

Karen Sue gasped and paled. "But why would I be on that list?"

"Mrs. Murphy the best way to get someone to comply is to threaten their loved ones."

What he was saying shook Karen Sue to her core. She looked back up to Colt who was watching her closely. At least she was getting some answers.

"Okay so he was doing something for this Pallone guy that was preventing us from being hurt. So what went wrong?"

Colt looked at the man called Sarge. "I don't know. Sarge, did you listen to the tape yet? What went wrong?"

Karen Sue remembered them saying her house had been bugged.

"We haven't listened to it yet. We were too busy extracting your ass."

"What does that mean extracting your... You know...ass."

Colt smiled again. He didn't know why, but

he thought it was adorable that she had trouble saying the word ass out loud. Shit! Did he just mentally use the word adorable? He was an idiot.

US Marshall Mann stepped alongside of DA Barrett. “I guess that’s my cue.” He said. His voice was deep and hard toned like he probably smoked. “I’m here because Colt’s cover has been blown and you are both witness’s. We have to keep you both safe now.”

Karen Sue tilted her head indicating she didn’t understand. Agent Sargent spoke up.

“After Colt left your house he was with Pallone. He had phoned in a distress call to us indicating we needed to get to your house right away. He also made an anonymous call to the local police hoping to get Pallone out of your house before you got involved and saw anything.”

Karen Sue looked back to Colt who stood silently watching her. His one hand was gripping her bedrail. Agent Sargent continued; “We were supposed to get to your house and shut down the scene before the local authorities got there. We had no idea what had happened, but we needed to protect Colt's identity. When we got there and found you were still alive we wanted to take you out the back door so Pallone wouldn’t know you were still alive, but EMS had already moved you into the ambulance. We probably could have still helped Colt stay undercover, but it appears one of your young neighbors used his iPhone to videotape everything and before we even knew this, he had sold his tape to a news crew that had pulled up. The news crew put it on air when they received it."

Colt took over the story. "I thought everything was okay. I drove Pallone and Big Tony to the warehouse where we picked up a few of the other guys and then went to the restaurant that Pallone eats at. He has a standing table that's separated from the other diners. There's a television placed on the wall just for his viewing. We sat down, the food came out and the news came on. Big Tony told the other guys that Murphy was out of the picture. He then told the guys that I was officially into the fold. They all knew that meant that I had killed someone for Pallone. The guys were all laughing and patting me on the back. I was feeling confident that I was about to get closer to nailing Pallone. Then the fucking news channel cut to a breaking news story. A reporter was talking over the video of you coming out of the house on the stretcher." Colt shrugged and sighed deeply.

"What happened?"

There was a long pause before Colt continued. "They knew I had missed on purpose."

"Oh my God. They shot you?"

“Yup.”

“I’m sorry you were hurt.” Colt couldn’t believe she was feeling sorry for him.

“He’s lucky that’s all that happened. If he hadn’t had a preplanned exit route he’d probably be dead.” Agent Sargent said with a little pride in his voice.

Marshall Mann tapped the bed rail to get Karen Sue’s attention. “We have put together a strong case against Pallone, Mrs. Murphy. With Colt’s testimony and hopefully yours too, we can put him away for the rest of his life. Pallone is going to find out soon enough that Colt was undercover DEA, his life is in danger, and yours is too. We need to get you both into protective custody ASAP.”

“But I have to work. Why would he want to hurt me? I don’t know anything?”

Agent Sargent cleared his throat. “He doesn’t know that you don’t know anything and he knows you saw him with the gun that killed your husband. Furthermore you saw him give the order to kill you. Trust me you need to be protected.”

“But work?”

“Mrs. Murphy we think you should be placed in Witness Protection until after Pallone’s trial, maybe longer.”

"Oh God." Karen Sue was beginning to panic. "My parents."

Colt looked down at the young woman whose life had unraveled in just a few hours. Well, if he was being technical, her dumb ass husband started pulling the thread a while ago, but today the whole spool had come undone. Her eyes were her tell. She was frightened yet mad. He admired her spunk but he still felt sorry for her.

The nurse chose that moment to come back into the room and Marshall Mann stepped in front of her before she could get to Karen Sue's bedside. He flashed his badge at her and said they wouldn't need her anymore. The nurse stood opened mouthed and said she was getting the doctor. Mann looked over to Karen Sue who looked confused.

"Pallone has pull." He said. "We can't trust anyone right now. We are going to move you to a safe house and bring in a doctor from the agency."

He looked at DA Barrett; "You need to go to give the hospital the paperwork so we can move her without drawing any undue attention."

DA Barrett left the room.

"Colt you need to get that arm taken care of."

Colt nodded. "It can wait. Whoever you get to look after Mrs. Murphy here..."

"Karen Sue."

"What?"

"Please call me Karen Sue. Mrs. Murphy is what my students call me."

"Okay then." Colt said giving her an awkward smile before looking back to Mann. "Whoever you get to look after Karen Sue can look at my arm."

US Marshall Mann and Agent Sargent moved towards the back of the ginormous hospital room to talk logistics leaving Karen Sue and Colt alone.

"Colt?" Karen Sue put her hand on Colt's hand that was gripping the handrail. He didn't look up; instead he looked at her small hand covering his.

"Colt, thank you. I know you saved my life. Maybe if I hadn't been so naive... Maybe if I had... Crud, I don't even know what I could have done. Maybe if I'd been a better wife."

Colt looked up his eyes slamming into hers.

"Don't say it. Don't you dare make excuses for your husband." Colt's voice was heated and his eyes bore into hers.

"I can't believe I didn't know how bad it was."

"Yea, well maybe that was his way of protecting you."

Karen Sue thought about that. It made it almost bearable to think about Ray if, in fact, he had been trying to keep her safe.

"What happens now? Where will they take me? Will you be there?" Karen Sue wasn't sure why she wanted to know if Colt would be with her. She did know that he made her feel safe and right now safe was good.

"I'm not sure. I'm DEA not Marshal Service. They need to make sure you have a doctor and I still need to get this bullet out of me so I'll probably get to go with you tonight."

Karen Sue felt the weight of the horrible day press on her and her eyes started to feel heavy. "You're tired." Colt said to her softly.

Karen Sue nodded. "I'm afraid to shut my eyes." She confided to him quietly.

"I promise I won't leave your side. You sleep, okay?"

"Colt, you're hurt too. Someone should be watching out for you." He smiled down at her.

"Don't worry about me. Things are going to happen quickly. I'll be looked after soon enough.

You get a few minutes of sleep."

Karen Sue lowered her hand from Colt's and Colt felt an odd bereft feeling. "Thanks Colt." Karen Sue mumbled his name as she drifted off.

Chapter 4

Karen Sue awoke to her bed being quickly wheeled down a hallway. Colt was walking right next to her. There were six rather encompassing men, not including Colt, Mann and Sargent that surrounded her mobile bed. She knew it was nighttime because there weren't many other people around, but then again, it also looked as if they were taking a less used hallway route. Where ever they were going the men around her were on high alert and the man in the front of their little convoy had a gun at the ready. Colt noticed she was awake and gave her a reassuring little nod.

Within minutes she was buckled into an SUV, no longer hooked to any IV bags or annoying beeping machine. Colt slid in next to her and some other beefy man sat on her other side. The driver had been waiting in the car and Mann got in the front passenger seat.

"Get comfortable kids," Mann said. "We have a bit of a drive."

They drove for two hours, cloaked by the dark night, and pulled up to a house at the end of a short cul-de-sac in a normal looking neighborhood.

"If we're targets," Karen Sue ventured. "Do you think it's wise to be in a neighborhood where others could get hurt?"

Mann turned around placing his left elbow on the center console so he could look at her when he spoke. "There are no other people living in the houses on the street."

"Oh...that's good." Karen Sue said softly. Mann smiled back at her.

"Marshall Mann I know Officer Ramsey had called my parents. I'm sure they are worried and want to see me."

"We spoke with your dad before we left the hospital. They have been placed in protective custody too."

"You are kidding!" She was astounded with the level of protectiveness these men were issuing.

"Karen Sue I can't stress how serious this is. If Pallone wants to hurt you he will put your parents on his..."

Karen Sue finished his sentence. "Red-list."

"Yea, his red list."

"When we get you settled we can call them.

They are eager to talk to you."

"Okay, thank you."

Karen Sue looked over at Colt. His eyes were closed but she knew he wasn't asleep just by how he was breathing. The man was handsome. She couldn't guess his age. He was a total bad ass, yet he'd shown her a softer side of himself. She got the feeling he wasn't used to showing that side too often and it made her feel sorry for the big guy.

The garage door attached to the little ranch house automatically opened and the SUV drove into the garage. The men didn't open their car doors until the garage door shut. Once the door closed the driver and the man on the other side of Karen Sue got out and entered the house through a door from inside the garage. About five minutes later one of the men returned and gave them the all clear sign. Colt helped Karen Sue ease out of the SUV. She was sore and her shoulder was on fire but she didn't want to complain.

They entered through a small mudroom that emptied into a large country kitchen. Mann came to stand by Karen Sue and led her by her elbow towards the hallway that presented off the large opened spaced living area. He stopped by a large room that was obviously the master bedroom. It was furnished and there was a bathroom attached.

“This will be your room.” He told Karen Sue.

“It’s too big for me. You should take it.”

Mann cracked out a laugh that came out more like a boom and Colt quickly appeared at Karen Sue’s side looking worried.

“What?” he asked.

“She told me to take this room. She’s the first woman to ever think about me first. Little lady if you weren’t so young I’d ask you out on a date.”

Karen Sue smiled and then the smile turned sad when she realized she was free to date if she wanted to.

“You ass Mann.” Colt hissed when he saw Karen Sue’s distressed face.

“Oh shit, I’m sorry. I just... You just shocked me.”

“No, it’s okay, really. It just kind of hit me.”

“You okay?” Colt asked her then he glared at Mann again. Mann said sorry again and walked back down the hall.

“Yea, I’m good. Truth be told I haven’t been in a marriage, like a normal marriage for the last two years so...”

"It doesn't matter he shouldn't have said it."

Karen Sue put her hand on Colt's good arm.

"Really it's okay."

Mann returned with a bag from Target. "We got you some things to tide you over. We guessed at the sizes. There will be a female Marshall here tomorrow morning."

Karen Sue took the bag. "Thank you. Can I get things from my house?"

"We'll see okay. Just let us know if you need anything. There is a doctor coming soon. He needs to check out your wound and Colt's."

"Okay. I...ummmm.... need to use the rest room. I'll be out in a few minutes."

"Take your time. We're making grilled cheese please tell me you eat that?"

"Yup, love them."

Mann was back to beaming at her and Colt stifled a groan when he saw Mann looking at her with big puppy dog eyes.

Karen Sue emptied the bag on the king-sized bed and sifted through the contents. They had gotten the basic necessitates: toothbrush, toothpaste, hairbrush, deodorant, shampoo, conditioner, body soap and lotion. There was a pair of soft pajamas complete with a button up top and elastic bottoms, a 3-pack of granny underwear. Karen Sue giggled when she saw that. The fact that she could giggle after her horrendous evening brought her up short and she instantly felt guilty. She knew if she and Ray had been in a normal relationship that she would be devastated and probably inconsolable. Truth be told, she was sad, but she had mourned the loss of Ray years ago. Karen Sue rummaged through the bag finding that they'd also provided her with a sport bra, a pair of yoga pants, two tee shirts and two pair of socks.

Karen put the clothes away in a drawer and headed for the bathroom. She brushed her teeth and after looking in the mirror and seeing how dried blood was grossly crusted in her hair she decided she needed to take a bath. Before she could start the water there was a knock at her door. Karen Sue walked over to it and opened it. One of the other men stood outside of it. “Hi, Mrs. Murphy.”

“Karen Sue.”

“Karen Sue, the doctors here.”

“Okay, thank you. What’s your name?”

“Bill, Ma’am. Bill Gifford.”

Karen Sue walked out to the living area. Colt

was sitting on a dining room chair without his shirt on. My God the man had a body. Karen Sue's mouth went dry just looking at his glorious chest and roped arms. Colt saw her and when she realized that she had been ogling his body she colored crimson and he gave her a quirky, cocky smile. His smile turned into a clenched toothed grimace as the doctor dug into his inner arm.

"You're lucky Colt; it's just under the skin here, no muscle damage. Now listen up hot shot. No lifting or anything for at least a week, okay." A sheen of sweat glistened on his forehead so Karen Sue grabbed a cloth from a kitchen drawer wet it with cool water wiped his brow and then placed it on the back of his neck. All five men stopped what they were doing and looked at her like she was an alien being.

"What? He's hurting and that will help." She told the other men.

"Thank you." Colt said.

The doctor dropped the bullet into a plastic bag that Mann was holding and they took pictures of Colt's arm and the bullet. The doctor finished with Colt by giving him a couple stitches and then wrapping his arm. He then gave Colt a shot of antibiotic and a plastic bottle containing pain meds. Karen Sue went to get Colt water but Bill beat her to it giving her a knowing smile, which she returned.

"And this must be the lady patient?"

"Karen Sue." She volunteered quietly.

"Well, Karen Sue let's have a look at that shoulder okay?"

Karen Sue pulled the neck of the scrubs she was wearing off to the side so the doctor could see her shoulder.

"I need to see it Karen Sue so why don't we take this in your room." Karen Sue wasn't a prude but she was a little nervous letting a man she didn't know, doctor or not, see her. She had no idea where the thought came from it just tumbled from her mouth.

"Can Colt come with me?"

The men in the room got quiet and the doctor just nodded his head as he packed up his bag. "Sure if that makes you feel more comfortable. I'm sorry we don't have the female agent here yet."

Karen Sue was so bright red that Colt thought she'd burst.

"Never mind, I don't know why I said that. I'm still out of sorts. I'm sorry it's okay."

Karen Sue stood up and quickly headed towards her room. A large warm hand grasped her hand from behind stopping her short. Colt stood behind her. “I can be in the room but keep my back to you, does that work?”

Karen Sue almost melted in relief and Colt saw it in her expressive eyes.

“Yes,” she whispered so low he had to lean in to catch what she said.

Colt followed Karen Sue into the room followed by the doctor who shut the door. Colt went to the ottoman and sat with his back to the room. Karen Sue went to the bed and sat down on the edge. The doctor placed his bag on the bed and helped Karen Sue take the scrub shirt off. Colt could hear her little moans of distress with each shuffle of movement. He knew she was in pain. He hated that she was hurting and that he was the cause of it. The doctor was talking to her softly as he examined her. Colt snapped out of his haze when he heard Karen Sue whimper in pain. He shot off the ottoman and turned to her. Her shirt was off and the doctor was reapplying some ointment. She held the scrub shirt to her chest but Colt could see the slope of one breast and a hint of its dusky areola. He quickly looked up to her face but his lower anatomy was already responding. Her eyes were closed and she was grimacing in pain.

Colt sat on the bed next to her and placed his arm around her back latching his hand on to her far hip. He tucked her body against his and she melted into his side placing her face into his side as she fought off the waves of pain. She was puffing out, “Ow, ow, ow, ow... Ohhhh owww.”

“Doc can you finish already?” Colt bit out.

“Karen Sue we are almost done here. Colt I had to change the bandage and clean the wound, come on man, you know the drill.”

The doctor fastened a fresh bandage over the wound and administered another shot of antibiotic to her, like he’d given Colt. “There. All done. Now Karen Sue don’t get that wet and here’s some pain medicine. Don’t use that arm either young lady.”

Karen Sue’s breathing started to come back to normal and she realized she didn’t have her shirt on. She also wanted to take a bath so she didn’t want to put her shirt on. She took her face out of Colts side and gave him the most dazzling smile Colt had ever seen. His stomach dropped to his toes and he fought the chubby that was about to press against the zipper in his dress pants.

“Thank you Colt. I’m sorry I was a baby. It kind of hurt.”

“You’ve been shot, that does hurt. Shit! I can’t believe I hit you. I’m so sorry.”

"I know Colt, but better a ding in the wing than a coffin, right?"

Colt looked at the little angel hooked to his side that was using police vernacular and sporting a bullet wound. "Man your something else little girl." He said with a shake of his head and sporting a tight smile. Karen Sue knew the guilt over shooting her was going to weigh heavily on this man for a while.

"I have a favor." She looked at him shyly.

"Sure, what?"

"Umm, this 'little girl' wants to take a bath." Colt's eyes grew twice their original size and Karen Sue would have giggled out loud if her shoulder didn't hurt so much. "Can you find me something to wrap my shoulder with so I don't get it wet and get me a cup so I can wash my hair please?"

The relief on Colts face was so apparent that even the doctor chuckled.

Karen Sue clutched the shirt to her chest and walked into the adjoining bathroom to run the bathwater. Her shoulder was slamming with its own heart beat sending waves of crippling pain down her arm and throughout her body. She was biting back nausea. Colt came back with a red solo cup and plastic wrap and handed it through the door that was opened about 5 inches.

"Karen Sue?"

"Hmmm?"

"I'm going to wait out here in case you need anything okay. I'm not being creepy okay I just... I want to help okay?"

"Thanks Colt, I won't take too long."

Karen Sue downed two of the pain pills the doctor had prescribed, slipped out of her scrub pants, wrapped the plastic wrap around her bandaged shoulder as best she could and carefully sat down into the tub with the water still running. Karen Sue dunked her short hair carefully under the spout trying to keep water off her shoulder. She washed her hair and rinsed it; thankfully her hair was short so it didn't take that long. She did not even bother with conditioner. She shut off the running water and grabbed the soap from the dish where she had placed it after unwrapping it. She soaped her body and quickly rubbed off the soap bubbles. Her stomach had begun to churn and she realized she was going to vomit. She needed to get out of the tub before she threw up in the water. The vomit pushed up her throat, and she clamped her mouth shut to hold it in. Karen Sue pulled herself from the tub, slammed onto the floor with a wet thud and crawled to the toilet where she lifted the lid and began to throw up.

The bathroom door flew open just as Karen Sue retched into the toilet. A towel was thrown over her back and strong hands held her hips and rubbed her back. Karen Sue felt so awful she didn't even care that she was naked under the small bath towel. She finished with remnant dry heaves and Colt left her side momentarily and returned with a wet washcloth. She lifted her head and Colt noticed how pale she was. He wiped her face as she clutched the porcelain bowl, her small frame shaking under his hand that had returned to support her. His other hand gently wiped her mouth and her face.

"Okay?" He asked softly.

"I shouldn't have taken the pain pills before eating. I hate throwing up." Colt nodded.

"Yea, me too. Let's get you dressed."

"I can probably do it." She smiled so weakly up at Colt his heart lurched.

"Little one I know you want to but I think if I help we can get you dressed faster. I promise to be a gentleman and look away okay." He chuckled as she reddened bringing a spot of rosy color to her otherwise pasty face.

"Why? Why are you being so nice?" For some reason his answer was important to her.

Colt paused for a second. "It's the least I can

do." His answer pissed Karen Sue off and she had no idea why.

Colt helped her stand. Karen Sue couldn't stop the quick jab of disappointment she felt at his answer and worse the anger it elicited.

"I think you just feel bad for shooting me. I don't want you helping just because of a guilty conscious thank you very much!" It came out so maliciously Karen Sue felt awful the second it slipped from her mouth.

Colt was momentarily stunned. "Wow, nice." He stood up from helping her slide her feet into her yoga pants and left her room with her pants still by her ankles.

"Fuck." Karen Sue said under her breath. "What the hell is wrong with you?" She said out loud, reprimanding herself.

Karen Sue finished dressing and ran the brush through her hair. She still felt like hell and because she had thrown up the pain pill her shoulder was still killing her. She padded out to the living room. Colt sat at the kitchen counter eating a grilled cheese; there was another plate next to him with a sandwich on it. Mann and Gifford were watching TV on the sofa. When she entered the room Gifford told her that her grilled cheese was on the counter.

Karen Sue murmured a thank you and approached the counter. She went to the counter and as she did Colt lifted up from his chair at the counter taking his plate with his partially eaten grilled cheese with him. Karen Sue reached out and placed her hand on his arm halting his exit. She looked up at him; even sitting down he was taller than her standing next to him.

“I'm so sorry Colt.” She whispered trying to hush her voice so the other men wouldn't hear her. She was embarrassed.

Colt just looked at her without emotion. His eyes were dark, scary and hard to read and Karen Sue realized that this mountain of a man had opened up a soft side of himself to her and she had ungraciously ripped him sending him back into tough guy mode.

“No problem. “He said without an ounce of feeling. He stood and took his sandwich to the couch.

“Shit.” Karen Sue whispered to herself.

While Karen Sue was trying to eat everything that had happened began to play through her head like a movie trailer. She couldn't believe Ray had gotten himself in so deep with such a bad man. Ray was smart, wicked ass smart. She wished she had made him talk to her, forced him too, but she also knew why he hadn't. The man she had married, the Ray that had been her best friend, would never have let someone hurt her and she knew that's why he had distanced himself.

Tears started to slowly slide down her face for the umpteenth time that day. Her appetite evaporated as Karen Sue picked at her sandwich. She took a few bites only to keep down the pain pill she had just taken. She didn't want the men to know she was crying so she sat at the counter wiping the tears as they appeared. She heard Mann click open his phone, she didn't hear it ring and she realized it was most likely set on vibrate. Out of the corner of her eye saw him leave the living room with the phone pressed to his ear.

Karen Sue kept her face hidden as she threw her mostly uneaten grilled cheese in the garbage. By keeping her head down and tilting her shoulder she managed to get to her bedroom without anyone seeing her face. Karen Sue climbed on to the bed and let her tears loose, burying her face into the pillow so that her sobs wouldn't be heard.

A knock sounded on her door and she heard Gifford call through the door that Mann wanted to talk to her in the living room. Karen Sue wiped her face and trudged into the other room. Colt noticed immediately that she had been crying. Her shoulders were slumped giving her a defeated look. He saw that she was trying to keep her face concealed. Her one hand cupped her elbow, supporting the arm of the shoulder that had been shot. What was it about her that had him twisted up inside? Was he feeling guilty? He didn't think so. He had been pleased that he had saved her life, minus the part that his bullet had made its way into her shoulder. She brought out some confusing emotions in him. Ones he hadn't felt in a long time. He didn't know why she had flipped out on him but she'd had a hell of a day. He could justify her outburst, he just couldn't figure out why he felt so distressed by her being upset with him.

The men were sitting around the table near the breakfast bar so Karen Sue joined them. Mann jumped up as she approached to pull out her chair and Karen Sue mumbled a thank you.

"The I.T. guys just went through the audio from the shooting. I want to share with you guys what they told me." Karen Sue nodded keeping her head down.

"Your husband had been working off his debt to Pallone with creative online bookkeeping. He must have been moving money for Pallone all over the place into and out of different accounts so the IRS and FEDS couldn't track anything. From what we know he'd been doing this for a while. This was keeping you guys off the 'red' list. Anyway from what we gathered from the audio, Ray wanted out of the arrangement, I'm sure it was getting dicey and maybe Ray grew a conscious." Karen Sue's shoulders slumped even more and she let out a deep sigh.

"Sorry, I'm sure this is hard for you to hear about your husband. Can I go on? Are you okay?"

Karen Sue nodded.

"So today Ray told Pallone he wanted out. Somehow your husband was able to secretly transfer a couple of million dollars from the accounts he had access to into one account that only he could get into. He told Pallone today, that he had a record of all of his illegal transactions, and the account numbers associated with the people Pallone dealt with. Plus, he told him about the millions of dollars he had secured in an account that only he could access. Ray was bartering for your lives, Karen Sue.

He told Pallone he wanted his debt paid in full and he wanted guaranteed safety for him and you. He said if Pallone agreed he would start to send Pallone increments of the millions each month after he had gotten himself and you some place safe. He also told Pallone that he had a personal safety net. He told him he had incriminating documents that he had hidden somewhere only he could access. Evidently these documents contain information that could bring down not only Pallone, but also some powerful people that Pallone does business with. These stolen files put Pallone's life in jeopardy. It was a decent plan.

He had Pallone over a barrel and Pallone knew it. What Ray didn't factor in was that Pallone knew the millions were nothing compared to the damage the information could do. We figure Pallone must have decided to just kill Ray and eat the millions. He thought if only Ray knew where the files were then he was safer with Ray dead and the information buried with him."

The information Mann had just told Karen Sue nudged everything she had seen and heard for the last two years into place. Ray, her Ray, was trying to save their lives. He was a smart man, and so ingenious when it came to computer stuff that Karen Sue had no doubt that Ray thought he could pull this off. Tears had again formed in her eyes, it was becoming almost too much for her.

"Karen Sue with this audiotape and with what Colt knows and with you being at the scene and seeing Pallone holding the gun and giving the order to kill you we can put him away. We need you to testify."

Karen Sue looked up at Mann with a dazed look on her face. "I want to help."

Mann nodded and then added, "We will have to keep you and your parents in protective custody until after the trial, maybe longer."

“What’s that mean?” She asked quietly.

“Pallone knows your testimony will be big. If he can get to you he will. Furthermore, and I don’t mean to be indelicate, but I don’t think Pallone knows you and Ray were weeks away from legally being divorced. Pallone thinks you were a happily married couple and he probably assumed Ray talked to you.”

Karen Sue could feel Colt's eyes on her. She looked up to him first and then to Mann and Gifford.

“Ray and I were just housemates for the past two year. He didn’t talk to me. Our lawyers had told each of us not to leave the house. I didn’t know what was going on.” She paused. “So I’m not going to be able to resume teaching at my school am I?”

“No, we will need to move you, probably a good distance away?”

“Can I be with my parents?”

“No, that is too risky. We can possibly manage some visits and there are ways we will set up so you can communicate safely with them.”

“After the trial can I go back to my old life?”

Mann was quiet for a few seconds. “Honestly, we wouldn’t recommend it.”

“God this sucks.” Karen Sue bit out.

“We will transfer you and give you a new name, a new identity; we will help get you a job, not teaching though. We will prep you for the trial and bring you back to Newark when you are needed to testify. The trial may not even come to docket for a couple years.”

Karen Sue thought about everything Mann was saying to her. She wanted to help. She knew Pallone was a major crime manufacturer. She knew her dad would want her to do this. When she thought about it she wasn’t leaving much behind. She didn’t have any close friends Ray had conveniently chased them away. She only saw her parents once or twice a year. She’d miss her house. Her house...

“What about my house?”

“That depends on you, there are options.”

“Like what?”

“Well, you can hold on to it in the hopes of going back. You can sell it and take the money into your new life. You can rent it, but that gets tricky because you can’t be a landlord.”

“Oh, this is a lot to take in. Is Colt going to be put in to protection too?”

Colt straightened in his seat. Why the hell was she worried about me he thought? Then he thought maybe she wanted to make sure he wasn't near her.

"Don't worry I won't be anywhere near you." He said stiffly forcing a bewildered look from Mann and Gifford.

"That's not what I was thinking Colt." She said with forced bravado.

"We can't tell you where Colt is going to be, but yes he will be in a form of protective custody."

Colt grunted out a "Yea, dandy." That forced Karen Sue to look at him. He knew where he was going already, she could tell.

"Is there anything else?" she asked.

"Not right now. We've gotten you a lawyer and you will meet with the Federal prosecutor who will be trying the case before we leave. Pallone has been picked up and is currently in jail. The female US Marshall will be here shortly and she will have more information."

"Like where I'll be going?"

"Like where you'll be going." Mann confirmed.

"I would like to talk to my Dad, can I?"

"Yea that's a good idea."

Mann dialed a number into his cell and waited. He said thank you and hung up. About a minute later his cell rang and after answering it he handed it to Karen Sue.

"Hello? Daddy?" Karen Sue started to weep and got up from the table walking back into her bedroom.

Karen Sue spent forty-five minutes, give or take, on the phone with her parents. They were taking their protective custody detail not only in stride, but she thought she heard a little excitement in her dad's voice. They had friends in their Florida community but they told her they wouldn't mind a new adventure; retirement was a little boring her Mom had said. They had been concerned that she'd been shot but the US Marshall's had told them that it had been a well-placed shot by the undercover agent, and the alternative would have been her being killed, so her parents being realists, were just happy she was alive. They were sad about Ray but they had known the marriage had been over for a while and like Karen Sue they mourned the old Ray and the life their daughter had once had. Her Dad said he brought this down on himself and it had almost gotten her killed.

Karen Sue said her good-bye to her parents buoyed with the fact that Mann had assured her she'd be able to talk with them again. She glanced at the bedside clock and saw that it was nearing 5:00 am. She hadn't pulled an all-night'er in years she glumly thought to herself. Walking back into the living room she walked towards Mann who was sitting on the couch. He held out his hand and she dropped his phone into his palm.

"Thank you."

"Parents okay?"

"Yea, they sound surprisingly good."

"You okay?"

"Better now that I've talked to them."

"You should get some sleep."

"Umm, I'm not sleepy for some reason. You can go to bed."

"It's my shift to be awake."

"Oh."

"You have any more questions?"

"What about all my stuff in my house?"

"You make a list of what you want. We'll pack it up and get it to you."

"That's simple enough I guess."

Colt appeared in the living room. He had on his dress pants, no shirt and he was barefoot. God, Karen Sue thought as she drank him in; he was a friggin' Adonis and how inappropriate was it that she was tingly just looking at him when her husband had just been gunned down in front of her about twelve hours earlier. Colt followed Karen Sue's eyes as they swept his frame. Her demeanor seemed calmer now. He knew talking to her parents probably had calmed her.

"Colt you got a big day ahead of you why aren't you sleeping?" Mann said to him breaking the uncomfortable silence.

"Got in an hour. I'm good. You go in."

"Don't have to ask me twice. If you get tired wake up Gifford, it's his turn."

"Got it."

Mann left the room and Colt took his place on the couch. Karen Sue was looking down at her hands that were twisting together in her lap.

"Colt I am sorry. I don't know why I said what I did. I swear I'm usually not a bitch."

Colt sighed. “You’ve been through a lot.”

“That’s not an excuse. I’m sorry, really. I was mean and you were helping me. You helped me when I threw up, you were helping me dress, and you saved my life and put yours on the line by doing so. Honestly I don’t know what made me say that. Oh God, I’m an awful person.” Karen Sue shuddered, disgusted by her behavior.

Colt shifted in his seat so he was facing her. He saw how weary and overwhelmed she appeared and he wished he could take some of the pain from her.

“Karen Sue when I first came through your front door I saw Ray laying there with blood pouring out of him and then I saw you were underneath him. For a second I thought I was too late. I thought he had shot you too and I did feel guilty that I hadn’t gotten to you fast enough. Then I saw your eyes looking at us from behind Rays shoulder. Your eyes were so large just watching everything. I knew you had to be in shock because you weren’t screaming your head off. I also knew I had to save you.”

“It was like an out of body experience.” Karen Sue confided in him. “I think I knew Ray was dead but I kind of pushed it out of my mind. I saw you come in and when they handed you the gun I heard what Pallone said but it wasn’t registering. When I saw you coming towards me with the gun, that's when I knew I was dead. Believe it or not I was pissed off."

"Pissed off?"

"Yea that I had wasted years with Ray. That my life was over and I hadn't lived yet."

"You said please."

"I did?"

"Yea, real soft like."

"I thought I saw you mouth 'play dead.' Then you aimed and I felt Rays body jerk and I felt a burn in my shoulder. Then I passed out."

"You passing out made it look like you were dead and Big Tony bought it so that was probably a good thing."

They both sat quietly for about a minute.

Karen Sue ran one hand through her closely cropped hair. "My life is about to change isn't it?"

"I would say that's a big yes."

"Why won't they tell me where you're going?

"It's not good for either of us to know where the other is. It's a safety thing."

"Colt I know this is weird but I need to know.

I don't know why. This whole thing happened because of my husband and his gambling. I feel responsible."

"You're not." Colt interrupted her.

"Not directly, but maybe if I had tried harder to find out what was going on. If I had let him sell the house..."

"Karen Sue we've been through this. It's harsh but you were collateral damage. My defunct undercover job became collateral damage. You need to remember you are going to help bring this man down. You're going to put a major kink into an organization that sells drugs, guns, woman, and who runs a major gambling operation that hooked your husband. You're going to do good."

Karen Sue took Colt by his hand and Colt felt a zing where she touched him.

"Thank you. You are a genuinely good guy Colt." She smirked at the shocked look on his face. "Don't worry, your secret's safe with me. Now tell me why I see sadness in your eyes. Tell me where they are sending you, please?"

Colt looked towards the hallway. "I can't tell you directly."

"Okay what can you tell me?"

"I joined the Marines out of high school. I served two tours. When I got out the DEA was hiring and I found a place with them going undercover. I look younger than I am, plus I have firearm knowledge, can speak street, and I'm a hell of a shot."

"And?"

"And... I don't want to be placed in Witness Protection and not be able to work as a cop again. Because I am a Marine that has prior Service experience, I have another option."

Karen Sue thought about what he had just said for about two-seconds before she realized what he was saying.

"Oh God no!" She squeaked out in a hushed voice. "Please Colt don't go back in. That's what you're saying right?"

"I didn't say anything."

"Colt please if anything happened to you..." Karen Sue had no idea why she felt so strongly about Colt staying safe. It was unexplainable. She felt a connection with him that intrigued her and scared her.

"Karen Sue, I'll be fine. I've been there done that. I'm not a rookie I know what to expect."

"But Colt..."

"Listen I probably shouldn't have even told you what I did. You can't let Mann know. If they don't let me go overseas I would probably die from boredom in whatever mundane job they would find for me."

Karen Sue nodded. She was still holding his hand. "Can we still communicate somehow? You know with you there and me wherever?"

"Yea there's a way. When I get over there I'll write you through the Marshals Service and you can write back the same way."

"I would like that. You won't forget right?"

"Scouts honor."

"Were you a scout?"

"Ha no, but I do promise okay."

Karen Sue laughed and said okay.

The two of them remained next to each and continued talking until both Gifford and Mann jolted them both back to reality when they entered the living room hours later. It had been years, literally, since Karen Sue had talked to anyone with the ease she talked with Colt that morning. He now knew so much about her; about her parents, her schooling, her marriage, and she even spoke passionately of her love of art. She had sketched a picture of Colt while they had been sitting and talking. When Colt saw it he asked if he could take it with him and Karen Sue was delighted that he wanted it.

Colt in return had shared with Karen Sue the mileposts in his life. How his Uncle had raised him after his parents had been killed in an automobile accident. He spoke fondly of his Uncle telling her how he had been a Marine and that he had done a great job raising him. Colt had played sports in high school and even had football scholarship opportunities but he had always wanted to be a Marine like his Uncle, so he signed up the day after he graduated high school. After two tours Colt had had enough and when he went stateside he was snatched up by the DEA. After finishing his DEA training Colt and been assigned the undercover opportunity to bring down Pallone. It had been his first and maybe his last assignment.

He had confided to her that he hoped after he finished this third tour, which would last fifteen months, he could to go back with the DEA and maybe even under cover again. Karen Sue also discovered he was twenty-eight years old. She felt so young compared to him. He was just two years her senior, yet he seemed older, seasoned, so much wiser than herself.

When Colt left that morning Karen Sue felt empty. They had hugged good-bye and Colt had promised to stay in touch. They knew they would see each other at the trial; Colt would be flown back from wherever he ended up, but neither knew when that would be. Karen Sue was fully aware of exactly how much he had sacrificed to save her life. Now he was being whisked away and would soon be in some war torn country just so he didn't have to go into Witness Protection. Karen Sue sulked around the house waiting for the female US Marshall to come deliver the news of her own fate.

To occupy her time and to alleviate the empty feeling crushing her chest she spent her time by making a list of things she wanted from her house. She knew she wanted her dining room furniture. She and Ray had bought it when they were first married from a Pennsylvania Amish store. It was a beautiful handmade table with chairs, a hutch and a server. She also wanted the furniture in the spare bedroom. She didn't want the furniture from the master bedroom, too many memories. She wanted all paperwork, any personal items and all the pictures on the walls, most of which were her own artwork.

She wrote down a few items from the kitchen including her new crock-pot and a top of the line Keurig. Of course she needed her clothes, shoes, and jewelry too. She finished by adding the cut glass lamp currently sitting in her living room, a wrought iron three tier plant holder, and a small nesting table that her grandfather had made.

When she finished the list she realized that it looked paltry but it was all she wanted. Mann had told her that what she didn't want would be sold and she'd receive the money. He also told her the government would be buying her house at an above market price and then they would put it on the market. This way she'd have the money from her house at her disposal immediately.

Evidently when you were placed in Witness Protection you were given a small budget to work within. They would pay your housing until you got on your feet and help you find a job. Karen Sue understood that should she want something more she'd have to use her own money. She wasn't sure what the market price of her house was but she lived in a good neighborhood in an affluent county so unless she was moved some place that was fancy smancy she figured she'd be okay.

Chapter 5

One year later – Witness Protection in Colorado

Kit Taylor gripped the neon green nylon leash that was attached to a matching collar as she jogged with Maize, the yellow lab she was currently boarding at her home which also served as her place of business. Kit had really lucked out when she had been relocated to Steamboat Springs, Colorado. A small town in northern Colorado that was a renowned ski resort. She didn't ski but it was on her bucket list to learn. When she had first been transferred out West she had been so nervous, she had only ever known east coast suburban life, but now she couldn't imagine living anywhere else.

Kit loved the textured mountains, some green and lush, some topped year-round with snow, and some boasting beautiful rock formations that jutted out of the fertile land to stretch into the open pristine sky. The fresh air was sometimes intoxicating and she, being an artist, marveled at how the sky could change into so many beautiful colors; like a blue that rivaled tropical ocean waters or a gray life a Confederate Soldier's uniform. The sky foretold the weather and Kit had quickly learned to read it.

Kit was pleasantly surprised with how happy and friendly the people were. The overall pace was slower than back east and it still startled her when random people, whom she didn't know, would say hello to her as she passed them. The new life she had carved out for herself in the charming ski resort was coming together much better than she could have ever dreamt. She often thought how something so wonderful, referring to her new life, had resulted from the nightmare she had experienced a year earlier.

She had chosen the name Kit because it started with the first letter of her old name. Witness Protection had given her the last name 'Taylor' somewhat generic but Kit liked it and she had decided she looked like a Kit Taylor. She had grown her hair out and it now hung softly at shoulder length. She had grown her bangs out, sans the fun color streak that had been her MO since college. The style gave her a more mature look.

Kit had bought a fixer upper Victorian home situated outside of town on a secluded street not far from the main road. The money the government had allotted her wasn't nearly enough for what Kit had envisioned the second she saw the house, so she used the money she had received from the sale of her home in New Jersey. After paying off the mortgage and her outstanding debts she still had enough to buy the home and fix it up so she could use it as a home and for her new businesses.

Kit replaced the roof, upgraded the heating, redid the wooden floors, modernized the downstairs kitchen, painted every room, hall and closet, and fixed the sagging wrap around porch. She had transformed the second floor into a separate apartment for herself. Walls had been removed so the main living area, kitchen and dining area were now one open spacious room. An upper deck looked out over her private backyard and further back she had a beautiful view of a sloping mountain with hiking trails. Kit would often sit on her deck, when the weather allowed, mesmerized by the brilliant colors brought on by the sun, snow and other natural elements.

Kit had turned the main floor into an adult drop in day care center. She was careful to comply with all the coded regulations so she could acquire the appropriate licenses to run her new business. She had a ramp installed and the doors widened to allow for wheelchair access. She had two bathrooms overhauled and the downstairs kitchen was downsized and protected so her clients could not wander in without her knowledge. There were a couple of rooms she had created for her elderly clients. She had a quiet room that had big windows looking over her backyard and there was a television room that had a Wii game. Once she taught her clients how to play they were addicted and often pulled Kit into a game of Wii bowl or golf.

Her second entrepreneurial venture was a doggie day care and kennel. For that she had changed the dingy basement into a dog paradise. An outside side door off her driveway was the dog business' entrance. That opened into a large mudroom. In the mudroom there were steps leading down to the doggie day care and another door that opened into the kitchen area of her adult day care. In the basement Kit had covered the floor in easy to clean linoleum, and then she carpeted low ledges and alcoves she had built for the dogs to lay on and in. One of her favorite projects had been painting murals of fields and mountains landscapes that successfully brightened the large open room. It effectively added to the natural ambiance she had created for her dog clients. In the back of the large room steps led up to a door that had a giant sized flapping dog door cut into it. Through that door a large wooden deck ran the length of her house. A sliding door off the deck accessed her adult day care kitchen. The backyard was fenced in and boasted trees, large boulders, and lots of room for her dog clients to run in.

The outside of her house she had professionally painted white with light green, light rose and light blue trim that brightened the entire facade and made it look like a charming homestead. She wanted the house to look like it was a one-family resident and not a place that housed two businesses and an apartment. She knew she had succeeded when new clients tried to find her and often thought they had the wrong address.

Kit had secured some loyal dog clients in her first few months, namely the hardworking, crazy scheduled single men in the local fire department. Their hours were 48 on and 72 off so they often needed someone to watch their dogs when they were on duty and Kit was the perfect choice. Her house wasn't too far from the fire station and when she had their dogs she would jog with them past the station so the men could see their beloved pets.

The guys thought Kit was awesome and some had even asked her out but they were gently told no thank you. Kit wasn't comfortable dating and she wondered if she ever would be. It did bother her that she was a healthy twenty-seven year old woman, yet she had no social life. She could be more social, but her protected lifestyle made meeting people and dating difficult. She just wasn't ready to put herself out there yet. Whenever she met someone, anyone at all, she had to call her US Marshal contact Lori and Lori would have to check the person out per Witness Protection protocol. It was a hassle but Kit knew it had to be that way.

Her adult day care was a little slower to get going but she had a few regulars. She didn't need the money right now. The sale of her house and its contents had netted her enough money to buy the Victorian house, renovate it to suit her needs, buy furniture and even invest some. She, of course, had to invest through the US Marshals Service but it didn't matter. She was comfortable, busy and for the most part happy with her new, quiet life.

Colt had written to her like he promised and she had written him back like she had promised. Every time she wrote him she always included a small notepad size sketch. The first drawing was of her and him sitting on the couch that first night. She had purposely left the faces slightly obscure but their body positions on the coach and the way their hands had intertwined that night were all visible. The next letter contained a sketch of her house. She had sent him sketches of the beautiful aspen on the mountains behind her home, of a dog she cared for, of his favorite quarterback in the pros, and the last one was of a US flag blowing in the wind with the majestic mountains in the background.

Neither could divulge where they were and the Marshall's Service always read the correspondences anyway, just to make sure they didn't reveal too much information. They kept their letters as generic as possible and Kit always looked forward to them. Colt had started to include stick drawn figures on the back of his letters, which was his version of art, and never failed to make Kit laugh.

Kit turned down the road that lead to the fire station and Maize knew where they were headed so she moved her cream colored legs faster forcing Kit to pick up her pace. When they got to the firehouse Maize's owner came running bringing her a water and Maize a dog biscuit. The men were washing one of the rigs and they all waved to her. Kit noticed a new man washing the front end of the truck. He looked up from his task and sent her a lazy smile before returning to his grill scrubbing.

Bud, who was currently on his knees petting Maize his beloved dog called out towards the truck. "Jess come here, you need to meet Kit."

Kit looked up to see the new guy drop his sponge in the bucket near him and walk, make that swagger, towards them.

The guy was drop-dead gorgeous. His body commanded serious space. He had to be 6'4' easily. His shoulders were wide under his blue uniform and she could see his arms were muscled as they stretched the blue fabric tight around his bicep. Back east some men purposely wore smaller sized shirts to accent their muscles, but Kit knew, without a shadow of a doubt, this man did not play that game. He was perfectly sculpted and all male. She inadvertently wondered what he looked like out of his clothes. Kit had to slam her eyes shut to force that random thought away. She was reminded of Colt's gorgeous body and she had to push that vision out as well, because it was his body and face that she conjured up late at night when pleasuring herself.

The man Bud had called Jess, had honey blond hair that reached the back of his blue uniform collar. It looked soft and Kit wished she could run her fingers through it. He had indigo blue eyes that twinkled in the morning sun. His white-toothed adorable smile looked casual but mischievous too. Kit knew this man was trouble just by how he already had her heart thumping. She didn't normally react to most men, but then she thought he was not your garden-variety male either. She knew he was one of those men that had woman at his beck and call, twenty-four -seven.

The man walked to where they stood on the station's paved drive and Bud introduced them. "Jess Ryan this is Kit, she's the one we were telling you about that boards dogs."

Jess stuck out his hand and Kit wiped her sweaty hand on her shirt before placing it in his larger one. "Hi." She said shyly. Jess smiled when she had wiped her hand. His first think he noticed upon seeing her was that she was cute, however the closer he got to her he realized that she was gorgeous. When she wiped her hand he thought she seemed almost timid.

“Hi, any chance you have room for my dog too?” Jess asked.

“Hi, sure, what kind is it?”

“She’s a German Shepard, Lulu. She is well behaved I promise.”

“Lulu, cute name. Just call me with your schedule. The guys can give you my number. Will Lulu like our walks to the station too?” Kit was trying to appear nonchalant but for some ungodly reason her mind wasn’t working and her mouth had dried up. She took a large gulp from the water bottle Bud had given her and the water went down the wrong pipe. She sputtered helplessly embarrassed as it spilt out of her mouth and sloshed down her shirtfront.

Bud laughed. “Kit no need to chug I’ll get you another.”

Jess continued to look at her with his brilliantly beautiful eyes, smiling away with a knowing grin.

Cripes! Kit thought he knows I’m attracted to

him. She turned crimson under their scrutiny and lowered her eyes to Maize trying to calm herself.

Jess decided to help her out. “She craves to be outside and I run with her daily. Lulu will love jogging here and honestly I’ll love seeing her. I haven’t been separated from her too often in the past two years so leaving her has been hard.”

Kit looked at him and tilted her head giving him a questioning look.

“Lulu is a war dog, a bomb sniffer. I was her handler in Afghanistan. She was retired when I finished my tour so I was allowed to adopt her. We’ve spent a lot of time together.”

“Wow, I promise to take good care of her.” Kit was impressed and talk of Afghanistan reminded her of Colt. She prayed every night before she went to bed and every morning when she woke up that he stayed safe.

The fire chief came out from the open garage door and told the men to finish up and to head upstairs for a meeting. Bud gave Maize one last pet and Jess said he’d call her. Kit said good-bye and she and Maize took off jogging back towards her home. Jess watched the pretty little thing practically sprint away and he smiled; something he hadn’t done much of since returning from Afghanistan.

Chapter 6

The next day Kit did receive a call from Jess. He asked if he could check out the kennel before committing to anything; so Kit invited him over when he got off his shift the following day. She would still have Maize with her. Bud was picking her up when he finished with his shift that same afternoon as well. Her only other commitment for the next day was an adult day care client, Mr. Peterson, who was being dropped off for a few hours while his daughter ran errands around town.

At first, Mr. Peterson had been obstinate about staying at the day care. He insisted that he could be left home alone and he griped incessantly that he was being treated like a child. His good-natured daughter attempted to appease him by explaining that she was more comfortable knowing he was with someone. That had been three months ago, now Kit had trouble getting him to go home.

When Mr. Peterson arrived the next day, they played Wii for the first hour; then he dozed while Kit got their lunch started. Bud arrived while she was heating up the soup and she asked if he wanted to join them, which he immediately accepted. Bud went downstairs to play with Maize for a few minutes while she finished getting everything together.

Kit placed the lunch on the dining room table just as Mr. Peterson walked in after his short nap. He grimaced when he saw there was another place setting and practically growled when Bud came back upstairs to join them. Mr. Peterson did not like to share his sweet little caregiver. Kit playfully swatted his arm telling him to be nice. They ate their meal of soup and sandwiches while Bud regaled them with firehouse stories; how Kirby had burnt the dinner the night before and how Chad's wife was getting ready to go into labor and he was a nervous wreck. He also gave a detailed accounting of a call they had responded to the night before. A car had crashed out on the interstate and he described how they had used the Jaws of Life. Luckily there was no loss of life. When they finished eating Mr. Peterson excused himself from the table to watch his story on television. Bud helped Kit with the dishes.

"Kit I think Jess was kind of taken with you yesterday." He told her a little hesitantly.

"Oh Bud come on. He's just happy to find someone to watch Lulu."

"No, he asked about you. He wanted to know if you were single. He tried to ask me quietly but some of the guys heard him and gave him the business."

"Well, thanks for what... The warning? He doesn't look like he'd be hurting for female company." Kit replied jokingly.

"Why Kit Taylor did you notice how he looked? I can't believe it. Seriously if you hadn't told me you'd been married before I might have thought you played for the other team."

"What?" Kit cried out with a laugh.

"Come on, I know you've turned down dates from some of the guys, me included, and some of them are decent looking. Well, don't want to sound weird, but I think they are anyway." But chuckled at his little joke causing Kit to giggle. She then paused her dish washing and looked soberly at Bud.

"I just... I don't know. I'm not good socially." Kit replied candidly.

"You aren't social at all Kit!" Bud snapped the kitchen towel at her.

She laughed. "You don't know that!"

"I beg to differ. I have my ways and I am sure you haven't gone on one date since you moved here. Plus, I never see you at any of the local bars."

"Like I said, I'm not a big social butterfly, and I would never go to a bar alone."

"Do you even have any girlfriends?" Bud asked as he leaned his hip on the counter drying the last dish.

Kit became uncomfortable with his questions and fidgeted while she wiped down the sink area.

"Bud, I'm good. I'm happy. I'm concentrating on my businesses right now. If it's any consolation I signed up for ski lessons when the mountain opens up."

"That's a good start. You know I'd be happy to escort you to a bar one night."

"That's sweet Bud but that's probably not a good idea."

"As friends, just friends." He put both hands up in the air using an 'I surrender' gesture.

Kit thought about it. She chewed her lower lip and contemplated his offer. She was a little lonely, but she didn't want to lead Bud on.

"Maybe okay? Can we leave it at maybe?"

"A maybe's good, just friends. You can be my wingman... Well, wing woman."

Kit giggled. Bud was a good guy and he was probably the closest thing she had to friend. The front doorbell rang and she knew it was Mr.

Peterson's daughter coming to collect him. Kit sighed; didn't she realize she was coming in the middle of his story and he wouldn't want to leave.

"That's Mr. Peterson's daughter." Kit stated.

"I'll collect Maize and take off. Thanks for taking such good care of her. I'll see you in three days okay?"

"Three days." She repeated back to him.

"And Kit if you want to venture out, really, I'm here for you okay?"

"Okay Bud, thanks."

Jess knew he was at the correct address because he saw Bud putting Maize in the back of his pick-up truck that was parked in front of the house. The place didn't look like a kennel. It was the only house down the little secluded road. He could tell it had been recently painted and looked to be in good shape for a home in Colorado, considering the harsh winter season. When Jess had gotten off shift he had gone to his parents' house first to pick Lulu up to bring her with him. His parents had been watching Lulu for him while he worked. He knew her being there was not a long - term solution. Lulu needed more activity and his parents were more on the go than ever.

He put Lulu on a leash, something he rarely had to do, but he didn't know if there were other dogs or people inside and he preferred to be cautious. Jess rang the front bell and Kit opened the door giving him a shy smile. He heard loud voices coming from a room off the foyer and Kit motioned him inside and then excused herself, telling Jess she would be right back. He could hear the conversation from where he stood.

"Confound it girl, you know my stories on!"

"Dad come on I told you I DVR'd it for you."

"I hate that machine and you know it.

"Dad please, Kit has company. Let's go I promise to put it on the second we get home."

The voices moved closer until an elderly man appeared followed by a woman, who Jess assumed was the man's daughter, and then Kit brought up the rear.

The old man stopped before Jess.

"Who are you?"

Jess was slightly taken back with his aggressive tone, but he recovered quickly.

"My name is Jessie Ryan, sir."

Jess respectfully held his hand out for the

man to shake.

Mr. Peterson took the outstretched hand and shook it. “I like a boy with manners. You gonna board that dog here?’ Mr. Peterson asked.

Jess smiled that the man had referred to him as a boy. “I’m thinking about it.” Jess replied.

“Humph.” Mr. Peterson grumbled. “Another distraction. Kit you’re taking on too many dogs.” He said looking at her.

“Dad!” The woman chastised him.

Kit laughed and gave him a little hug. “Don’t worry Mr. Peterson you know you’re my number one client.”

Mr. Peterson smiled. Mollified with Kit’s comment, he let his daughter lead him out the front door to the car in the driveway.

“Sorry about that.” Kit said turning towards Jess.

“No problem. I take it he’s a little possessive of you?”

“Yea, he grumbles a lot but he’s all growls and no bite.” She laughed.

Jess chuckled at her analogy.

"So," Kit said as she knelt down so she was eye to eye with Lulu. "This must be Lulu."

Kit carefully let her hand dangle in front of Lulu's nose for the requisite sniffs. Then Kit advanced to petting her. Lulu gave Kit's arm an appreciative lick and then looked up to Jess as if to ask if that had been okay.

"Why don't I show you two around?" Kit said as she stood. She first took them to the side door to show Jess where the dog businesses entrance was. They toured the downstairs and then walked up the steps to the outside. Kit pointed out the doggie door explaining how the dogs could move about freely. Jess was impressed and he could see why the other guys had raved about boarding their dogs with her.

Jess asked a few questions regarding the business; like how many dogs did she have at one time and what the rates were.

Kit told him that the most dogs she'd ever had at one time was three, but there may be more if her business picked up. She also quoted the costs of her services, explaining that it was a special rate she gave to firefighters and police officers. Jess thought the fee was low, but he didn't comment about it. Kit also described how she would occasionally bring the dogs up to her apartment, which was upstairs, at night; especially if she had only one. She told him she lived alone, that they were good company, and she liked how safe they made her feel.

Jess asked if he could see her apartment and he observantly noticed that Kit was momentarily taken back. Kit was unnerved by Jess' request. None of the other clients had asked to see her apartment. She regained her composure realizing she had opened to door for it when she told him that she sometimes brought the dogs up there. The request alarmed her because despite being in Wit Sec for an entire year, Kit was still guarded with her personal life.

"Umm... I guess so." She replied. It wasn't lost on Jess that she had all of a sudden become a little nervous. She was a curious little thing he thought. A beautiful, intriguing, curious little thing he mentally added.

Kit walked them through the sliding door attached to the downstairs kitchen. She first showed him around downstairs as she explained that she also ran an adult day care business, which Jess had already pieced together after meeting Mr. Peterson. Jess was impressed with the homes lay out and with her entrepreneurial spirit. They ended up back in the main foyer where they walked up steps that Jess had noticed earlier. At the top of the steps, a larger than normal landing had been built and on that landing there was a door. Kit turned to her left and slid back a well – concealed small piece of the wall, exposing a top of the line burglar - fire alarm system. Jess knew from experience this was no ordinary home alarm; this one was serious. Kit nonchalantly commented that she needed to keep her private home secure from her business. Jess just nodded but his inner antenna was twitching big time.

Upon entering Kit's apartment the first thing Jess noticed was how it had clearly been renovated. He saw the large sliding door that led to a private balcony. The kitchen included a breakfast bar, which was one of the only things separating the well - designed room. Furniture had been placed to create a homey atmosphere. Jess noticed her dining room set immediately and knew it was handmade. He went over to the table running his hand over the expert craftsmanship.

"This is beautiful." He commented.

Kit's tummy did a little roller coaster dig. She was, for some odd reason, happy that he had noticed it. It was her favorite piece of furniture. She watched his eyes focus on the artwork that hung on the walls.

"I like your art too." Jess moved from one framed picture to the next. "I love these landscapes." Jess commented about one that she had just recently framed and put up.

"This charcoal drawing is beautiful." Jess

said as he stopped in front of a piece she had done a little over a year ago. It was the drawing of her hand on top of Colt's. It had been such a powerful moment for her that she drew it from memory. When she had completed the drawing she had copied it at Staples, making it much smaller in size and had sent it to Colt. He said it was his favorite so far of all the drawings she had sent him.

"Thank you" Kit said.

"Who's the artist?" Jess asked genuinely interested.

Kit looked away from his gaze and fixed her eyes on Lulu who stood obediently next to his owner.

"Me." She said so quietly Jess wasn't sure if he'd heard her correctly. Somehow he knew that it was Kit's hand in the picture. A foreign feeling washed over him as he acknowledged her hand lay tenderly on top of a male's hand. Judging from the size of the hand he was a large man too. For some reason Jess was hoping it was her father.

"I like these, Kit, you're talented." Jess looked away from the sketch of her and Colt's hand and watched the self-conscious woman as she looked apprehensively out the large window.

"Thank you." She said again.

"Kit, you're like an onion. You have so many layers."

Kit laughed out loud and swung her gaze to where he now stood in front of a colored pencil sketch she had done recently of a beautiful mountain scene. The sun had just set and the mountain shimmered with hues of purple and rose. Jess thought it was stunning.

"Wow, I like this one. Would you sell it?"

"Really?"

"Yea, I know exactly where I'd hang it."

"Umm, I guess. I haven't sold anything like this before; I'm not sure how to set a price."

"Why don't we hash it out over dinner?"

There, he'd done it. He had wanted to ask her out the second he saw her but there was no way he'd do it in front of the guys. Then he had tried to discretely ask about her but, of course, nothing is sacred at the station house so he was razzed for the rest of the day about his interest in her. The guys confided to him that they thought she was remarkable but had kept herself off limits. The men, whose dogs she watched, were happy with her kennel. Their dogs liked her and Jess knew dogs were great judges of character. It was also divulged to him that a couple of the firemen had asked her out and all had been politely turned down. She wasn't married, but Bud said she had been. He had no idea if she was divorced or widowed. The girl was an enigma.

"Jess that's probably not a great idea."

"Why not?"

"Well, for one, I'm hoping you'll board Lulu here when you're at work and that would make you a client. I don't date clients. I can't afford to lose customers because of a bad date."

"I haven't decided whether to board Lulu here yet, so technically I'm not a client yet." Jess grinned at her like a Cheshire cat.

"Yes, but still."

"What?" Jess was looking at her with a serious expression on his face. "It's only dinner. I'd like to get to know you better. Peel another layer, you know?"

Kit laughed again. "Do you even like onions Jess?"

"I friggin' love them! Honest!" Now Jess was laughing; again something he had not done much of in the last year.

Jess stepped towards Kit and she

unconsciously backed away keeping some distance between them. Her step backwards was not lost on Jess who quickly stood still. His first thought was that someone had done on a number on this doe-eyed girl because she suddenly appeared to be frightened.

"I don't date." She said softly.

"Don't or haven't?" Jess stood his ground but softened his tone.

"Well, I haven't. Not for a long time. God, I don't even think I remember the last time I went on a date." Kit said quietly. She worried she had probably just revealed too much information to him. Not Wit Sec too much information, just to a guy she didn't know, too much information.

"I haven't been on a date in a while either. Why don't we just call it two friends having dinner and see how it goes, okay?"

Kit kept the couch between them as a personal space buffer, but it did nothing to stop her from being physically attracted towards this handsome man. She was surprised he said he hadn't been dating. Maybe he was a hit and run type of guy. He seemed to get her though. He recognized how hesitant she was and he managed to say things to put her at ease. His large frame stood still behind her blue couch and he rested his hands on the back of it. Lulu stood patiently to his side.

"All right, dinner, when?" She relented somewhat nervously.

"How about tomorrow?"

"That's good. I'll have Mikey D's dog so we can't stay out late okay."

Mikey D was also a firefighter - Mike De Angelas and one of Jess' best friends.

"Lulu and I have hung out with Mikey D and Crank. They sometimes run the same trail we do."

"Crank's a good dog, a little hyper but he sure does love Mikey." Kit added.

"Yea, Crank's all right. Crank's the first non-military dog Lulu got to know."

"Why don't you leave Lulu here with Crank tomorrow night while we go to dinner? This way both Lulu and Crank will have company."

"That would be good, actually great. I'm not comfortable leaving Lulu alone. She's not use to civilian living yet. Even when I wasn't with her in Afghanistan there was always someone around. I didn't have to crate her too often."

"Crank doesn't like to be alone either." Kit smiled thinking of the first time she tried to leave

Crank in the basement while she ran errands. He had squished himself on the top of the basement steps waiting for her to return.

“Okay so dinner tomorrow, I’ll bring Lulu. Are there any foods you don’t like?”

“Are you saying it looks like I like food?” Kit playfully bantered. Kit blushed. ‘Oh my gosh’ she thought to herself, ‘did I just flirt?’

Jess smiled at her with full cheek-to-cheek smile. He thought to himself; ‘and there is another layer.’

“Ah and the lady has a sense of humor too. You know exactly that is not what I meant.”

Kit's blush deepened and Jess watched as the dusty rose color spread from her cheeks to her small neck. He had the most ridiculous urge to place his lips on that delectable neck and lick the blush off of her. God he bet she tasted great. His dick chose that moment to come out of hiatus, making its presence known within his work slacks. He changed his stance and before emerging from behind the couch made sure he was decent. Luckily for him Kit had turned to head to the door.

“Ummmm, I guess the only food I’m not into is spicy stuff.”

“Okay, good to know. I’ll swing by around

7:00pm tomorrow is that good?"

"Yes, that's good."

Kit opened her apartment door and waited until Jess and Lulu had passed her. Then she stepped out onto the landing with them, shut the door and keyed up the alarm hidden in the small paneling. She then turned and the three of them walked down the steps and out the main door and onto her front porch.

Jess could tell Kit wanted to say something. He hoped she wasn't having second thoughts about dinner already. On the porch with Lulu waiting protectively at his side Jess turned to Kit. The top of her head reached only to his sternum. He noted she really was petit.

"What Kit? I know you want to say something."

How did he do that? Kit thought.

"I, well, it's silly."

"It's probably not, come on ask away."

"Jess could you not tell anyone, right now anyway, that we are having dinner?"

"You want to keep it a secret?"

"Just for a day or until afterwards anyway. I

have to see Mikey D tomorrow and will be running past the station, I just..."

"No worries, Kit. I don't want to share you with anyone just yet anyway."

With that loaded statement Jess turned and walked down the steps with Lulu at his heels. Jess knew what he had said would put her a little on her heels but he wanted her to know she meant something to him. He didn't know what, my God he had just met her, but there was something about her. He wanted to unwrap her like a gift and start playing with her like a kid with a Christmas toy. She made him want to learn everything about her.

Jess sucked in a deep breath as he shut his car door. Trying to get a handle on the unfamiliar sensations zipping through him. He looked back to where Kit stood on her porch and envisioned pulling her close, threading his fingers through her golden blond hair and kissing her little pink lips. His first impulse was to protect her and he didn't even know from what. His second thought was that he wanted to bury his head in her thighs and feast on her. Then explore her adorable mouth with her sweetness still on his tongue. God she made him want things he hadn't thought of in years, and she made his dick jump, and that hadn't happened in a very, very long time either; despite what the guys thought.

Chapter 7 Jess

Jess grew up in Steamboat Springs the only child of two loving parents. He had wonderful friends, had made good grades, played sports, and enjoyed his share of woman. He hadn't been in many long-term relationships and had never thought of any of them as serious. When he was in high school he had dated an older girl who guided him through a year of wild sex. During that initial, experimental year he learned how to please a woman and he also discovered he liked to dominate when it came to sex. Nothing with pain but he enjoyed binding his partner and driving her crazy before blowing her mind. He quickly earned a reputation as a ladies man and often had woman openly proposition him, much to the awe of his firefighting brethren. Woman talked and word was he could deliver so woman was not shy about approaching him and he had no problem obliging them, until he had gone to Afghanistan.

Jess graduated from Colorado State with a degree in Criminal Justice. He played football there and enjoyed the camaraderie of being on a team. He was never without friends or women, but Jess preferred small gatherings opposed to wild parties. After graduating he moved back home and in a surprise move, instead of applying for the State Police or Sheriff's Department, he applied for and accepted a job with the local fire department. They sent him to firefighter's school where he excelled and specialized in combatting forest fires. After five years on the job Jess was a well-known member of an elite group of smoke jumpers. An extremely dangerous job where he and his team are required to jump into the middle of forest fires to battle the blaze from within.

Jess was happy with his life but he had become restless. His career was going well but he was an adrenaline junky and although he didn't wish for fires to break out, he loved the charge it gave him when he fought them. His love life was another kind of fire. He never felt the pull to settle down, even though many of his peers where doing just that. Like in college woman flocked to him and he would occasionally take one on a date, but he always kept them at arm's length. He never gave them false hope and because of this he had gotten the reputation as a womanizer. It was simply that he had never met someone who he wanted to spend his free time with. He liked sex, he liked sex a lot, but he didn't want the entanglement of a relationship even if it meant hot sex all the time. So Jess fought fires in his hometown, jumped into forest fires whenever he and his team were called in and he fucked woman, lots of women.

A few years earlier while working a particularly nasty forest fire in California, Jess met a man who changed his life. Vince Holmes, a retired FBI agent that had been in Viet Nam and who was also a retired smoke jumper. Vince wasn't actively fighting fires anymore but he still was involved as a consultant and was often flown in to aid with strategies to fight the unpredictable fires. Vince and Jess had bonded one night over beers at a hotel bar. The fire they had been working on had been downgraded to 'under control' so the team of smoke jumpers Jess was attached to were told they could go home. That night Jess learned that Vince had a particularly unusual skill. He was a bomb expert. Vince told Jess about some of his personal experiences. This included the dangers he had faced, some of the bad shit he had seen and then, of course, the good, which outweighed the bad. Jess was intrigued so Vince encouraged him to sign up for courses that were offered through the fire department that trained men and women to handle bombs.

Jess did just that and within a year he had taken and excelled in his training. He learned about different types of explosive devices, how to assemble and disassemble them, and most importantly how to spot them. When he tested off the charts in aptitude and character traits Jess was sent to Washington, DC to further his education. In DC he surpassed his classmates, especially when he was paired with a K-9. Jess knew his life was about to change. He loved being a firefighter and a smoke jumper, but working with bombs was a different kind of rush, a challenge he couldn't back down from.

When he graduated from an intense four-month course in DC, the Army sergeant who had been teaching most of the classes approached him. He asked if Jess had ever considered serving. Jess told him he hadn't and told the sergeant that he was twenty-seven and he assumed he was too old. The sergeant told him he wasn't too old and that his country and the men and women serving needed a man with his unique qualifications. Good men were being hurt and killed every day and people with Jess' skills could make a difference. So Jess enlisted in the Army. He suffered through boot camp with guys that were fresh out of high school and then completed two, fourteen-month tours overseas.

While Jess had been in Afghanistan he and Lulu, the K-9 that had been assigned to him, were responsible for sweeping areas for a Marine unit he'd been placed with, making sure it was safe, well as safe as any war torn area could be anyway. After scouting out front, he and Lulu would fall back while the squad cleared the area of insurgents. Jess and

Lulu didn't just sit back idly, he and Lulu dropped behind securing their flanks, the rear, and that usually meant dealing with anyone that had slipped past the well-tuned Marine force that was surging forward.

Jess' first priority was to keep Lulu safe. She wore a flak jacket like the men did. Lulu had saved countless lives with her well - honed sense of smell. If she stopped and barked that meant there was an explosive. Then Jess would secure Lulu away from the area and he would either shoot at the bomb to detonate it or he would have to dismantle it. The bombs were often simple homemade devices and unless they were staying black, which meant quiet; he just cleared the area and shot them.

During one mission, one that continued to haunt Jess, he and Lulu had swept and cleared a partially caved in building. He then stood watch outside. While he and Lulu stood attentively, guarding the entrance and small dirt ally way, he heard muffled cries coming from what appeared to be an open storefront a few buildings up the vacant main road. He and Lulu cautiously made their way to the building and slipped inside past the vacant wooden stands. They crept up an isle to where a dirty curtain hung across a doorway partitioning the front neglected stalls from whatever was in the back.

Jess quietly drew the curtain to the side. What he saw inside, to this day, still had him jolting awake at night. Two men were holding down a young woman and raping her. Not with their cocks, which he saw were out of their pants, limp, glistening and obviously just used, but with a long and dirty rifle barrel. The girl was moaning and bright red blood ran from her vagina down to her thighs and butt, which were being held firmly down on a seedy wooden table.

Jess fired off two quick shots and the two men were dead before either one knew he was there. His shots brought the men from his squad running. They too saw the young woman, who Jess figured couldn't be more than twelve or thirteen, laying on the table, with blood dripping off of her and onto the dirt floor.

The young girls eyes rolled to the back of her head and she mercifully passed out. The medic in his squad cleared everyone out of the room except for Jess who still held his gun, white knuckled, as he stood staring at the poor girl on the table. Jess watched the Doc go to work. He was an EMT, but no matter, he knew his shit. One of the men in Jess's squad came back with an older woman who was crying. When the woman saw the young girl she sobbed even louder and Jess felt such intense sympathy for her and the young girl that it gutted him. He knew he would never be the same.

The brutality of what those men had been doing and the fact that it happened all too often in war torn countries was becoming too much for him. He knew then he would not re-up for a third time and he prayed he could somehow; someday, forget the image of the girl on the table.

Another one of Jess's squad mates spoke with the overwrought woman and was able to discern that the young girl had been raped a year ago, no one knew by who, and because she was now considered 'unclean' she was given to men to do with what they wanted, as long as they paid her father. Jess was disgusted and fought the bile that was threatening to surface. Doc told the soldier to relay to the young girl's mother that she needed medical help, that she was hemorrhaging badly and then, as if the scene hadn't been gruesome enough, the young girl began to convulse on the table as thick crimson blood gushed from her vagina. Within minutes she bled out and died. Doc said the men had ruptured something inside of her with the rifle barrel. The scene was horrific and it sobered his entire squad for days.

When his second tour ended he was thirty-one years old and after seeing some shit he knew would haunt him forever he was ready to go back to a quieter life, fighting fires in Colorado. That wasn't to say his bomb dismantling skills couldn't still be used and the DEA, FBI, and HLS knew exactly where he lived and how to get in touch with him. He had been called in to use his skills twice since he'd been back. Once at a high school to a bomb scare call. He wasn't involved with the actual sweeping of the school but he had been brought in, in case they had found anything; he was there to decide how to deal with it. Luckily it was a false alarm. The second time he had been called upon had been just last week. There had been an explosion in a small plant and he had been asked to walk through, as a favor to a US Marshal, to determine if it had been a bomb or an accidental explosion. It had been accidental.

Jess thought about Kit as he drove his jeep up the small mountain road before turning onto his private drive. Since that incident in Afghanistan Jess hadn't had sex, and even worse, when he had tried to it had been a colossal bust. When he was first discharged, he had a leggy, large chested wet dream practically chase him into his hotel room in Hawaii. After a few minutes of hot and heavy kissing and petting, Jess realized he wasn't getting hard, not even a little. Luckily for the leggy blond he was gifted in pleasing a woman and she never even knew how he ailed. Although he was more than a little concerned about limp appendage, he simply satisfied her a couple times in other ways before sending her away.

After a few more 'dates' with the same

dysfunctional results he knew he was in trouble and he sought out professional help. The good news, he was told, was that it was in his head. It wasn't anything physical. The bad news was his doctor couldn't say how long it would last. Although Jess didn't think about sex as much as he had before going overseas, it weighed heavily on him that he might never be able to have sex again.

Until today that is, when his cock suddenly jumped to life in Kit's living room. Jess had been so shocked that he almost blurted out to Kit, "Hey look I've got an erection." Luckily he regained his senses and was thankful he'd been standing behind her couch. Jess smiled to himself as he entered the welcoming tunnel of aspen that bracketed his dirt driveway. When he made the slight turn at the bend his home came into view. He was still astounded at how perfect this place was for him. He had his parents to thank for that.

Before Jess had gone to Afghanistan he had already accumulated a descent sized nest egg from working at the firehouse and living at home. When he went overseas he had given his parents power of attorney for two reason's; one, the obvious, in case something happened to him and two; if his mother, who happened to be a Realtor, found the perfect house for Jess she was instructed to buy it.

During one of his Skype sessions with his parents his Mom showed him a picture of a beautiful cabin, surrounded by aspen. She told him where it was located and what the owner was asking for. It was within his means and so his parents bought it. It sat on forty acres of wooded land. The best part was that the back and sides of his property joined with National Forest land, so no one could build anywhere near him. Jess liked his space, his privacy, he always had. He wasn't a recluse. He enjoyed being with people, but more often than not; he maintained a distance that he hadn't before. Especially now, upon returning stateside, he often found himself exasperated with stupid little things that some people did. Unkind people were a major pet peeve, but loud persons, braggarts, people who flaunted money, he just couldn't stand being around them.

Jess stopped the jeep on the gravelly spot near his barn turned garage. The small-detached barn structure was something he had added when he had moved in. In bad weather he could park inside of it, also it held a plow he could attach to his jeep along with some second hand tools he had picked up. The barn still had that new lumber smell to it and Jess had plenty of extra room inside for whatever project might call to him in the future. Jess enjoyed using his hands and hoped to build some furniture. It was one of the reasons he was so taken with Kit's dining room set. He'd love to be able to make something that beautiful.

Jess slid out the driver side door and Lulu bounded down right after he did. She wandered over to a patch of lawn near a tree that had become her favorite spot to pee. Jess walked to his front door and after unlocking it and stepping inside he moved immediately to his alarm system, keying in the numbers to negate the alarm going off.

He loved his house. A rustic log cabin with a front porch and that boasted beautiful wood trim. The bottom floor, like Kit's apartment was open and airy. Large sliding doors in the back led to a stone patio. Another addition he had made when he moved in. A grand stone fireplace to the right with a wooden beam jutting out over it that served as the mantel. On the left was a kitchen area with a breakfast bar completed with four stools. His living area had an L shaped couch that was positioned so when you sat on it you could see the fireplace and the large flat screen that he had had installed on the wall in the far corner. Steps ran up to the loft hallway along the back of his home. Upstairs he had two bedrooms and a large full bathroom with a stacked washer and dryer.

The house was decorated with furniture that had wood accents, which kept the decor natural and carried the charming wooden theme throughout it. His Mom and Dad had outdone themselves and outfitted his kitchen with everything he might need. He still hadn't figured out how the damn Panini thing worked yet. The colors that ran throughout his home were predominantly in the brown family and that highlighted the wooden floors and wooden ceiling beams that ran throughout the home. Blue and green accent colors added a splash of color to each of the rooms. His chocolate brown leather couch was smothered with bright pillows that often ended up on the floor or under his feet when he propped them on the old cobbler's bench he used as a coffee table. He had two large overstuffed chairs one green and one blue, each having brown throw pillows accenting them.

His Mom had also fancied up his place with a dried flower wreath and some candleholders keeping the color theme alive. Steamboat Springs had an abundance of artists that turned out beautiful crafts. Jess' Mom filled his home with local flavor. When Jess had arrived home a few months ago he had been wowed by what his parents had done for him. His place was move in condition and it suited him to a tee. The privacy, the rustic features of the cabin, the decor, everything was perfect and Jess had spent much of his free time working on or around his home making it his safe haven. The picture he wanted to buy from Kit would hang in his living area, between the two sliding doors. He hoped she'd sell it to him.

Just thinking about her made him smile again. This dinner date with her was going to be a sort of first time for him too. Since coming home he hadn't been on a date. He'd had one drunken hook-up, with an old friend named Tina. He had been hoping his cock would work, but it hadn't, so he gave her a couple of orgasms and distanced himself. Unfortunately she had his number and he found himself frequently dodging the woman when he ventured out. He had not had anyone spur his interest in a long time and along with the fact that he had a major body function issue, he had been more comfortable being alone, until he met Kit.

Chapter 8

Kit called Marshall Lori after Jess left so she could check him out before her date. When Kit told her his name Lori told her she already knew him. Kit wanted to ask how she already knew him but Lori started telling her about Jess and she didn't want to miss anything she said so she didn't interrupt her.

Lori told Kit the man was A plus perfect. He was a firefighter; a smoke jumper and he served two tours in Afghanistan as a bomb specialist. Lori explained he'd only been stateside about three months. He had spent his first few weeks after being discharged in Hawaii waiting for his dog to be officially retired and then to clear customs. When his dog got to Hawaii they flew home together to Colorado. He took some personal time before rejoining the fire department about a week earlier. According to Lori he was highly regarded by everyone that met him.

Kit confided in Lori that she was nervous about her date and Lori laughed telling her she'd be fine. Lori then got serious and reminded Kit not to talk about her past and stick to the story guide they had set up the year before. Kit had become good at deflecting questions about her past.

When she hung up with Marshal Lori, Kit rifled through her closet trying to decide what to wear and when she didn't find anything she knew she had to go shopping tomorrow in Steamboat Springs after she got Crank settled.

Mikey D brought Crank at the ungodly hour of 5:45 am but his shift started at 6:00 so it had to be. Before Mikey D left he hesitated, and then as if revealing a secret, he confided to Kit that Jess had been asking questions about her. Kit thought it curious that both he and Bud thought she needed to know this tidbit of information.

"Mikey are you trying to warn me or something? Because Bud told me the same thing."

"I don't know, maybe. Jess is a great guy. He's always been popular, especially with the ladies. He's one of my best friends, but I have to tell you he's not the relationship sort. He's also changed a bit since coming back."

"Changed. How so?" She asked her interest piqued.

"He's different now, more serious, and quieter."

"Well, he's probably seen a lot that you and I

can't even imagine."

"Yea, that's what the Captain said. I just...I just wanted to tell you. Jess is one of my best friends. Shit, he's a fucking, oops sorry." Kit smiled. "He's great and really great at what he does. I just wanted to let you know, okay?"

"Okay and Mikey D, thanks."

"So we're good?"

"We're good. Have a good shift. I'll jog by later this morning."

"Thanks Kit, you're the best."

Mikey D left and Kit led Crank upstairs into her apartment. She allowed the dogs to walk through the downstairs rooms when no one was there when she brought them to her apartment but because of health code regulations she never let them stay there.

Kit made toast with apple butter jam for breakfast and watched TV with Crank lounging at her feet. The stores in Steamboat Springs opened at 10 am so Kit had it planned that she'd jog with Crank at 9:00, come home, put Crank downstairs, then shower and shop.

At almost exactly 10 am Kit was climbing into her Subaru Forrester to find the perfect date outfit.

She wished she knew where they were going and almost called Jess to ask but instead she decided to wing it. Her first stop was at a small boutique store right in the middle of town where she found a simple white spaghetti strapped dress. She'd have to wear her sticky boobs since the back dipped low but it was July and that was fine. She loved July in Colorado; so far it was her favorite month. Cool enough for sweaters in the morning and night, but warm enough to swim or tube on the Yappa River during the day. Her next stop was into Lightfoot, a renowned western wear store, where she bought a pair of cowboy boots with a blue, green and rose-colored flower patterns swirled into the soft leather.

Last stop was to Maribel's, a small shop that specialized in jewelry. Kit bought a silver cuff with a large turquoise stone and silver dangly earring that had turquoise stones as well. Pleased with her purchases Kit rewarded her with a small mocha swirl cone and then she headed home.

Her first couple of months in Steamboat Springs, Kit had been too nervous to venture out much. The Marshal's service had set up an online account for her and most of what she had needed she had purchased on line. She intentionally shopped for groceries at off peak hours because she wasn't comfortable being around many people. It was a rude awakening when she realized the fraternizing she had done in college was all because

Ray had dragged her with him. Granted she wanted to go with him. Heck, back then she would have followed Ray anywhere. Kit sighed at the painful memory. She hated when they would pop up randomly, sometimes triggered by a smell or a song. Lately, she assumed because she was happy with her new life, the memories didn't cut her to the quick like they use too.

Kit welcomed another adult day care drop off that afternoon, Mrs. Pritchard. Her daughter Nancy, was a little tiny woman whose spouse had just recently ran off with his secretary, very cliché, Kit felt sorry for her. Mrs. Pritchard was starting to get dementia and Kit saw that her daughter was having a hard time dealing with her lapses. She also knew that Nancy was looking for full time work and had inquired if Kit could take on her Mom full time if that happened. Kit was not comfortable making that commitment. She loved her dog business and she enjoyed the freedom she had with her schedule, something she hadn't had when teaching. So Kit had been researching other options for her. Nancy was on her way to an interview to be a receptionist in a Doctor's office. Kit wished her luck and then settled Mrs. Pritchard into the TV room by the large window. Mrs. Pritchard loved to watch the birds so Kit had put up a large bird feeder outside the window. The only problem was, unlike in her old suburban town of New Jersey, Kit had to remember to bring the feeder in at night so it didn't attract other animals, namely bear.

Nancy picked up her Mom after an hour and a half; she had also used the time after the interview to food shop. She paid Kit and told her the interview went well and she'd let Kit know if she heard anything. After Mrs. Pritchard and Nancy left, Kit went to the side mudroom door and called to Crank who came flying up the stairs. She put Crank on his leash and told him they were going for a short walk so she could start to get ready for her date. Kit laughed that she was talking to Crank like he was a human and good old Crank just cocked his head to one side and listened to her.

Kit was becoming more nervous with each passing hour and came really close to canceling, but there was something settling about Jess. He seemed like a good guy, he had wowed Lori. She was a little leery that Bud and Mikey D felt like she needed to be warned about him though. She hoped it was simply a case of them acting brotherly.

After giving Crank a good walk up the trails behind her house Kit re-showered and dressed in her new outfit. Her hair was down and fell gently along her exposed collarbone. Her new dress was flirty and fun with pearl like buttons that ran down the front bodice stopping at her waist. The dress' skirt was A line and stopped a couple inches above her knees. She applied mascara and pink lip-gloss, which was all she ever wore. Her new cowboy boots were a bit of whimsy. Everyone else wore cowboy boots with dresses she decided she would too, besides she loved the look. Her new jewelry finished her outfit. Kit looked in the mirror and decided she liked how she looked. She hoped Jess did too.

Jess rang her bell at precisely 7:00 and Kit scooped up her small bag, engaged the apartment alarm and ran down the stairs. Kit opened the door for Jess and Lulu. Lulu had a small bouquet of wild flowers in her mouth. Kit laughed when she saw it and promptly fell to her knees taking the flowers from her mouth and hugging Lulu before giving her a kiss on her black cold nose before standing back up.

"If I'd known you were going to give out hugs and kisses for the flowers I would have given them to you myself." Jess chuckled.

Kit laughed and Jess decided she had a great laugh. For some reason he got the impression she didn't laugh often enough. He hoped to change that.

Kit looked at Jess peering over the small, beautiful bouquet. "Thank you Jess. This was sweet of you." Kit's stomach was doing little flip-flops and she knew she was blushing again.

Kit invited them in and turned towards the mudroom door. "I'm going to put this in water would you mind putting Lulu in the basement, Crank's going to be so happy he has a playmate." Kit went into the kitchen and Jess led Lulu downstairs. As Kit had predicted Jess saw that Crank was excited to be with a friend as the two dogs darted all over the basement playing hide and seek dog style. Jess walked back upstairs as Kit came out holding a vase with the flowers in it. She placed the vase on the table in the front foyer. She moved a bud and rearranged a stem and when she finished she graced Jess with such a dazzling smile that he stopped breathing. God she was gorgeous and Jess didn't think she even knew it. Kit eyed Jess nervously. He was standing still and was staring at her, it made her hyper aware that she was on a date.

"Ready?" She asked, hoping her voice wasn't shaking as badly as her knees were.

Jess was jolted out of his haze and gulped in a much-needed breath.

"Yea, uh Kit I gotta tell you, you look great. I mean you probably always look great but, woman right now you look...you're beautiful."

Kit blushed and again Jess marveled as he watched her creamy skin changing to a rosy hue.

Kit thanked Jess in a tiny voice and he smiled at her obvious discomfort on being complimented. He wondered how someone so beautiful could not be accustomed to men complimenting her. She was such a mystery. They left the house but not before Kit had engaged the security system near her front door. Jess was curious about her hyper cautiousness. He led Kit to his jeep and opened the door for her and even helped her with her seat belt being mindful of his hands. He wanted her relaxed not skittish.

When they got on the road Kit asked where they were going and Jess told her it was a surprise. He confessed to her that at first he thought to take her to the rodeo. In Steamboat Springs there was a rodeo on Friday and Saturday nights in July. However, he thought better of it because he was sure they would run into people they both knew there and he was honoring her request for privacy. Kit nodded and told him she had never been to the rodeo but she was glad they weren't going there tonight. Jess smiled and said he would love to take her to it another time. Kit smiled and told him she would love that. That set well with him that there was already a possibility of another date.

He drove them through Steamboat Springs past the Hayden airport until they got to a small town Kit hadn't visited yet. Jess parked and led Kit into a small barn turned restaurant. There was a beautiful horseshoe shaped bar with the requisite stools. Tables and chairs were scattered around a dance floor and beyond the dance floor was a small stage that already had a band setting up on it. Kit could see through another opening that there was a game room. The place was bustling with the dinner crowd. Jess leaned in and spoke softly into her ear that this place has the best burgers in northern Colorado. Kit turned and her nose brushed his cheek as she whispered to him that she loved burgers and she hoped they had fries too, because nothing pissed her off more than a place serving chips with a burger instead of fries. Jess laughed out loud which brought a few stares from nearby tables making Kit giggle. She liked the fact that she had made him laugh. As he had thought with her, she liked his laugh and she hoped to hear him laugh more often.

A hostess seated them and after sending Jess blatant sexual signals she sauntered away with a little more sway to her tush than necessary. Kit couldn't help but roll her eyes. "Tell me it's not always like this when you're on a date?" She asked.

"Like what?" he asked seriously.

"You know, woman fawning all over you."

"Did you think she was 'fawning'?" He laughed.

"Big time fawning." Kit countered.

Jess looked at her and then left his side of the table to join her on her side. Kit moved over to make room. It seemed like an odd thing to do but maybe it was a western thing. Kit looked at him as he slid in then lowered her eyes to the menu in her hand.

"We can talk more discretely this way and if I want to hold your hand it's a lot easier." Jess said his voice dropped an octave and then he released a seriously heart stopping grin on her. Kit's stomach plummeted. Oh man this guy was good she thought.

Jess took her menu from her hands and made her look at him. "I have a confession to make." He said earnestly which put Kit on edge. Kit nodded so he'd continue. "I haven't been on a date in over two years. I'm a little nervous." Kit looked at the gorgeous man sitting at her side and couldn't believe he had just told her that.

"Jess, I know you've been overseas but since you've been back, nothing?"

"Nope, nothing."

"I'm a little shocked. I mean you obviously don't have a problem attracting woman. Can you tell me why?"

"No interest until now."

"Puhhhleezze... that could be the best line ever." Kit elbowed his ribs with a giggle.

"Honest Kit. I know I have a rep, I know what the guys think, but..."

"You've changed." She said. It wasn't a question.

Jess nodded. "I'm glad you said yes to dinner Kit." His smile reached all the way to his eyes.

"Me too Jess." Jess handed her back her menu, gave her a sexy ass wink and then picked his own menu up.

Dinner was perfect. The burgers were excellent and she and Jess spent much of the time getting to know each other. Kit adhered to the story the Marshal's Service had constructed for her. She was widowed, not a lie, which was a good thing because she was a terrible liar. She moved to Colorado Springs because she decided to start fresh somewhere. When he asked where she had gone to school? She said Rutgers, she and Ray had attended William Patterson. Where had she grown up? She said Chester, New Jersey, when, in fact, she'd grown up in Morristown, New Jersey. It helped with keeping her cover story straight that she knew the areas. It made it easier for her.

Kit learned Jess grew up in Steamboat Springs and had attended The University of Colorado where he played football. He told her how he first became a firefighter then how he then became a Smoke Jumper. He explained that when the team of smoke jumpers that he was assigned to was needed; his firehouse would lend him out. That's the way it was with all the smoke jumpers. He told her how he hoped to be a team leader one day and get his Instructors Certification.

Then Jess told her about meeting Vince Holmes and how he became interested in disarming bombs. Jess told her how he became a member of the Explosive Ordnance Disposal (EOD), and how he had been paired with Lulu. Like Lori had said, he had spent 28 months in Afghanistan and he'd been home for about three months. Kit mentally noted that the man had three different jobs and all of them were dangerous. Jess divulged that he only recently rejoined the fire department because he had wanted to spend a little down time working on his house. He then told Kit all about his house and she noted how his eyes lit up when he described it.

Kit felt comfortable with Jess. He had put her at ease and she found him easy to talk to. The waitress had tried to garner Jess's attention but he had barely taken his eyes off of her. He made her feel special and she knew that put a silly smile on her face but she couldn't help it. After dinner when they were drinking coffee he did hold her hand. When he had reached for it under the table he could feel her tighten and slightly pull away, but Jess smiled gently at her and wrapped his large fingers softly around her littler ones, letting the entwined hands rest casually against her thigh.

Their table had been cleared and Jess ordered them each a beer. The bar was beginning to get crowded and a band started to do a sound check. Jess turned to Kit keeping her hand firmly in his. "I was told this band was good. Would you like to stay for a bit?" Jess had put the ball in her court and Kit appreciated that he asked her and hadn't just assumed she would want to stay. Ray would have told her they were staying and then, of course, she would have.

"Sure, let's hear them." She said enthusiastically.

Jess was psyched and relieved that she had agreed to stay. His next move would be to see if he could get her to dance, preferably a slow song, which would allow him to wrap her up in his arms, something he'd wanted to do since he'd first met her. More people filled in the bar and soon it was standing room only. The band started playing and the bars patrons whooped their approval. There were two main vocalists; a male and a female, so they were a great cover band playing many of the current country hit songs. Kit watched the dance floor fill up and her toes started tapping out the beat to the songs. She loved dancing but she didn't know any line dances and she had never two stepped either. There were some songs that people free styled to and Kit found herself wanting to join them.

The band started playing one of Kit's favorite songs by Luke Bryan, Country Girl. Jess turned to Kit and asked if she'd like to dance. Kit was hoping Jess was a dancer, some guys weren't. She nodded back at him with a huge smile on her face and they slid out of the booth. They found a spot on the dance floor and Kit discovered the man could move. He kept his eyes on her face and grinned when her eyes locked in on his hips that were naturally keeping perfect rhythm with the upbeat song. Kit's smile lit up her face as she looked up to the sexy man in front of her, moving in tune to the music. Kit clapped her hands together like she had just received a grand present, let out a small delighted whoop and joined the happy party on the dance floor, wiggling her hips and losing herself in the vibrant atmosphere.

Kit and Jess stayed on the floor for three more dances. The second one had a great beat and she found herself grasped tightly and within minutes Jess had taught her the two-step. She simply had to follow his lead to the two quick steps followed by two slower steps. Jess kept great time with the music and he was easy to follow. The third song was a slow song and as other couples separated to leave the floor Jess pulled Kit in closer. He placed her hands so they rested on his shoulders then he put one hand on the small of her back and the other hand just above that. He had been waiting all night to hold her close. He drank in her smell and how soft her body felt against his. It took Kit about thirty-seconds before she relaxed in Jess's arms. Jess felt the second she let herself go. Her body fit him like a lost puzzle piece and she swayed gently against him as she looked up into his eyes with a shy smile. Jess couldn't help himself and he placed a quick and chaste kiss upon her forehead. Kit took her hands off of his shoulders and wrapped them around his strong back and then she leaned her cheek against his chest and melted into Jess's strong embrace as they continued to dance.

This was exactly what Jess had hoped for. They had gotten to know each other; she had relaxed and shared personal information about her earlier life. She liked dancing and so did he so that was a definite bonus. She was smiling and seemed relaxed; mission accomplished. When the slow song ended Jess led her back to the table where they finished their beers and headed out.

When they got back to Kit's house she needed to walk Crank so Jess accompanied her while he walked Lulu. Kit hooked Crank to the leash, picked up her iPhone engaged her flashlight App., grabbed a small plastic bag and relocked the house after re-alarming it.

"You walk the dogs at night like this all the

time?" He asked.

"Yea, most of the time. I want to keep their run clean and it helps if they do their business before bedding them down for the night."

"I don't know how comfortable I am with you doing this at night, alone."

Kit put her hand on her hip as Crank sniffed out a tree she knew he was partial too. "Jess, I've been doing this for a while, you know." She told him teasingly.

"I know, I'm sorry. Just being honest." His voice had become more stern almost tense.

Kit praised Crank on completing his business and they continued walking down the deserted, unlit road.

"Jess, I had a good time tonight. It was a great first date and I want to thank you."

Jess knew there was a 'but' coming.

"But?" He pressed her.

"Not really a but...it was a date, a good one, please don't go caveman on me now. I went from living with my parents to living with my husband. I'm learning to live by myself, on my own and it's refreshing to only have to answer to me, to only be responsible for me."

"I get that, but you walking in the dark, alone at night, it's not safe. I'm only stating a fact, not telling you what to do." Jess was feeling a little exasperated. The date had been awesome and he didn't want the tone to change because he had stated the obvious.

"I'm careful Jess."

"I'm sure you are. I just..." He stopped walking and touched Kit's arm so she stopped walking too. "It's just that... I've seen so much shit. Now that I know you do this." His arm gestured at the solitary dark road. "I'm going to be thinking about you walking a dog alone at night, on this road and I'm going to worry."

"Jess, you don't need to worry. I can't imagine the horrible stuff you've seen. Believe it or not I've seen shit too." The second she said that she wished she could take it back, but she couldn't so she hoped he wouldn't think too much of it and she plowed on. "Point being; I'm cautious. I carry my cell, see." She waved her iPhone in front of him. A little smirk quirked her pink lips making her appear adorable and mischievous.

Jess pulled her in close for another quick kiss this one on her lips. "Okay, I get it. You are woman hear you roar." He laughed "But I'm still going to worry about you." He said as he nuzzled her ear and then sexily bit her lobe before releasing her.

The small kiss on the lips she handled well, but when he nuzzled her ear an unfamiliar whirl hummed towards her core and then when he gently bit her ear lobe she audibly moaned and felt her thong dampens forcing her to clutch her legs together. Kit playfully swatted his arm. She was hoping her knees wouldn't give out.

Jess was laughing at her adorable reaction, rubbing his arm like her playful swat had hurt him. Kit was giggling at his fake hurt expression. He was grateful for the darkness since his cock had decided to come roaring back to life after an eight-month vacation. He was rock hard. Jess took Kit's free hand in his and they headed back towards her house, grateful for the darkness. Kit opened the front door and punched in the code. She turned to face Jess who stood on her porch with Lulu obediently waiting at his side. "So can I call you again?" He asked.

"Yes, I'd like that. I'll see Lulu right?"

"If Lulu becomes a client will you still go on dates with me?"

Kit thought about it for a second and Jess's started to worry that she might say no. Then he saw her smile.

“I can’t believe I’m going to break my rule, but yes I would like to see you again and take care of Lulu. Just please let’s not broadcast it, okay?”

“No problem there. I have two more days off and then I’ll bring Lulu by.”

Kit was surprised that she was a little sad that she wouldn’t see Jess for two more days and then it would be in the capacity of a client. She hadn’t enjoyed speaking with someone like she had tonight since that fateful night with Colt, almost a year ago. Jess broke through her melancholy.

“Kit would you like to go on a picnic tomorrow?”

“I could do a dinner one. I have adult clients tomorrow and another dog coming also.”

“A dinner one would be great.” Jess said, his voice barely containing his excitement. “Can you leave the dogs here or will you need to bring them?” He asked trying to be considerate.

Kit laughed. “I can leave them here. It might get a little crazy with Crank and Misty.”

“Your call, whatever gets you to say yes I’m happy with?” He told her honestly.

Kit ducked her head as a rose-colored blush crept up her neck and spread to her cheeks. She couldn't remember the last time anyone, well Ray, had said something so sweet that it made her blush. Jess stepped to her making his next intention obvious. He took Kit by the nape of her neck and put his other hand on her hip guiding her towards him, tilting her head with his thumb on her jaw. Staring down into her sapphire eyes making sure there wasn't a 'no' lurking in them. He bent his head and his mouth captured Kit's lips in a kiss that was so hot and consuming that she was sure the person who invented the phrase 'panty melting' must have kissed Jess.

When they pulled apart Kit was breathing hard, her lips were puffy and Jess ran his thumb over them loving that he was the one that made them appear so delectable. Her heart was thumping and she was sure he could hear it. Kit watched Jess compose himself too. She saw him take a calming breath, running his hand through his hair as he took a step back from her. It was obvious that he had been just as affected by the kiss as she was, especially seeing his jeans now sported a very noticeable bulge. Jess said good-bye and he and Lulu walked off the porch. Kit stood in the doorway waiting until he was in his jeep before shutting the front door, locking it and engaging the alarm.

Chapter 9

Kit and Jess's picnic was what Kit would remember as a perfect date. Jess took her up a mountain pass to a private bluff that had a spectacular vista and would soon give them an unfettered view of a summer sunset. Jess supplied a simple dinner of fried chicken, coleslaw and a bottle of Pinot Grigio wine. Dinner conversation was easy and revolved around what they had done that day. Jess enjoyed hearing about her adult day care people and their antics. He laughed as she recapped a few funny stories. He in turn told her that he was spending his free time working around his home adding his own personal touches to it.

As the sun slipped lower in the pristine blue sky, Kit snuggled into Jess's warm chest. She'd worn a lightweight skirt and Jess covered her bare legs with the ends of the blankets as they cuddled and watched the glowing colors cascading across the sky. When the sun had set a sliver of natural light cast a glow on their picnic spot giving it a romantic atmosphere. Jess picked Kit up as if she were light as a feather and turned her so she was straddling his hips and they were face to face. A thick aspen tree bolstered his back. Kit placed her hands on his wide shoulders, her thumbs grazing gently along his neck. Kit was closely watching his face and Jess was studying hers, neither of them moved.

Jess took the initiative and leaned in to taste her delicate lips. She returned the gentle kiss and softly stroked his lower lip with the tip of her tongue. Kit heard him stifle a small groan. One small, almost ticklish lick later and he opened for her, welcoming her warm tongue as it wreaked havoc on his libido. His cock fought for space, so Jess lifted Kit's little body slightly off his lap so he could reach down and adjust himself.

Their kiss started as a sweet, exploration but exploded into a hot, wild, 'can't get close enough' surge of passion. Kit ran her hands through Jess's thick hair and suckled him with her lips. Jess played with her, nipping and stroking inside her warm mouth until moving to taste her neck. His hands were everywhere, first her hips then roaming her back, and then, hesitantly, moving to fondle her small breasts through her thin tee shirt. Her nipples were aching as they pushed outwards and Jess swept over them roughly with his thumbs sending delicious waves throughout her system.

Jess placed his hands on her hips and encouraged her to rock on him. Kit needed no further prompting as she rubbed her wet cleft up and down his thick cock, trapped and full in his jeans. The friction she was feeling through her satiny thong and the way Jess was rubbing her sent the heady whirl of a pre-orgasm racing towards her core. Kit moaned into Jess's mouth and leaned her forehead on his as the sensations became too intense. The feeling was so foreign, so forgotten, she became timid. Jess felt her stiffen and knew she was nervous about letting go in front of him.

"Give it to me Kit, let it go baby. I want to feel it."

Kit's head fell back exposing her delicious neck and Jess leaned in to erotically suck on her soft skin. His hands caressing her breasts and the gentle way he was sucking on her neck sent her over the edge. Her back bowed and an epic orgasm crashed through her, causing her hips to buck uncontrollably. Kit moaned out Jess's name in such a husky voice Jess almost came himself. Kit collapsed, boneless against his heaving chest. Jess held her tightly rubbing his hands up and down her back and softly kissing her hair and shoulders, anywhere he could reach without disrupting her.

Kit regained some semblance of coherent thought and sat up pressing a soft, shy kiss to his lips. "Jess... That was...it was...thank you."

She felt the hard ridge of his jeans pressing against her damp thong and realized he was stone hard. She stuttered, unsure of how to continue.

"You didn't... You're still...hard. I..."

"Kit, relax." Jess said tenderly. "I loved making you come. I'm hard because you are such a sensual person it's a turn on."

"Yes, but don't you want to... I mean... Can I please you now?"

Jess tucked a stray hair that had fallen on her flushed cheek behind her ear.

"Not tonight baby. Tonight was all about you."

"Sure?" She asked quietly too boneless to argue.

"Sure." He confirmed. Then he pulled her gently into his chest, her cheek using his strong shoulder as a pillow, his cheek resting on her forehead. Jess would have loved to relieve the powerful throbbing of his cock but for some reason he knew it was more important for Kit to know she was his priority and not his sex drive. They sat content just holding each other, his dick finally softening.

The next few days flew by. Jess had gone

back to work but she saw him every day when she walked Lulu to the station. He also called and texted her when he had downtime. He was quickly becoming very important to her and it was a little scary, but also something she had no control over. She liked him a lot. Just thinking about him sent shivers through her. Kit appreciated Jess's effort to stay in contact and she often found herself smiling randomly when she thought back to their date.

Kit's businesses were keeping her busy. She had adult day care customers stopping in at all hours. She had also picked up a new dog client. Everything seemed to be coming together and she mentally patted herself on the back for choosing two businesses' that brought money in yet afforded her free time to pursue her art. Kit sketched when she was emotional, happy or sad. An image would implant in her brain and she had to put it on paper. She'd always been that way.

Kit found time to draw a picture of Jess leaning against the aspen tree on the bluff during their picnic. She drew him with one leg stretched out in front of him and one leg bent at the knee. One of his hands rested on the bent knee while the other lay on his denim clad thigh. His hair looked slightly mussed and very sexy. Her favorite part of the sketch was how she had captured his eyes. Slightly hooded and twinkling, the way they look after he had given her that tsunami of an orgasm. His lips were slightly open and turned up in a tiny, knowing smile. When Kit finished she knew she had captured him in that private after moment. She wasn't going to show him the sketch. It was one she would keep, a private, special memory.

She did, however sketch one for Jess. She drew a charcoal sketch of Lulu as she sat regally in her backyard. The sketch was done on a 9 by 11, thicker, more expensive piece of paper than she usually used, but she wanted it to be a special gift for Jess so she went all out. She couldn't wait to show it to him when he came to pick Lulu up later that day.

Her last adult day care client had finally left and Kit ran upstairs to wash up and change into a nicer outfit before Jess came for Lulu. When she heard the doorbell ring she skipped down the steps and pulled open the front door. Instead of her gorgeous Jess standing on her porch U. S. Marshal Lori and a suit clad gentleman greeted her.

"Oh, hi." Kit was taken back. Lori always called before coming over.

"Kit, hi, can we come in?"

Kit stepped back and motioned them inside.

"Is something wrong?" She asked them. Her gut churned and she knew this couldn't be good.

“Kit, this is Fred Grossman. He’s a lawyer, your lawyer.”

“Oh.” Was all Kit said and then she suddenly knew why they were there and said. “Oh,” much louder.

“It’s time, isn’t it?”

“Yes, Pallone’s lawyers have been working to move quickly since Pallone has been sitting in jail. The trial is starting next week and we need to move you tonight. Pallone would love to... Well...not have you testify...so we want to be hyper vigilant with you and how we move you.”

Kit’s head was spinning. She knew this day would come and she had known she would be nervous but now, right when everything seemed to be so good both in her business life and her social life.

“Tonight? Wow that’s not giving me much notice.” Kit spit out.

“Has to be Kit.” Lori said to her trying to sooth her with a rub to her shoulder.

“My business? I have dogs, I have clients.”

“We’ll wait for you to contact those people and for you to pack and then we have to leave.”

"Oh God." She groaned this is going to happen. Then she thought about Colt.

"Will Colt Andrews be there?"

Lori who only knew about Colt because of the letters she curried between the two of them shrugged her shoulders and deferred to Fred.

"Yes, he's being flown in as we speak." Fred told her.

"Will I see him?"

"Maybe, you'll be kept in separate locations."

"Oh, I would like to say hi to him."

Although Jess had thoroughly invaded all of her thoughts and private fantasies Colt would always be special to her. They had never kissed, only briefly hugged good-bye but he was her Colt. He had risked everything to save her life. Then he had provided the stability she needed in the crazy hours after she left the hospital. The man had put everything in prospective and kept her grounded. She owed him her life and through their many letters had become good friends.

Kit told Lori and Fred to help themselves to anything in the downstairs fridge and asked Lori to toss out anything that would spoil. Then she set about calling her adult and dog clients. While the phone was pressed to her ear, she called out to Lori. "How long will I be gone any idea?"

"A few weeks at least, maybe more, maybe less. There's no way to tell."

Kit groaned and then continued calling her clients delivering the bad news. She told them there was a death in her family and she had to go help her parents. She told them that when she got back she'd call them. She hoped they wouldn't make permanent other arrangements in her absence, but she wouldn't blame them if they did. Just as she finished her final call the doorbell rang and Kit's heart plummeted, Jess.

She opened the door to see the sexy firefighter still dressed in his blue uniform and was instantly lifted into a consuming bear hug, then peppered with tiny kisses that made her laugh out loud. Jess looked over her shoulder and saw the two people staring at them from the couch. He had noticed their car but when he had seen Kit he couldn't help but embrace her. Jess lowered her to the ground and stepped inside keeping hold of her hand. He approached the two people. "Lori?"

Oh God! Kit realized they knew each other. "Jess." She smiled at him and the green-eyed monster punched Kit in the stomach forcing her hand to her stomach.

"You know each other." Kit said. It wasn't a question.

Jess looked at Kit. "We've worked together."

"Jess helped us during a bomb scare that was called into a plant that, umm, I had an interest in. Jess, this is Fred Grossman." The two men shook hands.

Jess swung his gaze back to Kit who was looking almost pale. Something's started to click into place for Jess but he kept his mouth shut as his mind mentally shuffled through what Kit had revealed about her personal life.

"Lori, I need to talk to Jess...alone okay?"

Fred spoke up, "We need to get going Kit."

Jess's mind registered the word 'going' and he looked back to Kit.

"Just give me a minute. I'll talk to him while I pack."

"Good idea." Lori chimed in. "We'll wait here."

Jess and Kit climbed her apartment steps. Kit was physically feeling ill. She liked Jess, really liked him. The 'what if?' scenarios where bouncing chaotically through her thoughts. Kit led him to her bedroom and he sat on the bed, heavily, he knew what was coming.

Kit looked at Jess, a man that jumped into fires and disarmed bombs and knew for some reason this was going to be hard on him. She saw such anguish in his face and she knew he needed her, needed reassurance, so in a very un-Kit like manner she took the lead. Kit stood between his legs and took his face in her hands so she could look at his eyes. He looked so sad.

"Jess I have to go away for a few weeks. I hope it's only a few weeks."

"You can't tell me where, can you?"

"I can tell you what I've told everyone else; that there was a death in my family and I'm going home for a while to support my parents."

"But that's not the real story? I know what Lori does for a living Kit."

"I know you do and no, it's not the real story and I shouldn't have even told you that much."

"I'm worried about you."

"I'll be okay. I'll be protected."

"Oh God Kit what the hell are you involved in?"

"Jess, please, you know I can't say."

"Baby, my gut is telling me you might be in danger and it's killing me."

Kit smiled that he had called her 'baby.'

"Jess, I'll be protected."

Jess placed his forehead on her chest and reached around to hug her.

"I'll miss you, you know that right? I know we have just met but Kit… there is something between us. Please tell me you feel it too?"

"I feel it Jess. It's wonderful and scary too. I'll miss you too. This past week and a half, you've brought me back to life Jess."

Jess wished he could tell her how much she had brought him back from a living hell, and he wasn't just talking about his renewed sex drive. He had slept a few nights without waking to his usual nightmare. Instead his dreams were of her, sweet and sexy.

Jess lifted her away from his chest and granted her a tender smile. The smile made her remember the drawing of him that she had done.

"I have something for you."

Jess let her back away from his embrace

and Kit walked to her closet pulling out the drawing she had matted and framed of Lulu. She handed it to him and stood back to see his reaction. Jess looked at the framed sketch and his heart swelled with emotion.

"Kit this is beautiful. It's so... Lulu. I love it. Thank you."

Jess stood and pulled her in for a hug. This time he tilted her head up and found her mouth with his. They devoured each other and Kit finally had to push on his chest to put a stop to the steamy kiss threatening to become something more difficult to halt. Something they both wanted to spend more time exploring.

"I have to pack Jess."

"I know." Jess sat back down on the bed holding the picture frame in his hands.

As Kit pulled out a small wheelie suitcase she told Jess that she had called all her clients and she hoped she wouldn't be gone longer than a couple weeks.

Jess was somber and realized Kit was probably scared. He tried to appear more in control than how he was actually feeling; inside his gut was twisting, his head was reeling and he felt nauseous. He couldn't lose her now. What if she didn't come back? There were so many not good scenarios running through his mind.

Kit saw how worried he looked. “When I get back Jess can I call you?”

“Fuck that Kit you’ll call me every day you’re away, you understand?” He blurted out a little louder than he meant too.

Kit giggled at his machismo and sat down on his lap after placing the frame gently at his side.

“You get bossy sometimes you know?” She whispered into his ear.

“Baby when it comes to you I could be a downright bear.”

“I’ll call Jess, if I’m allowed okay?”

“I’ll talk to Lori.”

Kit smiled for him. “Now there is my take charge man.”

“Kit... Please call me. I know they aren’t going to let you take your cell.”

“I’ll try to borrow one, I promise.”

Jess gave Kit another searing kiss before lifting her to her feet. He zipped her bag for her and carried it down the steps. When they got downstairs

Jess looked directly at Lori.

"I need to hear from her, get her a burner." It wasn't a question and he knew it sounded demanding but his mind was still whirling, he was already worried, and he didn't have time for the niceties.

"I'll try Jess, sometimes we can't."

"You can and you will Lori. You owe me."

Lori nodded and Kit wished she knew why she owed him. Kit engaged the final alarm after Jess retrieved Lulu from the basement. Lori and Fred were waiting in the car. On the porch steps Jess turned to Kit one last time.

"Be safe Kit, please come back to us." Kit nodded as tears rimmed her eyes, thinking how adorable he was and how unfair it was that she had to leave now. He walked her to the sedan and watched as she buckled in. Fred had already put her suitcase in the trunk. Jess bent down and kissed her again and then he straightened and shut the car door. Kit watched out her window as they pulled away. Kit saw Jess push his hand through his hair and she realized that when he pushed his hand through his hair it was his tell. Jess was upset.

Chapter 10

They flew out of Hayden and after being in the air for two hours they landed at another small airport. A black sedan car met them on the tarmac and Kit, Lori, Fred and the driver, who was also a US Marshal drove east. Like a well-oiled machine, before they hit a state line, Kit, Lori and Fred were transferred into a different car, with a different US Marshal driver. They never stopped and only used rest rooms when changing cars. The ride was exhausting and the further Kit got from Colorado and Jess the heavier her heart felt. When they reached the Pennsylvania, New Jersey State line at the Delaware Water Gap, Kit began to feel the pressure of testifying.

The further east they drove on Route 80 Kit felt the confines of suburban living closing in around her, strangling her. There were more cars, more houses, and more people. One of the things she liked best about where she lived in Colorado was how spacious it was; no traffic jams, her house was not sitting on top of someone else's, it was simpler and less hurried and she already missed it.

Tiny niggles of 'what if' scenarios had been plaguing her the entire ride. She was worried about her businesses, but she figured if she was gone too long and her small client base had to find other options she would simply start up again. Thankfully money wasn't an issue at the moment. What she kept coming back to was Jess and their newness. What if he found someone else? What if he realized she had baggage? What if he just liked her because she was new to him, a conquest? Kit just hoped the trial would be quick, at least her part in it, and that she could go back to her new life that she was just becoming comfortable with. It seemed like it had been so long since she had been this content. Her new life made her happy, her dogs, and her elderly clients…Jess.

The car arrived at a hotel that was found near Newark Airport. Kit knew exactly why they had chosen it. From this location there were many different routes into Newark, where the Federal Court House was located; they were keeping her safe. Lori had told Kit that when it was time for her to testify that they would bring her to the Court House alternating their routes daily. She would be wearing a bulletproof vest when they traveled. In the court building she could monitor the courtroom proceedings through a closed circuit TV while she waited, secured in a nearby room. After she testified she would continue to go to the courthouse until the judge deemed it reasonable that she could leave, that usually took a couple days after testifying. She thankfully did not have to wait around for the verdict to be read.

The car pulled up closely to a side door of the hotel and the driver pulled out his cell. Within a minute the side door entrance was opened and they were quickly ushered inside with their suitcases. The man, who had met them, also a Marshal, took them to a service elevator where he produced a key that he slid into a special keyhole and once he punched in the top floor number the elevator began to move. The elevator made no stops and Kit deduced it was because of the key.

When the elevator did stop they were led to a door at the end of the hallway and the Marshal unlocked it and ushered them inside. Once inside he handed separate key cards to Lori and Fred, it was not lost on Kit that she did not get one. Kit glanced around the room and was pleasantly surprised. They were in a large suite. There was a spacious living room complete with a huge TV, a desk and comfy furniture. There was an eat-in kitchen and the Marshal told them that there were three bedrooms all with private bathrooms. Lori told Kit to choose a room so she did; they were relatively all the same. She chose the one painted blue; the color always calmed her and it reminded her of Jess' eyes, so she figured the room had chosen her.

Lori told Kit to settle in and when she was

done to come back to the living room for a brief meet and greet. When Kit finished putting away her clothes and toiletries she freshened up and joined walked back out to the main room.

"Kit this is Sam Maddox." Lori said pointing to one of the men, "and this is Tom Mahoney." She said directing Kit's attention to the other. Tom was the one who had met them and let them in the hotel. "

We have another Marshal assigned to our team but she isn't here yet."

Kit acknowledged them with a nervous smile and a nod.

"Here's the game plan. As you know Fred is here as your personal lawyer. The State has their own lawyers and the Feds have theirs. The Feds are trying the case so they take the lead. Their lawyers will want to question you and prep you for trial. Fred here will make sure nothing you say is incriminating."

Kit nodded a lump of fear lodged in her throat. This was happening and she was getting scared.

Lori continued. "I'm here as your personal Marshal. You need anything, want anything I'll try to get it for you. Sam, Tom and Gina, that's the female

Marshal joining us later, are here as your security detail. They will be your round the clock surveillance team, here, in court, and driving to and from court. You won't be allowed to use the hotel phone or Internet and obviously you can't go anywhere. Do you have any questions?"

Kit started to shake her head, then thought of one. "So the trial starts soon?"

Fred took the lead on that.

"Yes, the day after tomorrow, Monday morning, first thing. The other lawyers will be here later today and probably even tomorrow to ask you some questions. When the Prosecuting attorney thinks it's time to call you to the stand he will let me know and we will take you to the courthouse to wait there."

"Okay." Lori said. "We should all get comfy. I'm told the kitchen is stocked, we won't eat out, it draws too much attention, if anyone wants to cook great, otherwise eat what you want when you want and we can order out too." The meeting was over and Fred and Sam went to the kitchen and Tom left because he wasn't on duty yet.

Kit sat at the table and looked over at Lori who was rummaging through some papers. "Lori, can I call Jess?"

Lori stood and motioned her into the hallway. "Listen I'm not supposed to do this but I know Jess and I do owe him. Do not and I mean it Kit, do not tell him where you are or anything about the case okay?"

"Okay."

Lori took out her cell and scrolled through her contacts. Finding what she wanted she hit send and handed the phone to Kit. Then she left telling Kit to leave the phone on her dresser when she was done. Kit walked into her bedroom and shut the door.

Kit heard the phone ringing and then she heard Jess. "Lori, is she okay?" He hadn't even said hi, her man was worried.

"Jess, it's me." She said quietly. Not wanting the others to hear her she turned on her TV and then went into her bathroom.

"Kit... Wait a second." She heard shuffling and figured he too had opted for some privacy. "Kit are you okay?"

"I'm fine Jess, promise."

"How are you?" She asked sincerely.

"Honestly, I'm a mess worried about what you're involved in." Jess's voice had taken on a gentler tone.

"Jess please don't worry."

"But I am worried and I'm going to tell you the truth here Kit; I have some favors hanging around and I know you can't tell me anything but I guarantee by the time you get home I will know everything."

Kit sighed, "Listen to me Jess, please don't stir the pot, it's really important that I don't have any attention directed towards me and my life in Colorado. You get that right?"

"I do and I'm not happy about it and just so you know, when you get home we are going to have a little sit down, just you and me. Don't worry I'll clear it with Lori first, okay."

"That would be wonderful." Kit said and she meant it.

"So are you being treated well?" He asked.

"Yup, I have my own room and bathroom too."

"Nice set up." He bantered playfully. "Kit I have to go we just got a call. Call me tomorrow okay?"

"Okay, be safe Jess."

"You too babe." Then he disconnected.

A week passed and then another and still no word from court. Kit was restless. Fred was antsy and watched the worst shows on TV. Lori was on her computer a lot. Kit fell into the routine of making breakfast and dinner for everyone. What ingredients she didn't have Lori was quick to retrieve. The Marshals and Fred appreciated her cooking and they always handled the clean-up. Kit had been allowed to call Jess almost daily but the conversations were stinted and Kit began to worry that Jess was pulling away.

Kit was sketching every day out of sheer boredom. She had completed a few drawings that she had used colored pencils on and she was pleased with the results. One of her drawings was of her home in Colorado. She knew exactly where she would hang it after she matted and framed it. Another sketch was of the view she and Jess had of the sunset on their picnic. She tried to capture the exact moment the sun had dipped behind the ridge and had left a glorious golden hue that appeared to make the mountains shimmer. Kit had successfully encapsulated the color of the sky that she remembered had turned a dazzling rose, almost pink color. This picture took almost a week to complete. She wanted the details of the mountains and the colors to be exact so she spent hours working on it. Kit was also working on a charcoal of her face. She didn't often try to sketch herself but she was bored and so she sat in her room at the desk that had a mirror over it and tried to put to paper what she saw in the reflective mirror. She had thrown four or five start up sketches away already but this current one was better so she decided to keep going.

Finally at the end of the second week Fred got the call they'd been waiting for. Kit hadn't talked to Jess in two days. Lori had been using the phone almost constantly one of the days, and the other day she had gotten absorbed in her sketching and then fallen asleep. Kit had also lost track of Jess' on and off days and she didn't want to bother him at work. Fred relayed the information at dinner that night that Kit's presence was required in court the next day. She asked if she'd testify right away and Fred said he doubted it.

After dinner Kit excused herself and went to her room. Instead of drawing she turned on the television and lay on her bed trying to lose herself in mindless sit-coms. Lori knocked on her door and told her they would be leaving at 7:30 am and asked her if she wanted her to wake her up. Kit told her she was sure she'd be ready and Lori shut the door.

The next morning Kit's Marshals', which she had begun to refer to them as, and Fred moved somberly around the suite. Lori handed Kit a bulletproof vest and helped her secure it. She then handed her a dark wig, an oversized belted trench coat and large sunglasses. Kit put on the wig and the trench coat and then placed the sunglasses on her face. She modeled her new look for her Marshals and they gave her the thumbs up sign. They took Kit downstairs in the same elevator they had come up in using the special key that by passed all the other floors.

Kit hadn't been outside in more than two weeks and she welcomed the early morning rays, as she was discreetly and quickly loaded into a sedan with tinted windows. Their small party headed to court.

Kit was sitting in the backseat between Lori and Fred, Sam and Gina were in the front seat, Tom was in a car behind them looking for possible tails. When they arrived at the courthouse they were allowed to use a gated parking lot found on the side of the building. Sam parked and everyone looked at each other and within seconds they had Kit out of the car, surrounded on all sides and were quickly moving her towards a side entrance.

Inside the building they were ushered through metal detectors and then the Marshals placed her at their middle again as they continued through the building. Fred stayed in front and after they had climbed a set of white marble stairs they were met by one of the Prosecuting Attorneys assistants. He was a young, handsome African-American man, dressed impeccably in a dark suit and red tie. The young man said hello to everyone and shook Fred's hand. He then led them down a hall, past a sign pointing to Court Room #1, and to a door guarded by a State Trooper. He unlocked the door, handing the key to the Trooper and then he held the door open for everyone to enter. Once everyone was situated inside the tiny room he shut the door and locked it using a dead bolt. Kit looked around the room, which was very different from the hotel suite she had just left. Inside the room there were no windows but there was a door located in the middle of one of the putrid green walls that was currently closed. The room contained a TV, a small table with two chairs, and a plaid, very worn, love seat.

"Kit, I'm the Assistant Prosecutor, Nix Jones." He held his hand out for her to shake, which she did.

"You are Mr. Grossman, and Marshal Frost?" Mr. Jones nodded at Fred first then to Lori. They nodded. "Both of you and Mrs. Murphy will stay in here and monitor the proceedings from that closed-circuit TV. We will have a State Trooper outside of your door at all times and no one will be allowed in unless Mr. Grossman or Ms. Frosts allows it. Needless to say no one can leave the room." He walked to the one other door in the room and opened it revealing a toilet and sink. "We hope to have you take the stand today, but Pallone's lawyers know your testimony will be damaging and they may try to delay it."

The use of her former named jarred her. Kit stared glassy-eyed at the young man. He was so exuberant; she recognized that for him, this was probably an exciting case, trying a mob boss. The press was following the case closely and for a young ambitious lawyer it could be a career definer. To Kit, however, it was a nightmare. She silently wished she had called Jess last night because she didn't know when she'd get to talk to him now that she was stuffed away in the courthouse. She was so tired of waiting. Lori reached down and grabbed her hand. "You'll be fine Kit." Kit smiled at her but it was a forced smile and they both knew it.

Sam, Gina and Tom left the room and Kit settled on the couch after removing her vest, wig and sunglasses. Lori turned the TV on and she and Fred sat at the table watching the courtroom as it filled with people, and lawyers. Pallone was brought in from a side door and the shock of seeing the slimy man that had shot Ray and ordered her death sent Kit running into the bathroom. She dropped to her knees and puked what little breakfast she had eaten into the brown stained toilet. Two minutes later Kit stood on shaky legs and wiped her face with a paper towel soaked with cold water. Lori knocked on the door and asked if she was all right. Kit replied meekly that she was and Lori opened the door to peek in. She handed Kit her phone, “It's Jess.” Lori closed the bathroom door giving her privacy.

“Jess?”

“Baby, are you okay?”

“Jess...” Kit started crying softly. “Jess, I'm scared.”

The phone was quiet and all Kit could think of was that she was probably pushing him further away.

“Kit, take a deep breath. This is the worst part, the waiting. What happened?”

Kit didn't question how Jess knew she was waiting. She was too distraught.

“I saw him. I saw him on the closed circuit TV in the room I'm in.”

“I'm sorry babe, that had to be rough.”

“Do you know Jess? Do you know now?” He knew what she was referring too. Did he know what she was involved in?

“I know Kit. I don't know everything. I know where you are and who you're up against.”

"Jess what if I lose it? How am I going to be in the same room with him if seeing him on TV makes me physically ill?"

"Kit you can do this. You need to do this."

"I know. I just feel so alone. They are being so cautious, it's almost scaring me more."

"They better be cautious."

Kit realized it was early in the morning in Colorado.

"Did Lori call you?"

"Yea, she knew you were freaking out."

"It's early there?"

"Yea but I'm glad she called. I haven't heard from you." The last statement kind of hung for an ugly second.

"I couldn't use the phone one day and... Jess, you don't need someone in your life that..."

Jess exploded and Kit pulled the phone back from her ear. "Don't you say it Kit, don't you dare try to pull away from me because you think it will be better for me."

Kit was so surprised at his outburst that she remained quiet.

Jess was breathing hard into the phone. “Kit, talk to me.” Jess’s voice was filled with anguish. “Kit!”

“I’m sorry Jess.” Kit started crying again and Jess felt so helpless. His woman needed him to hold her and calm her down and she was clear on the other side of the country.

“Shhhh, baby, please stop crying, you’re killing me. Kit please, it will be all right. You’ll be home soon and we’ll put this behind us.” Kit fought the tears and wiped her face again.

“I can’t wait to come home Jess.”

“I’m going to plan some fun dates for us. You think of some things you’d like to do too okay?”

Kit sniffled, “Okay.”

“That’s my girl.”

They said good-bye to each other and before she hung up he asked to talk to Lori. Kit walked out of the bathroom and handed the phone to Lori. “He wants to talk to you.” Lori took the phone from her and went into the bathroom and shut the door. She came out a minute later. Kit looked to her to see if she’d tell her what she and Jess had talked about but she didn’t volunteer anything as she placed her phone on the table and sat down in a chair to continue watching the monitor.

"Thank you Lori."

Lori smiled at her. "He's a good guy and he's worried. We're all worried about you Kit." Fred nodded his agreement with what Lori had just revealed. "I knew he'd be able to calm you down so I called him."

"Well, again, thanks." Kit settled back on the couch and braced herself to watch the trial.

Kit was soon caught up in the proceedings. There was a ton of legal jargon spewing from both lawyers; some of it did not even make sense to her. Seeing Pallone on the tiny screen became bearable. She realized that it was probably a good thing she had seen him beforehand on the monitor, before she went into the actual courtroom, because it would not have been a good thing if she had freaked out the way she did in front of everyone. The trial broke for lunch and within a few minutes there was a knock on the door. Lori looked through the peephole and then opened the door to let Nix Jones in. He carried a large bag, which contained sandwiches, chips and sodas for the three of them.

Nix looked at Fred and then to Kit.

"We're going to call you after lunch. I just wanted to give you a heads up." Kit's appetite went out the window and she put down her still wrapped sub.

"You just need to tell the truth, remember don't embellish, don't say how you felt, just describe what you saw."

"I remember." Kit said with a bit of a quiver in her voice.

"Pallone's lawyers will cross-examine you and they will try to attack your character, they will try to make you confuse your facts but honestly, we think they are going to want you off the stand quickly because you are a normal, everyday person and the fact that you were tragically effected by what Pallone did will not sit well with the jurors."

"Hope so." Kit said.

"Kit, you need to put the wig and sunglasses back on. We want to keep you as disguised as possible during this circus." Lori stood and handed Kit the wig. Kit stood and took the black wig and went into the bathroom. Kit pulled her blond shoulder length hair into a ponytail and put the wig on making sure none of her natural hair was visible. The wig did make her look different. It was much longer and thicker than her natural hair length giving her a more exotic look. Coupled with the large sunglasses much of her facial features were hidden.

When the trial resumed Kit was ready. She was looking forward to getting it over with and she silently gave herself a pep talk. She was doing this for Ray and especially for Colt. She reminded herself that her parents would be proud of her too. Kit found more resolve in the fact that she didn't want Jess to worry about her and she knew, not for sure, but she thought Jess was keeping tabs on her through Lori.

When Kit heard her name, her old name, Karen Sue Murphy, being called to the witness stand her knees buckled slightly, she had almost forgotten they were going to be using her birth name. This man she was going to testify against had changed her entire life. She'd even had to change her Goddamn name! Kit was ready and as Fred accompanied her to the courtroom she grew calm, like before a storm, and she knew she would be fine.

After she was sworn in the Judge asked her to remove the sunglasses. The Prosecuting Attorney started by asking her some general personal questions, name? Marital status, age, where she'd grown up and lived? Were her parents still living? What did she have a degree in? How had she met Ray? How long had they dated? How many years had she been married? What was the status of her marriage at the time of her husband's death? He took the jurors through her life in a matter of minutes. The only thing he did not reveal was her new identity or the state she lived in now. She had been prepared for this line of questioning. Fred had told her it was so the jurors could identify with the normalcy of her life, until the murder anyway. Kit answered all the questions as they rehearsed, simple answers and as unemotional as possible, but not cold like either, no embellishments.

Then he started to delve into the day in question. He asked Kit to take the jurors through the event as it happened. Kit told the courtroom how she came home from school one day and heard loud voices, one of them Ray's. The courtroom was so quiet that it was eerie. Kit knew she had the attention of all the jurors and they were sympathizing with her and they hadn't even heard the worst of it.

Kit shot a glance to Fred who was sitting at the long Prosecutors table, took a deep breath and continued. She told the court how before she could push through the kitchens swinging door Ray fell back through it and landed on her. She described to the jurors how she fell and was trapped underneath him. How she saw the blood on his chest and felt it seeping on to her. She told the room how she looked into her living room to see the defendant pointing the gun at where Ray had just been. The prosecutor interrupted her and asked her to point out the defendant and with quiet resolve Kit looked over at the small, well-dressed, oily looking man and pointed at him for everyone to see. The Prosecutor then said; "Let the records show Mrs. Murphy has identified the defendant, Mr. Vincent Pallone as the man holding the gun."

The prosecutor asked Kit to go on so she did. She explained how Pallone had handed the gun to another man and then how Petey had come through the door and told Pallone they needed to leave because the cops were coming. She described how Pallone had then taken the gun from the man known as "Big Tony" and handed it to Petey and he was told to kill her. The prosecutor stopped her and said, "Were those his exact words, 'kill her?'" Kit nodded and said yes they were his exact words. Kit then told the jurors how Pallone had left through the front door while Big Tony remained behind. She then explained to the jurors how Petey had approached her and mouthed 'play dead.' then fired the gun at, what she later learned had been Ray, but she'd been hit in the process and had fainted.

The prosecutor asked a few more questions making sure the jurors had a clear idea of what had happened. He then asked if Ray had been killed, and she told the jurors yes, her voice raspy as she remembered the heavy feeling of Rays body as he lay motionless on top of her. She shut her eyes as she envisioned the amount of that blood that had been seeping on her. Kit felt an odd whirling force begin to suck her breath away. The prosecutor asked if she needed a minute and the judged looked at her sympathetically. Kit said, "No I'd like to finish, but thank you."

The prosecutor asked what had happened after that day and Kit told the court that she's been in Witness Protection ever since. He asked if she'd seen her parents or friends and Kit quietly but firmly said no. The prosecutors wanted the jurors to understand the depth of how much Kit's life had been altered because of Pallone. Satisfied with his questions to Kit and her answers the prosecutor told the court he was finished and he relinquished her to answer the Defendant's lawyers' questions.

Kit steeled herself; she knew this would be the hard part. Then something made her look up and there in the back of the courtroom stood Colt. Teaming with muscles, large and formidable, dressed in a suit and tie and looking larger than life and more dangerous than she remembered. His eyes held hers and he gave her a slight nod. His face held a hint of a smile. That tiny acknowledgement gave her an abundance of confidence. His life had been altered too and worse yet, he had to go to Afghanistan to be free from Pallone's reach. Kit took a deep breath and looked away from Colt right into the Defense lawyer's eyes. She mentally thought to herself. "Bring it."

Pallone's lawyers first tried to find out her new name and where she was currently living but her lawyers squashed those questions before she even tried to answer. Next he began to attack her character, but it only made him look like a bully to the jury because she was of exemplary character and had never even gotten so much as a speeding ticket. Her school records were clean and she had received Honor Roll grades. She had worked with other college students as their tutor, often not taking any payment. She volunteered at the local Food Cottage during her Christmas and spring breaks. Kit, Ray, and her parents also served Thanksgiving and Christmas dinner to the poor at an outreach Church, before they went home and enjoyed their own Holiday.

Pallon's lawyer, realizing he was doing more harm than good, switched tactics and tried to get Kit to say she had hit her head on the floor, when Ray had landed on her, and that she couldn't be sure of what she'd seen. Kit steadily repeated what she had said earlier, that her head hadn't touched the floor. She stated calmly, that her view had been unobstructed since she had been looking over Ray's shoulder and he hadn't been moving. The Defense attorney then asked if she had seen the defendant pull the trigger, to which Kit answered honestly, she had not.

Capitalizing on that he began to argue the time line the Prosecutor had established, suggesting there had been enough time for someone else, namely Big Tony, to pull the trigger and hand the proverbial 'smoking gun' to his client. Kit didn't answer because it wasn't a question and she was not going to let him open the door to hypotheticals. His last few questions were different in nature. He kept asking Karen Sue in different ways if Ray had given her anything to hold? If he had established accounts anywhere other than locally? If she knew where he kept personal papers? Karen Sue had responded no to each one. Her lawyer finally halted that line of questions with an objection that the judge agreed with.

The judge told Karen Sue she was done and thanked her. Kit stood up from the little stand she had been placed in, her legs were shaking but she felt euphoric. She knew she had done a good job. She caught Colt giving her the universal 'good job' thumbs up along with a sexy wry smile. She wanted to run to him, to bury her face in his massive chest and rejoice. She was almost finished with this horrid affair. Kit wanted to feel his muscular arms around her and have him tell her she'd done well, but instead she and Fred walked back out of the courtroom to their little room nearby.

When Kit got back into the room Lori jumped into her arms and squeezed her in a very un-Lori like way. "You did great! I mean great!" Kit smiled; her head was still tumbling over everything, especially seeing Colt.

"Thanks."

Fred had relocked the door behind them and he added to Lori's jubilant praise. "Kit, honest to God you were a dream witness. After this morning, you know, you seeing Pallone and freaking out... I got to tell you I had my doubts, but kiddo you were top-notch. The jurors ate up your story. Kit took off the wig and sunglasses, which she had promptly put back on once she was off the stand, and shook out her hair.

"One time I thought I was going to lose it but then...I saw Colt. He was in the back of the courtroom and I knew I had to be strong for him."

"You were kid, you were."

The courtroom monitor showed court ending for the day. Lori told Kit they were going to sit tight for a bit and make sure they could move her safely. A knock on the door halted conversation and when Lori opened it after seeing who it was and Colt stepped in with Marshal Tom.

"Colt." Kit said with a rushed breath. Lori looked from Kit to Colt and then to Fred.

Tom spoke up. "Colt here wants to speak with Kit for a few minutes alone. Kit's given her testimony so it won't be a problem legally. Kit would you like to speak with Colt alone?"

"Yes, please." She said softly never taking

her eyes off him.

Lori, Fred and Tom left the room telling them they have five minutes.

"Kit, huh?"

"Uh, yea, my new name. Kit Taylor."

"I got to keep mine, but then Pallone had only known me as Petey anyway so I was good."

"I'm glad you're safe." She said.

"I worried about you too you know?"

"I wasn't being shot at daily."

Colt grinned at her. "Your letters and pictures, they were the best part of being there. When I got a letter I'd go to my bunk and read it in private. I hung up all the pictures you drew, but when I had to go somewhere I folded them and took them with me. Thank you."

Kit laughed happy that she had brought some joy to him. "I liked your pictures too." She quipped and they both started laughing.

"So..." He started with a lowered voice. "Is your life good Karen Sue? I mean now? Are you okay? Are you happy?"

Colt stepped to her and tilted her chin up so

he could look into her blue eyes. The same blue eyes that had stunned him when he'd first seen her, the ones he dreamed about.

"I am Colt, I'm happy. I have a good life now. I guess that 'every cloud has a silver lining' saying is true."

"I've thought about you Karen Sue."

"Kit." She corrected.

"Kit, I like it. If Pallone gets what he deserves and you come out of this okay, happy, then it's all been worth it."

"What about you Colt? Are you okay? What's next?"

"I'm good. I hated going back to Afghanistan but it would have killed me to be in Wit Sec. When the trial ends I'll be back with DEA. I'm hoping to go undercover again if my face doesn't get plastered all over the papers."

"Wear a disguise, like I did."

Colt laughed. "That was a good disguise; you didn't look anything like the girl I'd met over a year ago. That long hairs kind of sexy." Kit laughed. "But I like this hairstyle best I think." Colt said as he fingered her blond hair. "No color streak?"

"Nope I guess I've grown up."

"I have to testify tomorrow. I'm hoping they'll let me see you again." Colt said never taking his eyes from hers.

"From what I understand I will be here for a couple more days. Good luck tomorrow."

"If I'm half as good as you were Pallone doesn't stand a chance." Kit beamed at the compliment. Colt drew her in for a quick hug and kissed the top of her head. "You're pretty awesome Kit, stay safe."

"Back at you Colt, you stay safe too."

Colt stepped back and Kit's hands fell to her sides missing his warm embrace. Colt knocked on the door signaling he was opening it and then the Trooper opened the door letting Colt leave and Fred, Lori and Tom back in.

Chapter 11

They sat in the dingy room for a half hour longer until Gina finally came for them. Kit once again put on her bulletproof vest, her wig and sunglasses and trench coat. Her Marshals team surrounded her and they left the building the same way they had come in. Sam had pulled the sedan right up to the side door and she, Lori and Fred piled in. Tom left to ride trail. They took a different way back to the hotel and again Kit marveled at the difference between the busy east coast city life and her quieter existence in Colorado.

Back in the hotel Fred proclaimed Kit was not cooking and as a celebratory dinner they ordered Chinese. Kit excused herself before the food arrived and went to soak in a warm tub. The hard part was over. She had done it. There was a possibility she'd be called back in for a redirect but Fred said he doubted it since she had 'kicked ass,' as Fred put it, on the stand. Lori had been quiet, abnormally quiet but Kit just chalked it up to her wanting to go home as much as she did. Kit finished with her soak and as she was throwing on comfy clothes Lori knocked on her door and asked to come in.

"Hey, what's up?" Kit asked as she brushed out her hair. Lori stood next to her watching her reflection in the mirror.

"Jess called."

"When?" Kit asked wondering why Lori hadn't let her talk to him.

"When you were talking to Colt."

"Oh...did you tell him I was talking to Colt?"

"I can't tell him anything, you know that."

"What did you say?"

"I said you were talking to someone."

"Lori what's going on, spill it, you're acting weird."

"Christ Kit! I like Jess. I know Jess likes you and now you I see you have another super handsome guy who couldn't take his eyes off you. What's up with that?"

"Lori, I like Jess too, a lot. Colt and I, well he saved my life. When he chose to save my life he threw his in the shitter. You know we've been writing to each other. He's special, but we are just friends. Good friends."

"I know, but I didn't know what he looked like before or how he looks at you like you're Christmas dinner."

Kit laughed. "Christmas dinner, really?"

"I think Jess, well I was so floored I think Jess knows you were talking to a guy, someone special."

"Crumb Lori! Let me call him please." Kit's stomach churned.

Lori handed Kit the phone and left the room.

The phone rang three times and then went to voice mail.

"Uh, Jess it's me. I did it. I'm hopefully done. Fred thinks I may get home by Friday. Call me."

Kit attended court for three more days. She watched Colt testify but they could only talk one other time at it was very brief. Colt hadn't worn a disguise but cameras weren't allowed in court so Kit hoped he'd be fine. Jess had never returned her call and Kit started to think Lori had maybe said a little more to Jess than she had originally indicated. The judge called Thursday night and said Kit was free to go. The trial was continuing with other counts that

Pallone had been charged with. Kit, Fred and her Marshalls were happy they were all going home. It had been three long weeks and everyone was in need of some personal space.

This time Kit was allowed to fly directly into Denver. Lori swapped out the black wig giving Kit a long red one, Kit giggled at how she looked. Red was not a good color on her. The other three Marshalls along with Lori and Fred had flown with Kit to Denver, but there they parted ways. Kit realized for all the time she'd spent holed up with them, she didn't know them very well. She had no idea where they even lived. In Denver a car met her, Lori and Fred and drove them the three hours back to Steamboat Springs.

Kit still hadn't heard from Jess and it weighed heavily on her. She had been looking forward to putting this behind her. With the added bonus of meeting someone who she really, really liked, her coming home should have been a joyous occasion. Kit valiantly hid her unhappy mood from Lori and Fred, but she had a feeling Lori was feeling a little guilty herself. The driver dropped Kit off first and Lori walked her in. After Kit disengaged the alarm Lori touched her arm signaling she wanted to say something. "You did great Kit, really great. I know you haven't heard from Jess, I haven't either, in case you're wondering. I'm a little surprised to be honest."

"Lori did you say something that would, you know have Jess upset with me?"

"No, I keep replaying the conversation over and over in my head. He likes you. I know he does. I'm sure there's a reason he hasn't called."

"Yea, maybe." Kit hung her head, her heart hurt, was that even possible?

"Kit we'll have to talk, you know about you and staying in Wit Sec. The deal was until after the trial. Personally I think you should stay in, but it's your call. Think about it, okay."

"Okay, thanks Lori, thanks for taking care of me."

"You're welcome. I wish all my people were as easy as you."

Kit smiled but Lori saw it didn't reach her eyes. What should have been a happy; upbeat homecoming had been marred by Jess' lack of communication. They hugged good-bye and Kit stepped into her home, reengaging the alarm. She carried her bag upstairs to her apartment and let herself in keeping with the routine of reengaging the alarm once safely inside. After Kit unpacked she called her clients, including Jess and told them she was back. Jess' phone went directly to voice mail again. Kit decided if this was what lay ahead in the land of dating she didn't want any part of it. Bud and Mikey D had been right to warn her from him. He had obviously rethought his association with her.

The next few days flew by. Her elderly clients were happy she was back and on Monday she even had two new adults who arrived at the same time. They got along well and entertained themselves by putting a puzzle together. Mikey D had dropped Crank off and Kit wanted to ask about Jess but their relationship had been private and she just couldn't bring herself to poke Mikey D for information. Besides if Mikey D told her that Jess was dating someone she didn't know if she could handle it. Kit had to remind herself that she and Jess had only dated for a little over a week. So then why was she so disappointed?

When Crank arrived he was excited to see her and even more excited when Misty arrived. Misty's owner was a detective in Steamboat Springs. He had asked Kit out the first time he had met her and like the other men, she had told him no, that she had just moved there and wasn't ready to date yet. Today when Tim Barns, Misty's owner came he lingered a little longer than usual and Kit had the feeling he was going to ask her out again. As predicted he asked her to breakfast the following morning, when he'd be back to pick Misty up.

Although she didn't use the 'I just moved here' excuse she simply said, "Thank you but no thank you." She could tell Tim wasn't use to being said no to and she could feel his demeanor towards her cool.

The rest of the day was smooth sailing except for the nagging empty feeling Kit was dealing with. Mr. Owen and Mrs. Channing, her two adult day care people for that day, left within minutes of each other. It was still light enough outside that Kit decided she had plenty of time to take the two dogs on a run up the trail behind her house before it got too dark. They jogged up the small dirt trail. Kit loved being able to exercise outdoors again; it was something she had missed while in New Jersey. About a half hour up the mountain trail and thoroughly winded she and the dogs turned around to head home.

As they walked briskly down the trail Crank saw a deer and bolted. Kit held tightly to his leash yanking on it hoping he'd slow. Crank was strong and he pursued the deer pulling Kit and Misty behind him until he jumped off trail taking Kit and Misty with him through the brush. Kit was using all her strength to hold on to him and Misty as they crashed through the woods swerving around trees and rocks and prickly thickets of brush.

Crank turned sharply and leapt over a large rock. Kit had no choice but to release his leash, but not before she went careening into a pine tree, which she bounced off of, landing into the thick pricker bushes nearby. Kit jumped up untangling herself and Misty's leash from the grabby long branches. Disregarding the scratches to her arms and legs. She ran after Crank, calling for him and fighting the panic that she was going to lose him in the darkening woods. Mikey D would kill her, not literally, but it wouldn't be good. It was almost too dark to see as she continued bushwhacking down the mountain having lost track of the trail. Kit wiped wetness from her tingling cheek and realized the wetness was blood. Her heart started booming in her chest as she was instantly transported back to the day Ray had been shot. How the blood she had wiped from her face that day had belonged to him.

Kit fell to her knees gripped with a body clenching panic attack and Misty stopped alongside of her happy for the break from their previous pace. Kit couldn't catch her breath and she was afraid she was going to pass out. Black spots swam in front of her eyes and there was a roaring in her ears she couldn't keep out even when she pressed her palms against them. Her back seized in a spasm that rendered her immobile. Tears streaked her face as she tried to pull herself out of the wicked time warp but all she saw was Ray lying on the kitchen floor covered in his warm sticky blood.

Kit finally pulled herself together after a few terrifying minutes. She struggled to her feet making sure she still had Misty's leash and stumbled down the dark mountain. It was one of the few times she had not taken her cell phone with her and she cursed herself knowing the flashlight app would really have helped. Her anxiety began to escalate. She had lost Crank and she was lost. She knew she was headed down the mountain, but she couldn't see more than a few feet in front of herself. She worried she'd be spending the night on the mountain and even in the summer it got cold.

Kit was walking with her hands out in front of her, feeling her way. When she felt a tree she would sidestep it. She continued in this fashion slowly making her way downhill. Her fingertips brushed bark and but this time when she moved to the side her foot never touched anything solid and she found herself tumbling down a small ravine. She felt the brush tearing at her exposed skin. Kit's last moment of lucidity was hearing Misty yelping as she tumbled down with her. Kit's head collided with a tree and although she tried to fight it, her world faded black.

Jess arrived at Kit's house after stopping at his parents to pick up Lulu. He had finally heard her voice mail from the week before and then the latest one telling him she was back and opened for business. He had been away fighting a forest fire in

Utah and had no cell service. His last conversation had been with Lori and she had sounded sketchy. Lori had hesitatingly relayed to him that Kit couldn't talk. When he'd ask why she had fumbled over her answer and then said she was talking with someone. Jess got a hinky feeling in his gut. He thought he'd be able to talk to Kit before he left but luck had not been on his side.

He had hoped to call her but in the backwoods of Utah but his cell phone had no bars, none of the men had service. They were housed in trailers so there were no landlines either. It was not until he was heading home at the airport that his phone started to ping with missed messages but then he had had to run to catch his flight so he hadn't heard Kit's voice mails or Lori's either until he had landed in Hayden; that had been an hour ago.

While the plane was taxiing in he listened to Kit's message, the one from last Monday. Then he listened to Lori's message as she bitched him out, wondering why he was being a dick and not calling Kit. Next he heard Kit's message from Friday saying she had returned and taking clients again. Her voice had been quiet and her tone was apprehensive. He knew she would be upset not hearing from him, but in his defense he hadn't realized he wouldn't be able to talk to her. He tried calling her as he exited the small prop plane lugging his duffel bag, but her phone went directly to voice mail. He left a message telling her he was home, he'd elaborate later, and that he wanted to see her. He decided he'd go to her house after he picked up Lulu from his parents' home. It was 9:00 pm when he arrived on her doorstep; he figured she'd be home and still awake. He couldn't wait to see her, he had missed her and he was going to make sure she knew it.

He rang the doorbell and when she didn't answer he went around to the side dog client door and rang that bell, again no answer. He then went around back thinking perhaps she was in the backyard, but Kit was nowhere. He sat on her front porch hoping she had just run a quick errand, but he saw her car was in the driveway. Jess had no idea if she were watching any dogs that night. The house was eerily quiet. He knew if she were watching dogs that she wouldn't leave them alone for too long so he sat down and continued to wait. A queasy feeling took up residence in the pit of his stomach.

After waiting for an hour Jess was on edge. Maybe she was on a date, which would suck if she and her date pulled up. He would look like a chump sitting on her porch waiting for her. He pulled out his cell and punched in her number again. It rang to voice mail yet again. Jess waited for fifteen more minutes before heading to the firehouse, maybe Mikey D or Bud knew where she was.

When Jess got to the station he left Lulu in

the jeep and climbed the station steps where the guys were sitting in the living area watching TV.

The guys welcomed him back asking him questions about the fire. They had been monitoring it on a scanner. Jess answered a couple of the basic questions as he scanned the room looking for Bud or Mikey D.

"Hey Jess welcome back, you bored? You're not scheduled for another two days." The captain teased him. Jess spied Mikey D sprawled out on the lazy boy.

"Uh, I need to talk to Mikey D for a second."

The guys all looked at Mikey D and he shrugged his shoulders indicating he had no idea what Jess wanted, before getting up from the comfy chair and following Jess to a corner in the front of the room.

"Hey man what's up?"

"Mikey, do you know where Kit is?"

"Home I guess. She's watching Crank. Jess, don't go there man, she's a good girl."

"Shut it Mikey, she's not at her house. I'm getting worried." Jess's tone was harsher than he intended but he was worried, especially now that he knew she was watching Crank.

Mikey D hesitated a second taking in Jess' tone of voice and his aggressive stance. "Maybe she's purposely ducking you." Mikey D reluctantly pointed out.

"No, I don't think so, I..." Loud barking coming from the front of the station house cut off Jess's response. The two men looked out the window, looked at each other and dashed down the station house stairs.

Crank was wagging his tail and jumping all over Mikey D obviously delighted to see him. He had twigs stuck through his collar and looked like he'd been playing in the woods. Jess picked up the leash Crank was dragging behind him. He held it up for Mikey to see and both men muttered, "shit" at the same time. Crank had been in the woods and with his leash still attached that meant Kit had been with him.

Jess got back in his jeep and raced back to Kit's house. Mikey D was going to tell the captain what was going on and then head over, with Crank. Jess arrived at Kit's house and pulled his flashlight out from behind the back seat. He let Lulu out of the jeep and they waited until Mikey D pulled up. Mikey D wrapped his hand around Cranks leash not wanting the high-strung dog to get away from him. He took a flashlight from his truck bed box and the two men and two dogs headed up the trail behind Kit's house hoping that had been where she'd gone.

It was pitch-black out as clouds covered any stars or moonlight that might have helped. Once they entered the woods it was ominously dark. Jess's gut clenched and he sent a silent prayer to the big guy upstairs asking for guidance in finding her.

They started calling Kit's name and about a half-mile up the trail they heard a dog barking. Jess realized it wasn't coming from anywhere on the trail so they ventured off the small path and followed the barking. It was slow moving; their combined flashlights guiding them, their speed hampered by the rocky terrain and thick brush. Lulu started to whine and that clued Jess in that something was directly ahead of them. He picked up his pace and almost fell down a small ravine. He flashed his light over the rocky ledge and his beam landed on Misty standing next to Kit who lay unmoving. Mikey D leaned over to look. "Holy Shit."

Jess' heart was pounding and he had to tell himself to breath.

Both men carefully climbed down the rock formation. Mikey D released Crank knowing he'd get down safer, using another path rather than if he were to try to lift him down. Lulu wasn't on a leash and made her way down to them on her own as well. Jess saw that Misty's leash was wrapped tightly around Kit's hand so he unwrapped it and handed the leash to Mikey D. He knelt by Kit and felt for her pulse, which thankfully was beating away. Jess nodded that she was alive to Mikey D who said, "Thank God."

Jess knelt down and carefully looked her over for injuries before moving her. Her head had a small gash in it near her hairline that had thankfully stopped bleeding. Her arms and legs were scratched and she was shivering. Jess pulled his flannel shirt off his body and wrapped her in it. He then carefully lifted her shoulders off the cold ground and rested her back against his torso, supporting her gently with his large frame. He put his cheek against hers and spoke in a hushed, calmed voice.

"Kit, Kit baby wake up. Kit...Kit, its Jess wake up baby."

Mikey D looked on realizing his best friend cared for Kit and not like wham bam, later ma'am, but cared for her.

Kit turned her face into Jess's shirt and mumbled out "Jess." Jess released his pent up breath that she was coming to. He caressed her face as he continued to encourage her awake.

"Kit, honey please wake up, it's Jess." Lulu leaned into Jess's side and licked her face. Lulu's cold lick acted like Prince Charming's kiss.

"Jess" She mumbled weakly. Then, as she fought through the haze and her eyelids continued to flutter with her efforts, she spoke his name with more emotion. “Jess... Jess, you’re here.” She finally opened her eyes and reached her one hand up to clutch Jess’s arm. When she realized her other hand was free she cried out, “Misty.”

Mikey D leaned over Jess’s shoulder, “I got her kid.”

Kit had tears in her eyes as she started to come back from la-la land. “I lost Crank.” She gulped out. “I got him too.” Mikey D grinned as he held up his other hand showing her Crank’s leash. Her relief was visible and she melted back into Jess chest.

After a minute of pulling herself together she tried to stand up but was too unstable. Jess promptly lifted her into his arms and kissed her cheek. Kit was surprised but loved how his arms felt around her. Jess’ tense coiled muscles began to unknot as he held her gently in his arms. He had been scared; no doubt about it, this slip of a girl had thrown him for a loop.

He hadn’t been able to stop thinking about her after their first date. He’d had to relieve himself that night, twice. Kit was, of course, the vision he had beat off to as he pictured tasting her, pleasing her, and his favorite image was her gently tied and immobile begging him to let her come. He was also ecstatic and relieved his cock was working again.

Jess held her protectively and Kit relaxed into his chest, leaning her head against him.

"Baby, what happened?" Kit didn't even notice his endearment but Mikey D did.

"I wanted to walk the dogs before it got too dark. Crank started running after a deer and went off trail. I tried to stay with her, I had Misty too, God, Misty must be hungry."

Jess smiled. "You're worried the dog might be hungry?"

Kit smiled at him. It dawned on her that Jess was continuing to carry her down the mountain.

"You can put me down now. I can probably walk."

Jess just grunted out a "No way."

Kit kept her arm around his neck and fiddled with his hair near his collar. "It's dark, what time is it?"

Mikey D looked at his watch and shined the light on the dial. "10:35."

"Oh wow." Kit said almost under her breath.

"You hit your head" Jess said.

"I...I must have." She saw that Jess was

staring down at her as he picked his way back to the trail while Mikey D led the way holding the two flashlights and Cranks and Misty's leashes.

When they got down the mountain Jess reluctantly let Kit stand on her own. Mikey D called the firehouse and said he'd be there in a few minutes. Kit unlocked the side door, unarmed the alarm and signaled for the guys to follow her. Mikey D told Kit he'd feed the dogs and he took them both downstairs. Jess turned Kit to him and pulled her in as he stroked her back.

"We need to take you to Urgent Care, you took a good hit on your head and it knocked you out. God, I was so worried." His voice was soothing and Kit rested her cheek on his damp tee shirt savoring his spicy, woodsy smell. At that moment she remembered he had not called her.

"I'm sorry you were worried." She said gently.

"I'm just glad we found you."

Kit nodded numbly afraid if she spoke she'd start weeping.

"What's the matter?' He asked seeing her fretful expression, still not allowing her to leave his embrace.

"Why didn't you call me?" She asked

uncertainly.

"Kit, I was fighting a fire in Utah. I had no cell service. I got home a few hours ago. I came right here."

Kit started crying. She was embarrassment that she was appearing to be dramatic and she burrowed her face deeper into his shirt. Jess was a little out of sorts. "Kit, why are you crying? I thought you'd want to see me."

Kit wrapped her arms around his waist and placed her chin on his chest looking up at Jess who was now so distraught it tore at her physically.

"Jess you have no idea how happy I am to see you. These were happy tears. I thought...I thought maybe you didn't want to see me anymore, that you were just cutting line." She smiled weakly up at him.

"No fucking way Kit and for the record baby I don't think I like happy tears. You just scare the shit me." Kit chuckled and wiped her hand across her face. "I must look a sight."

"You look great, but you need to see a doctor before you clean up."

"Really, I just a have a headache and ummmm, a couple other aches. I think I'll be fine."

"No chance Kit, we're going. Then after you see the doctor and I know you're okay how about if I come upstairs and while you shower or take a bath I'll cook you some supper, you have any eggs?" Kit nodded.

"I have eggs, are you sure?"

"Kit, believe it or not I would appreciate you letting me cook you dinner. I need to settle my nerves and the only way I'm going to be able to do that is by being around you and knowing you're okay."

Kit was quiet for a second and then looked up at him shyly. "You say some sweet things Jess."

"I don't say anything I don't mean Kit." He leaned in and kissed the top of her head as he rubbed her upper arms.

Mikey came back upstairs and said the dogs were fed, watered and had already settled down. Kit thanked him and Jess walked him out to the driveway. They spoke for a second and then they shook hands and Jess came back in. Kit was standing in the doorway. Lulu had remained at her side.

"What did you say to him?" Kit asked as she set the alarm.

"I thanked him and I told him he could tell the

guys what had happened but asked him not to reveal how I felt about you."

"Felt? About me?"

Jess put his hand at the small of her back walking her to the stairs leading to his jeep.

"Kit, I like you, you know that right?"

Kit shrugged her shoulders.

"Really, you can't tell I like you?"

Kit let out a loud deep breath debating how to tell Jess what she wanted so badly for him to know. She decided to just tell him and see how he reacted.

"Jess, I've only ever dated one person, only ever any-thinged with one person. Maybe what we did on our two dates is normal, but I don't know normal. Maybe what I'm feeling isn't what you're feeling. I just don't know."

Jess helped Kit into the passenger seat of his jeep and buckled her in. Then he leaned in with his muscled forearms arms resting on the roof. "Kit, we need to talk. Let's see the doctor first, and then we'll talk."

Jess drove Kit to the Steamboat Springs Urgent Care facility that was open 24-7 and the PA confirmed, as Jess predicted, that she had low-grade concussion. She then used a clear liquid adhesive on Kit's cut. The PA told Jess that Kit was to be woken up every two hours for the rest of tonight and she wasn't to do anything that would cause her head to bang around for the next week, which included jogging. They thanked the PA and drove back towards Kit's home in silence. When Kit's eye lids began to droop Jess made her talk to him, which she found quite annoying and Jess found her rather adorable that she tried to act mad.

Kit unlocked her apartment door, waited for Jess and Lulu to get in, set the alarm and headed towards the bathroom. She spoke over her shoulder. "Jess there's dog food under the sink." She then stopped in her tracks, turned around and walked slowly back towards him. She placed her hands on his chest and peered up at him, her eyes betraying her emotions. "And Jess...thanks. I'm glad you're here." Kit turned back to the bathroom and Jess stood where she'd left him. God did she have any idea how sexy she was? Jess shook his head and ran both his hands through his hair. Then he turned to the kitchen to see what he could rustle up for their midnight dinner.

Jess made scrambled eggs, bacon and toast and he had everything dished out and on the table when Kit reappeared twenty minutes later. Her hair was damp and she wore a Keep Calm tee shirt with black yoga pants.

"Smells good." She said as she sat down. "Thanks for cooking." The PA had given Kit four Advil and she didn't have a headache anymore, but she was tired and hungry.

"Don't thank me until you taste it." He chuckled.

They both started eating and neither spoke while they cleared their plates.

"Jess that was good. You can cook me breakfast anytime."

Jess looked at her with a sly grin on his face.

"That's the plan."

Kit's face registered the shock of what he said and Jess started laughing. "Kit you should see your face."

Kit blushed and looked down at her empty plate. Jess stood and took both their plates to the sink.

"Jess I'll clean up, you cooked."

"Everything's already clean, just needed to do these two plates."

"Okay, thanks."

"You're welcome. Here you dry." Kit took the towel from the fridge door handle and dried as he washed. The entire process took only a few minutes and Kit remembered back to a time when she and Ray had shared chores like this. Her heart started pounding with the latent memory and tears filled her eyes. Jess looked over to her as he handed her the final utensil and saw the tears.

"Jesus Kit, you're not okay. Why didn't you tell me?" He took the towel from her and led her to her sofa.

Kit followed him and sat down. She folded her legs underneath herself. Jess sat next to her and took both her hands in his. He sat with his one knee bent so he could face her.

"Kit talk to me, please."

"Please Jess I'm okay. I don't want to talk about it."

"Not an option." He said so seriously and in such a tone that Kit knew it wasn't.

"Can I plead headache?" She said keeping her head down looking at their hands.

"Ha, you're good woman. Do you have a headache?"

"Ummmm..."

"Kit, don't you lie to me. It's the one thing I won't tolerate, lying."

"Geez, you are pushy. No, my headache is surprisingly gone." She looked up at him playfully and rubbed her thumbs over his hands causing Jess's heart to swell along with another part of his anatomy.

"I just had a stupid memory. I guess with the trial I'm just remembering things that I hadn't thought of for a while."

"Kit I told you I did some digging. I know you were married to a guy named Ray Murphy. I know he was killed in front of his wife, I figured you were his wife. I'm also certain you're in Wit Sec. Seeing Lori with you was kind of a giveaway. I followed the trial, until I got called away."

"When did you get called away?"

"The afternoon after I spoke with you. I called to tell you and that's when Lori told me you were talking with someone. She was annoyingly cryptic. She rushed me off the phone before I could tell her I was leaving. I thought I'd be able to call you from Utah but they have seriously no service anywhere. Honestly after talking with Lori I got a weird vibe from her, like she was hiding something. Is there anything I should know?"

"Like what?"

Jess hesitated for a second but he needed to know the truth.

"Like are you…," he hesitated. "Is there another guy in the picture?" He finally spit out. That had been hard for Jess to ask. It had been on his mind for a week. It would rip him up if she said yes.

"Oh Jess, no. I can't tell you who I was talking to, but I'll be honest, he is special to me."

Jess momentarily stopped breathing. For the first time ever he'd let a woman wiggle her way into his heart and now she was about to tell him about another boyfriend.

"Special?" He asked somberly. "Boyfriend special?"

"No." She said honestly. Jess relaxed, not sure what to make of her answer. Jess decided it was time to show her exactly how he felt. To hell with this 'special' guy. He pulled Kit on to his lap so she was straddling him. Her hands wrapped around his neck and she played with his hair running it through her fingers. He placed his hands on her cheeks and gently, oh so gently pulled her mouth down towards his. Before he touched his lips to hers he whispered. "Good." Jess touched his lips to hers and softly ran his tongue over them coaxing them to part.

Kit moaned and Jess hardened painfully, trapped beneath her as she opened her pink soft lips to stroke his tongue with hers. He fought to keep the kiss gentle when what he wanted to do was to strip her naked and slam possessively inside of her. Kit began to grind on him as she made little mewling noises. God she had no idea what she was doing to him. For the second time he prayed he wouldn't spew in his jeans.

Kit lifted from his mouth and leaned up to suck on his neck. She'd suck then nibble then lick, then move to a new spot and suck, then nibble and lick again. Jess felt himself tighten and knew he had to change things up so as not to embarrass himself. He lifted Kit off of him and she groaned frustrated that she'd lost contact. He placed her on her feet and stood up. Then he grasped her sweet little rear and lifted her. Her legs wrapped naturally around his lean hips as he walked them towards her bedroom. He watched her eyes darken with emotion as they drank him in and he held his breath hoping she wouldn't redirect him.

When they reached the bedroom he told Lulu to stay and he shut the door. Kit tilted her head at him. "No Lulu?"

"Not this time."

Kit smiled and Jess knew he was going to fulfill at least one of his 'Kit' fantasies. He didn't even care which one, but he knew which one he was going to start with. Jess lowered Kit till her feet hit the floor. "If it's too much, too soon, you can tell me, okay?" He really, really hoped she wouldn't. Kit didn't know if he meant because of her hit on the head or Ray, but she didn't care and there was no way she was stopping him. She wanted this, she craved this, she'd dreamt of this.

Kit whispered out a husky, "Not going to stop you." Her eyes were hooded and she had a rosy glow gracing her cheeks.

Jess pulled her tee shirt over her head being careful of her head wound. He realized he probably should be letting her relax but he'd waited too long and he sensed she wanted this and needed it as much as he did.

Kit watched Jess as he pulled her shirt over her head. She wasn't wearing a bra and when he saw her breasts his mouth dropped open and he grinned down at her. They were perfect, round and perky with stiff dusk colored nipples.. She was beautiful and Jess felt himself press agonizingly against his zipper. Her areolas were the color of a ripe peach and darkened under his gaze. Her yoga pants were soaked in the crotch area and her senses were becoming a jumbled mess of electrical synapses.

Jess bent down to pull her stretchy pants off but Kit swatted his hand away and began to unbutton his shirt.

“Need this off.” She bit out.

Kit then began to undo his jeans. He let her unbutton his top button and moaned when she slid the zipper down, relieving the pressure. She ran her hand down the front of his boxers cupping his length and her gentle touch almost unmanned him.

“Oh, God Kit, don’t...” Jess choked out.

Kit looked up at him surprised and embarrassed. She tried to step back out of his arms.

“No baby, no.” He pulled her back to him forcing her to look up to his face. “Honey I am so turned on that you touching me, well let’s just say I won’t last, and baby... I want to last.” Kit nodded and gave him the sexiest, most angelic smile he’d ever seen.

Jess shed his jeans and boxers and led Kit to the bed. She lay down on her side, her head on a pillow. He lay alongside of her, facing her and ran his strong hands tenderly over her body, exploring her soft curves. Kit was equally transfixed as she traced the muscles on his arms and chest and finally the six delicious indentations on his abdomen. They didn’t kiss, or talk, they explored with their hands, and it was intimate and sensual.

"Jess?"

"Ummmm?"

"I'm not...I'm not very experienced and I'm not on the pill or anything."

"Do you want to be with me Kit?"

"Yes, but I haven't been with anyone in a long time."

Jess waited for her to continue, he knew there was more.

"Ray and I dated in high school and college. He's the only guy I've ever been with in any way. When he was killed we were two weeks away from our divorce being finalized. We hadn't been together as husband and wife for years, sexually or emotionally, we just cohabited together."

"I'm sorry baby that had to be rough."

"I just didn't want you to think that I was, you know, slutty."

"Slutty?"

"You know, I bury my husband a year ago and now I jump into bed with a guy I've only known for a few weeks."

"Babe, no one in their right mind would accuse you of being slutty."

"I want to be with you Jess. When we were on our picnic...what we did...how you made me feel; it was...it was so unbelievable." Jess' heart was hammering in his chest. He was experiencing a dichotomy of emotion. He wanted to dominate her hard and fast, but he wanted to make slow tender love to her too.

"I'm going to try hard to make you feel unbelievable again Kit, tonight, and with any luck, more than once."

Jess pulled Kit's small delectable little body towards him and kissed her with so much passion Kit melted into his arms. She placed her one leg over his hip without realizing she did it to pull him closer to her. Kit splayed her hands on Jess' chest loving how he felt. She let her one hand trail lower. Jess groaned as her small hand fisted him and he tilted his head back, exposing his neck that Kit immediately latched on to with her lips.

Jess gave himself over to her sweet strokes. He grasped her face and began kissing her passionately. He was losing control and he had to stop kissing her so he could breathe. He hadn't been with a woman in years and until a month ago his cock hadn't even worked. He stilled his hips, gritting his teeth, forcing himself not to come.

"Am I not doing it right?"

"You're perfect babe; again you've brought me to the brink."

"Let me finish you Jess." Kit whispered to him. Her gentle touch and whispered plea sent him over. Jess groaned, "Oh God, Kit...KIt..." She felt his body go ridged and his muscles clench and then he moaned so deeply, he sounded as if he was in pain. Jess felt like he had cum for minutes instead of mere seconds. His body languid from the tremendous orgasm she had pulled from him. Kit continued to hold him delicately in her small hands. He was acutely sensitive so he took her hands in his and held them gently.

"Kit, that was, it was awesome. Thank you."

Kit leaned up on her one elbow. "I believe I did owe you one." She teased as she pulled out of his grasp and swung her feet off the bed. Kit padded to the bathroom and cleaned herself with a warm washcloth before bringing it back to gently wipe Jess off too. When she finished she dropped the wet cloth on the floor and climbed back on the bed.

Jess pulled her to him and lowered his mouth capturing hers in a passionate kiss. He worked his way down her body, using the licking, sucking and nibbling technique she had just used on him. Kit started to feel the pre twirls of an orgasm.

Her hips moved wantonly seeking relief. She had never before experienced such an erotic onslaught of sexual foreplay. Jess continued to kiss his way down her body. When Kit realized where he was headed she tugged on his hair making him stop and look up.

"Jess..." Her voice was shaking she was so heated up. "Jess, I've never...I..."

"Shhh, baby relax. I'll make it good. I promise."

The fact that no one had ever gone down on her before was such a turn on for Jess. He was going to take his time and feast on her. He wanted to drive her crazy until she begged, which he was thought she'd probably never done before either. He slowly wrecked havoc on her with his tongue. Kit was almost convulsing. His warm breath was heating her and she knew if he'd just touch her there she'd explode, but he didn't.

Kit felt so exposed and part of her thought she should be embarrassed, but what he was doing to her, how he was making her feel, she didn't want that to stop. Instead she grasped his thick hair and held on.

Kit was beside herself her hips were starting to press upwards and Jess knew she was close.

"Jess, Oh my God Jess...please."

Jess smiled to himself and then felt her come unraveled. Kit was wildly bucking against him; unabashedly chanting his name over and over as she death gripped his hair. "Jess...Jess...Jess."

He never let her fully come down from her shattering and he continued to pleasure. He felt her body tighten and release again

"Oh My God!" Kit groaned huskily.

When Jess was satisfied that he'd wrung every tremor from her he kissed his way back up her body. and slowly pushed deeply inside of her. Kit moaned out his name again, "Oh God Jess yes. That feels so good."

Jess filled her then retreated. Her legs were wrapped tightly around his hips and she was clutching his back, her nails dug into him as she urged him deeper. Jess picked up his pace and felt himself grow heavy. "Oh. God. Kit I'm going to commmme..."

Kit was milking him from the inside. He remembered he needed to pull out; he hadn't put a condom on. He'd never gone bareback before, ever. Jess pulled out and began rocking against her. Kit's head was slashing back and forth on the pillow, her hands gripping his tight ass pulling him closer to her.

Her body relented and she began to buck uncontrollably as she came for the third time, keening out his name in an incoherent groan. Jess came with her, his cum spurting out, once, twice, three times painting her erotically.

"Kit...Kit....Kit." He thickly moaned her name as if it was a mantra.

His face was buried into her soft neck and he sucked on her salty skin. Kit rubbed his back, her thighs still cradling his strong athletic hips. They were both so physically spent that neither moved for a while. Reluctantly Jess got up, retrieved the wet cloth from the floor and walked into the bathroom. He washed himself off and then he brought back a cloth to wipe Kit off. She was already starting to fall asleep. Jess started to wipe her clean and she tried to protest, saying that she could do that herself, but he pushed her hand away. "Let me do this Kit. I want to take care of you." He told her in his soft Dom-like voice.

When he finished he walked back to the bathroom, peed, washed his hands and then let Lulu into the room. Jess climbed into Kit's bed as Lulu made herself comfortable on the rug below him. Jess pulled Kit to him, covered them both with the sheet and blanket, gave Kit a kiss on her cheek, set his watch for two hours, and fell into the best sleep he'd had in two years.

Chapter 12

As promised Jess prepared breakfast again, this time it was two bowls of cereal and coffee that awaited Kit when she came out from her bedroom. Jess grinned sheepishly when she looked at the meager offering and gave him a cute little eyebrow rise. Her little attempt at disapproval had him laughing out loud.

"I'll do better next time. I'm running late." He replied sheepishly.

Kit laughed too and then told him she was content with cereal and coffee. Kit heard her dog client doorbell ring and she went downstairs to let Tim in. Kit told Jess she'd be right back. Tim had worked the night shift and usually she had coffee waiting for him. She felt a little guilty that she wasn't going to offer him any today. On top of that she felt obligated to relay to him what had happened the night before because it involved his dog.

Kit opened the basement door after letting Tim into the kitchen. Tim knelt down to give Misty a few obligatory loving rubs. Kit then told Tim what happened the night before. After hearing what had happened Tim stepped towards her and placed his hand on her neck so he could better view her wound that had begun to turn purple. “Are you okay?” He asked genuinely concerned.

“I’m fine, thanks. Misty is too, I promise.”

“I know Misty is fine. I’m concerned about you. You should have called me I would have come over. You shouldn’t have been alone.”

The kitchen door opened and Jess sauntered in. “She wasn’t.” Jess said his voice hard and sure. Kit groaned at the chest thumping posturing Jess was displaying.

Tim glanced down at Kit who was now beet red and thoroughly embarrassed. Tim’s eyes searched her face and she shivered. She felt his disapproval and he dropped his hands from her shoulders as if she were a leper.

Jess walked to Tim and stuck his hand out. “Jess Ryan.” The two men shook hands. “Tim Barnes, I’m a detective with the Sheriff's office.”

“You must have come on after I left a couple years ago.”

“Yea came over from New York City.”

Kit’s eyebrows raised, she knew he wasn’t from around here but he didn’t have a New York type accent.

"I didn't know that?" She quipped nervously interrupting their little bonding session.

"There's a lot you don't about me." Tim said with a chuckle. She knew he meant it to be funny but it came out sounding creepy.

"Well I guess you are being taken care of." Kit knew he was inferring to more than just her well-being and his comment made her cringe she was so mortified. Tim started out the door but stopped and turned back. "Glad you're okay. I'm on Wednesday night can Misty come?"

"Of course, I love having Misty here." Kit said as she bent to pet Misty's head.

The men shook hands again and Tim and Misty left. Neither spoke until they heard the side door close. Kit whirled to face Jess who was standing with his arms crossed leaning against the counter looking at her with an amused expression on his face.

"You should have stayed upstairs Jess that was embarrassing and kind of awkward."

"I know but I'm not going to apologize." Kit humphed and turned to go back upstairs.

He reached out and grabbed her arm before

she could escape.

"You do get that I don't share Kit?"

Kit looked first to where his hand was wrapped around her slim bicep and then up to his face.

"This is my work Jess." She bit out.

"He likes you."

"Jess." Kit said exasperated as she tried to shrug his comment off.

"Kit, I won't share." His tone was even and dark.

"You keep acting all cave dweller and that won't be a problem." She shook her arm free from his grasp and left the kitchen. Jess followed her upstairs.

Kit turned towards him. "Listen, last night, thanks for staying, I have to get ready for work now so..."

"Kit, don't be like that."

"Like what Jess? Upset that you just butted in on me when I was simply talking with a client, just so you could let him know you stayed here? Upset that you just made me feel like a tramp!" Kit was getting heated.

"No, I didn't mean for you to feel like that. You're not like that."

"I know that, but Tim doesn't. I've tried to maintain some barriers and now that he's seen you...well."

"Are you always going to keep us a secret?" Now Jess was mad.

"No...No it's just, it was embarrassing."

Jess stepped to her and reached for her but she backed away. Shit! This was not good Jess thought.

"I didn't mean for you to feel uncomfortable Kit. I'll admit that I wanted him to know I was here though."

"Why? So he would know you nailed me last night. So he could attest that the infamous Jess Ryan, God to woman legend, was alive and well?"

"Is that what you think? Son of a bitch!"

Jess turned from her, grabbed his jacket off the back of the kitchen chair, gave Lulu a quick pet good-bye and walked down the steps and out her side door. Kit watched him leave from her bedroom window. She fell backwards on her bed and hugged her pillow to her stomach. She felt hollow. Jess had made her feel special last night and then like a tart this morning. Kit decided if this was what the dating scene offered she was going to be single for a long time.

The day crept by at a ridiculously slow pace. Kit kept checking her phone, hoping Jess would call, yet was relieved when he didn't. She couldn't get a handle on her feelings and that scared her. Bud dropped Maize off and Mikey D picked up Crank. Mr. Peterson was her only adult day care client and she busied herself by helping him make a birthday card for his granddaughter.

Kit ran the dogs past the station house the next morning only because if she didn't Bud would notice and she didn't want to invite any questions. Bud came out to greet them bringing her a water and Maizie and Lulu a biscuit.

"Where's Jess?" Kit asked cautiously. Part of her was relieved and part of her was disappointed that he hadn't come outside.

"Picking up supplies." He told her without thought as he rubbed Maizie.

Kit mumbled weakly, "Oh."

"I told him you'd be by with the dogs soon but he volunteered to go anyway."

Kit knew he was avoiding her and she realized this was exactly why she should not have mixed business with pleasure.

Another lonely day passed, another day of no Jess. Was she wrong? She wished for the umpteenth time she had a girlfriend she could talk to. They had argued, yes, but she didn't think he'd walk away forever. The mere thought of never being with Jess again left Kit feeling empty inside. The only bright spot was that Lori called and said Pallone's trial had ended and that the jury was out.

Bud picked Maize up and then surprised her by taking Lulu too.

"Why? Where's Jess?" She asked trying to sound nonchalant.

"He has someone flying in and he went to meet her at the airport. I'm taking Lulu to his parents for him."

Kit was rocked, her stomach clenched and she paled. Ouch that hurt. She thought.

"What's the matter?" Bud asked noticing that she had paled.

"Oh, nothing, just, just a little tired."

Bud eyed her wearily. “I’m going to Rooney’s tonight, care to join? As a wing man of course.”

Kit thought about it, she wouldn’t have any dogs. “Sure, why not?” She couldn’t live the life of a hermit forever she thought.

Bud was floored that she’d agreed to go with him. He knew they were just friends but he was glad if he could help her socially acclimate to the Steamboat Springs bar scene.

“Really, wow that’s great. I’ll come get you around 8:00 okay?”

“Okay, see you later.”

Kit wasn’t sure why she agreed to go out, but she knew sitting around waiting for a call that may never happen was not how she wanted to spend her night. She dressed in a flirty skirt that was a little shorter than what she usually wore a simple white V-necked tee that dipped between her cleavage and her new tan cowboy boots that coordinated with the colorful edging around her skirt. She put on dangly silver earrings and her new silver cuff bracelet. She then applied her makeup of mascara and lip-gloss. Kit knew she looked pretty good and the outfit made her feel sexy. The bruise on her head had now taken on a gross yellow hue so Kit applied concealer to cover it up and then stood back from her full-length mirror behind the door to scrutinize her appearance. Not bad, she thought. She wished her mood matched her fun outfit.

Bud arrived and Kit left for her first night out on the town ever. She had agonized a bit over what to wear, but she knew she had nailed it when Bud's jaw had dropped when she'd opened the front door. After he recovered he playfully said.

"Maybe I'll have to be your wing man!"

Kit laughed thinking perhaps this night out diversion was exactly what she needed. There were a couple different bars in town but Kit knew Rooney's was the one most of the locals hung out at. During ski season the others got packed with tourists hoping to sample the local flavor, but Rooney's was the town's people's favorite haunt. It served bar food but it wasn't known for its cuisine. It was the fun bar that the locals loved. It had a long curved bar with ample seating. Scarred tables sporting fake flickering candles surrounding a wooden dance floor. A raised platform housed the nightly entertainment, including a weekly karaoke night, which the guys had told her had some good local talent. A room off to the right held pool tables and dartboards. The clientele was a potpourri of ages and the dress ranged from ripped jeans and tee's to night club, eye popping, 'come and get me' numbers that a few of the ladies wore.

Kit sat with Bud at a table with a bench seat

that curved around all but one side of the table. Mikey D arrived and joined them. Kit tried to relax and enjoy their company. They were conscientious about including her in their conversation and Kit appreciated their attempts to make her feel welcomed. Kit danced with each of them a couple times but never a slow one, those she sat out. Tim was at the bar with some friends and she even danced with him once. He asked where Jess was. His exact words were “Where’s your boyfriend?” in a bit of a snotty tone. Kit replied evenly that she didn’t know and after the dance she excused herself and returned to the table.

An extremely large and very handsome man had joined their table and Bud introduced her to his friend Cole, who she garnered from their conversation was a well-known rancher in the area. Their little table continued to grow and two chairs had to be brought over when three women, who the men all knew, joined them.

Kit listening to the easy banter criss - crossing the table that good friends enjoy. She’d had that a long time ago; when she and Ray would double with other couples, and for the first time in ages she missed something from her previous life. The dull ache reminded her just how much she missed being with people. She looked around the table. Bud was making googily eyes at the one woman named Krissy and Kit noticed she was just as googily eyed when she looked at Bud. Mikey D and one of the other girls were currently pressed together on the dance floor and the third woman, a very buxom blond was trying her damnedest to get Coles attention but he was politely keeping his distance. Kit realized he was focused solely on her.

Cole was ruggedly handsome and big in every way. His body was large framed, shoulders that stretched forever and a thick impressive chest that tapered to strong lean hips with a shelf like ass. He was genuinely impressive in the body department. The man didn't have an ounce of fat on him that Kit could see. His large hands wrapped casually around his beer making it appear small. His personality was as large as his body. He was a teddy bear of a man. He entertained Kit with stories about life on his ranch and never once boasted about himself, although she learned in the rest room from one of the girls, that he had once played pro football, his ranch was top-notch and he was seriously wealthy. He had Kit laughing and she was happy she had come with Bud. This was just what she had needed.

He and Kit danced a two-step and when the music slowed Cole pulled her gently into his large frame. His eyes looked down into hers making sure she was okay with dancing close with him and Kit decided why not? She hadn't heard from Jess and although just thinking about him made her heart clench, she stayed on the floor welcoming the distraction Cole offered. Cole was sweet, attentive and beyond handsome. He had wavy light, brown hair and hypnotizing hazel eyes. A constant smile adorned his expressive face and he had that cool chin dimple which only enhanced his handsome features. He put Kit at ease with light, fun conversation and she marveled at his dancing as he twirled her easily around the small dance floor.

Kit was enjoying her until she saw the bar door open and a beautiful young woman entered followed by Jess. Her heart slammed violently against her chest causing her to stumble on the dance floor but Cole righted her easily. Kit saw Jess hold the door open for the woman who turned slightly towards him, intimately wrapping her fingers around his strong bicep. They were both laughing at a private joke they apparently shared as they entered the bar.

Jess had been in a foul mood since arguing with Kit. He knew he'd been an ass. He'd spent most of the last two days figuring out how to apologize to her. He didn't even know if she'd let him. She tied him in knots. He had wanted that cop, Tim to know she was taken. Yet, he understood why Kit had been upset, he'd embarrassed her and afterword's he felt like an even bigger jerk remembering how shy she was to begin with. She had just pushed his buttons with her remark about him being a womanizer had hit a sore spot. The one thing he was sure of was that he missed her and if he needed to grovel to get her back he would.

He had talked to Mikey D earlier that day and knew he and Bud were meeting at Rooney's so he decided to stop in for a beer. He had run into Tina in the parking lot. She was an old friend who he had occasionally hooked up with before Afghanistan and one of the women he had unsuccessfully been with since he'd returned, the one he kept dodging. As they entered the bar together she had made some witty remark, which made him laugh. Jess knew she was giving him the 'I'll do anything you want' signal. Her hands were all over him, but Jess had no interest what so ever.

Jess entered the bar, holding the door open for Tina and the first thing he saw was Kit dancing with his good friend Cole. His heart thudded and he had to hold himself back from stalking over to them and ripping her out of his hands. Kit had seen him walk in and he saw the distressed look on her face. She turned away from him and it was then he realized Tina had her hand possessively wrapped around his arm. He mentally kicked himself. He gently extracted himself from Tina's tight grip, said good-bye to her and walked to the table he saw the guys at.

He kept his eyes on Cole and Kit as he made

his way to the table that Bud and two women were occupying. He grabbed one of the empty chairs and that's when he realized Tina had followed him to the table. She snagged the chair nearest to him and sat down making sure she was close enough to touch him easily. She gave Jess her best flirty smile and then turned to say hi to everyone at the table.

Kit felt like she'd been punched in the gut. She'd been having a good time with Cole. Hell that wouldn't? The man was great looking, could move on the dance floor, was seriously a sweetheart, plus he was humble. She enjoyed dancing with him and he had made her feel welcomed in the large group, but seeing Jess only confirmed what she had known all along. The painful fact that being with Cole was only a temporary band aide.

Kit missed Jess and even though gorgeous Cole was every other woman's dream in the bar, he wasn't hers. Jess had been a jerk and had seriously overstepped when he decided to come downstairs. He had shoved Tim's nose in the fact that he'd spent the night with her, but she'd been harsh to him too.

The slow song ended and Cole led Kit back to the table keeping his hand resting lightly just above her butt at the small of her back. Jess saw the intimate contact and was fighting the jealousy that was threatening to unhinge him. Jess stood when they approached the table and the two men shook hands before Cole slid in next to Kit on the bench seat. Kit watched the two gorgeous men thinking, of course they knew each other, and everyone knew everyone here. Then Cole said hello to the girl seated almost in Jess' lap calling her Tina. Wow, if this girl just flew in and she was no stranger to Jess's friends that must mean they'd been dating for a while. Kit felt like the village idiot and wished she had listened to Bud and Mikey D.

"Kit." Jess said acknowledging her. He was looking around Coles big frame his eyes seeking hers forcing hers to lower to the table.

"Hi Jess." She murmured quietly.

The beautiful woman named Tina grabbed Jess's arm with both her hands, squealing as a popular slow tune began to play. "Jess, baby come dance with me."

"No, Tina." Jess said shaking off her hand as he continued to stare at Kit.

Jess never took his eyes off Kit and Cole became aware of the strained interaction he sensed between his longtime friend Jess and the sweet young thing he'd just met.

Kit watched Tina's face fall with Jess' abrupt rejection and then she leveled Kit with a scowl that made Kit feel self-conscious and out of place. She thought Jess was being rude to his date and not wanting to be the cause of friction between them she decided to distance herself. She quietly asked Cole to let her up so she could use the Ladies room. Cole stood and watched her walk away. He could tell she was for some reason uncomfortable around Jess. Cole watched Jess watch Kit until he couldn't see her through the crowd.

Tina was wrapping herself around Jess' arm. Jess stood abruptly successfully disengaging himself from Tina's grasp and left the table to go to the bar. Cole watched Tina frown and then she left the table walking into the adjacent poolroom. Cole decided to join Jess at the bar.

"Hey man how ya been?" He asked Jess.

Jess turned to him and asked directly. "You here with Kit?"

"No, just met her tonight. She came with Bud, some joke about him needing a wing man."

"What's up Jess, you know her?"

"Yea, we've been on some dates." Jess hated that he couldn't claim her.

"Pretty little thing."

"She's mine, Cole, mine." Jess voice was barely restrained as he warned off his good friend.

Cole looked at him, gave it some thought and then decided he needed to point out the obvious.

“Uh, Jess, you came with Tina. I’d never move in on a girl that was yours, but as far as I’m concerned right now, she isn’t your girl.”

“I didn’t come with Tina.” Jess hissed. “She was in the parking lot when I arrived.”

“Sure looks like you came with her.”

“Well I didn’t. Shit! Kit probably thinks I did though.”

“Be a reasonable assumption, my man.”

“Shit!”

“You really like her Jess?”

“You have no fucking idea. The woman is so far under my skin I don’t even know what I’m doing.”

“She is something special, I’ll give you that. Sweet little thing and her body…”

“Shut it Cole.”

“Geez man, chill out.”

Jess bought himself and Cole a beer. They talked for a few more minutes catching up with each other before they walked back to the table. Kit reemerged from the restroom hallway and slipped into her spot at the table. Before either Cole or Jess could slide in next to her Mikey D and his woman came back from the dance floor and claimed the spot forcing Kit to slide further around the curvy bench seat until she was now next to the buxom blond who still wasn't looking too happy.

Jess's date came back from wherever she'd disappeared to and stood behind him splaying her hands possessively over Jess's shoulders. Kit could feel hot tears pressing against her eyelids. She was such a loser she thought as she fought back the tears. She could feel Jess' eyes on her and when she glanced at Cole he looked so concerned she knew she had to pull herself together before she became an emotional mess. She kept her head down as she held her beer, peeling the label off the bottle.

It was her own damn fault she chastised herself. She had let Jess into her heart and her bed, and now, while she was feeling broken and lonely, he had efficiently replaced her with in forty-eight hours.

Cole couldn't stop looking at Kit as he spoke with Bud and Krissy who were seated to his left. He felt like laying Jess out knowing that somehow he had hurt the pretty little thing that had turned his head.

Kit finally looked up after focusing her eyes on her beer, willing the tears away. Mikey D leaned into her and quietly asked, “Are you okay?” and when she shook her head no he sighed sadly and took her hand telling the table they were going to dance. His woman didn’t look happy but he quickly whispered something to her that placated her. Mikey D guided Kit to the dance floor where Kenny Rodgers, Lady was playing. He gently pulled her in to his frame and she rested her forehead on his chest.

“I should have listened to you. I’m such an idiot.”

“Kit, you’re not. I know he likes you.”

“Who? Cole?”

“No, Jess, but shit probably Cole too.” Mikey looked back at the table and saw both men staring at them, neither looked happy.

“Yea, well...um in case you haven’t noticed he’s got himself a hot date sitting right next to him.” Kit said glumly.

“What happened?” Mikey D asked her softly.

Kit unburdened her telling Mikey D

everything. Well, almost everything, she left out the part about Jess giving her three fantastic orgasms in one night. She decided to let him think what he wanted regarding Jess spending the night.

“Kit he hasn’t stopped looking at you, and it’s a good thing Cole is a gentleman because if he touches you again I think Jess is going to lose it.”

“Mikey, he’s with a woman, who has not stopped touching him. Bud told me she flew in to see him.”

“I don’t think Jess is with Tina, Kit.”

“It doesn’t matter Mikey, I’m not with him either so...”

A large shadow fell across them as Cole appeared at their side. “Mind if I cut in?”

Mikey looked at Kit who nodded and he relinquished his hold on her. Kit and Cole danced for a few seconds in silence before Cole tipped her chin up so he could look at her.

“You upset about something sugar?” He had that wonderful sexy drawl and it probably would have melted the pants off any other woman.

“I...I have a bit of a headache. I would like to go home.”

"Did you drive here?"

"No, I'm Bud's wing man, remember?" She said with a tiny smirk making Cole laugh.

"How about if I give you a lift? I'm done here too."

"Are you sure Cole? I don't want to mess up your night."

"Darlin', I have chores before the sun comes up. It's way past my bedtime."

"Okay if you're sure."

"Let's just tell the table we're leaving."

"Um Cole I'm going to just meet you outside, can you tell them please?"

"Sure thing. I'll meet you by the door."

Before Kit made it through the bar doorway she heard a disturbance coming from the bar. When she looked behind her she saw that Jess was standing facing Cole, shaking out his hand and Cole was rubbing his jaw. What the hell? She walked awkwardly back towards the table where the men were now standing uncomfortably in silence and a pudgy bouncer was making his way towards them as well.

Jess looked at her and exploded, “You are NOT going home with him.”

Kit stilled taken back by Jess serious tone of voice. Tina had a firm grip on Jess’ arm again and Kit winced.

“Jess” Cole started to speak still holding his jaw. “I said I was driving her home, not taking her home.”

The table was quiet, Mikey D and Bud had jumped up to stand between the two men. The bouncer decided it would be in his best interest to stand down, and as Kit looked from Jess to Cole and then to the beautiful woman staring adoringly at Jess, the pain in her heart splintered inside of her and became more than she could emotionally handle.

Her first night out and she has to run into Jess, with a girl, no less. She wasn’t that strong. She should have never agreed to come out. Kit turned away from the table and hustled out the front door of Rooney’s into the jammed packed parking lot. She didn’t know what to do; it wasn’t like there were any cabs waiting around to hail. She picked her way through the cars thinking the walk back to her house would be about a ten miles.

Kit heard the gravel crunching behind her and turned to find Jess bearing down on her. He stopped when he reached her, his hands fisted at his side. “I’m sorry.” He said his voice strangled and tense. “ Okay, I’m sorry I should have stayed upstairs.”

Kit looked at Jess, he was so handsome and he looked so distraught. Tears stung her eyes. “Jess you’re here with a date, please go back inside.”

“No, no way, I need to talk to you.” He ran both hands through his hair.

“No Jess, go back inside. I suck at this boy girl stuff and I can’t stand feeling like this. You hurt me. I can’t believe how much I hurt.” Tears were now dripping down Kit’s cheeks and she was embarrassed that she couldn’t even talk without her silly emotions ruling her body.

“You hurt me too Kit.”

“How? How exactly did I hurt you Jess?”

“You hurt me because you think I’m some womanizer. That all I’m interested in is a roll in the sack. How can you think I’m that shallow?”

“I never...”

“You did...and after a night that was damn near perfect.”

Kit didn’t respond right away, she wasn’t

exactly sure what to say.

"I'm sorry if I hurt your feelings Jess. You just made me so mad."

"I get that. I was wrong Kit. You just make me feel...possessive."

Kit let a few seconds slip by. Jess was breathing hard and she felt uncomfortable.

"Okay Jess. Apology accepted and I'm sorry too." Jess looked at her, his eyes revealing how upset he really was.

"Really apology accepted?"

"Yea. Now, umm, would you mind telling Cole I'm outside? He offered to drive me home."

"No fucking way!" He snarled.

"Jess!"

"I'll take you home."

"Jess you're here with a date and I may not have dated much but that's really uncool."

"Kit I'm not here with anyone."

"Jess I saw you walk in together, I know you picked her up at the airport. Please tell Cole to come out." Kit's lower lip was quivering as her unrelenting tears threatened to become harsh sobs.

Jess gripped her upper arms so she couldn't pull away. "I didn't pick Tina up at the airport. I picked up my cousin Alexei."

Kit got quiet. "You're not with Tina?"

"No way. Kit you may have made me mad, but I'm not that much of a jerk to be with someone right away after being with you. The old Jess maybe, but not now, no way."

"Does Tina know you're not with her? Because I watched her looking at you and I don't think she does."

"Oh God, we need to talk."

"No Jess, not now we don't. Please don't do this to me."

"Kit I'll go get Cole but you need to hear, really hear me and get what I'm saying. I am not romantically involved with Tina. I care about you and it's darn near pissing me off that you can't seem to get it through that beautiful head of yours how much I do like you."

"Jess... Okay, maybe we do need to talk, but right now I just want to go home."

"I'm taking you Kit."

"No, you are NOT!" Kit stamped her foot like a penchant child to emphasis her point.

More gravel sounded from behind them and Cole and Tina appeared.

"You okay Kit?" Cole asked her.

Tina sidled up to Jess and put her hands on his forearm in a comforting gesture. Kit watched as her hands wrapped around her Jess and she sickened. Jess noticed Kits face start to crumble and pulled out of Tina's grasp.

"Yes, please Cole, will you take me home?"

"Yup, come on."

Cole placed his hand at the small of her back and Jess grabbed his wrist. "Cole." He hissed so lethally that even Kit gulped.

"Don't worry Jess I know. I know."

Jess dropped his hand from Cole and after looking at how distraught his girl was, he turned back to return the bar. Tina followed behind him like a puppy.

"Sorry about all the drama Cole." Kit said to him as they drove the quiet dark streets back to her home.

"No problem just disappointed."

"Disappointed, with what?"

"I was enjoying your company and you're the prettiest thing I've seen in a long time. I'm disappointed that Jess has dibs or I would have asked you out."

"I'm not sure how to respond to that Cole. Jess and I, I'm not sure what we are. Thank you though, I think?"

"Kit I've known Jess for a long time. He's a good man. I've never, I mean never, seen him look at a woman the way he looks at you."

"Um that maybe so, but that doesn't mean he wants to be with me. For Gosh sakes Cole we just broke up, I mean not that we were going out that long but...what it took him all of two days to find another woman!"

"I've known Tina about as long as I've known Jess. She and Jess have a little history but most guys around here do, regarding Tina that is."

"Ugh, not helping Cole. Maybe they'll rekindle their affair." Kit said glumly.

"A man can only hope." He said with a cute ass grin as he pulled up to her house.

Kit thanked him and told him to sit tight, when he tried to walk her to the door. Cole watched her unlock her door and she waved good-bye to him before he pulled away.

As Kit relocked her door and set the downstairs alarm her phone pinged and she looked down to see a text from Jess.

Breakfast tomorrow please?

Why drag this out? Kit responded.

You know why!

You may be otherwise occupied tomorrow morning.

Kit knew that was a snarky comment but she was tired, jealous and hurting.

I am not with anyone nor will I be. Please let's talk.

Okay, tomorrow. She finally relented.

Kit shut her phone and twenty seconds later it rang. She saw it was Jess again.

“Hello?”

“I’ll be there in five minutes.”

“Jess, what?”

“Breakfast, you said you’d have breakfast with me.”

“Jess I meant tomorrow.”

“It’s 12:01 Kit, it is tomorrow.” And he hung up before she could reply.

Jess arrived at her front door in ten minutes, not the five he had anticipated. Kit let him in and reset the alarm. When she turned back towards him he handed her a brown bag. Kit looked inside and started laughing.

“The only damn place open was Gas Mart.” He said sheepishly.

Kit reached into the bag and pulled out the S’mores Pop Tart box. “Your breakfasts are getting worse each day Jess." Kit said blushing.

Jess took two steps towards her and before Kit could move he had her wrapped in his arms, cupping the back of her head with one hand gently holding her face into his chest as he rested his chin on the top of her head. Kit melted into him for a wonderful two seconds before remembering why he was there so she pushed lightly on his waist to back him up.

"We were going to talk Jess, remember?"

"We are." With that he grabbed her hand and led her upstairs to her apartment.

Once inside Jess propelled Kit to the couch, opened the box of Pop Tarts, unwrapped a foiled pouch and handed her one out of the two-pack. Kit took it and started nibbling on it while Jess ate its twin.

"First off," he began, "I'm going to apologize again for coming down stairs and embarrassing you with Tim."

"You really did Jess, he even made a snide comment tonight."

"That bastard what did he say?"

Jess, forget it."

"God Kit I am sorry." Kit nodded.

"Furthermore, the person I picked up at the airport was my cousin."

"Okay."

"Third, Tina was in the parking lot when I arrived and we just walked in together, I swear."

"K." She answered monosyllable for the third straight time.

"I'm not kidding you Kit. Just to be clear here, I've been with her in the past, but it was sheer coincidence that we walked in together tonight."

Kit's head was tucked towards her chest. Her body language portraying how insecure she felt.

"Well it's not like we were together and she touched you like you were together. When you walked in she sat with you at the table. It was a reasonable assumption on my part that you were together."

"Yea, I get that and Cole said the same thing. Tina, well, she's not easy to shake off. Trust me I tried. I would never hurt you Kit. I'm so sorry. Do you believe me?"

"Jess, if it's one thing I do know it's that you

aren't it's a liar. I believe you." Jess relaxed seemingly relieved.

"Okay now for you."

"Me?"

"Bud talked you into going out tonight?"

"Yea, I was his wing man." She grinned lamely. "It was the first time I've gone out, you know unattached, since I got here over a year ago." Jess smiled sadly at her then blew out a breath.

"How much do you like Cole?"

"What? Hey!"

"Answer me."

"You're doing that pushy Neanderthal thing again."

Jess' voice got quiet. "I've known Cole almost my whole life. He's one of the best guys I know. The guy has everything going for him, looks, personality, and more money that you can shake a stick at, plus he's got a great spread just outside of town. If you like him I'm going to bow out now, even though it'll kill me. I can't compete with him, never have and never will."

Kit was blown away by what he said. Jess truly believed someone was better than him. Her heart tore apart for her handsome man looking so serious and troubled. Quickly wiping the crumbs of her pop tart off her skirt Kit took his hand in hers. She looked into Jess' eyes and saw how uncertain he was as to how she might answer his question.

"Jess I can't believe you just said that." Jess didn't answer her and she knew the ball was in her court. "Listen to me mister."

She took Jess' face in hers two hands bracketing his cheeks, her fingers spread, and her thumbs on his cheeks. She made sure he was looking into her eyes when she spoke.

"Cole may have all those things but he's still not you and for the record, I knew that he'd never even come close to replacing how I feel about you within the first five minutes we were together. He is a great guy, but Jess he could never measure up to you."

Jess looked at her and she saw the shock register across his face, as he understood what she'd just admitted. He couldn't talk. He tenderly pulled Kit to his chest and gently cupped the back of her head with both hands as he leaned towards her. "That's the nicest thing anyone's ever said to me Kit."

"Not too heavy for you?" Kit asked him seriously

"Uh-uh." He shook his head gently. "Baby I'm going to kiss you now, okay?"

Kit's eyes welled up and she nodded. Jess found her lips with his and their worlds collided unleashing days' worth of pent up emotion.

Scorching sexual heat leapt off their bodies as they both struggled to get closer. Jess lifted his mouth from hers and choked out, "Clothes." They went for each other's shirt stripping them off and tossing them on the floor. When they reached for each other's pants, in Jess' case her skirt, they conked their foreheads against each other. "Ow." Kit said as she rubbed her brow. Jess straightened and leaned in to kiss her head. "Are you okay? How is your head anyway?"

"I'm fine. Clothes remember?" She whispered in a soft syrupy voice.

"Clothes." He repeated.

They stood naked and facing each other in less than a minute. Kit was surprised at her brazen behavior, but geez the man had her so hot it was a relief to get out of the hindering garments. Jess took one look at Kit from toes to eyes and groaned as he smashed his body to hers. Kit crawled up his frame and he helped her hitch her legs around his waist. Jess walked them to her kitchen table dropping her butt on the wooden top.

"Jess?"

"In you, now." He panted.

He pushed her knees open with his hands and stopped for a moment to stare at the erotic sight of Kit utterly exposed and waiting for him.

"Jesus you are beautiful woman."

"Jess...Jess...now." She whispered urgently.

His body reacted accordingly hearing her sweet pleas and he pressed slowly into her. Kit moaned her approval.

Jess needed her in the most primitive sense. This was not going to be a slow coupling. Kit's body was already over-heated and she answered Jess' ardor fervently. Their emotional roller coaster of a night fueled their passion and they quickly found their release together.

Jess lowered Kit's legs and leaned over her putting his clean hand on the table. "God woman you are frigging kill me." He kissed her mouth sweetly. In his post orgasmic bliss Jess decided he needed to buy some condoms…soon. Kit's body was limp from the mind-blowing orgasm Jess had given her. He helped her sit up and rested his forehead on hers careful not to touch her sore spot. Kit handed him a napkin and he wiped his hand off.

“We still need to talk Kit.” He said softly.

Kit just nodded too spent to speak. “Can I sleep over?” He asked carefully.

She pressed a palm to his cheek. “I’d like that.”

Jess helped Kit off the table and they walked into her bedroom.

“I need to clean up Jess.” Kit said her shy demeanor surfacing.

“Me too.” He said following her to the bathroom.

“Oh Jess no, I’ll just jump in the shower real quick.”

“Yea, shower...you and me. Come on.”

Jess turned the shower on and when he was satisfied that the water was warm enough he stepped in and extended his hand to Kit. Kit took his hand and joined him.

“Are we just going to shower Jess?” Kit asked bashfully.

“This time yes.” He grinned at her.

They quickly rinsed off and then Jess toweled Kit off before using the towel on himself. Kit went to put on her PJ's and Jess took them from her hands and tossed them in the corner. "No, PJ's darling. I want to hold you and touch you. I've been missing your sweet body." They both slid under her covers and faced each other. Jess hooked her top leg over his hip and trailed his hands up and down her side. Kit crooked one arm under head and the other she used to trail her fingertips around Jess' chest.

"Jess."

"Ummm?"

"I missed you."

"Honey I missed you too."

"I don't want to fight with you anymore."

"We won't, we're going to settle some things tonight, establish parameters."

"Like what?"

"Like you are mine Kit. I told you before I don't share. It 'bout killed me when I saw you dancing with Cole."

"Yea well I think I know how you felt. I wasn't feeling so great when you showed up with Tina."

"Yea and that's why we need to get some things straight."

"It goes both ways Jess. If I'm only with you, you're only with me."

"No problem here."

"Really? Okay what else?"

"We are not going to keep our relationship a secret."

"Are you sure?" Her voice wavered.

"I'm sure. I want everyone to know you're mine that we are together. I want to walk into Rooney's next time holding you next to me. I want to dance with you, sit with you and kiss you regardless of who's around."

"I'm not comfortable with PDA Jess."

Jess chuckled. "I'm not either but for some reason I think you're going to change that for me."

Kit smiled up to him and ran her fingertips over his jaw line.

"So does this mean we're going steady?" Kit asked in a little voice that told Jess part of her was teasing but part of her needed to have a straightforward answer.

"Yes, baby we are going steady. Is that okay with you? Will you be satisfied with just me?"

Kit knew there was a little insecurity mixed in his loaded question.

"Jess, I only want you. Don't I make you feel like you're special?" Kit asked seriously.

"When we make love, when you look at me yes, but I won't lie I'm still picturing you dancing with Cole, and Kit it's not something I'll forget anytime soon."

"Jess I told you, he doesn't do anything for me. He doesn't make me weak-kneed with just a look like you do. He doesn't make me lose my breath with his touch like you do."

Jess pressed his palm to her cheek and kissed her so softly it felt like little butterfly wings were playing on her lips.

"Kit I care for you. You have turned my world upside down." Jess said after he pulled back.

"Is that a good thing Jess?"

"It's a great thing."

"I care for you too Jess." Kit whispered back. She tucked her face into his neck and Jess held her to him. They fell asleep holding each other, entwined, their bodies joined like interlocked puzzle pieces.

Chapter 13

One month later

Kit's days began to fall back into some sort of normalcy. The difference now was that when Jess was off work they would spend most of their time together. He had shown her his cabin and although Kit loved her home she adored Jess'. Their sexual exploits ranged from making slow sweet, traditional love to adventurous, erotic explorations that left them speechless and quivering. Jess was wonderfully dominant in the bedroom and because Kit was a little bit of a sub they meshed perfectly. Jess was experimental and Kit loved all the inventive ways he came up with for them to pleasure each other. They had made love everywhere in Kit's apartment, everywhere in Jess's cabin, outside on the trails, and one time, when they couldn't wait, they had pulled over in Jess's jeep. Their sex life was beyond great. They could not get enough of each other. Jess was hands on in public too and never failed to make her feel special. His firefighting brothers knew their brother had fallen hard.

The weather had begun to change into the cold and snowy Colorado it is famous for. Kit had been through one winter in Steamboat so she was better prepared this time. One afternoon Lori visited her and after her last client had left they sat in the adult day care kitchen. Kit had been following the trial on the Internet and she already knew Pallone had been convicted. Lori started the conversation that Kit realized was probably long overdue.

“Kit, Pallone’s been convicted. I’m sure you know this. He was convicted yesterday.”

“Yes, I read it on the internet.”

“I’m sure national TV will pick up the story. I just want you to be aware.”

“Okay thanks.”

“We need to discuss if you want to stay in the program or not?”

“I know I’ve been thinking about it, a lot.”

Kit heard the side door opened and she knew it was Jess coming home. More often than not he would come to her home after his shift and either stayed with her or he picked up both, Lulu and herself and they would go to his place. It all depended on if she had other dog clients.

“Wait one-second Lori, that’s Jess.” Lori was

aware that they were dating. Jess walked into the kitchen.

"Hi Lori, everything okay?" He leaned down and gave Kit a kiss before sitting in a vacant chair.

"Yes, we were just discussing business."

Jess looked to Kit but she remained quiet.

Lori stood "Okay then let me know what you decide okay?"

"I will. How much time do I have?"

Before Lore could answer Jess asked. "For what."

Kit laid a hand on his and replied easily. "If I'm staying in WitSec." Jess nodded. Lori figured Jess knew what was going on.

"One month." Lori said as she dug into her large purse and produced two regular mail envelopes that looked like they'd already been open. She handed them to Kit. "Letters from Colt." Lori said looking nervous as she handed the letters to Kit. Kit took the envelopes and walked Lori out.

When Kit turned to go back to Jess in the kitchen she found him standing in the foyer with Lulu beside him. He looked upset and his usually sparkling blue eyes were flashing darkly.

"You have something you want to tell me?" He said tersely, nodding at the letters in her hand.

"They're letters, from my friend Colt."

"I didn't know you corresponded." Jess's voice was clipped.

"Jess let's take this conversation upstairs okay?"

Jess nodded and followed her upstairs to her apartment. Kit could feel the anger radiating off his large frame.

Kit walked to the couch and sat down expecting Jess to follow on the couch but he didn't. He stood with his back against the wall, his stance ridged. Kit got off the couch and walked to him.

"Jess they are just letters."

He still didn't speak.

"Jess." Kit took his hand and placed it over her heart. "You have my heart Jess, only you I promise."

Kit watched Jess relax a little but not completely.

"Come sit and I'll tell you about Colt. How he saved my life."

That piqued Jess's interest. He had been hoping Kit would tell him about her life before moving to Colorado. What had happened that forced her into Witness protection. He knew much of the story, but no personal details. He'd been waiting patiently for her to open up to him so he followed her to the couch and sat down. Kit surprised him by sitting astride him and she took his face with her delicate hands and bestowed a sweet soft kiss on his tense mouth.

She then took a deep breath and launched into her private story. She began by telling him in detail, about the day she had walked in on Ray as he was shot. She explained how Colt had saved her life by firing at Ray, but he had accidentally shot her too. Jess already knew she'd been shot. One night after they made love he had traced her scar with his finger and she had told him it was from a bullet. He knew she wasn't ready to share the story then so Jess spent many minutes afterwards kissing her scar until they had made love again.

Kit told Jess how they had bonded that first night in the safe house. Kit explained to Jess how Colt chose to go back to Afghanistan instead of going into Wit Sec and that they have kept in touch with each other through the US Marshall Service.

"Does he like you Kit?"

"I know he likes me as a person. That he

was proud of me at the trial."

"He was there." Jess went ridged again.

"He was there but I only talked to him that one time."

"So he was the person you were talking to when I called that time?"

"Yes."

"Why do you two keep in touch?"

"I guess, at the time, we both needed someone."

"You have me now." Jess said stoically.

"I know and I love that, but Colt risked everything for me, his job, and his life and then he had to go back to Afghanistan. The man has made some incredible sacrifices."

"For you?" Jess finished for her.

"Yes, and because he wants to continue to be a DEA agent."

"He saved your life and for that I will be eternally grateful. I am just confused why he would continue to stay in touch with you?"

"I guess we've developed a friendship over

the past year. Remember when I moved here I was alone for a while. He was alone too."

"If he were here Kit, would you want to date him?"

Kit kissed Jess again adding a light flick of her tongue to his lips.

"Do you need to ask that Jess?"

"He sounds like one hell of a man."

"He is, I told you he's special, but so are you Jess. Honestly you two would probably be best if he lived here."

"Besties." Jess smirked, but he then finally smiled. "Kit, men don't have besties."

"Well, you'd be the male version of it then." She nipped his lips with her teeth.

"So are you going to read the letters?"

"Are we a little nosy?"

"Yes, when it comes to you we are excessively nosy."

"Sure we can read them together." Jess was delighted with that response and he gave her a huge grin. Kit picked up one of the envelopes opened it, looked at the date and then opened the other. A small frown touched her lips and then she picked up the first one again.

She started reading:

K,

Got put on desk duty until trial ends. Not so happy about that. Loved the last pic you sent me. I wondered if you'd go back to the short haircut after the trial. You sound like everything is going well. Don't let those public servants get bossy with you. There he drew a smiley face.

A case is coming up in (whatever he had written next was slashed out) I'm hoping to be put on it. No ties to you know who so it should be okay. I hate sitting at the desk. Here's me. Kit showed Jess the doodle of a large man at a small desk with a big frown on his face.

Thinking of buying some property in (slashed out) always wanted a quiet place to go to between gigs. Hope all is well with you little one.

C

Kit put that letter down and said, "See." Friends. Jess grunted and shrugged his shoulder.

"You send him pictures?"

"Yes. He told me when he was in Afghanistan they cheered him up. I sent him one that I'd drawn of myself last month, during the trial."

Jess had grown quiet.

Kit picked up the other letter and started reading.

"Hey little one this will be short. I got the assignment, finally! Trial will be ending soon so I'm off desk and prepping. Won't be able to write as often just didn't want you to worry. I know you worry! Wish me luck.

Yours, C

Jess wasn't as happy with the second letter and he was still bristling that she had sent him drawings. He knew he was being unreasonable but when it came to her he was.

"It sounds like he cares for you Kit."

"He does Jess, like I care for him."

"He lives a dangerous life."

"I know. I worry about him." She said as she brushed his stubbly jaw line with her thumbs.

"I don't want you hurt." Jess' hands rested lightly on her hips. Fidgeting, he slid them to her waist and back down again.

"Jess you live a dangerous life too. I worry about you all the time. You fight fires, you jump into forest fires, and if that wasn't scary enough, you do shit with bombs. Pot - kettle, dude."

"Dude? Your Jersey is showing 'little one,'" he teased.

Kit smiled and gave him a slobbery fun kiss that Jess wiped off his mouth.

"Hey!" she exclaimed indignantly.

"That's not a kiss! This is a kiss." Jess grabbed her face and delivered a kiss that was explosive. Kit was breathless when he pulled away.

Kit rested her forehead against his. "You're the best kisser, Jess."

Jess kissed her again. Then still lip locked he walked them to the shower where he stripped them both naked and guided them under the warm spray.

Jess' chest had a tight, heavy feeling and he felt a little out of sorts. This woman was fast becoming a part of him. When he wasn't with her he thought about her constantly. His buddies knew how special she was to him. He took all the teasing from the guys in the firehouse that accompanies a new relationship. The Chief had simply slapped him on the back and laughed. "Been there, done that, and kid, it's awesome." The Chief had been married for twenty years. The only time Jess had drifted from his good-natured, 'I can take it' demeanor regarding the teasing, was when one of the rookies made a glaring mistake and jokingly said, referring to Kit, "I'd tap that too if I had a chance."

Jess was on him in a heartbeat, his forearm crushing against the younger firefighter's windpipe.

"You won't go anywhere near her." He spoke so calmly, so lethally that even his long time buddies were surprised at the emotion. They dragged Jess off the dumb rookie and the rookie dropped to his ass, his back to the wall as he rubbed his neck.

"Geez Jess, I was teasing man. What the fuck!"

Jess ran his hand through his hair and stared down at the kid he'd just scared half to death.

"That's not something to tease about."

His face was hard and his eyes almost feral.

The men that had pulled Jess off the rookie were bracketing his sides, but not holding him. Jess wasn't a hot head so what he'd done had startled even them. They knew he was a bad ass, though he rarely showed it. Jess could fight with the best of them. His size alone often had others backing down before shit even began. Once he'd taken on two bikers at Rooney's and came out the victor. Jess reached down and helped the rookie up.

"Okay?" He had said.

"Yea, okay." The kid had replied. "Sorry."

Jess remembered that scene as he watched his slip of a woman beaming up at him with her 'having sex' smile that made his heart swell. Jess took her head in his large hands and pressed his lips to hers. His tongue made love to hers as his hands braced her head, not allowing her to move, he took total control of her.

Jess suckled an earlobe which garnered a small whimper from her. He saw that Kit's eyes were closed, her pink well kissed lips were parted slightly and Jess tasted them gently before pulling back.

"Kit, open your eyes. Watch me love you."

Jess made love to her with so much tenderness that it took Kits breath away. Never had she experienced such physical and emotional fervor. He pleasured her so completely that Kit would have collapsed had Jess not been holding her. Jess' own release left him shaking and they sank to the shower floor together.

Kit's found his blue eyes, hooded beneath his black thick lashes. Jess splayed his hands against her back and Kit held on to his shoulders as she placed her forehead against his chest. She couldn't speak and her heart was hammering. They had had lots of sex and Kit was always amazed at the wild orgasms Jess could pull from her body but this one had been undeniably the most powerful one yet. The first one had rocked her leaving her breathless, the second one slammed unexpectedly through her had made her eyes roll up into the back of her head.

They sat on the shower floor for a few minutes, Jess knowing she needed to hold him and he was just as happy to hold her. His forty-eight hour shifts were forty-seven hours too long to be away from her. The water began to turn cooler so Jess kissed the top of her head rousing her from her dream like state. "Babe got to move."

He heard a small groan and it made him grin with male pride. He loved that he could make her come undone.

They dried off and redressed into comfy clothes. Kit turned to Jess before they left her bedroom and wrapped her arms around him. She looked at him shyly, her cute face sporting a pink blush.

"Ummm, Jess, thank you." She said softly.

Jess tucked a wet strand of her hair that was caressing her cheek behind her ear.

"I love making you come. I love watching your face, it's so expressive.. I love that I can do that to you, so Kit, thank you."

Kit snuggled into his chest emotions that had been dormant for so long bubbled to the surface and tears splashed down her face.

"Sweetheart, what's wrong? Are those happy tears? Please tell me those are happy tears?"

Kit nodded indicating they were happy tears. Jess tilted her chin upwards and used his fingers to wipe the errant tears off her face.

"I feel it too Kit. I feel it too." Jess's voice was thick and edgy.

Kit turned her head so she could nuzzle his palm. She looked back up to his face that showed that he was feeling emotional too and that gave her the confidence to tell him what she'd been feeling.

"It's almost too much." She said quietly keeping her eyes on his.

Jess was taken back and took a small step back from her, his muscles tensed and he moved his hands to her waist.

"You and I? Too much?"

"No, you and I, we are perfect." She said gently watching him relax his posture. "How I feel, about you, about us, sometimes it feels overpowering like I'm falling off a cliff." She stepped back into his protective embrace. "I don't want to crash." She whispered.

Jess let out a calming breath. He was choked up and knew exactly how she felt.

"I know." He told her. "When I saw you with those letters and I knew they were from your friend. I felt almost out of control. I'm falling too Kit, it's heady and overwhelming at times, but it's good, really good."

Kit nodded and reached up to pull his mouth to hers. She kissed him softly her hands wrapped in his damp hair. "It is very good Jess, the best."

Jess knew that was a big thing for her to admit. She'd been married before, been in love before and he was chest thumping happy that she had just catapulted her feelings for him over that of her late husband. Jess had never been in love before, not even close. He'd been in lust, but this was different. They had phenomenal sex and he loved that she was open to his slightly kinky side but he recognized this was more.

He liked spending time with her outside of the realm of having sex. He loved being able to read her body language and that he knew when she was wanting to say something, but not sure if she should. She was kind and well-liked by all her clients, dog and human. He'd learned that she had eclectic music taste that ranged from the Beach Boys to everything country. He was floored that she liked muscle cars and that she knew how to fire a pistol, compliments of her dad she'd told him. He was filled with pride that she loved his house and that she'd blushed and grinned like a loon when she saw that he'd hung the sketch of Lulu in a prominent place in his living room. Jess was falling and was glad she had admitted that she was falling too, even though she'd said it metaphorically.

Chapter 14

Kit and Jess's relationship continued to grow stronger on every conceivable level. With Pallone behind bars now and with the Marshall's service not hearing any inside chatter about retaliation, Kit stop setting the alarm to her apartment. She had trusted Jess with the code to her downstairs alarm so that when he was late, because his station house had responded to an emergency, he could let himself in. When Lori visited in the last week in November, Kit had told her that she had decided not to remain in Wit Sec but she wanted to keep her new name and new social security number. Kit had to sign a ton of paperwork releasing her from the program and Lori thoroughly went through the specifics with Kit.

Not being in Witness Protection anymore would bring forth changes that Kit hadn't even thought about. She could now travel and the first thing she knew she would do when she got the chance was to see her parents. The other changes involved her banking, bills, and mail. Up until now everything had filtered through Wit Sec.

That very day Kit had gone in to Lori's office to sign the papers to officially release her from Wit Sec; Kit arrived home to find Jess' jeep sitting in her driveway. She assumed he had gotten off early to welcome her into the world of unfettered social living. He knew today was the big day and how much she was looking forward to it.

Kit climbed the stairs to her apartment to find Jess sitting on her couch, with Lulu at his feet waiting for her. She knew the second she saw him something was wrong and her heart began to pound with anxiety.

"Jess? What wrong?" She said as she crossed to him and sat down giving Lulu's head a loving rub before settling in.

"That obvious, huh?"

"What is it?"

"It's not bad, really it's a good thing. The Chief just told me I have been invited to attend Smoke Jumpers Instructors class in California."

Kit looked at him still not understanding what the problem was. "Okay. I thought that was what you wanted?" She waited for him to continue.

"It is. I've been hoping for the invite. It's an awesome opportunity."

"But?"

"Kit I'm going to be away training for a month and then, as long as I pass, I'm being sent to Australia to train a group of jumpers over there."

"Wow. How long? How long will you be gone in Australia?"

"Another month."

"Wow, two months." Kit couldn't think of anything else to say. She was floored and her throat had tightened. Her old insecurities were zinging up her spine and she was afraid of what this meant to their relationship.

"Kit, I have to go. I've wanted to do this." Jess said softly. "When I finish the training in California they are promoting me to a Captain and I'll get a major pay bump."

"I understand Jess." Kit said quietly her hands rubbing his. "I'm proud of you, you deserve this."

Jess pulled her into the side of his body and rested his cheek on the top of her head.

"Thank you. Thank you for understanding."

Kit didn't respond and she fought her tears. "When do you leave?"

"Next week. Can Lulu stay with you?"

"Of course." Kit said quietly.

"I'll be gone for Christmas and New Year's." Jess said sadly. "I was looking forward to spending the Holidays with you."

"Yea me too. Well, I guess it's a sign for me to go visit my parents for Christmas." She said trying to sound cheerful.

"That's a great idea. I'll feel better knowing you're with your family. If you can't take Lulu with you just drop her with my parents."

Kit had met his parents at Thanksgiving the week before. They were the epitome of wonderful. Jess got his looks from his Dad who was ruggedly handsome and he got his personality from his Mom who was fun and outgoing.

"Kit you know this separation is temporary right? Maybe now that you're out of Wit Sec… You're out right? All the papers are signed?"

Kit nodded.

"Congratulations honey." Jess said softly before kissing her forehead. "Now that you're a free agent you can fly to California before I leave for Australia and we can spend New Year's Eve together. I'd love to spend New Year's with you.

What do you think?" She knew he was trying to be positive.

"I think I miss you already Jess." and then she sniffled and Jess held her tenderly knowing this was going to be a hard two months and a real test of their relationship.

Jess had the rest of the week off and he and Kit were inseparable. Kit had learned one of the other firefighters from Jess's house, Dusty, was going to California to train to be a smoke jumper, but he did not have to go to Australia. Jess was training to be an instructor and it was a big deal. The men and women who completed their Instructors training and passed the harsh physical test were given their own teams of jumpers to command. Kit learned his training was to be held on a large compound in southern California, near Mexico, where smoke jumpers from all over the United States and jumpers of all levels were trained.

They spent most of the nights at Kit's because she had dog clients. Every night they made love savoring their time together. Some nights Jess would be so tender and unhurried drawing out their love making until one of them needed the release. Other nights he would take her fast and dominant, owning her body.

Kit's favorite night was when he showed his kink. It involved her dining room table, a feather, a strand of pearls, and scarves. It was also the first time she ever passed out from sheer pleasure. Afterwards Jess talked to her in a gentle voice as Kit slowly regained consciousness. When she came to she saw that Jess was lovingly staring down at her and gently caressing her cheek. Kit dissolved into tears. Jess picked her up and took her to the couch where he cradled her on his lap after throwing a small, quilt over them.

"Baby its okay. I've got you. Did I hurt you?"

Kit gulped down her tears and she shook her head back and forth.

"No Jess it was spectacular. I love how you make me feel. It's just...so powerful and then I thought about you leaving. I'm sorry. I swear I'm trying to be strong."

"You are being strong. You have been wonderful Kit. Not moping around and helping me get ready. You have no idea how much I appreciate it."

"I'm going to miss you Jess, so much."

"But? I hear a 'but' Kit. What is it?"

"Okay I'm going to just say it because we're better when we're honest with each other. I hope you don't think worse of me."

"I won't, spit it out."

"Okay, well two months is a long time. Did you want to date other people when you're gone?"

Jess was not expecting that question and he was momentarily thrown by it.

"Are you telling me you want to date while I'm away Kit?" Jess' tone was even and he tried not to sound harsh but he knew he did.

Kit looked at Jess as his body tensed around her. She realized he thought she'd asked because she wanted to date.

"Jess look at me." Jess had been averting her eyes he was so upset. When he was finally looking at her she answered his question.

"Jess I have no desire to date anyone regardless of how long you're gone. I don't want to be clingy; I don't want you to feel like I'm strangling you from afar. I'm still new with this having a boyfriend thing. We have been spending so much time together. I don't want you to be sick of me. It's just, God I'm being honest here. If you were to be with someone else it would kill me. I wouldn't be able to be with you again. I couldn't handle it. I just wanted to give you the option of being able to date."

"I don't understand, if you wouldn't be with me again if I was with someone else, I don't understand why you'd even suggest it?"

"I needed to know. I didn't want to ask you to be loyal to me, to us and have you running for the hills. I figured I had to offer it to you, as an option, and just pray you wouldn't want to."

"Kit I will not be with another woman while I'm gone. I don't want to be. I want to complete my instructors training, train the Aussies and get back here as fast as I can, to you."

Kit leaned her head into his chest, her relief palpable. "Thank God." She murmured and Jess chuckled his relief as well.

That was Kit's favorite night. Jess had made her feel special and she knew where they stood relationship wise when he left. In addition he had outdone himself with his kinky dining room table sex. Yes, that was her favorite night.

The last night before Jess left they had gone to his parent's for dinner and then afterwards they stopped at the fire station so he could say good-bye to the guys. The Chief asked to speak with Jess privately and he gave Kit's hand a squeeze before leaving her side. One of the older firefighters approached Kit and told her if she needed anything while Jess was gone all she had to do was ask. The men and their families were tight and they took care of each other. The older firefighter gave her shoulder a small pat. “And you are part of our family, okay?”

Kit nodded appreciating the warm gesture. The other men were watching TV and Kit heard them complaining that they had no sweets to munch on. Kit decided she would spend some of her free time each week making the firemen treats. It would give her something to do at night.

They left the firehouse hand in hand as the guys wished him luck. Kit didn’t have any dog clients that night so they were able to spend his last night at Jess’s house, which was perfect because he still needed to pack. Back at Jess’ cabin Kit helped him push clothes into his green duffle. She teased him about rolling all his clothes before handing them to her to shove in. He assured her that rolling clothes before packing them helped them not to wrinkle. When Jess went to the bathroom to get his shave kit, it gave her the opportunity to sneak the sketches she had made for him inside his duffle. Kit also hid a note she had written him in his bag. It was a little on the sappy side, and she hoped he wouldn’t unpack in front of any of the other men.

They didn’t get much sleep that night. Jess couldn’t keep his hands off her and she didn’t want him too. They would make love, doze, and then whichever one of them woke first, would initiate another bout of lovemaking. When the alarm went off at 6:00 am they both groaned. Kit kissed her way down his body sending him off with a pre-planned mother of a blowjob that she knew he wouldn't soon forget.

They had already decided that she would keep his jeep at her house so she could start it every couple of days to keep the battery charged. Jess dumped his duffel in the back, Lulu jumped into the back too. When Jess got in he handed Kit his house keys. Kit gave him a questioning look and he simply told her he wanted her to have access to it. He didn't have plants that needed watering and he had a P.O. Box since he was too far up the mountain for mail to be delivered, so she knew the keys were a symbolic gesture. Kit took the keys and gave him a tender kiss.

At Hayden airport Jess grabbed his duffle and told Kit to wait in the jeep while he checked in. He'd then come back out to sit with them before he needed to go through security. Neither wanted to wait in the airport, they wanted the privacy that being in the jeep would afford them. The heaviness of him leaving was starting to weigh on Kit and she tried to occupy her thoughts with things she would do while he was away. She was going to join the gym, take ski lessons, bake goodies for Jess and send them to him and bake for the firehouse guys too. She had some art projects planned, and she planned to visit her parent, who had also opted out of Wit Sec.

Jess sauntered back out of the terminal. He was so handsome that it took her breath away every time she looked at him. His muscular thighs were encased in his faded Levi jeans, and he wore black combat boots making him look like a bad ass. He had on a down vest covering an off-white thermal and a flannel shirt. His blond hair was tousled and because of her pre-planned morning attack he hadn't had time to shave so he sported a day's growth that only enhanced his chiseled features. Jess got into the driver's side and drove the jeep to a far corner of the lot, away from prying eyes.

"I have to go back inside in about twenty minutes.' He said as he parked.

He jumped into the back seat signaling Lulu to get in the way back and then he gave her another hand signal so she lay down. He grabbed Kit's hand and pulled her into the back with him. Kit snuggled into his possessive arms.

"I can't believe I'm not going to be able to hold you tonight." Jess said somberly.

"Will you call me?" She asked as her hand filtered through his hair.

"Babe I'll be calling and texting you all the

time."

"I have to get a new number soon, Wit Sec orders."

"When you have it call me right away so I have it."

"I will."

Jess adjusted her so she was sitting across his lap. Her back was resting against his shoulder and arm, which cushioned her from the side door. He softly gripped the nape of her neck and pulled her in for a kiss. It started out gently but Jess couldn't hold off the raw emotion surging through him. He was head over heels for this woman and he was already hurting and he hadn't even left yet. Kit's arms were wrapped around his head as she kissed him back with equal emotion.

When it came time for Jess to leave, Kit drove the jeep to the front of the terminal and Jess turned to her before getting out, giving her a kiss that they both knew needed to last them both a month.

"I'll miss you Kit. Take care of my Lulu." Lulu jumped into the back seat again, reclaiming her normal spot and Jess rubbed her head. "Lulu takes care of my girl."

"Be safe Jess. You'll do great. Don't worry I'll

take good care of her."

Jess kissed Kit one more time. "You're mine Kit. You have my heart." He exited from the jeep as Kit fought the tears. When he disappeared in the doors she let the tears fly. She had to pull over before leaving the lot to get a handle on her emotions. She felt as though her heart was splitting in two. She prayed these two months would fly by because she didn't know how she was going to get through the next day much less the next sixty days.

Chapter 15

The first week Jess was gone Kit had busied herself by enrolling in a yoga class in the local gym, baking for the firehouse and working on a sketch she was going to give Jess as a Christmas gift. These were added ventures along with running her dog and adult day care business, which continued to thrive. Jess called her every night and they both admitted the calls were the best part of each day.

Jess told her there were thirty new jumpers in the training program including three women. He was training with five other men who were also getting their instructors certification. Part of their training was working with the rookies. He said it was hard work and part of his final practicum would include a tough physical test so he was spending any downtime hours he had running, lifting weights and training on a mountain trail that had exercise stations.

Kit told Jess how she had signed up for yoga and was enjoying the gym. She animatedly described to him the new dog she was now watching compliments of Tim's endorsement of her business. The dog's name was Dune, a beautiful female yellow lab that belonged to a pilot that had just moved to Steamboat. He had opened a business catering mostly to hunters, fishermen, and skiers who choose not to deal with public airlines.

During week two of no Jess, Kit took two yoga classes that left her sore in places she didn't even know she had muscles. She also took her first ski lesson and had Jess laughing out loud as she described how she had face planted not once, but twice. Jess in turn told Kit about his days but she knew he was leaving out some of the more perilous things he was doing. Jess had received two care packages from Kit and he thanked her. He loved how thoughtfulness she was. The other guys, some who were married had not received any packages yet and he'd gotten two. Jess told Kit and was hoarding his treats away, which made Kit laugh. He said he had heard from Bud and he knew she was baking treats for guys at the station house. He told her that she had thoroughly endeared herself to the men. Kit savored their talks but she could tell Jess was tired, his voice giving him away. He sounded stressed so she kept her conversations with him light, trying to keep their talks up beat, when she was feeling hollow inside without him.

Week three was Christmas week. Kit had scheduled a flight to visit her parents who were in a little town, just north of Dallas, Texas. She mailed off her Christmas presents to Jess wishing she could see his face when he opened them. She had sketched two pictures for him but did not send the original of either one. The first one was a picture of Jess and Lulu. Jess was sitting on the front steps of his home and Lulu was sitting next to him. Kit had captured the natural beauty of Jess's home and her sketch of him portrayed him being in a peaceful, thoughtful mood. With his hand propped on Lulu's back he looked handsome and virile, yet totally at ease. She had drawn him with a slight smile on his face, the smile he used on her that made her tingle.

She had taken a picture of that sketch and sent that, because she had already mounted and framed the original and she did not want to send that. She placed a sticky note on the back of the picture saying that she had put the original, framed sketch in his house. Kit also sent him another picture. This one was of a present she had bought for him, a large multi drawer tool chest. She took photos of the red, five-drawer chest and of the tools housed inside. She also included a photo of where she and his dad had placed the toolbox in his garage/barn area. Another gift she sent him was a large Ziploc bag filled with his favorite candies. Her man had a bit of a sweet tooth.

Her final gift was one she was a little nervous about giving him, and she hoped he liked it.

Kit had sketched herself in the nude, sitting on a chair. Her one knee was bent and her foot rested on the chairs edge effectively hiding her private area. Her hands were entwined and resting on her bent knee. Her arms casually hid her nipples from view but the swells of her breasts were visible. Her chin was resting on her hands and she had captured a look on her face that she thought was a cross between thoughtful and 'miss you.' She didn't want it to look sad because she knew that would upset him, and she didn't want it to be too erotic either. Kit felt she had captured her mood perfectly, especially how her eyes were slightly hooded and her smile was small and knowing. Kit didn't frame this picture. She didn't want to send him the original either. She went to a local office supply store and made a high-resolution copy of the sketch. She then converted it so it was the size of a postcard, which she copied onto heavy high-grade paper. Kit was pleased that she could still see the details in the sketch, despite its smaller size. On the back of the print she wrote. 'We (the original full sized picture and me - the original) will be waiting for you when you get home,' she added a smiley face and signed Love, Kit underneath.

Kit's adult day care schedule was light due to the Holidays. She had told her clients that she'd be gone until the twenty-sixth. Only Bud and Mikey

D were going to be effected and only for one day. Kit was relieved she hadn't put them out too much by leaving town. Jess had sent a box to her house that arrived by UPS. Jess had informed her in one of their nightly conversations it was going to arrive and that it contained her Christmas presents. Kit decided not to open it until after she returned from her parent's house so she set the box off to the side.

She dropped Lulu off at Jess's parents, thanking them for watching her until she got back. She told them she'd pick Lulu up on the when she got back. Kit drove herself to Hayden where she hopped a prop plane and only had the one stop in Denver before heading straight to Dallas. Her parents met her at the airport and she and her Mom shed happy tears at their long awaited reunion.

Her parents had decided to leave Wit Sec, but unlike her they had chosen to take back their own names and social security numbers. They drove Kit to their home that Wit Sec had provided and two things were obvious as they pulled into the driveway. One was that her parents were going to move. That was apparent with the sold sign that was planted on their front lawn. Secondly, they were going to be traveling. Kit figured that out when she saw a large, brand-new mobile home sitting in their driveway.

Her parents looked at her and both said, "Surprise." Kit started laughing, putting her parents at ease. They had been anxious that she wouldn't understand, but Kit understood and applauded their adventurous spirits. At dinner that night they explained what prompted their decision. They'd lived most of their lives in Jersey before spending a few years in Florida. When they'd been transferred to Texas they found they liked that State too. When they opted out of Wit Sec they decided they wanted to travel, to see the country, to see what other states thy may like. So they bought a top of the line Cruiser and were planning to leave the day after Kit left, which was the day after Christmas.

Kit spent a wonderful Holiday with her parents. The only hard part was how dealing with how much she missed Jess. Although they talked every day it was wearing on them. Kit needed to hold him, to kiss him; she missed speaking with him face to face so she could read his emotions. She felt empty at night, almost lost, as she remembered how their bodies meshed so perfectly together.

Jess called her on Christmas Eve. His time there was coming to a close and she thought he should have sounded more enthusiastic that half his trip was over, but instead he sounded weary, drained, and his voice hinted at him being distressed. She wished she could comfort him somehow. He told her he was getting ready to go into town with everyone. The rookies had finished up and were celebrating before most of them flew home to their families. He told her Dusty, the rookie from his station house had something he had given him to give to her. Kit playfully tried to find out what it was but Jess brushed her questions off. He wasn't acting like himself and it ate at her. She didn't want to add to his stress so she tucked her fears away.

Before they said good night Jess told Kit that the day after Christmas he and the other five men going for their Instructor's Certification were going to be given a practical test. Jess said he had no idea what that entailed but they were told they would be off line and out of contact with anyone for at least five days. They were to be ready at 5:00 am with a back pack containing items that they were instructed to pack. They could bring nothing but what the list indicated. Kit tried to justify Jess's somber mood by telling her he was getting mentally prepared for whatever he was going to face in the field. That night insecure feelings found their way into her dreams. Kit was worried that the separation might be too much for them handled.

On Christmas Day Jess called her but his mood was one Kit could only describe as distracted and foreboding. Kit's 'spidey' senses kicked in and when she questioned him, asking if there was something else bothering him he had snapped at her, telling her he was fine. He then apologized and said there were some things he had to work out and that he would talk to her when he got back. Kit's fears escalated. She didn't want to press him, but she wished she knew if he meant when he got back from the entire trip, or got back from his test? Kit changed up the conversation and asked if he had opened his presents yet and he admitted he'd been too busy and not gotten to them. Kit had been hoping they would have lightened his mood. For the first time since he'd been gone, Kit was feeling a sense of unease. Kit wished him luck and told him to call her when he got back.

Chapter 16

Kit's parents drove her to the airport the day after Christmas and she hugged them good-bye with less tear shedding than she expected. They were going to be starting a new adventure and because they were connected by cell phones and their access was now unrestricted, Kit knew they were a mere phone call away. One of the presents her parents had given her was new Mac book pro. Kit had turned her old computer in to Lori last month; it had been given to her by Wit Sec and had been highly monitored. Kit had used it sparingly.

Kit was looking forward to going home to Colorado. It had become her home. She loved the new life she had built; her house, her business and she loved Colorado with its intense beauty no matter what time of the year it was.

Kit arrived home still apprehensive from her last stilted conversation with Jess. She hated how their last two phone calls had left her feeling anxious. She hoped it was due to him being worried about his field test.

Jess' presents to her sat like a whale on her on the kitchen table but she decided she wanted to open it while she was on the phone with him, so she left it unopened. Kit was tired from traveling and her last two conversations with Jess had made it impossible for her to asleep. The fact that she wouldn't be hearing from him for days, because he was currently being physically and mentally tested, doing God knew what, wasn't helping either. She was happy to be back in her own bed and she hoped she might get to sleep but she found herself missing Jess more than usual and sleep continued to evade her.

That first morning home Kit went to the gym and then to the food store. After she brought the food inside and put it away, she ran her final errand, which was picking Lulu up. Jess's parents were delighted to see her and she stayed for lunch chatting amicably with them.

The next day Kit had Mr. Peterson scheduled to come for an hour while his daughter got her hair done and she also welcomed Maize and Crank back to her home. Bud and Mikey D arrived together with their dogs and they handed Kit a gift certificate, as a Christmas present, to a local spa. Kit thanked them then teased them asking them if they thought she looked like she needed a day at the spa? They laughed and told her no but they weren't good at gift giving so Krissy, the girl Bud had been seeing, had suggested it. They asked if she'd heard from Jess and she said not since Christmas Day. They told her Dusty had returned and passed his smoke jumper training. They relayed to Kit that he said it had been hard but he was excited and glad to be home.

The men said good-bye, leaving her with their beloved dogs and Kit eased into her normal daily regime, which now included time spent in the gym doing yoga or kick boxing. She had walked into the kick boxing class by mistake and was too embarrassed to leave once it got started. She discovered she enjoyed the work out so she kept attending.

The next day was the day Kit had scheduled time to get a new cell phone. After she took Lulu, Maize and Crank on a long walk, she whipped up a batch of brownies to bring to the fire station and then drove into Steamboat Springs to buy an iPhone. The new iPhone boasted a great camera and she couldn't wait to set up Face Time. She'd been using her new Mac to research different Apps she could buy too. After a long one-on-one, impromptu tutoring session with the young man from the Verizon store, Kit headed for the firehouse. Packed with a delicious double batch of brownies and a gift she had for the station house Kit was excited to see the guys. Visiting the firehouse made her feel closer to Jess and now, not being able to talk to him, left her needing to feel that connection.

The gift she had for the firehouse was a colored pencil sketch she'd done of the firehouse, showing eight pair of rubber firemen boots lined up outside the closed firehouse garage door. Kit remembered seeing it the day after they had responded to a small restaurant fire. Kit had decided to sketch that scene and frame the picture as a gift to all the guys.

Kit arrived at the station house with her wrapped gift and the plate of brownies. She met the Chief who was walking out of the firehouse heading to his car. He gave her a quick hug, asked how she was and asked if she'd heard from Jess. Kit told him what she'd told Bud and Mikey D that he was off grid taking his final test. Kit tried to hand the Chief the brownies and gift but he told her he was headed home and ask if she would mind bringing them upstairs. Kit happily said she'd love to see the guys anyway so it wasn't a problem.

Kit walked up the station house steps to the upstairs living area. She saw the guys looking at pictures on the TV screen and realized Dusty was showing them pictures from his training session. Kit watched quietly for a second from the doorway enjoying the men's brotherly camaraderie. Just as she was about to make her presence known she saw a picture of Jess standing next to an absolutely gorgeous brunette who was smiling up at him. It was the same way Kit knew she smiled at him, like he was everything. Her throat constricted and the whirl of a panic attack threatened to engulf her.

She heard someone say, "Who's that? She beautiful."

Dusty answered, "That's Bess and she was fucking gorgeous."

Dusty changed the picture and it was one of him with a group of his new friends, but in the background Kit saw Jess with one hand on the beautiful Bess' shoulder. He appeared to be speaking to her and his face was leaning down so they were looking into each other's eyes. Dusty changed to the next picture and it was a wonder that Kit didn't vomit where she stood. It was a picture of Bess sitting on Jess' lap and they were kissing.

"What the fuck." She heard Bud say.

"Dusty was Jess with that chick?" Mikey asked his voice tense.

"I didn't think so man. She was totally hot for him though and she let him know it. Honestly I didn't believe he'd go for her but my roommate saw her coming out of his room that night sooooo."

Kit knew she needed to leave before she embarrassed herself by passing out. She quietly placed the present and the brownies down on the table next to her that was just inside the door and fled down the firehouse stairs.

Bud was upset and Mikey D was livid. The second he heard Jess was back Mikey D was going to rip him a new ass hole. Mikey stood up heading for the stairs, needing air. He saw that there was a package and plate on the table by the door. When he looked closer and yelled, “Fuck!”

Bud jumped off the couch coming to Mikey D’s side and when Mikey showed Bud the brownies and present, he too said, “Fuck.” They realized Kit must have been there and the only reason she wouldn’t have spoken up would be if she had seen what they’d seen and heard what they’d heard.

Kit somehow managed to get back home without crashing her car. She could barely see through the tears that blurred her vision. Her chest was tight and she was desperately fighting for each breath she could pull in. She numbly got out of her car and ran inside to the security of her home. Kit didn’t release Lulu from the basement like she normally did when she got home. Lulu was always privy to her apartment, but Kit was so overwhelmed, so hurt that Jess had cheated on her that she couldn’t even bring herself to look at Lulu.

Kit crumbled onto her bed into a pile of unchecked emotion, sobbing salty, hard tears. She knew something had been wrong. She realized the thing he had 'to work out' was telling her he'd met someone else. Eventually she cried herself to sleep; Kit didn't know that was even possible. When she woke up it took her a second to remember why she was laying in her bed in the middle of the day. The awfulness of what she'd seen and heard surged through her system and Kit ran for the bathroom, puking up what little food she'd eaten. After finally pulling herself together enough to stop throwing up she washed her face and forced herself to go downstairs to the dogs. It was time for their dinner so she fed them and then took all three of them for a walk.

Lulu sensed something was wrong. During the walk and when they got home she refused to leave Kits side, she was glued to her. Kit wrapped herself in a big quilt and sat outside on her back deck watching Maize and Crank dash around the gated yard. Lulu however, would not budge from her side. She rested her chin on Kit's leg as if she knew she needed to provide comfort to her.

After a half hour of sitting in the dark with only the glow of her house illuminating the deck Kit brought the dogs back inside and settle them down for the night, all except Lulu who refused to be left downstairs. Kit allowed her to come up to her apartment even though seeing her just poured gas on the fiery pain lodged in her heart. Although it nauseated her to think about it; she tried to justify what Dusty had said and what she'd seen. With a sinking feeling she knew she had lost Jess. He had met someone else. The evidence was crystal clear as far as Kit was concerned.

Kit sat on her couch and picked up her new iPhone. Hoping to push away the sickening images of Jess with his new girl. Kit busied herself by playing with her new phone. Unfortunately the images kept flashing in her brain like a three-picture horror show. Kit continued to try to distract herself. She downloaded Apps and put her client's phone numbers into the contacts area. The only contact she omitted was Jess'. Kit then texted or called each contact separately, giving them each her new number.

Back in her rumpled bed Kit turned on a mindless TV show. She was feeling ridiculously sorry for herself and tried to give herself a pep talk but it wasn't doing much good. She kept thinking how could he do that to her? She kept seeing his beautiful face as he had leaned into the jeep at the airport and he told her she had his heart. Kit tried to calm herself, not wanting to cry anymore. She looked around her bedroom thinking about how much her life had changed yet, she thought, sadly it hadn't. She was once again devastated, let down by another man she had let herself care about, love. Lulu lay on the carpet below her and Kit stretched down giving her head a rub. While straightening back up Kit's eyes landed on her rocking chair where Hannah, a cabbage patch doll she'd been given on her first birthday sat.

Hannah, as she had named her, had heard every one of Karen Sue's elementary school secrets, agonized with her over all her junior high crushes, and been privy to every detail regarding her and Ray, including the night she lost her virginity. Hannah had even gone to college with Karen Sue, which opened her up to some good-natured teasing from her friends, but the fact remained that Hannah, even though she was a doll, had been through thick and thin with her.

Kit climbed out of bed and picked up the little doll, deciding she needed some Hannah time. Kit returned to her bed, cautiously stepping over Lulu and snuggled under her covers. As she had done so many years before, Kit poured her heart out to the little inanimate doll, while she cried more tears than one body should even contain.

Feeling slightly better and altogether silly Kit hugged Hannah to her as she thanked Hannah for listening to her. Kit smiled realizing she would look like a crazy loon if anyone saw that she was talking to the doll. Giving Hannah one more loving squeeze Kit felt something hard inside the dolls soft fabric body. Kit lifted Hannah's well-worn dress and felt the dolls front. There was a pouch like area built in where the doll used to have a small plastic heart but Kit had lost that many years ago. Kit fingered opened the cavity and pulled out a small USB drive.

Kit placed Hannah back on the rocker she inhabited and walked into the living room where she had set her new Mac book up. Kit wasn't computer savvy like Ray had been and she knew, without a shadow of a doubt, that there was only one person that would have put that little black drive into her Hannah, Ray.

Kit inserted the drive and an icon appeared on her desktop labeled Karen Sue. She double clicked on the icon and several file folder icons appeared on her screen. They were all labeled. One was labeled with the number 1, so she opened that one first. A letter appeared. Ray had written it and it was addressed to her. A fresh wave of tears surfaced and Kit angrily wiped them away, "OMG what else is going to fucking happen today." She said out loud to herself. Kit swiped the annoying tears away and read the letter:

Dear Karen Sue,

I know if you're reading this that I'm obviously not able to talk to you. First, make sure that you are reading this alone. It's for your eyes only. I want to first apologize for the colossal mistakes I made that affected our life so drastically. I never meant to hurt you. As I write this I can assure you that you were my one and only concern. I love you with all my heart, even now as we wait on our divorce to be final. I can only hope that you will find it in your heart to one day forgive me.

My gambling has led me to places I wish I had never ventured. I owe so much money to so many people that it is mind-boggling. I owe a significant amount to a man named Vince Pallone. He's a very bad man Kit.

Pallone has something called a 'red list.' If you're on that list you might as well kiss your ass good-bye. We were on that list, yes you too, and it's all because of my gambling.

I tried everything to pay him back but I just kept getting in deeper. I finally hit on an idea to try to keep you safe. I told Pallone I would work for him if he didn't touch you.

My job involved using my computer skills to move money around for him so it wasn't seen by any government agencies. I was privy to his accounts and business contacts. I was always watched when on the computer but I had to try. I had this idea that if I could steal some of Pallone's money and hide it away, plus gather information regarding Pallone's business associates; I could barter for our safety and get me released from my debt without either of us being killed.

I am so sorry you had to go through all of this crap. I'm giving you all the information I collected along with the offshore accounts I set up. There are fifteen accounts in all. Each account contains $150,000.00. That's the most I could skim without it looking fishy. The money is yours to start someplace fresh if you want to. I was adamant with Pallone that you knew nothing about what I'd done. I only hope that by giving you this information you will use it, or not use it in whatever manner you wish.

I love you Karen Sue. I always have and I always will.

Yours,

Ray

Kit dissolved into a mass of body wracking sobs. He had been trying to protect her like she'd been told. Kit wiped her tears off her face and clicked on the folder labeled 2.

It contained a series of numbers and symbols Kit didn't understand but figured they were overseas bank account numbers. Folders 2 through 16 were all the same, each containing numbers for coded bank accounts.

Folder 17 was a spreadsheet containing names, dates and more bank account numbers.

Folder 18 was another Word document describing how Kit could use the numbers in folders 2 through 16 to access the money.

Kit was blown away with the magnitude of Ray's scheme to barter for their lives. He must have been planning this daring scheme for a long time.

Kit wished she could talk to Jess but as she thought of him she glumly realized that that wasn't an option anymore. She decided she would call Lori in the morning. Kit already knew she didn't want the money and she didn't want to have access to the names of Pallone's business associates either. She wished she'd found this earlier so they could have used the information at his trial.

Kit went back to bed but sleep never fully claimed her. She slept fitfully thinking first about Jess and then about Ray. She mentally made a note to never fall in love again because her track record sucked.

Chapter 17

The next morning at the fire station Bud and Mikey D were talking quietly when the Chief strolled in. “Boys, everything calm here last night?”

Bud and Mikey D shrugged their shoulders and the Chief knew immediately something was wrong.

“Spill it.” He said as he pulled out a chair next to them at the kitchen table.

“Kit came by yesterday.” Bud said.

“Yea, I saw her. What did she bake?”

“Brownies.” Mikey D said.

The Chief looked at them.

“Were they bad or something?” He chuckled.

Bud shook his head and then they unloaded, telling the Chief what Kit had walked in on.

“Damn.” Chief swore softly. “Doesn’t sound like Jess.”

"Yea that's what we thought too, but Chief you should see the pictures Dusty has. Jess is kissing the girl in one of them."

"Maybe it's not what it appears." The Chief defended Jess.

"Chief, Dusty told us that his friend saw that same girl leaving Jess' room that night."

"Shit. Did Kit see and hear all of it?"

"Not sure. We're sort of debating how to handle this."

"Poor thing, you guys didn't go after her right away?"

"We were on duty and you were gone. We didn't know what we could say anyway. I'm totally fucking him up when he gets back." Bud bit out angrily.

"Bud relax." The Chief said. "We have to hear Jess' side of this."

Bud and Mikey looked at each other.

"I'm serious men; do not do anything until you hear what he has to say. Are we clear?"

"Yes sir." They chimed begrudgingly.

Kit – New Year's Eve Day

It was New Year's Eve afternoon and Kit was alone except for Lulu. Bud and Mikey D had picked up their dogs that morning and tried to talk to Kit about what she may or may not have heard. She effectively shut them up by telling them in an eerily calm but terse voice that if they brought his name up to her one more time, even accidentally, that she would not care for their dogs anymore. She was dead serious.

They knew not to cross her so then they tried to persuade her to join them at Rooney's that night but she begged off. When they were outside and far enough away from her accidently over hearing them, they both commented on how poorly she looked. She was thinner, her eyes lacked the luster they'd once had, she didn't smile once, and worst of all were the dark circles under her haunted eyes. Jess was a dead man walking when they heard from him, despite what the Chief had said.

Kit had called Lori the day after she found the USB drive and the office relayed to her that she was out of the office and wouldn't be returning until February. Kit didn't trust anyone else with the drive so she tucked it back inside Hannah where it had remained safely hidden for all the time before.

New Year's Eve, God how stupidly she had looked forward to spending it with Jess. She knew he was probably back from his test now and according to his previous schedule, he was due to fly to Australia the day after tomorrow.

Kit took Lulu hiking up the snowy trail behind her house before settling in for what she figured would be a long, difficult night. It was still early afternoon but Kit had no plans to leave her house except to walk Lulu again. She was well prepared to spend a cozy night alone watching Dick Clark's Rocking New Years.

Jess - New Year's Eve Day

Jess and the other newly certified instructors had finally been returned to the barracks at base camp, a day later than planned. One of the new instructors had broken his leg while on his mission and when he hadn't shown up at the designated pick up site after the practicum the other four instructors naturally volunteered to go back into the mountainous terrain to find him. This time they were supplied with walkie-talkies, food and water. They were air dropped at the same location the missing instructor had been dropped five days earlier and they were given the coordinates he was to follow. It took a hard day and half of climbing before he was finally located. He had broken his leg repelling and luckily he had the training to find shelter and wait for help. A chopper was able to airlift the hurt man to the nearest hospital.

Jess peeled off his dank clothes that he'd spent almost seven days in and headed for the shower. He wanted to talk to Kit. He knew he'd been an ass to her on Christmas but he had been so stressed. He hadn't wanted to tell her that he was stressed because one of the female rookies had been all over him the entire four weeks. At first Bess had been coy, asking him for extra help with things like packing her chute. Jess would always find her sliding in next to him for meals. When he worked out at night she'd appear next to him, running and laughing about what a coincidence it was that they were training together. Jess grimaced as he remembered her thinly veil attempt to rub against him when she pretended to trip and then proceeded to plaster her body to his after he had helped her up.

It all came to a head the night of the Christmas Eve sendoff party. He was missing Kit and he knew she knew something was wrong. He had been so thrown by what Bess was doing that it was messing with his training. Jess was pissed at himself that he had taken his frustrations out on Kit on the phone. The one person who had always made him feel better.

At the party Bess was all over him. Finally he had to tell her sternly, for the umpteenth time that he had a girl and he was not interested. Unfortunately Bess did not get the message as she delivered the first of a one-two punch when she jumped on his lap and gave him a very unwanted kiss in front of all the guys. He practically threw her to the ground and then quickly left the party. The second blow came when she showed up at his room hours later, falling drunkenly inside when he opened the door. She had wrapped him in a smothering hug and professed her love for him. God what a mess! He quickly got her out of his room and hope no one had seen her.

Jess went to the commanding officer the next morning and relayed what had happened. He didn't want to be responsible for her being kicked off the smoke jumpers unit, she had passed her training, but she had really crossed the line and he thought his superiors should to know.

Jess had debated whether or not to tell Kit about Bess, but he didn't want to upset her. He was going to be away for five more weeks, and that in itself, was going to be difficult enough. So Jess decided he would simply explain everything when he was in Australia. Jess was all about trust and deep down he knew he'd never given Kit any reason not to trust him. He'd even gone to his C.O. so it was on record, not that he would need that; he was confident his girl would understand. He knew he would need to apologize for being short with her on the phone though.

Jess showered quickly and sat down to call Kit. He missed her so much that he ached. He had served with men that had spouses and girlfriends and his respect for them grew monumentally. He understood now the sacrifices they had made by being away from their loved ones for so long. He had barely survived a month without Kit. He couldn't imagine being away from her for six.

Jess pressed the #2 button on his cell, which was her preset number. An automated message told him that the number was no longer in service. Jess pressed #2 again thinking that he had made a mistake and he heard the same response. Jess checked his message application and email seeing if Kit had left him a new number. He knew she was getting a new cell. Jess then punched in her number, instead of using his preset and again he was told that the number he had dialed was no longer in service.

Apprehension churned in Jess' gut and not knowing whom else he could reach out to he called his station house. He hoped one of the guys could tell him what was up with Kit's phone. Dusty answered after a couple rings.

"Station House."

"Hey it's Jess."

"Jess, hey, you done? You passed right?"

."Yea, I'm back at base camp. Hey, umm Dusty is Bud or Mikey D there?"

"No, they're off, lucky bastards, its New Year's Eve you know."

"Yea, I know." Jess heard a little commotion on Dusty's end and the Chief got on the line.

"Hey Jess how'd it go?"

"It went well Chief. I'm certified and ready for Australia."

"That's good son." The Chief paused momentarily. "Jess you talk to Kit by any chance?"

"No that's why I called the house. I'm not getting through to her." The Chief paused before answering.

"Jess, it's not my business but are you calling her to break up with her?"

"What? Hell no! Why? What's going on?" The line was quiet and then the Chief spoke.

"Boy you better sit down and listen and

because I'm sticking my neck out here I'd appreciate an honest answer from you, okay?"

"What? An honest answer to what, Chief, is she okay?"

"Sit down boy and let me tell you what happened here. Then it will be your turn to talk, got it?"

"Okay, got it." Jess knew something was really wrong.

The Chief relayed to Jess how Kit had shown up with brownies and a present for the station house while Dusty was showing pictures that he had taken at training camp. He explained that the pictures included some from the final party.

Jess' mind was reeling.

"Jess, Dusty was showing them to the guys running them from his computer onto the station house TV screen. The guys didn't realize Kit was in the room."

Jess' heart began to clench and he dreaded hearing what he knew the Chief was going to say next. The Chief told Jess that he was in some of the pictures and he described those in great detail, since the Chief had personally made Dusty show them to him.

The Chief could hear Jess breathing, but the line was silent. The Chief then relayed the conversation that Kit had overheard.

"Jess, Mikey D and Bud were livid when they saw the pictures. At first they had they stood up for you, telling the guys that you would never cheat on Kit, but Dusty told them how his buddy had seen the girl coming out of your room that night."

Jess swore. This was bad, very bad.

"Jess, Kit saw the pictures, she heard what Dusty said about the girl coming out of your room."

"Holy Shit! Chief it wasn't like that. I even filed a complaint. Oh my God, Kit must hate me."

"Tell me what happened Jess."

Jess retold the entire story and by the time he finished the Chief knew Jess was telling the truth.

"Son, I ain't gonna lie. Mikey D and Bud said she's really hurting."

"Chief, I leave in two days for four more weeks. What should I do?"

"I guess that depends on how you really feel about her Jess."

Jess thanked the Chief, quickly packed his duffle and went to his Commanding Officers hut.

Chapter 18

Kit was lying on the couch. It was past midnight and she was too restless to go into bed. At midnight she had given Lulu a kiss on her head and promptly burst into tears thinking about Jess. She rubbed her hands over her face trying to wipe away the heart-ripping image of Jess kissing the girl that continued to flash through her mind. Suddenly Lulu sat up; ears back as she growled towards the door. Lulu never growled, which alarmed Kit prompting her to quickly stand up. Kit looked quickly around her apartment for something to defend herself with. Her first thought was wondering why her alarm hadn't gone off. She placed a nervous hand on Lulu's head that had stopped growling and was now whining. Kit's apartment door flew open banging hard against the wall and Jess walked in looking exhausted and disheveled.

Neither of them spoke, they just stared at each other. Kit immediately noticed how haggard he looked. His eyes were dark and foreboding, he had a day's growth on his face and his clothes were wrinkled. Jess drank in Kit's image and was startled at how tired and sad she looked. Jess dropped his duffle and took a step towards her.

"What the hell. Get out of here!" Kit choked out when he stepped towards her. She was shocked that he was in her apartment. Lulu had left Kit's side to bounce around Jess with her tail wagging hard side to side so happy at seeing her master. Jess knelt to pet her before whispering something to her that caused her to walk away from him and lay down.

Jess stood back up and looked desperately at the woman he had inadvertently caused so much pain to. "Kit we have to talk."

"No Jess we don't!" Kit hissed back.

"Yes we do. I know what you saw in the pictures. I know what you heard. Now you need to hear what really happened."

Kit grabbed her new phone off the coffee table; she was sobbing now and slowly backing away from him. It tore him up that she acting as if she was frightened of him. Kit punched in a number on her phone and weakly cried "help" into the phone. Then, before Jess could stop her she raced into her bedroom and locked the door behind her.

Jess banged on the door and pleaded with her to let him in. Lulu was whimpering sensing the anxiety in the room. Jess didn't know what to do. He didn't have much time and he needed to explain what had happened. He sank to the floor by her door and tried to talk to her but she wouldn't even acknowledge him. Ten minutes later he heard feet pounding up the stairs. Jess stood up alarmed. Mikey D and Bud charged through the door. They were breathing hard and they looked pissed. Jess realized two things, one; in his haste he hadn't reset the alarm, and two; this was who Kit had called.

Mikey D, who rivaled Jess in size, took two steps towards him before Bud grabbed his arm to halt him.

"We ought to whip your sorry ass." Mikey D said threatening him. Bud was glaring. The tension in the room was palatable and Lulu jumped up to protectively stand between the three men.

"Lulu down." Kit heard Jess say from behind the door. She knew Bud and Mikey D had arrived.

"Guys I know how it looks, but it's not what you think."

"How could you Jess?" She heard Bud say.

"You fucked up brother." Mikey D said.

"Guys please, hear me out. I swear. If you don't want me here afterwards I'll leave. We've been friends forever, you know me."

Mikey D and Bud were still breathing hard as they looked at each other, and then Bud nodded to Mikey. Both men still gave Jess berth as if he were contagious. Mikey D stepped to Kit's door.

"Honey we're here."

'Honey?' Jess shot him a lethal glare and Mikey D mouthed back 'fuck off.'

"Can you get him to go?" She asked quietly through the door.

"If that's what you want we will, but Kit we owe him to hear him out. Come out here with us. You deserve to hear this too, even if it sucks. We'll be here for you. Open the door, baby."

Jess was white knuckled listening to the endearments Mikey was using with Kit.

They waited outside her door cautiously eyeing each other and then finally Kit reluctantly opened her bedroom door. She stepped into Mikey D's protective arms, burrowing into his chest, hiding her eyes away from the man who had been the cause of so many tears. Jess ran his hands through his hair as he watched the woman he was so madly in love with hold on to his friend for support. Support he should be giving her.

Mikey D guided her to the couch where he and Bud possessively sat on either side of her. Bud patted her thigh and Mikey D continued to hold her against his chest. Jess was fuming. He was as much a victim in this too; the problem was that the evidence was stacked against him. Jess knew he had to tell them from the beginning what had been happening and hope that his years as their friend and his short-lived tenure as her lover would carry some weight.

Jess sat in the chair opposite the couch. He was gripping his hands together. Bud and Mikey noticed that he looked like he hadn't slept in days. Jess told them everything. He started from the beginning, describing how the woman, Bess, from day one had been harassing him. How at first he had just brushed it off, but he'd been naive where she was concerned. He told them how he had been working and training hard, doing his job, but he was constantly finding himself being cornered by her. Jess told them that he had told Bess that he had a girlfriend and she needed to focus on her training and not him. She had laughed him off saying she was just interested in being his friend.

Jess described how she continued to plague him daily and it was beginning to affect his training. He reiterated how he had attempted to avoid her but she always popped up where he was. Jess looked directly at Kit when he explained how he had wanted to tell her what was happening but he was afraid she'd over think it. He swore to her that he was going to tell her but he didn't want her upset over something that was a nonissue as far as he was concerned.

Jess relayed to them the incident that happened while running on the trails and her ridiculous attempts to seduce him. He then told them how at the Christmas party she had dogged him the entire night. He said he even got in her face and harshly told her to back off.

Mikey D interjected, "Did you have your hand on her shoulder then?"

"Yea, Chief told me that it's in the background of one of Dusty's pictures." Jess continued. "I was feeling cruddy because I had been short with you on the phone." He nodded at Kit. "I'm so sorry. "This woman was wreaking havoc on my training and she would not back off."

Jess continued. "So I was getting ready to leave the party when she jumped onto my lap and kissed me. I swear I was so taken back. The other guys were hooting and hollering thinking it was some big deal. I'd been sitting there talking with some guys and hadn't expected her to pull a stunt like that. I pushed her off me and stood up. I was livid. I left her on the floor where she fell. The guys thought it was funny, but I was beyond pissed. I went back to my room and started writing out a formal complaint to the CO."

Jess watched Kit hoping for some sign that she believed him. Her breathing had evened out and she was still sniffling. She looked so pale and small between his two best friends. Jess continued.

"Then there was a knock at my door and when I opened it she tumbled in. She was shit faced. She was climbing on me, begging me to kiss her. She told me she loved me and wanted to show me just how much."

Jess saw Kit tense up, her lower lip quivered and she placed her forehead into Mikey Ds chest.

"I couldn't believe she was in my room. She started taking off her shirt. I was so taken back that I just opened my door and shoved her out."

Jess was breathing hard when he finished talking. Kit was crying softly and Bud and Mikey were silently contemplating everything he'd just said.

"Kit, I swear, I would never, ever cheat on you. I...I need you to believe me. All of you."

Kit continued to weep uncontrollably into her palms and Bud was rubbing her thigh as Mike D held Kit softly to him, caressing her shoulder with the hand draped around her.

"For Christ sakes guys, you know me!" Jess' voiced betrayed how emotional he was right then. His voice had cracked and his face was set with hard lines hinting at his anxiety.

Mikey D whispered something into Kit's ear and she looked up to him. After a few heavy seconds of silence Kit finally nodded. He stood up and Bud followed. "We believe you, Jess. Right Bud? We can't speak for Kit."

All three men stood up.

Bud gently slapped Jess on his back showing him that they were still his friends. Mikey D stepped to him and gave him a bro hug. "I knew you didn't fuck up man, I just knew it. The pictures you know? And hearing she came out of your room, it looked bad."

"I know how bad it seemed and it's why I wanted to explain it to Kit face-to-face."

"No matter how this ends up... We get it Jess, and we got your back, but know this; we got Kit's too." Bud added giving Jess a bro hug too.

"Kit honey we're going to leave you guys to talk. You call us back if you need us okay? I'll call you tomorrow." Mikey D said as he hugged her tenderly before giving her a brotherly kiss on her forehead. Bud did the same sans the kiss. Kit mumbled a soft apologized for wrecking their New Year's Eve and they waved her off saying it was no big deal, as they left her apartment.

Kit sat back down on the couch but still refused to meet Jess' gaze. He knelt down in front of her and put his hands on her knees.

"Baby I'm so sorry you thought I'd cheated on you, and honest to God I can see why you would, but sweetheart I didn't do anything with her. I wouldn't Kit I swear."

Tears continued to drip down Kits face. Was she an idiot? His best friends had believed him. She wanted to believe him. Hell, she did believe him, but the awful pain was still there. Kits wrung her hands together clearly stressed.

"I want to believe you Jess, God... I do believe you."

"But?" He said.

"It hurt so badly. I just don't know if I can..." Kit's eyes well with tears again.

"Can what baby?" Jess asked softly.

"Jess, I could barely function, I was shattered." She whispered honestly.

Jess put his hands on her hips and pulled her to him. She willingly slid off the couch and onto his thighs. Jess held her close, but she remained stiff in his arms. His embrace was healing and when she couldn't bear not touching him back another second she wrapped her arms around his neck and sobbed deeply into his neck. Jess stroked her back and talked to her softly hoping to soothe her. He felt her try to pull back and he let their bodies separate slightly, but not completely.

Jess cupped her face with his hands gently forcing her to meet his eyes.

“Kit if you leave me...you’ll destroy me.” His voice was straining with emotion. Kit started sobbing again. She buried her forehead into his chest and he rested his chin lightly on her head.

When Kit regained some control she looked up at him. Her eyes were wet and once again Jess noticed how tired she looked.

“I’m scared Jess. This scares me.”

“Me? I scare you?”

“No.” Kit paused. “You have the power to break me Jess. I’m afraid of not surviving losing you.”

“Oh baby.” Jess had tears in his eyes and he turned away from her for a second to gather his emotions. He then tilted her chin up so she could see how much she was affecting him. “Don’t you know you have the same power over me? I need you Kit. It scares me too. Please don’t give up on us.”

Kit's little shoulders shook as more tears slipped down her cheeks. Jess held her close and prayed they would get through this. They sat like that for a few minutes. Jess was just happy to be holding her. Kit was gathering her emotions, but she too loved that he was holding her.

"How are you here?" Kit asked trying to reign in her tears. Her head was down as she fiddled with the button on his shirt.

"Baby please look at me." He tilted her chin up again. "After I lodged an official complaint against the girl the next morning, Christmas morning, I had to focus on taking my test. I was so stressed over her, the test, you. I am so sorry I was shitty with you on the phone. I felt like an ass. I swear I didn't know what to do. The whole time I was doing my practical I thought about you, about us."

"Tell me about your test Jess. You passed right? Kit's hands moved to his shoulders and Jess audibly sighed that she was touching him on her own. He turned his face and kissed the top of one of her hands, letting her know how much he loved her touching him.

"Yea, I passed. It was tough. We parachuted blind into the mountains. We were given a series of coordinates that we needed to get to by the end of each day. There were also tasks we had to complete along the way. Five days later when we met back at the designated spot, we were told one of our men hadn't reported in. We were all tired but we had to go back out and look for him. The four of us were dropped where he had been originally dropped. We spent another night in the mountains looking for him. When I finally got back to camp this morning I tried to call you."

Kit interrupted his story. "Wait, Jess what happened to the guy that was lost?"

"He busted his leg repelling, so he set up camp and waited till we found him. He's okay." Jess loved that she always thought about other people, even when she was hurting. It was one of things he loved about her. Jess couldn't stop touching her. One hand rubbed her back and the other he kept on her cheek.

"When I couldn't reach you... You have a new number don't you?" Kit nodded.

"I was worried about you, so I called the firehouse. Chief told me what happened, what you saw, what you heard. I gotta tell you Kit; even he was ready to rip my head off. I was sick over it. I packed my duffle, ran to my CO, told him I had a family emergency and hopped on a military plane that was headed north. I then caught a flight to Denver and then I chartered a flight to Haydcn. My dad dropped me here. I told him what happened."

“That’s a lot of plane hopping.” Kit replied, her voice still soft.

“Kit I would have taken ten more if it meant I could see you.”

Kit smiled tenderly at him through her damp eyelashes and brushed one of her hands through his hair that hung over his forehead. Jess heart banged in his chest with the intimate contact. He took Kits hand and lifted it to his lips placing a sweet kiss to her palm.

“What are you thinking?” He prodded her gently.

“Honestly?”

“Honestly.”

“I’m just thinking that I appreciate your apology, and even though, I understand that you were harassed, and you have explanations for what I saw and heard; I can’t help but wished you had just told me. I wished you’d had faith in me.”

“Yeah, hind sight. I do have faith in you. I know how strong you are Kit. I was trying to protect you. Baby there was so much I wanted to tell you. I was afraid that if you did get upset that I was too far away to fix it.”

“Are you still leaving for Australia?”

"Yea the day after tomorrow, well tomorrow." Jess said looking at his watch.

"Jess?"

"What baby?" he said as he stroked her tear-stained cheeks with his thumbs.

"I really, really missed you."

"Oh honey, double back at you." He pulled her to him in a tender embrace. "Are we okay?" He asked tentatively.

"I don't know. Are we Jess?" He feathered his hands on her face and she looked up into his beautiful, tired blue eyes. Once again Jess became emotional and his voice hitched as he spoke.

"Kit I love you. I love you so much it hurts. Please don't leave me."

"You love me?" Kit was startled by his omission.

"So much. So very much." Jess leaned in and swept into her mouth, kissing her with so much passion that Kit felt her body roar to life. It was not lost on Jess that Kit hadn't reciprocated his proclamation of love.

Jess continued to consume her with his kiss, devouring her lips and stroking her tongue with his.

"Can I stay the night?" He asked nervous she might say no.

Kit nodded and he lifted her in his arms. Kit wrapped her legs around his waist and he walked with her into the bedroom. Jess placed her reverently on the bed and after taking off his boots and his socks he laid next to her facing her.

"Kit, are we okay? Please say we are okay." She had never answered him and he needed to hear her speak the words.

Kit looked at him and gave him a sweet loving smile. He fingers caressed his face. "Yes Jess we are good."

"Thank God." Was all Jess could reply.

Much like the first night they had spent together Jess took his time loving her. He was lost simply touching her. He noticed her hipbones were more pronounced and knew she'd lost weight. He kissed her mouth gently and then pulled back slightly wanting to see her face.

"Baby I need you. I need to love you." Jess' voice was husky with desire.

"Yes, Jess, I need you too. I missed us, I missed this."

They made love slowly and gently.

Reacquainting themselves with each other's bodies. Jess' was stronger now, leaner. His muscles harder and clearly defined from all his training. Kit's body was thinner, but her hours spent at the gym and in yoga class were evident in her flexibility and to Jess' delight in other ways. As Kit small body quaked from a drawn out detonation of epic proportions, she used her new yoga made muscles to clench tightly around his length. Jess immediately imploded inside of her. He was moaning her name as he released way to quickly into her. Jess collapsed on top of her.

"God Kit, what the hell was that?"

"Did you like it?" she asked seriously.

"Like it, I loved it; it felt amazing, like your fist was gripping me. Shit! You made me come. Oh God, I'm sorry, I didn't pull out." Jess was slightly panicked.

"I'm on the pill now." She said quietly stroking is back.

Jess rolled off of her and onto his back and then pulled her to rest on top of him. He gave her another kiss then he tucked her head into his neck and held her tightly. "I love you so much Kit, so much."

"I love you too Jess." Jess squeezed her against him.

"We are so not sleeping honey." He laughed as he rubbed her back.

Kit laughed. "Wouldn't dream of it." She answered.

Chapter 19

New Year's Day was spent watching football, taking catnaps, making love, and opening their Christmas presents.

Jess began by opening the envelope that contained the copy of the sketch of him and Lulu on the porch steps of his house. He was thrilled and Kit was delighted that he loved her artwork. Next it was her turn and she opened an envelope that contained a gift certificate for skis, bindings, and boots that she could redeem at the Mountain Ski Shop in town. Kit told Jess she had been getting better at skiing and she could now stem Christie her way down the mountain without falling. Jess opened the candy jar next and promptly told her he was not sharing them with the other Smoke Jumpers, which made Kit laugh. Kit opened a box containing all new sketching pencils, a new sketchpad and high-end colored pencils. Kit told him she loved it, which she did. She loved that he knew her so well.

Next Jess opened the envelope that contained the pictures of the toolbox. He flipped out, in a good way; grabbing Kit up in a huge hug, telling her it was spectacular. She was so in tune with him; it was an odd feeling to have someone know him that well. Kit opened her next gift, which was in a large box with an envelope taped to the top. Inside was a gift certificate for horseback riding lessons that would begin in the spring. There were ten in all. When Kit opened the box the certificate had been attached to she whooped gleefully pulling out a pair of stunning cowboy boots, in her size of course, and a beautiful cowboy hat with a turquoise band. Kit thanked him by diving into his lap and peppering his face with little kisses. Kit told him it was a perfect gift because she had been thinking of learning to ride. Jess insisted she open his last present before he opened her last one to him. Kit didn't mind because her last present to him was her seminude portrait and she was still unsure of how he would view it.

Jess handed her a long rectangle box and Kit unwrapped the delicate gold-foiled paper covering it. She peeked at Jess who looked like a restless little boy, as he waited for her reaction. Kit flipped back the hinged top lid to find a stunning charm bracelet. It had beautiful glass beads that Kit knew from the art world were expensive. She saw that charms could be attached between the colorful beads. Kit, "Oohed" when she took it from the white plush box. There were two charms already fastened to it and she looked at each one amazed at his thoughtfulness. One charm was an artist paint palette and the other was of a small heart.

Kit looked up at Jess and launched her again into his loving embrace.

"Thank you, this is so beautiful. I love it."

Jess held her to him, his cheek pressed against hers as he spoke earnestly.

"You have my heart. You are my heart. I love you. I can't see myself ever not loving you Kit." He watched as her eyes rimmed with tears.

"Happy ones right?" He said softy. Kit nodded giving him a reassuring smile.

Kit wrapped her arms around his neck and gave him a kiss of almost no return. She pulled back from him slightly. "You have one more gift." She pointed at the last manila envelope.

Jess opened the envelope and pulled out the thick, postcard sized piece of high quality paper. He looked at the small sketch and his eyes misted over. Kit saw him swallow, and she knew he was emotional. She turned the card over so he could read the back. Jess smiled and turned it back so he could see the front again. "It's beautiful Kit, you're so friggin gorgeous. I'm so lucky. Can you show me the larger one?"

Kit walked to her bedroom and pulled the original from her bottom drawer. She went back to the couch and handed it to him. Jess studied it without talking for close to a minute.

"Say something Jess." Kit was starting to get nervous.

"Kit this is probably the single most beautiful thing I've ever seen, excluding you in the flesh." He quickly added. "I love it. I love you. Thank you."

"I was worried; you know that it was too..."

"It's perfect. I'll need you to keep this one here for me though." He said indicating the original. "But I am taking this one with me." He said sending her a mischievous grin as he waved the smaller version.

Later that day while they lay draped around each other on the couch Mikey D called her, as he promised. Kit told him that everything was okay and they were back together. Mikey D asked to speak with Jess so she handed him her phone. When he hung up Jess was shaking his head.

"What?" Kit asked.

"It seems that my boys like you more than me."

"What?" She laughed.

"Mikey D just told me if I ever put you through shit like that again that he would pummel me senseless and then he'd kick my ass to Bud who would finish the job."

Kit giggled. "It's just because their dogs like me."

Jess stared into her enormous eyes.

"No honey, it's you. You are kind, and fun and sweet; everyone loves you, even my Chief. It's the very reason I've fallen in love with you. Along with your smoking hot body that is!" Then he smacked her tush playfully.

Kit blushed then squealed as Jess swung her over his shoulder fireman style and walked them past the dining room into the bedroom.

"No table sex?" She asked acting the minx.

Jess laughed out loud smacking her ass again since it was so easily accessible. "When I get back honey I am going to think up ways to make you come that will make our session on that table seem vanilla!"

"Oh my." Kit grinned pretending to fan herself.

Chapter 20

They tried not to waste their precious time together sleeping but after making love and talking for most of the night they both succumbed and fell asleep holding each other closely. Jess heard his phone buzzing in the other room. He rolled over and groaned when he saw the time on the digital clock. He had to leave. He realized the phone call had probably been from his dad who was taking him back to the airport.

"Babe..." He kissed her warm cheek. "Sweetheart, I have to go."

Kit opened her swollen sleepy eyes and placed her hand on his chest. "Already? Oh Jess you just got here."

"I know Hun, but that was the deal. I still have to report to duty in Australia. I just bought some time by not going on the military flight I was supposed to."

Kit sat up and the sheet fell to her waist. Her straw colored hair was sexily tousled and her lips were puffy from all the kissing they had done. Her breasts bore two tiny light purple love marks that he couldn't resist leaving on her pale silky skin. "Go shower Jess I'll get you something to eat okay?"

"Thanks I appreciate it. My Dad will be here in twenty minutes."

Jess went to shower and Kit made him a scrambled egg and a fried ham sandwich and wrapped it in foil. She placed that in a little brown bag and added cookies that she'd baked, a small bag containing carrot sticks, a granola bar and a water bottle. She then made him coffee and put it in a large travel mug. Just as she finished Jess came out of the bedroom dressed to go.

Jess glanced at his phone that was on the table and saw his dad had texted that he was outside. Jess texted he'd be right down. He threw his candy minus the jar into the duffle bag.

"Kit where's your phone?"

Kit handed it to him. Jess dialed his number and hit send it so he'd have her new number.

"Remember to email me later so I have your new email address okay?"

"Okay."

"I don't know how things are set up over there. I'm hoping we can Skype and email. Get that

Skype account set up okay?"

"Okay Jess."

"Can you walk me downstairs?"

"Yes." Kit was quiet and it worried him.

They walked downstairs and Lulu came too. She could sense Jess was leaving again and stayed close to him. Outside Jess' dad was waiting in the car. He got out of the car and took Jess' duffle. "Everything okay?" He asked looking first at Jess then at Kit.

"Yea Dad we're good."

"Phew!" Jess' dad hugged Kit. "We will have you out for dinner okay?"

"Yes, that would be nice, thank you." Kit responded trying to sound cheery.

Jess' dad excused himself and got into the car. Jess turned to Kit and pulled her into his arms. "We can get through this Kit. I'm going to miss you every damn second."

"I already miss you Jess. Here I made you breakfast and here's coffee." Kit said handing him both items.

Jess smooched her on her lips and smiled at her so sexily. "Thank you, you're awesome."

"Jess is safe. I need you to come home to me."

"I will baby. I love you Kit."

"I love you too Jess."

Jess bent down and ruffled Lulu's head. "Take care of my girl Lulu."

Jess gave Kit one final searing kiss and then got into the passenger seat. As the car drove off Kit knelt down and wrapped one of her arms lovingly around Lulu, giving her a hug as she waved good-bye to Jess.

Inside Kit cleaned the kitchen and put away the presents Jess had given her. She still had another one, according to Jess, that Dusty had for her. After giving her apartment a cleaning Kit dressed for the weather and took Lulu out for a walk. When they returned she sat on her couch and picked up her new phone. There were three texts from Jess.

I love u

Where are u?

I miss u

Kit texted him back. I love u 2 Took lulu 4 walk Miss u 2

Jess responded immediately: Always take ur phone with u k

She responded: K

He texted back: email me k

I will

Did you set your GPS yet

Not yet

Do it plz boarding love u tons

Love u xoxo :)

Kit loved her new white iPhone especially the camera. She and Jess had taken a few selfies together and Kit had taken a picture of Jess with Lulu and then a couple just of Jess. She scrolled through those pictures and sent them off to Jess along with a new one she took of herself with lips pursed in a kiss. She then busied herself by setting up the GPS and the Find My Phone App. She also installed a couple other Apps Jess had recommended. One had to do with navigating in case she ever got lost in the woods again and she still had cell service. The guy at the Verizon store had already set her phone so she could receive her emails on her new email account, when she'd receive one he had showed her how a little banner would pop up on her screen on her phone. Kit set up, Face Time, Skype and added her contacts to iMessage. Kit then made her screen saver a pic of Jess and Lulu. While she was looking at the cute picture and showing it to Lulu, she realized she'd forgotten to tell Jess about the USB Drive and what Ray had written. She picked up her phone and texted Jess.

Forgot to tell u something important call me before you leave Denver.

Jess never got the text. He was late for his connection and ended up running from one gate to the other.

Kit knew when Jess didn't call her that he hadn't gotten her message. She figured that he was currently in the air whizzing to Australia and she felt that familiar tug of sadness that he was moving further away from her, physically that is. Emotionally they had connected. Kit knew he loved her and she knew he was the real deal for her too. When she thought back to how she felt about Ray she knew she had loved him too, but it had been different. Ray had been her best friend, they had grown up together, and they had been comfortable with each other. They had good sex, but not anything near the chemical combusting kind she experienced with Jess. Jess made her heart speed up when she simply looked at him. She also loved how well she knew him and he knew her. Their Christmas gifts to each other proved that. She was pleased Jess had liked her seminude. She loved knowing that when he looked at the small replica while he was away, he would think of her in a special way.

It was getting dark and after one last walk with Lulu she climbed into bed earlier than she normally would. A sense of loneliness engulfed her and she called to Lulu and patted the bed net to her. Lulu hesitated for about a second before joining Kit on the bed. With one hand resting on Lulu's back Kit fell into a heavy restful sleep.

Chapter 21

Four long weeks had passed since New Year's Eve and Kit was already getting excited about Jess coming home in a few days. Their communication had been severely limited on this trip, unlike the month before when they could talk almost every night. Jess did not have Internet access as often as he would have liked and because of the time difference they were lucky if they connected with each other twice a week. She had told Jess about the USB drive but had not given him any real details about what was on it. She didn't want him to worry and she was just going to give it to Lori anyway. She wanted no part of the blood money or the memories it evoked.

Dusty had given her the other present from Jess. It was a delicate silver chained necklace with a delicate silver heart shaped charm attached. One side of the heart had Kit + Jess engraved into it. Kit wore it all the time keeping the engraved side next to her skin. She often found her self-absentmindedly rubbing her fingers on the small flat heart when she was contemplating something.

Bud and Mikey D took it upon themselves to keep her social. She understood they were her friends now too and she enjoyed spending time with them. They had taken her out to dinner a few times and Bud had brought his girl, Krissy along too. Kit had a good time with them and it helped pass the time.

One afternoon the UPS truck stopped outside of her house. At first, Kit thought the driver was lost but he handed her a package. Kit was surprised and checked the address thinking there had been a mistake. A happy thrill went through Kit as she realized all the Wit-Sec red tape was behind her.

Kit opened the small package thinking it was from Jess or her parents. She read the note first.

Hi saw this and it made me think of you. Merry Christmas, hope all is well. C

Kit unwrapped the white tissue paper surrounding whatever Colt had sent her and was surprised to see a beautiful leather snap cuff. It was decorated with intricate stitched colorful flowers. Kit loved it. On the inside of the cuff it was stamped Moapa.

Kit snapped the cuff on the wrist her right

wrist, the one that she didn't have Jess' beautiful charm bracelet on. She knew Jess would not be happy that Colt had given her the cuff. He didn't know Colt but the few times his name had come up in conversation Jess' eyes had clouded over and Kit knew he was controlling his jealousy. Kit figured she'd wear it for this week because when Jess came home there was no way he'd want her to wear it.

As Kit was getting ready to toss the small padded envelope into the garbage she noticed the return address was not crossed out. She'd never had his address before; she'd simply handed Lori the letters she wrote to Colt and Wit Sec took care of getting them to him. When she had received letters from Colt they had been in the original envelope but the return address had always been blackened out. Kit took out her phone and copied the address into the notes section in her phone. She then threw out the envelope and the note.

That day Kit had three dog clients dropped off, all new clients, so she had her hands full checking on them. One was only there for the day, a labra doodle named Chip. The two other dogs were terriers. They were yappy little things with an abundance of energy, belonging to a doctor in town who was going away for a weekend with his wife. Mr. Peterson had come in too, but he wasn't with her for long and luckily it was when his story was on TV so Kit hadn't had to entertain him at all. When Kit finished for the day she was exhausted.

She and Lulu retired to her apartment and Kit sat down to read the latest email she'd received from Jess. He said things were still going well but he was missing her and he could not wait to see her. He adding smiley faces to his email after that line. He told her that they had been given a rare night off and had gone into the dingy bar for a few beers. He described to her how secluded the place was and that his beers were served warm which he did not like. The entertainment for the evening consisted of a young woman collecting dollars in a mason jar and when the jar was filled she would take her top off. Jess assured her that he had not placed any money in the jar and he had left before she had, according to the other guys, taken off her top. Jess wrote that he had unknowingly stepped over a large poisonous snake and now whenever he was in the bush he carried a long stick with him. Kit shivered at the thought. She was not a fan of snakes either.

Kit replied quickly, knowing that he may not receive her reply before he left. She told him how much she missed him and what her days had been like; describing the two crazy terriers that Lulu was not a fan of. Kit decided she would be candid about Colt's letter and his gift to her. She carefully worded her email to ensure that Jess understood that Colt was just being friendly and that she was only telling him so there would be no secrets between them.

She wrote that she was going to write Colt back now that she had his address, and that she was going to tell him that she had a boyfriend, that she liked, she added a smiley face. Kit told him that she had tried the Wit Sec office again hoping to contact Lori, but she wasn't back yet from wherever she was, so she still had the USB drive.

After hitting send on her computer Kit wrote Colt a letter and printed it out so she could show it to Jess.

Dear C, I love my cuff thank you so much. I'm out of W.S. now and I'm really enjoying my new life. I take yoga, kick boxing and ski lessons. My dog sitting business is really picking up. I wanted to tell you a couple things. First and most important you were right about Ray, he was trying to protect me. I found something I wish I could talk to you about. Lori has been away and I haven't been able to give it to her yet. Here's a hint: I could buy a small island! I also wanted to tell you that I have met someone, someone I really care about. His name is Jess. He makes me happy. I think he'll be jealous you gave me a present but I really love it so I hope I can assure him that you and I have a special bond and we are simply good friends that share a unique past. Here is my cell and email address. Maybe it's easier for you to email me I have no idea. Be safe. K

Kit then included her new cell number and her new email address. Kit spell checked and then printed out the letter so she could mail it the next day, which she did.

It was Sunday morning and Kit was excited for Jess' homecoming. She knew his itinerary and that he was flying non-stop into Los Angeles in about twelve hours, but he had a killer layover before he could get on a plane to Denver and then another layover there before flying into Hayden. Jess wished he could fly directly into Denver but unfortunately he hadn't been able to arrange it.

Kit had had a relatively slow weekend regarding dogs. She had Misty who would be leaving in a few hours and then Crank and Maize were due to arrive that afternoon. Kit walked Lulu and Misty and then went to her kick boxing class. She stopped at the grocery store so she could bake for Jess' return. She also wanted to make him a good home cooked meal for his first night home. She had bought veggies for a salad, baking potatoes and a steak, which she was going to grill after she marinated it overnight. She also had his favorite beer chilling in her fridge.

As Kit was dropping her bags on the kitchen counter her iPhone pinged alerting her to a new email. She pulled out her phone and saw it was from an address she didn't recognize but the subject was 'C.' She immediately thought it was from Colt. He would have received her letter by now; he was only in Las Vegas, that's where his PO Box was anyway.

Kit put the groceries away and opened up the email on her iPhone. The email contained a photo imbedded in the body of the email. The blood drained out of Kit’s head and black spots flickered in front of her eyes distorting her vision. Although the photo was small Kit knew immediately it was a picture of Colt. The picture was dark but she could see that that he was tied in a chair. Kit ran to her computer and logged on to her email so she could see the picture better. When it came up she was chilled; she fought back the bile creeping up her throat at the heinous sight before her.

Colt's black hair fell in filthy strands to his shoulders. He was bound with his arms behind him to a chair. A hand was clutching Colts hair near his hairline forcing his beaten face upwards towards the person taking the photo. His right eye was swollen shut. A jagged cut was noticeable under his left eye and blood coated his left check and soaked the left shoulder of the shirt he wore, which was unbuttoned to his waist. His exposed chest and neck bore signs of purple bruising. Thin angry lines dissected his skin that she knew were caused by something sharp and painful. Colt's lips were pressed tightly together and Kit grimaced when she saw his top lip was spilt open. Colt looked horrible. Kits mind was racing and her heart was thundering inside her chest.

The message underneath the picture read: Bring it to us or he dies.

She couldn't believe it, that's all it said. Kit was shaking and her thoughts were scattered as she tried to understand what was happening. She typed a reply.

Bring what?

Nervously she sat at her computer looking at her email screen praying for a response. She was hoping this was a prank, maybe an elaborate hoax, but when her email pinged again, subject 'C' she knew it wasn't.

The money your husband stole. Bring it to Las Vegas airport in 15 hours or he dies come alone, do not contact the police, if anyone else is with u he dies.

Kit typed back: I don't understand

Even though she knew exactly what they meant.

Her emailed pinged again: 15 hours we will contact u

Another picture of Colt accompanied this message. She could see that they must have just cut the side of his neck, under his ear, and blood was pouring from the new wound. His one eye still opened was hard, dark and she could see the fury radiating from it. A filthy looking rag had been stuffed in his mouth.

Kit closed her screen and took calming breaths. She had to help him, but how? She'd give them anything they wanted if it meant keeping Colt safe. Kit couldn't understand how they knew about the money. It didn't make sense, unless Pallone's men had found Colt. She had so many questions. How could she do this without getting him killed, without getting herself killed? She didn't give a rat's ass about the money. They could have it all, but she was smart enough to realize that once they had what they wanted Colt was going to be expendable. Kit had to have a plan and she had to think of one quickly. Fifteen hours, that meant she needed to be in Vegas by 1:00 am.

The first thing Kit researched was how long it would take to drive to Las Vegas. She found out that was between 10 and 11 hours. She could make it there as long as there were no major delays. She then researched flights. There was one leaving that afternoon, two stops, that would get her there on time as well.

Kit's doorbell rang and she realized she'd just wasted a half hour of precious time. She ran downstairs trying to act normal; all she needed was Tim becoming suspicious. Kit let Tim in through the side door and opened the basement door where Lulu and Misty had been lounging. Misty ran up the steps and greeted her owner.

Tim was watching Kit closely. She knew she was acting odd, but she did not have the luxury of time or the good acting skills to attempt to act normal.

"Everything all right?" Tim asked.

"Yea, rough night."

"Why?" Tim asked.

Kit fumbled for an answer, "Oh not rough, just couldn't sleep. Jess flies in tomorrow. Guess I'm just excited." Even Kit surprised her with that off the cuff lie.

"Oh, yea well I can understand that. He's been gone a while."

"Yea, yea he has."

"Okay well let me get going then. I'll see you in two days, right?'

"Two days, yup."

Kit bent down and patted Misty's head before saying good-bye to Tim. She had been formulating a plan and she had so many different scenarios running through her head ached. The one thing she hated about her plan was that she was not going to be here when Jess arrived home. She knew he would be livid. She was going to be risking her life for another man. Hopefully the note she would leave for him would help him understand.

Kit ran back upstairs with Lulu on her heels. The first thing she did was place a call to her new client, Rick Jessup, the pilot and owner of Dune, the yellow lab. Kit quickly explained that she needed to hire him to fly her to Vegas. She used her family emergency excuse again.

Rick told her he could fly her there this afternoon. He was concerned for her fake emergency and Kit felt guilty about her lie but she had no choice. Rick explained the flight would take about 4 or 5 hours. He gave her his rate and she told him that it was no problem. He told her to meet him at Hayden by 2:00. That gave Kit two and half hours to get everything together. Her crazy plan began to solidify in her mind. If she could pull it off she could save Colt and not put herself in danger either.

Kit left her apartment leaving Lulu behind. She went to the Verizon store. On Sundays they were opened for 4 hours during the busy ski season. Kit ran inside and found the young man that had helped her when she bought her iPhone. Kit told him she needed two USB drives. She then asked if there was ways to password protect them. The young man said the best way was to password protect each document. In order to access them a password would be required. Kit thanked him and bought two

USB drives and headed home.

Kit inserted the original USB drive into her computer and first copied all the files onto her hard drive. The note from Ray she printed out and left by her computer. Kit then dragged each folder onto a new USB drive that was not password protected. She was leaving that one at her house. She repeated the progress with the other new USB drive. That one she was mailing to the US Marshals office with a short note explaining what was on it and that they should contact Sergeant Mann of the DEA office. Kit then converted the folders containing the bank account numbers, so that each one required a separate password to open. Kit dragged the newly password protected folders back onto the original USB drive. She tested the drive and found that it had worked. Each folder required a password. Kit had thought up the different passwords for every folder and she had placed the passwords in her notes section on her phone.

She then sat down to write the hardest letter she'd ever had to write to Jess.

Dear Jess,

First, please know I love you; I am so in love with you that I realize until you came into my life I hadn't known what true love was. I know it sounds sappy but it's true. If you're reading this you know I'm not here. I wish I were. Colt is in trouble, big trouble. I have to help him or at least try. He risked everything for me once and now I have to do the same. I'm headed to Las Vegas. I do have a plan. I know it would be pointless for me to tell you not to worry. I know this affects you too. It affects us and for that I'm sorry. I need to help him; it's not an option. I guarantee were the situations reversed he would do the same for me. I also know if you were in my shoes you too would do the same. You have my email address, here's my password feel free to look through my emails so you know why I had to go. PW: kitheartsjess4e (Kit hearts Jess 4 ever) get it :) With any luck I'll be able to save Colt and then come back here to you. I've missed you so much and this is def not the way I anticipated your homecoming to start.

Love always,

Kit

Kit printed out the letter and left it by the computer she then copied it and put it in an email that she sent off to Jess. She knew he was in the air and he would get the email when he landed. She also understood he may not forgive her for doing this and she involuntarily shuddered thinking she could very well lose him forever. Unfortunately she did not have a choice. If she did nothing and Colt died, there was no way she could make peace with herself over that, and that would ultimately kill her.

Kit took two sheets of blank computer paper and hastily wrote on one.

Sorry can't take your dog's today. Please come in, alarm off, take Lulu to Jess parent's love you guys. She hung that on the side door. On the other piece of paper she wrote Sorry cannot take anyone today family emergency, she taped that note to the front door.

Kit packed a small overnight bag. She took the envelope she was mailing to the US Marshals office, extra cash, her cell phone and charger, her wallet with ID's, and the USB drive that was password protected. She was traveling light. Kit knelt down to give Lulu a huge hug; she then got into her car and after stopping at the post office to mail the one envelope containing the USB drive she drove to Hayden airport.

After she parked at the airport and she found Rick waiting for her inside. He took her through a small back door and again conveyed his condolences to her regarding her family troubles. Rick walked her through a private security screening and then ushered through a door that led out to the tarmac where his private plane sat. He helped her buckle into the copilot's seat and placed headphones on her head so they could communicate.

Rick went through the preflight checklist and while he did that Kit mentally ran through a list of her own; specifically all the things she needed to do before the bad guys, as she called them, called her. She figured she'd arrive in Vegas around 7:00 PM and that left her five hours to get ready. Five hours for her to try to save Colt's life.

The flight was smooth. Rick was a natural tour guide and pointed out things they could see from the air. Kit feigned interest so as not to arouse suspicion. In actuality Rick just thought she was preoccupied with her family situation. When they landed Rick told Kit he had to head back right away and if she needed a ride back for her to call him. An airport security person met the plane and Kit was escorted into the main terminal through a private door.

She turned her phone back on and it pinged like crazy with texts and missed calls from Bud and Mikey D. Kit didn't stop to look or listen to them she needed to get her side of things squared away.

Kit first went to the car rental booth and rented a car. She drove the car into Vegas where she pulled into a large super market parking lot. Kit took out her phone and went on the Internet looking for two things; another rental car agency, not the same one that she had just used, and a motel that would not ask too many questions.

Kit found what she was looking for and put the address of the motel into her cell's GPS. Kit followed her GPS to the Sparkle Motel. Kit realized it may have sparkled at one time but right now it was anything but, however it would serve her purpose. She paid cash for a room and asked for two room keys. She requested a room that was around the back of the motel and out of road view. Kit then parked her car and walked to the other car rental agency, which was a half-mile away. Kit rented another car, she requested a two-seater. She drove that car around the neighborhood looking for a pharmacy. When she found the pharmacy she bought first aide items plus snack foods, waters, Gatorades and Advil. Her next stop was to a Wal-Mart where she purchased three prepaid cheap cell phones, small bottles of shampoo, conditioner, a bar of soap, scissors, a floppy hat that would hide her face, a razor and a set of clothes and flip-flops she hoped would fit Colt.

Kit went back to the motel and deposited all the things she'd bought on the bed. She took out the burner phones and put the number of the burner phone she would be using into one of the burner phones and she input the number for her real phone into the other burner. Kit had one hour before they were scheduled to call her. She needed to be fully prepared. Her cell phone was accumulating messages and she finally succumbed and looked at them. The first ones started with: where r u from

Mikey and they continued on with: we r worried call us by the time she looked at her last one she realized that they had contacted Jess and he was off the wall upset. Jess sent her a text: what's going on very worried. He had sent those four hours ago. Kit figured he was probably in Los Angeles now.

Kit texted Jess back email will explain everything

Little did she know Jess had already read her email and was currently landing in Vegas.

Chapter 22

Earlier

Mikey D and Bud arrived at Kit's house and when they read the note they knew something was wrong. There was no way Kit would take off with Jess coming home tomorrow. They took Lulu, as she had requested, and dropped her at Jess's family's house, using Kit's own excuse that she had a family emergency. They took their own dogs to Bud's girlfriend's house and told her about the note that Kit had left on her front and side doors.

After leaving Krissy's house they drove to the firehouse. They went directly to the Chief and told him they thought something was up. They knew Jess was in the air and they were worried. As the two men sat there the Chief made a phone call and then he made another and then another, by the third call he had Jess on the line using the Air Marshal, that was on Jess' flight, emergency phone.

"Chief?" Jess's voice crackled over the line

"Something up with Kit, Jess. Don't want to scare you but the boys are worried."

Mikey D then continued to tell Jess about the notes they'd found on Kit's doors. Jess's body became ridged he knew in his gut there was no way Kit would leave just leave without telling him especially with him coming home tomorrow. She also would have told Mikey D and Bud where she was going before she left if it was nothing to worry about. Jess thought about the trial she had been involved with. Something was wrong and Jess knew, he just knew it had to do with that damn USB drive she had told him about. He didn't want to worry her parents but if she did have a family emergency he needed to check that out first. Luckily he had her Dads number in his cell so Jess used the on board sky phone to call him.

When Kit's Dad answered he was slightly alarmed that he was calling but Jess simply told him that he would like to talk to him in person soon and asked what their schedule was. That appeased Kit's dad and he gave Jess their itinerary. Jess knew they were Kit's only family so Bud and Mikey's concerns about Kit were valid.

Jess told Mikey D and Bud the alarm codes to get into Kit's apartment. He told them to see if there was a clue as to where she was. He then swore under his breath. He couldn't tell them why he was so worried but he promised to explain it to them later. Jess had been given Internet access from the pilot and he read the email Kit had sent. He relayed what the email said to the guys and told them to get to Vegas. That was where he was now headed. He was landing in LAX within the hour and he would get himself to Vegas and meet them there. Fear cloyed at Jess. What had his woman gotten her into now? He was praying the time to pass quicker so he could get off the plane and try to call Kit.

Bud and Mikey D drove back to Kit's and let themselves into her apartment using the alarm codes they had been given by Jess. The first thing they found were the letters by her computer, one addressed to Jess and the other was from some guy named Ray.

Bud logged on to Kit's email and entered her password that she'd left Jess. He honed in on the two emails with the attachments. He and Mikey D were visibly shaken with the stark brutality in the pictures. They forwarded the emails to Jess's phone. They read the other emails which had told Kit she had 15 hours to get to Vegas and that was 10 hours ago. They had no idea who Colt was but they knew, without a doubt, Jess was going be terrified for Kit.

Bud and Mikey D drove to Hayden airport. Bud was calling all the private pilots they knew as they drove. When they arrived Bud had found a pilot willing to take them to Vegas even though it was very late. They were paying through the nose but the plane was a jet that would get them there about the same time that Jess would arrive and that was 1:00 am. Bud and Mikey D had no idea about Kit being in Wit Sec and her former life. The fact that she was involved with something that involved the kidnapping of some man, and that man had been brutally beaten, left them cold and afraid for her life.

While Jess was securing his flight to Vegas he called on the one person he thought he'd never have to talk to again, Bess. Bess' main job was with the FBI and she was a computer whiz. Jess punched in Dusty's cell number. He knew he could get Bess's number from the guy Dusty had roomed with. Dusty's roommate in training was from the same firehouse that Bess volunteered at. Within minutes Jess had Bess's number.

Jess called the number Dusty had texted him and when she answered and Jess identified himself, she warily said hello. Jess didn't waste time. "I need a favor, a big one and you fucking owe." He growled.

"What, what do you mean I owe you, you reported me!"

"Yes, and you needed to be reported, but I also saved your skin when I didn't press charges. You didn't lose your job and you still graduated Smoke School."

Bess was quiet. “I’m sorry I did that crap to you.” She confessed quietly.

“You can repay it now. I need a favor and it needs to be done fast.”

“What?”

“My girlfriend's in trouble. I need her phones GPS coordinates sent to my phone and I need all the places she’s been in the last 8 hours.”

“Ummm illegal much.” Bess countered.

“You can do this I know you can. I’ll give you her information and you have my cell now. I need the info in an hour, one fucking hour, Bess.”

“Okay, I get it. I better not get caught. You’re lucky it’s a Sunday and late, no one should be monitoring this shit on my end and I can do it from home.”

“Just do it.”

Jess gave Bess Kit's cell number and they hung up just as Jess was called for his flight to Vegas.

Before he got on the plane he dialed Kit's number but it went unanswered. He left her a message, ‘Kit I’m on my way. I’ll be in Vegas within the hour. Wait for me I’ll help you.’

Kit never listened to the message. She saw it was Jess calling and she knew he could potentially talk her out of what she needed to do. She had to remind herself that she didn't want him involved. She wanted him safe and untouched by the horrid crap that had crept into her wonderful new life, maybe staining it forever. She prayed he'd understand. She knew he well might not, and he was going to be beyond mad. She had to help Colt and that he was in the hands of men who thought nothing about inflicting pain on him. The thought of him being tortured nauseated her.

Chapter 23

Kit had everything all set, she hoped. She had already driven the two-seater rental car to the supermarket parking lot that she had originally pulled into. It was a perfect setting for what she had in mind. It had multiple exits and access to the main highway; plus there were a bunch of smaller streets that could be accessed in case she needed them. It was only about a mile from the hotel too. Kit had put a water bottle in the cup holder and one of the burner phones in the other cup holder. She placed one of the two motel room keys along with hotel address under the driver side floor mat. Kit then took one of the other burner phones and the password protected USB drive and placed them so they were visible on the front seat of the little car. She locked the car and put the keys on the rear back tire. She quickly ran back to the motel and got in her original rental car. She drove back to the same lot, but around to the side of the large building, parking in the small area reserved for employees. Kit positioned her car so she had an unobstructed line of vision on the other car. Kit had completed everything with ten minutes to spare. She anxiously waited to hear from the men holding Colt.

Kit's hands were trembling. While she waited she thought of how much she loved Jess. She worried that he wouldn't forgive her for doing this. It pained her physically to think they may not have a future. The fact remained that she had to do this and if he didn't understand that then he didn't understand her. Kit was beginning to panic as the seconds ticked away. She had to take control of the next communication that she knew was coming. She had to make them do what she wanted. If they wanted the money bad enough, they would.

Kit's cell buzzed, with an email. She pulled it up. Her hands were shaking uncontrollably.

You're in Vegas

She responded: Yes

Go to... Kit didn't wait to read the rest of that email and she sent off one to them.

No... Now we do it my way. She waited. Finally her email pinged.

You don't dictate this we do; your boyfriend is near dead now. You want to hurry that along

She wrote:

You'll kill him anyway. You'll kill me. I just want him safe; I don't give a crap about the money.

Kit thought she sounded tougher than she was feeling. Inside she was crumbling her phone quiet. It pinged again and Kit knew she had them.

Okay let's hear it

Kit: I have what you want. It's on a USB drive and it contains account and access numbers. Bring my friend to this address. 1124 Maple Lot M. Find the blue Mazda Miata - 2 door. Keys are on back tire. Take USB that's on the seat along with the cell phone. Bring a computer with Internet access and someone who can access the accounts using the numbers I will give you. Put my friend in the car, let him drive away alone and then press #2 on the burner to reach me.

The wait was unbearable. Her muscles were coiled tightly and she felt a headache slipping behind her eyes because of the stress. Finally her cell pinged with a response.

A half hour

In a half hour she would set her plan into action. Kit anxiously waited for them to get there. Minutes felt like hours. She was a nervous wreck. Her palms were sweating and her throat was dry she mentally kicked herself for not bringing a water bottle for herself. She also wished she had brought binoculars so she could see better across the dark lot. She was worried Colt might not be able to drive the car on his own and that would seriously put a kink in her plan if he couldn't. Kit put the floppy hat on her head and drew it down so the brims edge was at chin level effectively hiding her features. She kept checking her phone; she didn't want to use it in case they got there early and tried calling her. She itched to call Jess, to hear his voice.

Twenty five minutes into the half hour period Kit watched a Lincoln town car enter the lot and cruise the rows until it pull up next to the little blue rental car. Kit had to hold the front brim of her hat up so she could see. A huge Spanish looking man wearing a tee shirt, straining under ridiculously large muscles, emerged from the back seat, leaving the door open. He retrieved the key from the tire, unlocked the car and pulled open the door. He reached in and took out the phone and USB that she had left and walked back to the dark car. Kit waited; she had to remind herself to breath. Finally her burner rang and even though she had been expecting it to, her heart slammed with a jolt. She answered it.

"You bitch!" The accented voice said before she could speak.

"Did you think I would just hand it to you? I

told you I just want him safe. It's simple a trade for a trade."

"You have no idea who you're fucking with girl."

"I just want to trade, that's it." She heard the man sigh into the phone and mutter a quiet 'shit' that she probably wasn't intended to hear.

"Okay what now." The man's voice was tense and angry.

She told them each file contained an account and each account was password protected. She knew that he probably already knew that. She simply wanted to reinforce the fact that only she could give them what they wanted, not Colt. She told them to put 'her friend' in the car; she purposely did not use Colt's name. He was to be allowed to drive away, alone. Once he was away and she received word from him, she would give them a password for one account. For every minute he was safely away, she would give them a new password.

The man countered and asked how they would know the accounts weren't just dummy numbers. Kit said she would give them one password in good faith now and they could see for themselves. All they needed to do was open the file, input the numbers and passwords and then they would be able to move that money into their own account.

Kit could hear some shuffling in the background and what sounded like a moan. Her spine stiffened and she choked down a multitude of fears. God she hoped he could drive, she thought to herself again. Sweat was dripping down her back as her eyes strained to see what was happening. The phone was plastered to her ear as she labored to hear any background conversations they might be having. Kit watched as the large man leaned into the car, presumably awaiting instructions.

"How do I know once he's away you won't' take off too?"

"You don't. We both have to trust each other here. I'm telling you, I do not care about the money at all. I wish I didn't even have it."

The line was quiet and her reasoning must have satisfied them and.

"Give me the password for the first file." The man said harshly.

"Let him out of your car I want to see that he's alive."

The second she said it she knew she had tipped them off to the fact that she was nearby. A small Spanish looking man jumped out of the backseat and started walking around the lot. She knew he was looking for her. She couldn't leave, not until she was sure Colt had driven off. She heard the man on the phone say to someone, "Get him out of the car."

Kit watched as a thinner, wobbly Colt was dragged from the backseat and sandwiched between the large Spanish man and a third man that had stepped from the car. Kit held a nervous giggle thinking the sedan was like a clown car at a circus, as more men kept getting out of it. Colt could barely stand on his own. Kit knew he was in a bad way but she also knew he was a strong willed man. She prayed he'd be able to drive, even if only to get far enough away that he was safe.

"Give me the password."

Kit recited a series of letters and numbers to the man and waited. It took a minute but then the man came back on the line. "150,000.00." He said.

"Yes, now put him in the car and let him go, you've seen I'm not lying." Kit realized these guys were small-time thugs. Dumb small-time thugs. They were obviously floored with the $150,000.000 she had given them. It was probably more money than any of them had ever seen before

Kit heard him speak in Spanish to the men holding Colt and then she apprehensively watched as Colt was roughly dumped into the driver side of the car. Kit put the Spanish man on hold and dialed the burner she had put in the other cars cup holder with her iPhone. Colt answered quickly, his voice weak and wheezy. “What have you done girl?”

“Shut up Colt, I got this. Drive, when you are away reach under your floor mat there is a motel room key with the address, its close by. I’ll join you later. Go.” She hung up on Colt and pressed her ear back to the burner phone. She could hear the pissed off man swearing in Spanish. She calmly said. “I’m back. I had to talk to him.”

Kit watched Colt drive away and a surge of pride and relief swelled inside her. He was away. She’d done it.

“Give me another.” The man on the other ended demand, his voice thick with agitation.

Kit recited another number to him and within a minute she gave them another.

Kit had lost track of the smaller man that she knew was looking for her so she started her car. She could give them the account numbers now from anywhere, now that she knew Colt was safe. She turned to look over her shoulder to back out and a loud crack splintered her driver side window. As she turned towards the window she saw the butt of a handgun crashing through the already weakened glass followed by a hand peeling the jagged tempered glass away.

Kit tried to step on the gas but the man had reached through the now-unobstructed window and grabbed her hat along with a good chunk of her hair. He was aggressively pulling her head and neck out of the window. She could feel the sharp edge of the windows glass slicing the delicate skin of her neck. She slammed on the breaks and held her hands up.

"Okay, okay, stop!" She choked out.

The man kept a tight hold of her hat and hair and it reminded her of how one of these men had held Colt's hair in the horrible pictures she'd seen. Then her next thought was that Jess was going to kill her and she almost vomited because she knew, with such clarity that it overwhelmed her; that Jess would never get the chance to because she was going to die by the hands of these men.

Kit tried to stay calm and for some reason just knowing Colt had gotten away served to pacify her enough that she was more rational than she should have been given her situation. The man kept his gun pointed at her and refused to let go of her hair.

"Turn the car off and get out," He barked in a thick accent.

Kit opened the door carefully since her head

and shoulders were precariously being held out of the doors window. The man continued to painfully grip her hair. She turned slightly, avoiding the broken glass and placed her feet on the pavement. Slowly she pushed out of the seat. She remained in a hunched position because her neck was still sticking out the window. Blood dripped down her neck onto her shirt and again she was reminded of when Ray had bled out on her. The dark haired man reached his skinny arm around the doorframe and grasped her hair under her hat using the hand holding the gun. Kit went stone still, not wanting to risk the gun so near to her head to accidentally fire. He then let go of her head with his other hand, swiping the hat to the ground and simultaneously pulling her around the doorframe with his gun hand. Kit tilted precariously towards him. With no time to adjust her feet, she stumbled against the door.

The man wrenched up on her hair forcefully. Although it hurt it also helped her to regain her balance. Kit was pressed against his left side. The man was slightly taller than herself and he reeked of cigarettes. His left hand was gripping her hair at the nape of her neck and his right hand was across his stomach and under her shirt as he pressed the nozzle of his gun to her side. To anyone looking at them they would appear like two lovers walking.

So many things flashed through Kit's mind; Jess, her parents, she even thought about how mad

Mikey D and Bud were going to be at her for dying. She remembered Lulu comforting her that one night when she had let her sleeps on the bed and she hoped she'd comfort Jess too. Kit also knew Colt was going to agonize over the fact that she had saved him but gotten herself killed. In her heart of hearts she knew Colt would never forgive himself and in some way she knew it might destroy him.

As she was death marched towards the waiting town car she remembered her dad telling her to never, ever, get in a car with someone wishing you harm, even if a gun was pointed at you. He had told her that people had a better chance of surviving a gunshot wound trying to escape, than if they get into a car with someone wanting to hurt them. She could picture him saying. "Once you are in that car you're as good as dead."

Kit decided she wasn't getting in that car. She also knew she was going to get shot. She saw there were unsuspecting people walking to and from their cars in the supermarket's lot, even though it was frigging 2:00 am in the morning, what was up with that anyway? Kit realized the absurdness of her discombobulating thoughts, noting they would most likely be her last ones.

They were a row away from the town car now and Kit knew she had to do something before she got any closer. She feigned tripping and when the man fought to keep her upright Kit lifted her leg closest to him up and delivered a kick, her kick boxing teacher would have been proud of, to the man's knee. Kit twirled out of his reach as he lost his balance and swore. A burning sensation sliced through her shoulder. She recognized the sting. Kit stumbled for real this time and a blur of a body dove past her. Kit didn't even have time to see who it was since she was still hell-bent to get away.

Large hands latched her hard around her waist. Kit thought one of the other men had grabbed her and she fought against him. Her back collided with a large chest and she was roughly hauled behind a car where she was slammed to the ground. A large hard body fell on top of her. Her breath was knocked from her and she hit her chin on the pavement momentarily stunning her. She tried to move but was trapped.

"You are in such deep shit Kit!" Kit thought she recognized the hushed steely voice of Mikey D. She tried to look up to see his face but he kept her firmly flattened on the pavement. When she was able to draw in a breath she whispered, "Mikey?"

"Yea. Mikey, now shut up until this is over."

Kit's head was spinning. How was Mikey here? Kit listened to the uproar coming from the parking lot. After a full minute of cars skidding to stops, men shouting, and guns popping, the commotion seemed to quiet down. She heard a voice that she didn't recognize yell, "You have her?"

Mikey D answered, "Yea, we good?"

"We're good." The same voice responded.

Kit heard someone else yell, "All clear!"

Mikey D got off of her and then helped her to her feet. He noticed her chin was bleeding, "Oh shit did I do that?"

Kit barely heard him as she looked at the chaotic scene unfolding in front of her. Two sedans had boxed in the town car and three men including the very large one were handcuffed and lying flat on their stomachs in a nearby parking spot. Then Kit had to blink because she couldn't believe her eyes, Jess was delivering the limping man that had accosted her to the men in swat gear stationed near the sedan.

"Jess." Kit's eyes burned with tears just from seeing him. He was here; her Jess was here she thought as she sagged against Mikey's chest. Jess looked towards her and Mikey and when Kit saw Jess' eyes she knew they might not survive this as a couple. His eyes were set and hard, and he looked so mad. She knew how he might react. Kit's heart thumped hard in her chest. She deserved this; she knew what she had done.

Mikey walked Kit towards a group of men in

suits where Jess was already standing talking to them. He refused to look at her as she approached with Mikey D. When she reached them she wanted to bury herself in Jess's arms but he remained quiet, his arms were crossed effectively signaling to her that he did not want to touch her. Kit could feel the furious heat surging off of him and knew it was all directed at her.

"Jess?" She said meekly trying to get him to look at her. Jess turned his back to her and walked away from the group. Kit's heart sank as she watched him go to the group of men wearing swat gear. Kit started to shake and tears filled her eyes and spilled down her face. One of the men in a suit addressed her.

"Ms. Taylor you have some explaining to do."

Kit nodded her head and she wiped her tears from her face as she forced herself to meet the eyes of the man speaking to her. Mikey's arms remained supporting her. Even though she knew he was mad too, she was grateful for his strength, because honestly, her legs were about to give out on her. Kit drew in a deep breath. She knew she had done the right thing. Her plan had been good and if Colt had made it to the hotel room then she had accomplished her goal. If she got in trouble with these government men because of what she'd done, well fuck them! Jess was mad because she had done something that could have gotten her killed.

She knew damn well that he would have done the same thing, if he'd been in her shoes. Well fuck him and these government boys too! Kit's courage emerged and she straightened up, wiping the tears from her eyes.

"I know and I'll be happy to tell you everything I know, but there is a man in need of emergency care and he needs help first."

"I'm assuming you're talking about Colt Andrews?" Another man spoke to her now.

"Yes, Colt. He was badly beaten and I'm hoping he made it to the motel room I got for him."

The same man reached out to shake her hand. Kit looked at it slightly bewildered, and then she shook it. "I'm DEA Doug Foltham, Colt's undercover liaison. He's fine. He's on his way to the local hospital as we speak."

Mikey D looked down at her and spoke. "Bud was waiting at the motel room. He took him to the hospital."

What? Kit's mind was whirling and she was just now realizing she had no idea how Jess and Mikey had known where she was and who had alerted the big guns.

"Looks like I'm not the only one needing to explain things." She said looking at Jess's back but speaking to Mikey D.

DEA Foltham nodded. “Lucky for you we got a call or you wouldn’t have been alive long enough to explain anything! Do you have any idea who you were just dealing with?”

Kit shook her head back and forth. “No, I just had to help Colt.” She said weakly, suddenly tired. “Will he be all right? Can I go see him?”

“Yea, I think your chin needs a stitch and you’ve got blood on your shirt are you hurt?” DEA Foltham handed her a handkerchief to hold against her chin.

“Thank you.” She said accepting the white linen square. “No, I don’t think so.”

Jess looked over his shoulder at her and she welled up again, so much for her fortitude. Her bottom lip began to quiver and she knew she was about to become an emotional mess.

Jess was so angry with Kit that he was afraid to talk to her. He didn’t know what would come out of his mouth. He had regained a small amount of composure now knowing she was safe, so he glanced over at his little, brave, stupid, crazy ass woman who was leaning heavily on his best friend. Jess sensed she was about to crumble and even though he was still upset with her he also wanted to comfort her. He quickly walked back to the group and reached for her folding her tiny frame into his chest. Kit willingly transferred into Jess' welcoming arms and began to sob uncontrollably clinging to his shirt. The other men walked away, leaving Mikey D. with the embracing couple.

"Jess... please don't...be mad, please...try to...understand." Her voice was ragged and her words were pinched out between sobs. Jess smoothed his hands down her back and over her arms. His head rested on top of hers folding her against him.

"Baby stop crying please you're killing me." She heard Jess say. Kit felt another set of hands rubbing her back.

"Kit you're okay, its okay." Mikey D tried to soothe her. She could feel his hand on her back along with Jess'.

Someone approached them but Kit didn't look up. The man said they needed to question her. Jess replied for her, "We are going to the hospital with Foltham and Agent Marks. Can they question her on the way?"

Whoever had asked was satisfied with the answer and walked away.

"Kit we have to go to the hospital, Bud's

there, Colt's there." Kit noticed an edge to Jess's voice when he said Colt's name. "You need to be looked at."

Kit nodded refusing to remove her face from the comfort of his shirt.

"Kit, come on." He took her by her shoulders turning her away from his chest and then tucked her against his side as they walked to the waiting car.

"Wait. I need my wallet and phone." She said.

"I'll get them." One of the men in suits volunteered. When he returned he gave Kit her phones and her wallet.

Foltham drove and another man in a suit sat in the front seat. Mikey D and Jess kept her wedged firmly between them in the backseat. Jess' arm was around her and she partially relaxed bolstered by his presence.

The man in the passenger seat turned around and addressed her. "Ms. Taylor I'm FBI agent McGovern. Could you tell us what happened? Can you tell us from the beginning because we know nothing?"

Kit nodded and began her story. She told them how Colt had saved her life when he was undercover in Jersey. She described what had happened in detail, how he had shot her by accident but had really saved her life. She explained how Colt had to go back to Afghanistan and then when he came back he had to go on a desk job for a while.

She told them that she and Colt remained in touch throughout the year. Agent Marks interrupted her story.

"Ms. Taylor we know about Colt. Tell us about this, today, what happened, how it happened?"

"I will but you have to understand. I owed him. He saved my life, and then had his drastically altered because of that decision. He didn't have to, but he did." Kit was speaking to Jess now who remained silent at her side.

"Okay we get that. How did you end up here?"

Kit took a steadying breath. She explained to them starting from when she had received a letter from Colt and she had written him back. Then a she told them how little under a week later she had received the emails with the pictures of a severely beaten Colt tied to the chair. How the emails requested the money. Kit quickly explained about the USB drive that she had found and had tried to give to Lori her US Marshal, but she was away. Jess' body was tense and she leaned into him begging for his physical support. He relaxed a fraction but sent a silent look over her head to Mikey D.

"I had to help him. I knew what they wanted. I didn't care about the money I wanted to repay Colt. I wouldn't have been able to live with myself if I didn't try."

Kit described how she made three copies of the USB drive. One was still at her house and one she mailed off to the US Marshal's office in Steamboat Springs. She then told them how she password protected each file on the one she gave the 'bad men' and how she used that to barter for Colt's life. She saw Marks and Foltham smile when she described the kidnappers as 'bad men'.

She added that the men weren't too happy when they saw how each account was locked off with a password that only she had.

Jess 'humphed' next to her, "Ya think?" He said under his breath.

Kit continued her story explaining how she gave the men one account password, hoping to show good faith. When they got their first account and saw it was legit, they put Colt in the car and allowed him to drive away. For every minute Colt was gone she'd given them another password.

"How did you communicate with them?" DEA Foltham asked.

"I had bought three burner phones and when they contacted me using my email I changed the rules and told them to call the burner I was using. Then we would make the exchange, so to speak."

"Jesus Kit." Jess was radiating anger now and Kit didn't know how much more he could hear before he lost it.

"Jess, she's safe man." Mikey D said gently.

"Kit please continue." Marks prompted her.

"So once I saw that Colt was safe in the car and driving away I gave them another password. I had put a burner in Colts car too so I called him and told him that I had put the motel keys and the address to the motel under his floor mat. I had left first aid stuff and clothes for him there."

"Wow you were thorough, I'm impressed." Foltham volunteered.

"Once I gave them the second password or maybe it was the third, I can't remember, I knew I could still give them the passwords away from the parking lot, but before I could leave that skinny guy got to me."

Jess exploded next to her. "Got to you. For

God's sake Kit he had a gun in your side. Do you have any idea how easily you could have been killed?"

The men in the car went eerily quiet; Kit's eyes welled with tears hearing the sharp reprimanding outburst from Jess. She sniffled in her tears and then something snapped inside of her. It could have been the relief she felt that Colt was alive or the fact that she was alive, she didn't know and she didn't care. Kit turned to Jess with fire in her veins and unleashed holy hell on him.

"Yes! I know exactly how close I came to biting it. Yes! I know I risked my life. Yes! I know you're mad. Well guess what! Fuck you! You would have done the same thing. I had a good plan. Goal one was to get Colt safe. Accomplished. There was a risk! I knew it! I took it! I'm sorry if you can't handle that I handled something without going all 'I'm a girl...help me,' I did what I had to do and I'll tell you something else buster." God, she was vibrating with rage. Her finger was pushing into his chest as she finished her tirade. "I'd do it again!"

The car had stopped in front of the emergency room entrance and Mikey D had opened his door just as she finished ripping Jess. Kit climbed over Mikey's lap and stomped away from the car.

The four men sat for a second, stunned at

her outburst.

"Wow." Marks said. "She's something else. We could use someone like her."

"Don't even think about it." Jess bit out forcefully. "She's mine and she's not fucking joining any DEA/FBI or any other initial toting agencies!" When Jess jumped out of the car to follow his crazy ass woman it was to the sound of three men laughing inside the car.

Kit walked briskly into the emergency room and ran right into Bud. "Oh God Kit." He pulled her into his arms. "I'm so glad you're okay." Kit pushed away from him.

"If you are going to give me any shit Bud then you can just go join Jess in the car out front."

"Whoa, honey no. I'll admit I was mad at first, scared to death to tell you the truth, but I'm fucking proud of you now! You saved that man's life."

Kit pushed back into his arms. "Oh Bud thank you, thank you for understanding."

Jess walked in to see her snuggled in Bud's arms and Bud gently extracted himself from her hug when he saw Jess' face.

"Where's Colt, Bud?" Kit asked quickly.

“They’re waiting to take him to x-ray. He’s in the back.”

Kit walked through the door and when a nurse tried to stop her she gave her a look that would have put fear in most grown men. “Don’t even think about it, my brother's in there and I’m going in.”

“Who’s your brother?”

“Colt Andrews.”

It wasn’t lost on Jess that she had called him her brother. He knew they weren’t real siblings but if that’s how she thought of him, as a brother that sure sit better with him. He just hoped Colt felt the same way.

Chapter 24

Kit walked through the opening of the curtained room and saw Colt lying in the bed with his eyes, well one eye closed, the other had been shut for him. She leaned over his still form and grimaced over his battered face.

“That bad huh?” He said softly looking up at the woman who had just saved his life.

“Oh Colt.” Kit’s blue eyes glistened with the moisture.

“What did you do baby girl?”

“I saved your ass, bro.” She teased him gently.

“Girl if you ever do something that stupid again I swear I’ll blister your ass.”

That would be my job.” Jess said as he stepped into the room.

Alpha male testosterone swirled in the tiny room and Kit watched how they would interact.

“And you would be?” Colt asked.

“Jess Ryan”

“You’re Jess?” Colt directed that question to Kit.

“He was...”

“I am.” Jess said sliding his arm around her waist very proprietarily.

Colt's one eyebrow lifted in a questioning gesture and his lips slid into a very tiny smile.

DEA Foltham and Agent Marks walked into the room.

“Andrews you had us going crazy. What happened?”

Colt leaned back deeper into his pillow on the upright bed. Kit could tell he was tired and still in pain. “Do you need to do this now?” Kit asked.

Colt's mouth dropped open that she was still protecting him. Even more of surprisingly was his boss, instead of going ape shit on her just smiled.

“No worries Colt, we’ve already seen her in action. Just glad that anger wasn’t directed at me.” Foltham laughed.

“Kit its okay, it’s my job.”

"You can tell them later. Colt you should rest now."

"Actually little girl, I'll rest easier if I get it out now. Okay?"

"Okay, if you're sure."

Colt smiled at her. "I'm sure, but thanks for caring. It's been a long time since I've had someone fighting for me."

Kit beamed at the compliment and Jess's grip tightened on her waist.

She knew she needed to spread the love. She knew she had upset Jess. He was distraught that she had put herself in danger and then on top of that she had just verbally walloped him in front of the other men. The most important fact was that he was there. Somehow he had a hand in her surviving this ordeal and she needed to let him know how much she appreciated him and loved him. So Kit sank back into Jess's muscled chest, her back to his front, wrapping her arms around his arms that were circling her waist. The moment she did that Jess's entire demeanor changed and she felt his muscles relax as he continued to hold her closely to him. Colt began his recounting of events.

"So one of the guys I served with in Afghanistan was in a dive bar that I was in with some of the men I was undercover with. I saw him and as he came towards me I got up quick from where I was sitting to intercept him. He clapped me on the back a few times and called me 'Colt' before I could get him out of earshot. I told him I was using a different name now and I didn't want him using my real one. I told him it was PTSD thing. He bought it but one of the guys heard him call me Colt and started to watch me. I think the one guy recognized who I was. I should have worn a disguise like you had in court." He said nodding to Kit."

"I wasn't a trusted member of the group yet so I wasn't getting much useful information; I think I started to press a little more than I usually do. Anyway I was a dumb ass. I bought Karen Sue a present and I mailed it to her from the post office where I had a secure PO box. When I went back to the box like two weeks later..."

"Wait." Marks said. "Who's Karen Sue?"

"That was my birth name, before Witness Protection." Kit said.

"Anyway when I opened my P.O. box they tazed me, with my box open. I let my guard down, shit I never do that." Colt said his voice dripping with disgust. "They read the letter Karen Sue sent me telling me she had found something. They kind of put it together by going back through old newspapers, plus one of the guys had a contact in

Jersey."

"Beat you bad kid." Marks said

"Yea that they did."

"Kit, I got to tell you. They were pissed at what you set up. Very ingenious, but baby girl, you should never have done it. You put yourself at risk. You know if I had survived and you hadn't, well, it would have wrecked me, bad. It wasn't worth the risk."

Kit moved out of Jess' arms and leaned over Colt's bed running her fingers through his hair that was cascading over his closed eye and pushing it back.

"You're wrong Colt." She said so tenderly that Jess was blasted with jealousy. "You are very much worth it. You gave me a chance to live. I just returned the opportunity."

Kit kissed his forehead and stepped back to Jess as his arms opened and wrapped around her body so she was engulfed in his embrace. Jess kissed her neck and Kit rubbed his forearm letting him know she appreciated his gesture.

A doctor opened the curtain and looked around at the four people stuffed into the tiny curtained room. Before he could protest Foltham showed him his badge and the doctor acknowledged it with a sigh and a nod. “He’s going to x-ray now.”

“Someone has to go with him.” Foltham told the doctor.

Again the doctor just nodded. The doctor placed a clipboard on Colt’s covered legs and turned to Kit.

“Would you allow me to put a butterfly band aide on your chin young lady?”

Kit nodded and the room was quiet as they all watched the doctor administer to Kit's small cut. Kit quietly thanked him when he finished and he left the room. The previous conversations resumed.

“Colt we need to keep you protected. We arrested Mantus and the other men in the car but he’s probably already seen his lawyer and you know what that means.”

“What’s that mean?” Kit asked. “He’s not going to get out is he?”

Colt looked at Marks and Foltham then returned his gaze to Kit. “It means that he’s most likely put a hit out on me and you.” Kit felt Jess’ arm become bands of steel. Her body going ridged with fear.

“Oh God. But they don’t know who I am?” Kit felt a little light-headed. She couldn’t go through this again, she couldn't.

"Bones saw you and they have your cell and email address."

"Not my address. I didn't put my address on your envelope."

"You're right and I didn't write your home address down I had it memorized so you may be safe but you'll need to change your phone number and email right away and get a government techie to wipe your digital history."

"I can have that done." Jess said. Kit looked up at him wondering how he could manage that, but she'd ask him later.

"You also have another thing in your favor." Colt said. "Bones is blind in his left eye and he's right-handed."

The other men nodded but Kit still didn't understand. "How's that a good thing?"

Marks told her. "If he had his gun in his right hand that means he had to keep you on his left side which stands to reason he didn't get as good a look at you as someone else would have. Furthermore it was dark out and he only saw you under parking lot lights which often create shadows which distort images."

Kit relaxed a little. “When will you know if he saw me, you know, enough to identify me?”

“We probably won’t and if they put a hit on you it would be under your Karen Sue name since that was the only information they had.”

“Well, that’s good. I only signed my name K.”

“What about your email account?”

“I used a fictitious name and birthdate when I created it and it’s a benign address, my name isn’t in it.”

“Smart girl.” Marks said.

“I don’t want to go back into Witness Protection.” Kits said adamantly.

“You will if it means you’re safe.” Jess said quietly but firmly.

“Jess I don’t want to move.” Kit was already envisioning leaving everything she had built and more importantly, everyone she loved.

Marks stopped her from speaking further.

“Let's just see what happens. Right now it sounds like your new identity is still working and with that floppy hat and the precautions you took you may well be safe.”

“I hope so.” She whispered.

A nurse and an orderly opened the curtain and stopped short seeing how many persons were in the room.

“We need to take him to x-ray.” The nurse said.

“I’ll go with him.” Foltham said.

“Colt I’ll see you later okay?” Kit said.

Colt nodded but then for some reason Kit saw him look to Jess and a silent understanding passed between them. Jess nodded and gently pushed Kit out of the room ahead of him as the three left the room.

Out in the main waiting room Kit saw Bud and Mikey D waiting for them. It dawned on her that she still didn’t know how they had found her. The men stood as Kit, Jess and Marks approached them.

“How is he?” Mikey D asked.

“He’s gone to x-ray, but he’s talking and already looks better.” Kit told them.

“Listen folks I don’t think sitting here is a smart move. Folthom's already called in the head guys and Colt is going to be moved to a safe house when we can move him. I think you guys should 'get out of Dodge' so to speak, inconspicuously, if you get my drift."

"What about my car rentals, shit! I used my Kit Taylor name."

"We can take care of that." Marks said. "We'll get the cars back and wipe those records. They are only on their sites and not anything public."

"Thanks that would be great."

"Kit we need the rest of the passwords." Marks said.

"They're on my iPhone in the notes section."

Marks took her phone and after a few seconds had emailed himself that note to his phone. Ms. Taylor can we keep your phone? I know you're going to get a new email address and you should, of course, get a new phone number. I'd like to keep this for evidence."

"Yea that's fine." Kit said. "I don't want to testify again." Kit said. Bud's mouth gaped open he had no idea what her former life had entailed, Mikey D did though and Kit saw him smile at her in a knowing way that bolstered her confidence.

"Let's cross that bridge later okay. And Kit...Thanks, and again great job. What you did was crazy nuts but you're both safe and it resulted in a major bust so good job. You know..."

Jess interrupted, "Time to get going guys." Marks and Mikey D burst out laughing. Kit looked at them and just shrugged her shoulders at Bud who was as bewildered as she was.

"I need to say good bye to Colt." Kit said turning to Jess.

"Kit" Marks said. "We've already moved him. "He's being x-rayed somewhere else."

"That's what that look was for?" Kit said looking at Jess. "You knew?"

"I had a hunch, I guess Colt did too."

Kit was silent. She wondered if she'd ever see him again and the thought saddened her.

"Sweetheart, he'll contact you when he can. You saved his life." Jess knew her so well and that gave her a warm feeling. Jess placed his arm around her and led her out of the hospital's emergency room doors.

"We good Bud?" Jess asked.

"Yup all set." Kit had no idea what they were talking about so Mikey D volunteered. "We have a guy picking us up at an airfield outside of town." The men ushered her into a waiting taxi. "We'll be back in Colorado by lunch time."

Kit sat in the back bracketed by Mikey D and Jess while Bud sat in the front. She leaned her head against Jess' shoulder and watched the dark sky turn purple as the sun, still an hour away from rising, was close enough to emerging that it changed the color of the night's sky.

At the small airstrip Kit saw Rick's plane waiting for them. The four of them walked into the Quonset hut building, in front of the one landing strip, where Rick met them. They men shook hands and Rick's gaze settled on Kit. "You're family okay?" He asked.

"Ummm yea, thanks." She ducked her head embarrassed with her lie. Jess quirked eyebrows sending an inquisitive look to her.

"Is this how you got here so fast?' He asked.

"Uhh, yea I had a bit of a deadline." She said not wanting to start up a big discussion.

"Shit." He muttered as he ran his hand through his hair.

Rick settled them into his plane. Bud sat in the copilot's seat. Jess sat in a window seat next to Kit and Mikey D sat in the aisle seat across from Kit. Rick yelled back that he had to put his headphones on and if they needed him they just had to put theirs on and press the red button on the mouthpiece, which hung on an arm off the headphones. Bud had already put his on.

The take-off was smooth and as the plane took off Kit remembered she didn't know how they had found her.

"Guys, how did you find me?"

Mikey D looked at Jess so Kit looked at him too.

"Okay, so when you left those notes on your doors Mikey and Bud knew something was wrong. They got word to me on the plane. I was about an hour away from landing in Los Angeles. I gave them your alarm codes so they could go inside your place and try to figure out where you'd vanished too. Kit I knew it was something hinky. For anything else you would have waited for me. I called your dad to make sure you didn't have a family emergency." Kit started to say something but Jess held his hand up. "Don't worry he doesn't know anything.""

Kit nodded. "It killed me to leave knowing I wouldn't be there for you to come home too."

Jess smiled almost sadly and continued. "They found the letter from Ray."

Mikey interrupted. "At some point can we tell

Bud who Ray was and the history you share with Colt and about testifying?"

Kit looked to Jess who nodded so she said. "How about we tell Bud later? Maybe over dinner later this week, I'll cook."

"Deal." Mikey D said and they both swung their gazes back to Jess.

Jess continued. "So they found the letter you printed from Ray and the letter you printed for me and then they used your password that you'd left and went into your email. When they saw the pictures and emails you received they got back to me. When I got off in Las Angles I changed my flight and chartered a plane to Vegas. Mikey D and Bud did the same and we met here."

"But how did you know where I was?"

"I called in a favor and had the history of coordinates on your phone's GPS, sent to my phone."

"Really, that can't be legal who would do that?"

Jess' eyes flicked to Mikey D and his shoulders sagged ever so slightly.

"What? Tell me now." Kit demanded.

“I called Bess.” Jess told her quietly.

“You didn’t!”

“I had to!”

Kit got quiet and shut her eyes leaning back into her seat. She heard Mikey D excuse himself and put on his headphones to give them privacy.

“Kit, look at me.” Jess said firmly. His hand touched her chin careful not to touch her Band-Aid.

“Babe, please. She’s a computer whiz and had the access I needed to find you. She apologized for the shit she pulled in California. I told her I needed the information because of my girlfriend. She knows the score Kit, I promise. She owed me. Shit! She owed us!”

Kit turned to him. She was all of a sudden so tired. The entire evening's events and the enormity of what she’d done settled into her stomach like a rock and Jess watched her pale.

“Shit!”

He reached into the seat pocket and produced and opened a barf bag. Kit grabbed it and emptied the meager contents of her stomach into it. She mostly dry heaved. Mikey D took off his headphones and watched helplessly as Kit’s body racked violently with her heaves.

"Crap! Is she all right?"

Jess looked up at Mikey D, lines of worry creased his usually handsome face and he shrugged his shoulders as he helped Kit to hold the bag while rubbing her back.

Kit was finally able to lift her head from the bags edge. Her eyes were red and swollen and a few tears leaked errantly wetting her cheeks. Jess handed her a tissue and she blotted her eyes and then her mouth before tossing it into the barf bag. She folded the bag over and Mikey D took it and tossed it in a receptacle near him.

"You okay?" Jess regarded her with concern etching his eyes.

Kit nodded. "I guess I'm tired and then... Then you talked to that woman. Jess..."

"Sweetheart, listen, listen to me. I. Love. You. Only you. It was the quickest way to find you. She's nothing to me. You know that."

Kit nodded and smiled weakly at him. "I need to some water." There was a cooler in the cockpit and Kit got up to access it.

"She okay?" Mikey whispered.

"Yea, I think it's all starting to sink in, then when I said Bess' name I think it put her over what she could emotionally handle. She's tired. I need to get her home."

"Yea she looks beat-up."

Jess nodded.

"Jess, she did have a good plan." Mikey D said hesitating to voice his opinion.

"I know, man. It was smart. I just wish she had felt like she could have confided in someone. Is she that alone that there was no one she could talk to? I thought for sure she felt close enough to you and Bud. It's not healthy for her to feel like she has no one."

Nodding Mikey D agreed with him.

"I wonder if she would have told me if I'd been home." Jess's voice trailed off as Kit came back holding a small water bottle. Jess got out of his seat and sat in Kits isle seat. He reached up and gently pulled Kit down on his lap. He situated her so her back and head could rest on his chest and he lifted the center arm divider so her feet could stretch out onto his vacated seat. He took the bottle from her hand and stowed it in the seat by her feet.

"Comfy?" He asked.

"Thank you Jess. Yes." He kissed the top of her head and within minutes Jess felt her body soften and her breathing even out. She was fast asleep.

Chapter 25

The plane approached Hayden Airport and Jess gently nudged Kit awake. “Hon, we’re landing, I need to buckle you in.” He lifted a sleepy Kit off his lap instantly missing her body contact. He placed her in the seat he had been in and snapped her belt into place.

Leaving the small plane they each thanked Rick and he responded by laughing as he told them they’d get his bill. They walked down the planes steps and outside into the cold February weather of Colorado. None of them had coats on so they quickly walked to Bud's car that was parked in the lot. Bud dropped Jess and Kit off first. Kit hugged both Mikey D and Bud and Jess shook their hands, then she and Jess went inside Kit’s house and up to her apartment. It had not even been twenty-four hours and Kit felt like she’d been away forever. Jess had his duffle and he dropped it inside the apartment door before turning to Kit.

“Kit, we need to shower. Come on.”

He led Kit into the bedroom where he helped her take off her clothes. Kit was self-conscious being naked in front of him after their long hiatus. Which, of course, was ridiculous, considering the amount of times he'd seen her naked and they'd been intimate. Jess grinned at her sudden awkwardness and it only made him love her more. As Kit turned Jess saw an angry red mark underneath Kit's upper arm. He couldn't believe he hadn't seen it before. Jess walked to Kits discarded shirt and picked it up fumbling for the upper sleeve. When he saw the hole he audibly groaned.

Kit had no idea what he was doing with her shirt until she heard him groan.

"Kit you were shot!"

"No Jess I was only grazed, see." She turned her upper arm over so he could see her wound.

"That's a bullet wound." Jess was shaking he was so upset.

Kit stepped to him, quickly forgetting her shyness about being naked. She put her arms around him and felt him calm.

"I'm fine Jess. It hurts a little but I promise I'm okay."

Jess held her to him tenderly.

"Kit, I can't believe I almost lost you today. An inch in another direction and that bullet might have…" He couldn't finish his sentence.

"Please Jess, please don't. I know how close it came, I know how much danger I was in and I'm so sorry I put you in danger too."

"Baby I don't care about me I care about you."

"Well I care about you. I love you Jess. Thank you for coming for me. Thank you for saving my life."

Jess gave kiss a gentle kiss then shuffled her into the bathroom and turned the shower on. When it was warm enough he opened the glass door and placed Kit inside. Then he quickly stripped and joined her. Jess washed and rinsed her hair and then did the same for himself. Even though Kit had slept for two solid hours on the plane she was so physically tired and emotionally drained that she could barely lift her arms.

Jess washed Kit and then guided her gently down to the bench seat in the shower so he could quickly wash himself. When he finished rinsing he saw that Kit was looking at him shyly with an adorable smile on her face. Jess knew that smile well and his heart along with another extremity swelled in anticipation. Jess bent down and gave her a tender kiss.

"We have plenty of time for that later darling." Kit's coy smile turned into a tint pout causing Jess to chuckle as he helped her out of the shower.

Jess wrapped a towel around her and sat her on the closed toilet seat so she could brush her hair while he dried himself off. Then he walked them into her bedroom and helped her put on a tee shirt that she had laying out on her bed, he smiled when he noticed it was his. He then helped her put on a pair of underwear and gently guided her under her covers.

Jess grabbed a clean pair of boxers from his duffle and joined her under the covers. They found a blissful serenity wrapped tightly around each other, his leg draped over hers keeping her close. Within minutes they fell into a dreamless, much needed sleep.

Kit stirred first. She was sore and weighted down; she hazily realized the heaviness on her body was Jess, her Jess, home. She opened her eyes and looked at the handsome man sleeping peacefully on her pillow. She pressed a chaste kiss to his chest, over his heart. When she pulled back she saw he was looking down at her, with a sleepy beautiful face and he was smiling.

"Morning." She said softly. Jess looked over

her shoulder at the digital clock on her nightstand.

"Actually, it's evening. 7:00 pm to be exact."

"Oh yea." She giggled burying her face into his chest, breathing in the scent of lavender since he had used her soap.

They lay comfortably entwined, content to be holding each other again.

"Jess?"

"Ummm?"

"Can we go get Lulu? I miss her."

Jess gave her a kiss on her lips then one on her nose, then one on her forehead before pulling her in for a warm, tight hug. "God, woman, I love you. Yes, get dressed. Let's go."

They picked up Lulu and spent some time with his parents before leaving to spend the night at Jess' home on the mountain. Kit hadn't let her clients know she was back yet so she wasn't expecting anyone. On the drive to his house Jess told her she should close her email account and open another when they got to his house. He also told her it would make him happy, if she would agree to be put on his cell phone plan.

“Kit it makes sense. Your name won’t appear anywhere on the account.”

“But Jess, it's just. I don’t know. I don’t want to freeload off you.”

“How about if we barter.”

“How do you mean?”

“Well, how about if you watch Lulu for me once a week and we’ll call it even. I probably owe you about $800 for the last two months, so you don’t have to worry about paying me for...for quite a while.”

“Jess I’m not charging you for watching Lulu. I love Lulu.”

Jess smiled over to her as he turned into his drive. “I don’t want to freeload off you.”

Kit laughed at how he had turned it around on her and playfully swatted his shoulder.

“Okay, you’re right. It is smart and keeps my name off any contracts. As long as you don’t mind.”

“I was the one that suggested it remember.” He chuckled.

Inside they settled down on his couch and Jess brought his laptop over so they could close her email account and open another. When she opened her new account she again used a fictitious name and birthdate and her email account, like her last one, didn't contain her name.

They cuddled on the couch with Lulu at their feet and watched Monday Night football. Kit could sense that Jess wanted to say something to her and she began to feel anxious that he wasn't taking his usual direct approach.

"Jess, what? I can tell you want to say something. You're making me nervous."

"God Kit, its little disconcerting that you know me so well."

"Disconcerting?"

"Wrong word, sorry...wonderful...but spooky." She smiled at his fixed slip.

"Okay, now tell me."

Jess took a deep breath and muted the TV. Oh-oh, Kit remembered whenever her Dad had muted the TV to talk it was something big.

"I'm concerned you're unhappy here."

"Here? Like here with you?"

"Here, like in Colorado."

"Why do you think I'm unhappy Jess?"

“Are you?”

“No. Why do you think I am?”

“Because you had no one to confide in when this crap with Colt happened.”

Kit blew out the breath she’d been anxiously holding in. She’d been worried about he was going to say.

“Kit I thought you maybe could have told Mikey D or Bud. I know I was in the air...”

Jess took his eyes off her and she sensed he was still holding something back.

“Jess it happened so fast. I had 15 hours. They said not to tell anyone. I just couldn’t. I couldn’t risk them telling the police. I wouldn’t risk anyone getting hurt because of my problem.”

Jess contemplated what she’d said. He looked sad and Kit felt bad.

“Babe you know how much Bud and Mikey D care about you right?”

“Yes, I care for them too, and that’s precisely why I wouldn’t involve them. I wanted to keep them safe.”

Jess shook his head side to side. “That’s exactly how we feel about you, we want you safe too."

"Honestly Jess I still think it was the right decision."

"Would you have told me Kit? Be honest."

Kit thought about it. "I don't know, maybe. Jess...You need to understand how much I love you. I mean over the moon, can't stop thinking about you, you take my breath away, love you. If something had happened to you..." Kit paused. "You have no idea how much I worry about when you're working do you? If I were to ever lose you Jess…" Her voice trailed off.

"I feel the same way about you Kit. When I figured out you were trying to save Colt I was frantic. I was so afraid we wouldn't get to you in time."

"Did you call the DEA guys?"

"Yea, I called a friend when I landed in Vegas and told him what I knew. They put a swat team together in 10 fucking minutes. I was impressed. I knew where you were so I gave them your location and told my friend I was on my way. I texted Mikey and told him where I was headed. I paid the cabby a hundred dollars to not stop for anything, no lights, nothing and that I'd pay for any tickets. He dropped me at the parking lot, which was your last coordinate I was given. I was creeping around the lot when I saw Mikey and Bud doing the same thing. We sent Bud to the motel room. We knew the cavalry was coming but we had no idea what was going on. We didn't know if we'd find you or just your phone; we were blind. My friend knew it might not be anything more than a woman shopping in the market but, I alluded to the fact that you had been involved with some serious shit before so he didn't want to risk that it was nothing. God we were lucky, so friggin' lucky."

Jess ran his fingers through his hair. Kit was feeling awkward knowing she'd caused him so much distress.

"When I saw that man walking with you I about came undone. Mikey had to hold me down. Christ, I could have gotten you killed. You kicked him about the same time that swat team descended on the car. I leapt out from behind the car we were hiding behind and I tackled the guy while Mikey grabbed you."

"I remembered my dad always telling me it was better to get shot than to get into a car because once you were in the car you had less of a chance of surviving."

"Smart man and for the record you were fucking shot!" Kit calmed him with a quick kiss.

"I kicked him using a move I learned in kick

boxing class." She giggled.

"You were awesome."

"You were livid, if I remember correctly." Kit said gently.

"God I was seething. I was so upset that you had put yourself in so much danger."

"I know, but it hurt me Jess. It hurt so much when you turned your back on me when I needed you most."

"I'm sorry. I really am. Kit if you could have felt even half of the terror I was feeling, especially when I saw that man holding a gun to you."

"I won't apologize for doing what I did Jess. I told you I'd do it again."

"I don't agree with you honey. I'll never agree with anything that puts you in danger."

Kit started to argue but he hushed her with a quick kiss.

"However, I get it. I understand why you felt you had to do it. I wish you would have tried to ask for help, but again I get you not wanting anyone else's safety on your conscious. What I need you to understand is that you're not alone, ever. You have friends here."

“Thank you Jess that means a lot to me, and Jess... I’m happy here. Not so much when you’re gone mind you. And just in keeping with this full disclosure theme we have going on here; I feel the same about you Jess, I’ll never agree with you putting yourself in danger. Believe it or not I do know what that feels like.” She slipped her arms around his neck and gave him a delicate, loving kiss.

“I love you Kit. Over the moon love you.” Jess hugged her to him.

“I love you too.” Kit said as she snuggled into his arms.

Jess un-muted the game and Kit knew their serious talk was over.

Chapter 26

5 Months Later

July in Colorado was a gift from God to everyone, including Kit, who loved to be outdoors; hiking, tubing, horseback riding, cycling, and of course, the return of the rodeo! Kit had completed half of the riding lessons that Jess had given her for Christmas. She had a favorite horse, Reno that she rode during her lessons. Kit loved the trail rides the instructor would take them on the best. She also continued with her yoga and kick boxing classes.

Kit was proud of her toned and flexible body; she also loved how Jess couldn't seem to get enough of her. When she was near him he had to be touching her; holding her hand, walking with his arm around her, driving with his hand on her knee. He was always touching her, and Kit would not have wanted it any other way. She craved the contact as much as he did. When his work kept them apart, for those forty-eight hours, they practically melted together when they were reunited.

Kit's business continued to expand as she continued to add new adult and dog clients. In fact it had grown so much that she hired a woman named Liz and her 16-year-old daughter to help her. They would fill in as needed, sometimes walk the dogs, and interact with the adult clients. It gave Kit the flexibility she wanted to actively pursue her other interests. Kit still hadn't forged any new friendships. She had Jess and they spent all their free time together. On nights that she didn't have dogs they'd stay at Jess' mountain cabin, and the other nights they'd stay at her place. They joked that they had a country house and a townhouse.

Bud was still dating his girl, Krissy, and they had double-dated with them a few times. Krissy was a curvaceous, little brunette, spunky, with a great sense of humor and Bud was head over heels for her. Kit could see the feeling was mutual. She thought that Krissy was probably the closest thing she had to a female friend.

There had been no fall out over the whole 'helping Colt' event and her identity had remained secure. She had been relieved to learn she did not have to testify either. Colt was writing her once a month and Jess had resigned himself to the fact that Kit and Colt were always going to have a special bond. He reasoned as long as it stayed plutonic, on both ends, he could deal with her having a brotherly figure in her life. Kit was sketching when she could.

Jess was the proud owner of a few other pieces of Kit's beautiful art, which he displayed prominently in his home. All except her seminude, this was in his bedroom. Kit thought it adorable that whenever someone was coming to his house he'd run to hide the picture under his bed. She teased him as she pointed out that her private parts were tastefully hidden, but he'd simply glared at her and promptly tell her they were not hidden enough.

The only stress that peppered their relationship was when Jess was on the job and the firehouse would respond to a fire or other emergency situations. It started one evening back in March, when Jess did not come home from work at his scheduled time. Kit had become worried and called Bud, who was not working that shift. He told her that their station house had been called in to deal with a fire on a ranch that was threatening a forest line. Bud had said it was bad and some men had been hurt.

Kit sat up all night worried. When Jess finally walked in the door midmorning the next day Kit threw herself into his arms and sobbed. Jess wrapped her in his arms and after he had calmed her down he took her to bed. He made love to her with such tenderness, bringing her to orgasm twice before he found his release. The next day Jess bought her a scanner so she could monitor the police and fire calls. He explained she could listen to it when he was working and then she would know when he was on a call and when they were heading back to the house and therefore, hopefully not worry about him.

This would have been a wonderful solution and as far as Jess knew it was. However, now that Kit knew every time they were active, she was painfully anxious. Those times that Jess and the other men were responding to an emergency were agonizing for Kit. If it was during the day she continued to work bringing the scanner downstairs so she could listen to it. If it were at night she would remain glued near the scanner until she heard that Jess's company was leaving the scene. Those hours ate at Kit and it was during one of those anxious evenings that Kit finally understood how Jess must have felt when she had put herself in danger for Colt.

Kit never told Jess the severity of the anguish she experienced when he responded to a scene. If he came home late she'd pretend she was asleep so he wouldn't know how afraid she'd been. The thought of losing Jess was daunting to Kit. He was everything to her. She knew her fears were escalating and probably unhealthy but she couldn't help the terrifying thoughts that plagued her.

One beautiful day in early September, Kit

felt her house hake. After she made sure her adult clients were safe she ran downstairs to find Maize, Crank and Misty hovering in one of the carpeted alcoves. Lulu stood guard outside of it, uncharacteristically whining. An uncomfortable feeling crept into Kit's gut. Whatever that ground rumbling shake had been, she knew it was unnatural and immense. Kit comforted the dogs but they wouldn't budge from their little cave. Kit bolted back upstairs to her apartment grabbed the scanner and ran back downstairs to the adult day care kitchen. She had three clients that she needed to remain by.

Kit plugged in the scanner and immediately heard overlapping transmissions. After a few minutes she learned that there had been an earthquake causing a cave in at one of the nearby coalmines. Kit was riveted to the scanner listening to the horrific details that passed between the professionals on the scene. Jess and his station house were, of course, on the scene. Her adult day care clients Mr. Owen, Mr. Peterson and Mrs. Channing were glued to the scanner with Kit. She knew they were anxious so Kit struggled to remain cheerful and keep them occupied. The news stations had picked up the story so Kit and her clients sat watching the news and listening to the scanner. A reporter said that there were three known deaths, dozens injured and eight miners that were unaccounted for.

The afternoon slogged on and when her last adult day care client left she ran downstairs to feed the dogs, and after taking them out for a brief after dinner walk she grabbed the scanner and went back up to her apartment to continue listening. She turned the television on her angst was at an all-time high. The snippets of information coming over the airwaves painted a grim picture of the scene. News stations showed black smoke billowing from the mine. Kit kept the TV on mute as she continued to monitor the scanner. A banner scrolling under the TV images read that the walls of the mine were reported to be heavily damage and the owners of the mine were worried that another cave in was imminent. Then Kit heard something over the scanner that caused her stomach to lurch.

"Ryan volunteered. We're suiting him up now, over." The scanner was clicking and buzzing with white noise, but she knew she had heard correctly.

Ryan! Her Ryan! Suiting him up to go where? In the mine? Holy Shit! Kit was beside her self. Along with her fear for Jess' safety a new feeling pummeled her. In that instance, Kit was steaming mad at Jess that he had volunteered. He had chosen to put himself in harm's way; with no thought to how it would affect her if something happened to him.

A blistering moment of clarity seared through

her entire system. Kit knew she owed Jess a huge apology for what she had put him through when she helped Colt. If he survived this she was going to ream his ass for volunteering for such a dangerous mission. After she apologized, of course. Kit's phone rang and she hesitated to tie up the line in case Jess tried to reach her, but she saw it was Krissy.

"Hello."

"Kit, it's Krissy. Are you listening to your scanner?"

"Yes, it's awful."

"I heard Jess's name, he's volunteered for something."

"I know...I...I'm scared Krissy."

"Me too Kit. I'd come sit with you but I can't leave work, we're getting the injured people. It's crazy here."

Krissy worked at the small hospital in town as a registered nurse.

"I know Krissy, thank you. I'm all right."

"You can come here if you want."

"No but thanks, I'm better here, I have the dogs."

"Okay well call me if you need me, okay."

"Thanks Krissy. Umm can you call me if you hear anything?"

"Sure will do kiddo."

Kit's throat began to constrict and her lower lip quivered. She didn't want Krissy to know how upset she was. Her worst fears were becoming a reality.

"Okay... Thanks, bye."

Kit hung up and tears stung her eyes. Why would he volunteer for something so dangerous? Didn't he care about her? Kit knew she had done the same thing to him and he had been mad at her, but they talked about this. He knew she worried. She couldn't wrap her head around why, if he had been upset with her being in danger, would he turn around and do the same thing to her. Kit was furious and crazy worried. If he came out of this unscathed she didn't know whether she would hug him to death or beat him senseless. Right now she was leaning towards the beating.

Kit was irrationally overcome with the daunting thought that Jess must not care for her as much as he thought he did. If he loved her the way he protessed to, he shouldn't want her to experience the gut-wrenching agony she was currently feeling.

Ten minutes later a garbled, “He’s ready to be lowered.” Came over the scanner.

Kit sat curled on her couch clutching the throw pillow to her stomach. She felt so helpless and said a silent prayer. The scanner was eerily quiet and Kit was nauseous with worry. Kit's phone rang and she saw it was Krissy.

“Krissy?”

“Bud just called.”

“Tell me, is Jess okay?”

“They’ve lowered him into a small area to see if he can hand thread the camera through a crevice.”

Kit was silent picturing Jess in the dark mine.”

“Kit, are you there?”

“I’m here. Thanks for calling with the update.”

“Kit you don’t sound so good.”

Kit was silent for a second. “Krissy let me ask you something.”

“Okay, what?”

“What if Bud had volunteered to do what

Jess was doing?"

"I'd kill him. I'm sorry. Honestly Kit, it's their job I'd be upset but..."

"Krissy I sort of feel like Jess doesn't care about me the way he says he does if he could so quickly volunteer for something so dangerous."

Now Krissy was quiet.

"Kit I understand and I honestly have no idea how I'd be handling it, but Jess loves you. He's doing his job. He has explosive experience."

"Explosives!"

"Shit!"

"Krissy you tell me right now!"

"Bud's going to kill me."

"Krissy!"

"Jess is familiar with explosives and if he sees a spot to set off a small explosive that can open the tunnel where they think the men are trapped he has permission to do it."

"Holy Shit!" That tidbit of information was not on the scanner.

"Kit he's the only one with that kind of

experience."

"Oh my God." Kit's voice trembled and she abruptly hurried Krissy off the phone so she could get emotional without her knowing.

Kit struggled to understand why he had volunteered and yet she knew only too well why he had. He volunteered for the same reason she had helped Colt; he had too. Jess had the expertise with explosives, he was a professional firefighter, and he didn't have a choice. He would always help people, even if that meant putting his own life in danger. What Kit had to figure out was if she could stand by him while he did that every time he went to work.

Kit remained next to the scanner and watched the muted television. Every local network was now covering the news of the cave in. Kit lowered the volume on the scanner and listened to the on-site reporter.

A young woman dressed in a skirt and silk blouse, stood holding a microphone using the chaotic scene behind her as a backdrop. Kit could see the police cars and fire engines all with lights still twirling through the black sky. Large portable spotlights had been positioned to cast light on the mine's entrance. Professional men and women were either running to complete a task or huddled in groups at the ready.

"So to recap." The reporter said. "We've learned that an explosive expert from the local fire department, Jess Ryan, has been lowered into the mine. It's our understanding, although this has not been confirmed, that Ryan will be attempting to lower a camera and then detonate a small explosive that would open a sealed off area. We will keep you posted on his progress and our thoughts and prayers are with those trapped miners, their families and Jess Ryan. Back to you Dana."

The main newsroom was now on camera and anchorwoman Dana Buchanan assured the viewers that they would return to the scene should there be any more developments. Kit was a mess of emotional turmoil.

Her real fear for Jess' life was front and center in her thoughts.

She couldn't even fathom not having him in her life. He was everything to her. They could finish each other's sentences. He knew what she was going to say before she said it. He was so in tune with her and she with him that a small touch conveyed volumes of information. Kit could read his every mood by just looking in his eyes. She knew when he was troubled, mischievous and her favorite, of course, was how he looked at her when he was thinking about sex. Her feelings for him made what she had felt for Ray seem immature.

The depth of how strongly she felt for him rippled like a tidal wave through her body and she was bombarded with horrible visions of herself racked with pain, unable to function attempting to live without him. Kit stood from the couch quickly to force the nightmare like thoughts away. She went into the bathroom and washed her face. She needed to get a grip. Jess was alive; he was working, doing his job, and helping people survive. For God sakes he was a fucking hero. So then why did she feel as though he had severed himself from her? That he had chosen his job over her, over them.

Kit shut off the scanner and the television, grabbed her jacket and purse and walked downstairs ushering Lulu into the basement with the other dogs. She needed distance; she needed to figure out these contradicting emotions flooding her. She knew in her heart of hearts that she loved Jess, but did she love him enough to suffer through the countless traumatic events he would ultimately face? Did him putting himself in danger mean he didn't feel for her on the same level as she did for him, like the song said, 'can't breathe without you love?'

Kit reached her front porch and then went back inside to disarm the alarm. She texted Liz and told her she would be away for a few days, sorry for the late notice and that she needed her and her daughter to take over the care of the dogs and adults. Kit got in her car and started driving. She had no idea where she was headed but she knew it wasn't near the mine. When she hit the interstate she pulled over, it was past 10:00 pm and she knew it was late but she knew she needed to talk to Colt.

Colt was not undercover and as he had written her in his last email he didn't think he would be going under again. He was stationed in Texas and was busy aiding border patrols. Kit dialed his number hoping she would not be bothering him.

"Karen Sue?" he answered immediately. Kit smiled that he always forgot to use her new name.

"Kit, yea, hi."

"What's up baby girl, why are you calling me? What's the matter?"

"Colt I need to talk to you, in person."

"Are you okay? Where's Jess?"

"I don't want to talk on the phone okay?"

"Yea, okay do you want to come here?"

"Can I?"

"Of course kid."

"I'm driving to Denver I'll catch the first plane

I can. Where should I fly too?"

"Abraham Gonzalez International Airport if you have your passport."

"I don't."

"Okay then fly into El Paso International. Text me your arrival time and I'll pick you up."

"Thanks Colt. I hope I'm not being a pain."

"Never little girl. Travel safe."

"Thanks, bye."

Kit drove to Denver International. She knew Jess was going to be upset. Then she grimly thought she hoped that he would be upset because that meant he was alive. Kit chastised herself over her negative thoughts. She didn't turn the radio on because she was afraid of what she would hear. She turned her cell phone off too because she knew if she talked to anyone they would try to talk her into turning around and she knew she needed to work this out on her own.

By the time she got to Denver it was after 1:00 am. The airport was quiet and she had no trouble securing a ticket on the red eye that was going to leave for El Paso at 6:00 am. Kit sat in the airport and had no choice but to watch the news, which was on every screen in the waiting area. The first thing she noticed was there were not as many car and lights flashing behind the newswoman.

The anchorwoman was recapping: "Jess Ryan local firefighter blasted a hole into the tiny cavern where eight men were huddled. Their air supply had been close to running out when Ryan detonated the well-placed blast. The mission has been declared a success. All eight men along with Ryan survived. The miners along with Ryan have been taken to General as a precaution. Reports are Ryan suffered the worst injuries as the blast lifted his body and slammed him into a nearby wall. We have been told he is battered but otherwise unhurt."

Kit breathed a sigh of relief and tears prickled her eyes. She placed her palms over her face and kept her face hidden so as not to attract any attention. She breathed deeply some of the fear sliding away; he had lived, he saved those men. She was very proud of him. Guilt imploded within her as she realized he was going to reach out to her and she wouldn't be there. He would not know why. Kit turned on her phone and texted him.

You did great today. I'm not home. I have some things to figure out. It's not you, it's me. I love you, maybe too much. Kit

Chapter 27

It was 3:00am and the chaotic scene at the mine was slowly winding down. Jess sat in the ambulance he refused to lie down telling the EMS guys and his Chief that he was okay. His body had taken a pounding when the small blast had detonated but he'd had on a flak jacket. He knew he would feel a little sore tomorrow but he was perfectly fine. The Chief insisted he go in the ambulance and so to appease him he sat in the back of the rig talking with the EMS guys about the cave in, as they drove him to General.

Jess was proud of himself. He had found the perfect spot to set off the explosion so it didn't cause more of a cave in and it didn't put him in any danger. He also set it so the implosion would kick out towards him and not hurt the men below. After the dust had cleared Jess had looked below him as he dangled off a harness and saw all eight men were alive and huddled together in a tiny protected cavern. When they realized they had just been saved they cheered. Jess had keyed his walkie-talkie attached to his shoulder and told the Chief, stationed above, that the men were all alive, which set up a huge cheer from anyone standing near Command Central. Jess was then lowered further into the mine so he could fit his harness to each man as they were pulled up one by one to safety.

When the last man had been cleared, Jess hooked himself into the harness for the final time and when he surfaced it was to a rousing cheer from the men and woman working the scene. Jess was embarrassed that they were applauding for him. He didn't want the notoriety; it wasn't about him, ever. It was about saving lives. With his feet firmly on the ground Jess unhooked the carabineers holding the harness to the ropes. His firehouse brothers closed rank around him slapping his back and praising him. That's when the Chief had stepped in and told Jess he needed to ride in the ambulance to General, just to be safe.

When he got to General media vans were parked and clogging every conceivable open space available. Jess wanted nothing to do with the press so he quickly dodged the reporters and went inside with two EMS guys mirroring his every step. Once inside he was ushered into the back to a small curtained room where a young nurse asked him to strip to his boxers and then she gave him an open backed gown to put on. The nurse was gushing all over him and made Jess feel uncomfortable so he pretended to be preoccupied with tying his gown.

A doctor came in and as the nurse continued to hover he was thoroughly examined while being asked a barrage of questions. The doctor was satisfied that Jess was okay but told Jess to sit tight because he wanted to take his vitals again when the excitement died down. If they remained the same they'd release him. As the doctor left the room Bud came in followed by Krissy. The young nurse remained nearby and Krissy who out ranked her told her that she needed to concentrate on other patients. Which prompted her to blush profusely as she hightailed it out of the room.

"Jess we were so worried for you." Krissy said.

"I was fine. I've done this before remember?" Jess joked, down playing his role.

"Yea, well it still was nerve-racking and I know Kit was beside herself."

"Shit! I should call her."

Jess realized he didn't have his phone. "Krissy can you get her on your cell for me?"

"Sure." Krissy punched in Kit's number and it went right to voice mail.

"Her phone's not on." She told Jess.

Jess looked at Bud, his intuition telling him something was wrong, plus Kit never turned her phone off. Jess was reminded of the last time she had purposely turned her phone off. Shit! Jess told

Krissy to get the doctor he needed to leave. Krissy left the room and Jess looked at Bud.

"Something's wrong. I can feel it."

"Don't panic man, it might be something small."

"No, she listens to the scanner; I know she worries about me, about us. She doesn't say it but she worries."

The doctor came back in and after declaring Jess fit to leave, Jess changed quickly and Bud drove him back to the station house. They were both still on duty.

When Jess got to the station house there was more back thumping and when he was able Jess found his phone and a quiet spot to call Kit. When he took his phone off sleep mode he saw she had texted him. He opened the text and felt the hairs rise on the back of his neck. 'Not you, it's me... Loves me too much?' His head was spinning and his mind was racing. Where was she? His heart hammered in his chest. He tried to call her but he knew she had turned her phone off.

Jess walked back out to the living room and he sequestered Bud.

"Bud I need you to call Krissy and find out what she and Kit had talked about."

"Okay man, relax okay."

Bud called Krissy and put her on speaker. Krissy relayed to Jess most of her conversation with Kit. At one point she hesitated and Jess told her to tell him everything. So Krissy told him how Kit had said something about him not caring for her that much since he had volunteered for something so dangerous. Bud put a brotherly hand on Jess's arm that had tightened under stress. "We'll find her Jess."

Jess mumbled thanks and walked away from Bud who was holding his phone because Krissy was still on speaker. How could she think that he didn't care for her? She meant everything to him. Jess walked back into the main room just as the Chief called everyone in for a meeting. It was their debrief and after that they would eat and then go clean all the trucks.

The debrief took a half hour while two of the men cooked as they listened so when the Chief finished the meeting the hungry firefighters dug in to their meal. Jess wasn't hungry and told the Chief he needed to shower. The Chief told Jess no problem that he could take his time and clear his head. Jess desperately needed to think, but it wasn't about what the Chief thought he needed time for. Jess was fine with the mining disaster, well not fine, because men had lost their lives and he felt bad for their families. Jess needed time alone to try to process what Kit had meant by 'it's not you, it's me.' How could she even think he didn't love her, didn't care for her? Where the hell was she?

Jess went back to the locker room and tried Kit's cell again, and once again it rang to voice mail. He then texted her hoping she'd get it.

Kit, I'm worried. Where are you? I need to talk to you. Please call me.

He showered and rejoined the men who were lazily talking as they finished their meal of eggs and bacon. It was early morning; the sun hadn't broken through the inky sky yet. The Chief told the men they would take rests in shifts, but at noon it was all hands on deck washing down the trucks, double-checking the gear and resetting everything so they were prepared for the next call.

Jess was due to be off later that afternoon. He was going through the motions, his head not even close to focusing on what he was supposed to be doing. He kept checking his phone and there was nothing at all from Kit. The Chief called him into the office and told him the news stations wanted access to him.

"Chief, no way. I hate that stuff, you know that."

"Son I'm sorry but you have to. The Mayor is

proud of you; you'll be representing our House. We need good PR Jess. We need the taxpayers to see all the excellent work we do in the community. We're proud of you too Jess. You seem a little off. I know it was a dangerous thing you did..."

"I'm fine." Jess blurted out as he shoved his fingers through his hair. "It's Kit. I haven't talked to her. She's gone somewhere and she won't talk to me. I don't get it."

"Oh, woman trouble. You have no idea where she's gone?"

"No, none at all."

"I'm sorry Jess. You know I like Kit. Maybe it was too much for her, you know, what you did. There are some women who can't take that stress."

"I know, but I didn't think she was one of them."

"Well, I'm sure it will work out. Jess interviews at 7:30 am, prime morning news time. Get your head on straight for that okay?"

"Yes, sir thanks Chief."

Kit touched down in El Paso at 7:10 AM and of course the first thing she sees is a TV screen with an anchorwoman speaking to viewers in front of Jess firehouse. Kit pushed closer to the screen so she could read the banner running underneath. The anchor was describing the heroics of a Jess Ryan. She detailed how he had selflessly had himself lowered into the mine and set off a dangerous explosive that could have been fatal if done incorrectly. The anchorwoman was laying on how dangerous the mission had been. Then she said, "And we have that brave firefighter here."

Kit almost lost her balance as her handsome Jess filled the screen. A couple of women next to her were commenting on how 'hot' he was and that 'he could rescue her anytime', and 'I'd love for that man to carry me off.' Kit had to bite her tongue. He didn't look happy though and she knew he had most likely seen her text. Jess was wearing his uniform and his blue eyes popped against his tan skin. His blond hair was slightly rumpled and she watched him nervously thread his finger through it. He was stressed and she recognized she was the cause of it. God, she loved him so much. It hurt to look at him and not be able to touch him.

Kit read the interview:

Anchorwoman: So how dangerous was this Jess?

Jess: It was a well thought out plan. I just implemented it.

Anchorwoman: Were you afraid?

Jess: No I just wanted to help those men.

Kit watched Jess as he continued the interview. She noticed his eyes didn't have their usual sparkle and his smile was forced. Kit couldn't bear to watch anymore. She turned from the screen and walked out the gated security area. Kit stopped and looked around the terminal and saw Colt walking towards her bigger than life. He had a gorgeous smile plastered on his face, his hair was cut short again and he wore a black tee stretched over his muscled arms and faded jeans and combat boots. The man exuded sin.

Kit stood transfixed as Colt approached her. His brown eyes finding hers and a slow grin softening his foreboding bad boy look. Heads turned when he passed and why they wouldn't. Kit recognized how striking Colt was. He was the whole package, gorgeous, great body, and unassuming. He stopped a foot away from her and his eyebrow rose in a cute little question gesture.

"Hi." Kit said suddenly shy,

"Hi." His smile crinkled the crow's-feet at the corner of his eyes. "Flight okay? No luggage?"

"Yes, thank you, no, no luggage." Kit's fragile emotional state caused her eyes to mist up.

"Oh shit." Colt quietly said. He pulled Kit into his beefy arms. "Quick getaway huh? Did something happen with Jess?"

Kit nodded an affirmation into his tee shirt. She heard him sigh.

"Come on let me take you home." He took her hand and they walked in silence to the parking lot where he helped her into his jeep wrangler. The top was down and Kit leaned her head back against the headrest, shut her eyes, and let the early morning sun and balmy breeze caress her face.

Kit opened her eyes and realized she must have nodded off. Colt had turned the engine off and was turned in his seat looking at her thoughtfully. "We're here." He said gently.

Kit smiled at him and looked through the front window at a well-kept town home.

"This is where you live?' She asked the surprise apparent in her voice.

"Yea, do I even want to know where you pictured me living?" He smirked and that made Kit giggled.

"That's my girl. I love your laugh." He gave her thigh a light, playful swat.

Colt jumped out of his seat and came around

to help Kit out even though she was standing by the time he reached her. He took her hand and walked her up the short brick path to his front door. He pulled out a key, unlocked the door and then stood back so she could enter first. As Kit took in his living room Colt disengaged alarm.

"I have alarms in my place too." Kit said almost absentmindedly.

"Good precaution." He said and Kit nodded.

Colt gave her the grand tour. The downstairs living room and dining room areas were decorated with dark leather furniture accented with chrome and glass tables. A large flat screen hung over a fireplace and newspapers and remotes scattered the coffee table. The kitchen had a little used feel to it and Kit noticed it was sparsely equipped for cooking. The appliances were stainless steel and the counters were dark granite and fit with the rest of his downstairs decor. He had two bedrooms upstairs, one was the master bedroom outfitted with a king-sized bed and black shiny furniture. The spare bedroom was void of furniture and Colt just shrugged his shoulders when she gave him a little questioning look. Colt walked her back downstairs and then down another set of stairs to his basement. The basement was a perfect man cave boasting free weights, a bench, an elliptical, treadmill, and a heavyweight bag suspended from the ceiling with a chain. He had a small bar in one corner, a second refrigerator, an unbelievably large flat screen and a pool table. A black leather couch and a black leather recliner faced the TV. Now this room looked like Colt Kit thought to her.

They walked back upstairs and Colt motioned for Kit to sit on the couch. “I can offer you some water but honestly I eat most of my meals out.”

“No, I’m good, thanks.”

“So wanna tell me what’s going on, because I gotta tell you, you have me worried.”

Kit fidgeted and Colt pressed his large hand over both of hers that were knotted in her lap, hoping to calm her.

“I freaked out.” Kit mumbled, embarrassed.

“About what?”

“Have you seen the news this morning?”

“No, I just got off work. I haven’t had a chance, why?”

“Can we turn on the news?”

“Okay, but you’re still going to talk to me.”

“I promise.”

Colt turned on his TV and changed the channel so it was on one of the major news stations. The anchorman and woman exchanged pleasant conversation with a cheery weatherman before the meteorologist told viewers the forecast for lower 48. A banner running below the report read: Earthquake causes Steamboat Springs mine cave in 3 dead. Colt read that and then looked at Kit. “Is that it?”

She nodded, “It’s what triggered it.”

“Is Jess all right?”

“Yes.” Kit’s voice was starting to quiver.

The camera returned to the anchor desk and the newscaster began talking about the mine cave in. The anchorman told the viewing audience how an earthquake had caused the cave in and those three men were dead and eight others had been trapped. He then showed a still picture of Jess as he had been lifted from the mine. The anchor explained how fire fighter and explosive expert Jess Ryan had risked his own life to set off a small explosion that opened a hole large enough to lift the men to safety. The woman anchor commented that Jess was a true hero because the trapped miners had been running out of air.

The station then cut to a commercial and Colt lowered the volume on the television.

"Jess risked his life and it scared you." Colt said softly. It wasn't a question it was a statement.

Kit started crying and put her face into her hands, her small shoulders shook with the violent sobs coming off her tiny frame. Colt pulled her into his arms.

"Kit its okay, he's safe."

Kit regained some composure and wiped her wet cheeks.

"I know and I'm glad. Colt, I don't know if I can go through that again. It's me; I'm a selfish jerk. I ran because I couldn't handle it. Here's the worse part. I yelled at him when he was upset about me helping you."

"Well, that was stupid."

She slapped Colts arm and smiled up at him. "But I did appreciate it." He added with a grin.

"I'm such a hypocrite. I know it, but it doesn't change how I feel. I was barely hanging on listening to the scanner, waiting for updates. Him volunteering to do that, well it made me feel like he doesn't care for me. Not the way I care for him anyway."

"Oh Kar...Kit, it would have been abnormal for you not to feel afraid. As for Jess not caring for you, I can't answer that but I somehow don't think that's the case."

"I know, I swear I know."

"You love him, you were worried."

"I was scared Colt, so fucking scared and not just for Jess, but for me. I kept thinking how awful my life would be without him. He's become so important to me that losing him could break me. Like the 'can't ever be fixed again' break me."

"Kit, have you talked to him?"

"Uh-uh." She shook her head. "I texted him. I'm sure he's worried."

"What did you text him?"

"That I had to figure things out. That it was me, not him. That I loved him."

Colt shook his head. "God, the poor guy is probably out of his mind right now. What do you think you need to figure out?"

"I need to decide whether I should stay with him."

"Oh God, seriously? Kit you just said you're afraid if you lose him it will break you."

"I know. See? I'm so fucking up." She started

crying again.

"Okay listen, little girl, you're overtired and not thinking with a clear head. I have to get some sleep before I go back on duty. You go upstairs and sleep in my bed. I'll take the couch..."

"No way Colt I'll take the couch. I fit on it. You sleep in your bed."

"You sure."

"Positive, if you have an extra pillow and blanket that would be good."

"That I have." Colt ran upstairs and returned with a pillow, blanket, one of his tee shirts and a toothbrush still in its packaging.

"This conversation isn't over Kit, okay? I'm here for you. I always will be, but you and I need to talk this through."

"Okay Colt. And Colt...thanks."

"Sleep kiddo. Then we'll go enjoy a big Texas dinner before I have to head back to work tonight."

"Okay Colt goes get some sleep, night, well day." Kit giggled

"Yea, day, funny girl." Colt grinned at her.

Chapter 28

It was 10:00 am and Jess halfheartedly joked with his firehouse brothers that he had fulfilled his interview quota for the year. The guys had been great and as different networks in the driveway in front of the station house interviewed him, they had gone about their work in the background off the camera view. The Chief had been pulled in for a sound bite and a couple of the guys had added their praise as well, which the news people ate up.

Jess wasn't even close to being off shift yet and he was starting to feel the effects of working through the night. The adrenaline rush had ebbed away leaving him feeling tired and now his body was aching reminding him that he had taken a good hit. His mind was bombarded with so many scattered thoughts regarding Kit. Jess knew he needed to keep busy. He started to clean the rigs tool chest, but his mind kept wandering back to her text and to what Krissy had told him. He did love her and she knew he did. He couldn't understand why she'd just leave. His emotions were on a short leash and ranged from being pissed that she'd take off without talking to him, too worried sick not knowing if she was safe. He thought if she would just call him he'd at least know what he was dealing with, what she was dealing with.

His phone was vibrating in his pocket and Jess reached for it quickly, praying it might be Kit. The number wasn't one he recognized and was an out of area code.

"Hello." Jess said thickly trying to push the sleep from his voice.

"Jess, this is Colt Andrews. I've got your girl here."

Jess went still; fear throwing what little control he had left out the window.

What the fuck! Jess almost screamed into the phone, but because a couple of the guys were nearby he reined in his anger and walked to a more private place to have the conversation. He knew it could get ugly.

"Is she all right?" He asked stiffly. His mind was working at warp speed imagining her finding comfort in his arms.

"Physically she's fine. Emotionally she's a mess."

"What's going on Colt?"

Colt could hear the tension in Jess' voice. "Jess she's upset because you volunteered for a dangerous job and she feels like that's an indication that you don't love her."

"That's fucking bullshit."

"Yea, I agree but that's not all. She's not sure if she can handle the stress of you always being in danger, and before you go all bat shit she knows she's a hypocrite for what she put you through helping me and she's beating herself up."

"Oh God." Jess was quiet.

"Listen she's safe. I just wanted you to know. I'll talk to her some more. She just flew in a few hours ago. I work nights so we're going to bed now."

Jess inhaled sharply.

Colt heard and instantly understood what he was probably thinking. "In separate beds, man. She loves you."

"If she didn't?"

"Love you?"

"Yea."

"Do you want to go there man?"

"No, I guess not. I appreciate your call. I'm sick over this. I want to talk to her. I need her to know I love her."

"Yea I hear you. I'll try my best okay. I'm not the greatest when it comes to woman stuff."

"She trusts you Colt."

"I know. Jess, I'm not going to tell her I called you. I just wanted you to know she's okay."

"Thanks, where are you anyway?"

"El Paso Texas"

"Shit, when she wants distance, holy crap she gets it."

"Yea, she's something else." Colt agreed. "Jess, for the record, great job on rescuing those men yesterday."

"Thanks, group effort." And there it was in a nutshell, why Colt liked and respected the man his Karen Sue loved. He was a man's man, quiet, unassuming, an unsung hero, well until this morning anyway. Colt figured Jess didn't bask or probably even like being in the limelight. He was a good guy. Colt realized he and Jess shared many personality traits and he reluctantly thought that if circumstances were different they could probably be good friends.

"Okay well gotta catch some shut eye. I'll try to get her to call you."

"Thanks and Colt...I'm glad she has you, you know as a friend."

Colt chuckled at the unspoken meaning.

"Me too man and don't worry, I know she's yours."

Jess pressed end on his phone and although he felt better knowing Kit was safe. He was concerned over what Colt had told him. At least now he had some insight. The main problem was that it wasn't something he could fix. Like her text had said it was her not him. Jess knew he wouldn't be changing jobs. He wouldn't stop helping people in danger. He loved what he did and he'd worked hard to achieve his status as a bomb expert, his smoke jumper's instructors certificate, and he was in line to someday be Chief of the company.

Jess got off work at 3:00 pm and made the painful drive to Kit's to pick up Lulu. Jess knew she wouldn't leave the dogs unattended and Liz answering the door didn't surprise him in the least. What did surprise him was when she flung her arms around his neck and thanked him for saving the miners. Jess humbly told her he was just doing his job. She then asked where Kit was and he had to pretend that he had no idea where she was, in case

Kit checked in with her, which he knew she would. The look of shock that came over Liz's face said it all.

He quickly gathered Lulu and headed home. He called his parents after he showered for the second time that day. He fed Lulu and made himself a grilled cheese. Then he sat outside on his deck trying to pull himself together. He loved her so much and he began to prepare himself mentally that he might lose her. Short of quitting everything he loved to do, and his source of income, he couldn't give her the peace of mind she obviously needed.

Jess fell into his bed before the sun had even gone down and sooner that he thought possible his body succumbed to its exhausted state. His sleep, although not restful, was rudely interrupted. During the evening a forest fire had broken out in a heavily wooded area in Colorado Springs and he and his new Smoke Jumpers team had been called in. It was 9:00 PM; Jess had only gotten a few hours of shuteye. He jumped out of bed and took a quick shower. Grabbing his jumpers' duffel that he kept ready, he called his dad to come get Lulu and hastily drove to Hayden airport. In the small airport he met up with Dusty, who was part of his team. Dusty was nervous, but excited, this would be his first Smoke Jump. Jess remembered his first jump and he gave Dusty a reassuring pat on the back letting him know, he knew how he was feeling.

They were flying into Denver where they would meet with the rest of his team. From there his team would be helicoptered to Colorado Springs.

Chapter 29

Kit woke to the hum of the air-conditioner kicking on. She forced her swollen eyes open and glanced at the clock in the kitchen. She couldn't believe she had slept so long. She lay on her back staring at the ceiling. God she missed Jess. Her heart felt like it had a hole in it and she ached to feel whole again. She got off the couch, folded the blankets, used the bathroom and went to make coffee, which she soon discovered there was none. Geez, Colt you need a woman to domesticate this place. Kit giggled at the thought of Colt bending to any female's whims.

Colt walked down the stairs, it was early evening. Colt had been up for a while and had already tipped toed past Kit to work out in his basement before showering. When Kit still hadn't shown signs of waking, he lay on his bed and watched TV until he finally heard her padding around downstairs. He had to get something to eat and feed Kit too before he went to work. He wasn't used to houseguests and when he saw Kit looking exasperated at his meager food offerings in his kitchen he laughed.

"Colt, this is ridiculous. You have no food, at all."

"I have peanut butter!" Colt told her indignantly.

"Oh God, don't you ever eat at home?"

"I eat home all the time, take out." He chuckled.

"Hardy' har-har." She shot back at him, smiling.

"Get dressed little girl, we're going to eat."

Kit went into the downstairs bathroom and changed back into the only clothes she had. She washed her face, brushed her teeth, then her hair. When she came out Colt had his keys in his hands and he hustled her out the door and into his jeep.

The late afternoon sun was much hotter than what Kit was used to and she groaned when she stepped into the breath sucking humidity. Colt laughed.

"Little different from Colorado, huh?"

"I'll say. How can you stand it?"

"I love the heat. I have my best workouts mid-day. I get a great sweat."

Kit groaned again. “I’d never go outside.” She said. She pictured beautiful Colorado with its perfect summer weather.

Colt drove them about a mile away from his home before he pulled into a lot next to a shabby looking pub.

“Really?” Kit asked.

“Promise, it’s a hidden gem. Best Tex-Mex food around.”

“Okay, if you say so.”

“I say so.”

Colt placed his hand at the small of Kit's back and guided her inside. His touch was light and she knew he was being a gentleman and not sexual. She realized Colt's touch didn’t stir any passion within her the way Jess’ touch did. It was like a lightning bolt shaking her. One of the best looking and nicest guys she knew had his hand on her back and all she could think of was Jess.

They sat in a booth across from each other and he handed Kit a menu.

“You don’t need the menu?” She asked when he didn’t pick his up.

“Nope, I always get the Mexican burger. I

love it."

"Umm that sounds good. I'll have that too."

"The waitress came over and greeted Colt by name and asked if he wanted the usual and he told her two, ordering for Kit as well. When she left Colt leaned back in his seat and got comfortable.

"Kit let's talk about how you're feeling." He then laughed out loud. "God that sounded so girly." He said and Kit laughed.

"My feelings, huh, tough guy?"

"Yea." He was grinning.

"I already told you what I was feeling. When I heard he volunteered to go into the mine it hurt. I felt that he hadn't thought about me, about us, which I'm second in his life and I always will be."

"But you know you're not."

"I think I am Colt."

"You're confusing what he does for a living and the man Jess is, with his relationship he has with you."

"What do you mean?"

"Okay I thought about this for a while before I went to sleep. You love him right?"

"So much Colt."

"He loves you right."

"He says he does."

"He does...Kit, Jess has worked hard to become as accomplished as he is in three different professions. All three are rooted in saving lives. That's Jess; it's his thing, his passion. He doesn't look at it as putting himself in danger. I'm sure he knows it's dangerous, but he's not stupid. Part of the reason he is so good at what he does is because he is able to keep himself and his team, his firefighting brothers as safe as possible when he works."

"I know. I understand how good he is. I'm proud of him. It's insane, I'm nuts."

"You're not, kid. It's understandable that you worry when he's on a call. What you need to understand is that Jess is not going into these situations blind. He's trained for this. Everything is planned out. I guarantee if it was a bad situation something Jess might not survive; first his Chief would never let him attempt it and second, Jess would figure out another way to get the job done. He doesn't have a death wish. There is nothing more that he wants than to come home to you, his anchor, especially after something tough. Kit how he's wired is probably why you love him so much. It's a huge part of him."

The waitress brought their food and Kit pretended to eat as she thought about what he said. It made sense and she wished she had thought to talk to Jess about it way back when he'd bought the scanner. Instead she had bottled up her feelings because she didn't want him to know she was worried.

"Colt do you think it will get easier? You know when he's on a job?"

"I honestly don't know. I suppose it's never easy, and you'll always be anxious. But Kit you have to have faith in him."

Oh God she slapped her forehead. Suddenly all the horrible fears regarding Jess' job lifted from her leaving her thoughts clear. She realized the most important fact, the only thing that mattered that had always been right in front of her; she loved Jess, regardless.

"Oh God Colt I've fucked up. He's going to hate me."

"Kit he doesn't know what's going on. He deserves an opportunity to talk to you."

"You're right. I've been selfish, running from him. I was just so scared. I'm still scared. I know that I could lose him every time he goes out on call. I don't know if I can handle losing him."

"God woman, you're sitting here hundreds of miles away from him now. Can you honestly say you'd rather let him go, walk away from him because he might, might be killed someday? That makes no fucking sense!" Kit's head swam with the daunting reality of what her leaving Jess abruptly had presented.

"Oh Colt. You're right, you're so right. Will you drive me to the airport?"

"Yea, come on. Let's get you home to your man."

"I have so much to tell him."

"Are you going to call him?"

"No, I want to talk to him in person I need to talk to him face-to-face. I can read him better if I see him. God he may be so mad at me that he won't want to talk to me."

"That sounds nice."

"What, being mad at me?"

"No...Being so in tune with someone that you can know what they're thinking just by looking at them."

Kit thought for a second before answering. "Yea." She smiled goofily at Colt. "It is."

Colt drove Kit to the airport and walked her in. He gave her a brotherly peck on her forehead and warm hug before watching her go through security. Before he could text Jess, just to give him a heads up that Kit was headed home, his phone rang. An emergency at one of the border crossings had him running for his car and all thoughts of reaching out to Jess were forgotten.

Chapter 30

Jess

Jess sat on the little prop plane and ran through a mental list of things he needed to do when he got on-site as the team's leader. He was having trouble concentrating because his thoughts kept returned to Kit. It was 10:30 pm and he hadn't heard back from Colt, which surprised him. He knew he had to already be at work. He immediately thought that maybe Colt didn't have anything positive to tell him so he just wasn't contacting him. Jess decided he would send Kit another text, the pilot said they would get service on the short flight. As he rummaged for his cell he thought of all the things he wanted to say to her, most importantly how much he loved her. After a good two-minute search Jess realized he had left his phone on his nightstand. Shit! He thought about asking Dusty for his but Dusty was already asleep.

Jess and Dusty arrived in Denver at 11:15 pm and met up with the rest of their team. There were eight in all and all in pairs from the same area, he and Dusty from Steamboat, Ben and Jeff from Encampment, Wyoming, Denny and Luke from Manitou, Colorado, and Bess and Phil from Denver. Two months ago Jess had received a call from his commanding officer of the Colorado based smoke jumpers. He requested that Jess take Bess on his team. He knew about the complaint Jess had lodged about Bess and he didn't want that to be an issue. Jess said he was fine with it as long as she focused on their mission and didn't overstep his personal boundary line again. She had helped him find Kit.

The group shook hands and Bess sidled up to Jess causing him to tense up.

"Thank you Jess for giving me this chance."

"You're a good smoke jumper Bess I never wanted to hurt your career."

"I know I was such an idiot. How's your girlfriend? Everything turn out okay?"

"Yea, it's good. Thanks for getting me that info. It saved two people's lives."

"Good, good to know." Then Bess moved away from Jess and walked with Phil towards the private helicopter pad.

Dusty gave Jess a little 'what's up?' look and Jess walked over to him and told him it was all good. He quickly and quietly explained that she had helped him when Kit was in trouble back in January and he was returning the favor. Dusty was pleased with the answer because he smiled and clapped Jess on the back saying, "Good man, cause I'm not wanting anything to do with your girl being upset again. Damn near killed me."

Jess smiled sadly. Yea, his girl, right! God if they only knew the turmoil he was feeling right now. He loved that everyone loved her. They had been through so much already. He wished he could talk to her but now it was all about the fire and keeping his team safe.

The helicopter took them to a little airport in Colorado Springs where they were met with a sheriff who transported them in a van to a remote motel that was a near the fire. They all got out and checked into their rooms that had been set up for them. The Sheriff that drove the van said he'd be back at o-600 to take them to the command post. Jess instructed his team to get some sleep, be packed and to meet in the lobby at 5:45 am.

Kit

Around 9:00pm Kit caught the last flight that evening out of El Paso. Unbeknownst to her Jess too was also in the air. Unfortunately Kit's flight went to Cleveland and then Charlotte so by the time Kit landed in Denver it was after 6:00 am. She had no idea Jess had been called away the night before. She hadn't slept much on the plane, partially because she had slept during the day at Colt's but mostly because she was worried that she had driven Jess away with her selfish behavior.

She got into her car loving the cool crisp morning air that was so very different from El Paso. She turned her phone to find she had missed calls from Krissy and Jess and one text from Jess that he had sent yesterday. Jess had not called or text since last night and Kit knew he was probably hurt and angry. Kit knew she had no one to blame except herself if he was through with her. Kit text Colt to tell her she had landed.

When Kit arrived home it was to an empty house. Liz left her a note that all was well and she hoped Kit enjoyed her trip. Kit trudged up her steps anxious and really nervous to call Jess to ask if they could talk. She plopped down on the couch and pulled out her phone. She dialed Jess' number and it rang to voice mail. She left him a message that she was back and she hoped they could talk. Kit knew Jess wasn't working or Lulu would have been at her house. She took a shower and prayed her phone would ring.

As time slogged by Kit's fears escalated. She

decided to call Krissy maybe Krissy could tell her where Jess was or, God forbid, if he'd already written her off.

"Kit!" Krissy answered the phone out of breath. "Are you home now?"

"Yes, I got in a couple hours ago."

"Where were you? We've been so worried."

"Umm it's a long story and I promise I'll explain everything but right now, umm do you have any idea where Jess is?"

"Shit girl, where have you been?"

"On a plane, why?"

"Kit there is a major fire in Colorado Springs; it's all over the news. Jess' team was called in."

"Oh my God! When?"

"Bud said he got called in last night."

"Oh wow, okay, I didn't know I was on a plane all night."

"You need me to come over or anything?" Krissy asked.

"Oh no, no I'm fine. I'm going to catch up on some things here. Um Krissy, if you hear anything, you know from Bud about Jess call me okay?"

"Promise girlfriend takes care and glad you're back."

"Yea, me too, thanks."

Kit hung up and turned on the news. Krissy was right, the fire was huge and the coverage of it was pre-empting all regular scheduled programs. Kit sat transfixed to the TV. She was worried for Jess but what Colt had said made sense. Jess would never put himself or his team in a situation that was too dangerous. He was smart and well trained. He was in peak physical condition. Kit sat back on her couch and watched the news reports. Kit knew when Jess was fighting a fire in the forest he did not take his phone but she also knew if he could, if he wanted to, he would call her at night.

Chapter 31

Three days later.

Kit had resumed her jobs of caring for the dogs and her adult day care drop ins, but like many Coloradans she was glued to the TV about the forest fire which continued to rage. Bud and Mikey D called regularly to check on her but they never mentioned Jess, or asked where she had gone. They told her if she needed them they were there for her. She felt like they were cooler to her and she understood they were upset that she'd just taken off, again, without telling anyone where she was going. She knew she'd have to earn back their trust.

She had not heard from Jess and this wouldn't have worried her except Krissy said Dusty's girlfriend had spoken with him. So Kit knew Jess had had some downtime and cell service. Kit felt like her world was unraveling. She was suffocating in a blanket of self-pity. Colt called her and when she told him about Jess being at the fire he said he'd heard about the fire on the news. When Colt asked if she'd heard from him she'd told him no and then started crying, saying that she'd gone too far and pushed Jess away this time for good. Colt told her he didn't know why Jess wasn't calling her but he did tell her that if she loved him, she should give him the benefit of the doubt. Maybe he couldn't call her. He was, after all, the team leader and he was working. Kit thanked Colt for the pep talk and he laughed telling her anytime and to keep her chin up.

It was 7:00 pm and Kit had dozed off in front of the TV. When she awoke it was to hear that the fire had spread even further up the mountain. It was now threatening many homes and the news showed people packing their cars with their most precious possessions. The good news was that heavy rain was predicted and that would help fight the fire. She was halfway listening to the TV, thinking for the millionth time about what she'd say to Jess when they talked, when she heard the news anchor say they had a breaking report from the scene of the forest fire in Colorado Springs.

A young man dressed in jeans and a denim shirt held a microphone waiting to be cued. His backdrop was obviously far away from the actual fire but the viewers could see a trail of fire snaking up the wooded mountain behind him. The sun had lowered enough that the mountain looked dark and the contrast of the red and orange line of fire was easy to see.

"Yes, thanks Jim." The on sight report said

acknowledging the pass to him.

"We've just learned that command lost contact with a team of smoke jumpers about two hours ago." Kit's head snapped to the TV.

"The team was last heard to be up on the south side of the mountain. From what we were told their mission today was to set a back fire a half mile up the mountain to stop the progress of the fire on that south side. No word as to if they accomplished this before they lost contact."

Tears filled Kit's eyes and she wiped them furiously so she wouldn't miss anything on the television. The reporter continued. "The team of smoke jumpers consists of men and women from our own state of Colorado along with two from Wyoming and get this, its team leader is Jess Ryan, the same Jess Ryan that just recently saved the miners in Steamboat Springs. There are seven other jumpers with him and as of now, all eight, including Jess Ryan are unaccounted for. I'll try to find out their names. We're all praying for rain out here and now we should added those eight smoke jumpers to our prayer as well. This is Greg Burg on site in Colorado Springs. Back to you Jim."

This couldn't be happening. Kit fought the tears she pushed down the panic. Jess was smart. He was the best, she had faith he'd get his team to safety. Kit sat stunned on her couch. Her phone rang and she saw it was Krissy.

"Hello."

"You heard, I can tell by your voice."

"I just heard."

"They'll be okay Kit."

"I hope so. I've been such a fool Krissy."

"No, you have realistic fears. I do too, anyone dating or married to someone with jobs like our guys have those same fear."

"I wish I'd never bolted. I wished I'd stayed and talked to him."

"You'll get your chance Kit."

"Thanks for calling Krissy."

"Call me if you need a shoulder Kit."

"Thanks."

Chapter 32

Jess

Every morning his team had either parachuted or been choppered into the middle of the fire, where trucks and other firefighters couldn't reach. They would fight the blaze from within the walls of the fire. When they finished for the day a helicopter would pick them up or they would hike out. Except last night they'd had to spend the night on the mountain because it had been too dangerous for a chopper to land and they were too far to hike any place to be picked up. His team was tired but doing a great job and Jess was proud of them. The fire continued to damage homes and because of strong winds was changing paths unpredictably every hour. A storm was slated to roll in that night and hopefully the heavy rain, that was being predicted, would douse some of the raging fire and wet the dry timber to slow it down so that it could be brought under control.

Jess hadn't talked to Kit for five days if his count was correct. He probably could have borrowed someone's cell but the truth was he and his entire team was dropping into their beds; or like last night on to their sleep sacks. Jess didn't want to have a heavy conversation with her when he was physically dragging. The other reason he hadn't reached out to her was that he was afraid. Afraid she would tell him they were done. If she was going to break it off with him she was going to have to do it to his face.

Jess keyed his walkie -talkie asking his teams of two to report in. He was never far from his team but he still insisted they communicate regularly. Each team had walkie-talkies that were linked only to each other. His walkie-talkie was also linked to the command center. Jess and Dusty walked the line of timber that they had cut down to set as a back burn. They'd been felling trees and digging ditches all day. He knew his team was worn-out, especially since spending the night on the mountain required that everyone had to take turns at standing guard.

The teams of two reported back that they were ready to set the back blaze so Jess started the countdown over the walkie-talkie. Dusty, his partner had the long lighter at the ready. The first few minutes of a back blaze were the hardest to contain, a gust of wind, a branch not properly placed, a ditch not dug deep or wide enough all these things could cause the fire to move in a different directions than intended. "Light 'em." Jess called over the walkie-talkie and one by one his team yelled, "Lit." "Lit" "Lit."

Jess and Dusty managed their portion of the back blaze by walking back and forth pushing errant branches back into the blaze, shoveling dirt over little fires that fell over the barrier ditch. Jess' walkie squawked. "Jess Phil's down, help." It was Bess. He left Dusty watching the blaze and ran to where he knew Bess and Phil were. When he reached them Bess was leaning over Phil who was on his back with a heavy limb lying on his lower body. "What happened?" Jess asked Bess. "It didn't fall the way we thought it would. I swear we did everything right Jess."

"It's okay Bess let's deal with Phil. This shit is unpredictable, you know that."

Jess looked around and grabbed one of the small power saws they used to cut down the trees. He quickly used it to cut the heavy limb off of Phil's lower body so he and Bess could lift it off of him. Phil was quiet and Jess could tell he was not vocalizing the pain he was in because he didn't want to scare Bess. Jess bent to feel Phil's legs and realized Phil's lower right leg had been broken.

"Phil, we know this hurts man. Here swallow this." Jess gave him two Advil and quickly used the saw to create a makeshift splint. He then secured it to Phil's leg.

"Listen the good news is the break isn't compound."

Phil grunted and Jess saw the sweat popping out on his face. His skin looked pale.

Jess's walkie squeaked again. He heard Denny. "Jess winds blowing up here, really blowing. We've lost containment."

"Jess keyed his mike, get to Phil's spot he's hurt."

"Roger that."

Crap! Thought Jess they'd lost containment on the one section. Just as Jess began to think about how to move Phil the trees above him started blowing and before Jess could warn his team, swirling gusts ripped through the treetops that catapulted the fire sending it jumping over the man-made barriers. The trees above them lit up like fireworks and Jess knew they were in deep shit. He yelled into his walkie.

"Everyone out now! Meet at point B." Jess threw Phil, who thank God only weighed about 180 over his shoulder, Bess grabbed Jess' pack, hers and Phil's and they trekked down the mountain towards one of their planned exit routes. Jess was relieved when the other teams and Dusty converged simultaneously at the designated meeting spot. The sky was sprinkled with burning leaves that were floating around them like confetti.

Jess lowered Phil to the ground and Phil grunted in pain. Jess quickly told his team the plan he had formulated. Heading down the mountain was not an option anymore the fire was out of control.

"Okay listen and listen good. We're going to head back up the mountain."

"Up?" Dusty said

"Yea, up. There's a creek up there that runs strong. There are also rock formations on the side of the mountain near the creek. There may be some little caverns we can hide in till this blows over. We may have to split up to fit in those little holes and for God sakes check for animals before you go diving inside one because they're looking for safe cover too."

His team was stoic and Jess recognized they were frightened. Jess calmed them by turning their focus to Phil and making sure they were transporting him safely. The team took turns carry Phil. Two of them interlocked their hands to make an arm seat while someone else carefully held his broken leg, which Jess had stabilized with cut wood. There were no trails to follow and Jess used his compass and the laminated map he had to keep them heading in the right direction. The wind was beginning to blow stronger, bending treetops and aiding the red flames to move even faster through the thick forest. Jess knew the rain would come down in buckets once it started but now they were kept busy dodging fluttering pieces of fiery tinder from above.

They stopped under a ledge to catch their breaths. They'd been climbing steadily upwards and it was rough terrain. Jess tried again to radio to command post. Since Phil's accident all he'd been getting was static. He knew through his training that sometimes this happened. They may have moved command center and now they were out of range, there could be a wacky electrical charge in the air; there were a ton of reasons. He was trained to handle this. His main concern was everyone's safety and keeping Phil stable until he could receive medical attention.

The smokey forest was filled with eerie glowing shadows from the fire as the night began to engulf the weary group of eight. Jess knew because they hadn't checked in that they were going to be reported missing. God this is all Kit needed to hear. He had hoped he could get his team back before it made the news. His team was showing signs of stress and Phil had thankfully passed out from all the jostling his leg was taking. Another team member had to hold his back up. Jess surveyed the map and calculated they had to travel upwards about a half mile and then they needed to swing to the right for another half mile before they reached the creek and the safety he hoped to caverns would supply.

The group started moving again. The people not carrying Phil used their flashlights and helped clear the trail. Fire crackled around them and at one point they had to belly crawl under a tree that had fallen and was ablaze. Phil had to be dragged under the tree and Jess knew the man was in serious pain. The fire was chasing them. Their faces were red from being so close to the intense heat and Jess told his team to put on their oxygen masks. He and Bess helped Phil with his. The fire was gaining on them and his team was becoming skittish. He knew they were counting on him and he was not going to let them down.

Jess could hear the creek but he couldn't see it. Trees were falling all around them. He knew if he could get them to the creek they had a good shot of surviving. Denny was point person and yelled back that he was at the creek. The rest of the team made their way to the banks of the creek with Jess bringing up the rear. He had the men ease Phil to the ground and as the fire crackled around them they squatted in a circle keeping Phil in the middle to protect him from anything that might fall from the trees.

Jess had to yell over the roar of the fire all around them. “Okay here’s the plan. In pairs, you walk to the creek's edge and look for a little cavern or anything that will afford you and your partner protection. No one’s goes further than 100 steps up or down the creek or twenty steps into the woods.” An ominous thundering crack sounded above them and they looked up to see a giant pine tree, engulfed in flames slamming through smaller trees like dominos aiming right where they were huddled.

Jess yelled, “Jump.” He grabbed Phil by his collar and he jumped off the two-foot embankment landing him knee-deep in the cold, fast moving water.

Phil grunted clearly in distress but at least he was safe. Jess yelled to his team, “Hug the bank!” and then he pressed Phil, who was wet, against the curved bank and threw his body on top of him.

The huge flaming tree crashed with a deafening boom across the creek bringing smaller trees with it. Embers flew in every direction. The tree, which was engulfed in flames, lay sizzling across the creek, its limbs hissing as they poked into the cold water. Jess heard someone cry out in pain and his heart seized. Jess helped Phil anchor himself to the bank, so he didn’t wash down the fast moving creek and called out to his team. The water was freezing cold and the only light guiding him was what the fire provided. Everyone reported in responding to Jess calling for a head count. Even though he couldn't see them Jess sighed in relief. Jess yelled, asking if anyone was hurt and Dusty yelled back that he thought his arm was busted.

Jess shouted above the roaring flames dining on the trees, "Find a safe spot to hole up. Groups of two, stay within the confines of the original order. If you are safe from the fire no one moves until dawn or until I give the signal that includes taking a piss."

Jess could see movement through some of the fiery limbs and satisfied that his team was following orders he concentrated on getting Phil someplace safe. He dragged Phil through the cold water counting his steps. He knew the icy water would help with the leg swelling and he hoped he could find a place large enough for the two of them so he could care for him safely.

About forty steps by his count, the water had carved out a deep dirt ledge in the bank. Jess placed Phil on the rocks nearby and took his shovel and dug deeper into the side of the bank. Phil helped by pushing the dirt that Jess had cleared into the creek. It wasn't a cavern but it had a dry base and the overhang would protect them for now. Jess helped Phil into their alcove and raised his splinted leg up on a moss-covered rock. He then took off his pack and dug in to find his water bottle with the filter cap and two granola bars that he shared with Phil.

Jess was wet and Phil even more so. Jess rummaged through his backpack again and got his sleep sack, which was thankfully packed in a watertight bag. After taking off their soaked shirts he spread the blanket over Phil. It was then that Jess realized that his walkie-talkie was not only wet, but also bashed in. The walkie-talkie was water-resistant but the dent had allowed water to seep inside of it. The grim reality slapped Jess that now he had to get his team to safety without any outside help.

Jess got under the silver spread with Phil so they could absorb each other's body heat. If the fire hadn't been so close he knew he would have had to worry about hypothermia also but the fire was throwing off enough heat that they remained warm. The long night hours ticked slowly by, Phil was slipping in and out of consciousness He was in a ton of pain and Jess felt bad for him. He continued to make him drink water and gave him more Advil. Jess soaked his shirt in the creek until it was icy cold and then he gently wrapped it around Phil's splinted leg hoping to help alleviate some of the pain and take down the swelling. Phil was tough and didn't complain once. Sometimes he would jerk awake crying out in pain, but that was all the emotion he showed. Jess was proud to have him on his team.

The night dragged on and the fire around them started to die down from lack of fresh wood.

The wind continued to whip through the trees still standing and Jess could smell the rain as it started to find its way through the fire to the ground. Jess saw a fat raindrop hit the water next to him and within seconds a deluge followed, blanketing the area. The fire hissed and snapped as the welcomed onslaught of water soaked the angry blaze. Steam rose from the trees and ground as the rain suffocated the bright hot flames. Jess pushed in as close as he could to Phil to stay dry but it wasn't much use. The rain continued its assault for the rest of the night. Then, miraculously, as if on cue, it stopped when dawn broke, leaving tendrils of smoke spiraling into the sky.

Jess checked Phil who was thankfully sleeping and then he left their little hollowed out safe area. He took his damp shirt off Phil's leg and put it on before he picked his way up the creek, calling out to his team. With each answering 'here' Jess sent up a thank you to the heavens as he sought them out. Charred bodies of trees blocked the creek and Jess had to carefully maneuver around them looking for his unit. The last group he found was Dusty and Bess who were coming out from a deep thin crevice in a rock formation. Dusty looked pale and Jess saw that he had his arm in a makeshift sling.

"You okay?" He asked Dusty.

"Yea, hurts like a mother but I'll live."

Jess ushered his team back to where he had left Phil and he made everyone drink and eat before he issued his next plan of action.

"We need to find a spot where we can be seen. I know they'll start looking for us now that it's light out. My walkie-talkie is broken so we're on our own. The fire is, for the most part, out where we are but it could still be intense somewhere else. Also remember there are still hot spots. As we walk keep your shovel handy and throw dirt on anything still smoldering."

The team packed up their gear and then hefted Phil up again. Dusty even helped by using his good arm to hold Phil's leg up. The team walked, under Jess direction down the mountain at an angle. He had seen a service road on his map that was about five miles away and that's what he was aiming for. The terrain was rough and it was slow going. They broke to rest often and Jess didn't push them. They were all alive. Phil was still a major concern though. Dusty was handling his injury well so he let his team dictate the pace and by late afternoon they had made it to the road.

As they trekked towards the road the team didn't notice any new fires and they all hoped it was under control everywhere. When they finally reached the small dirt road they saw that the fire hadn't even reached it. Jess had the team set up camp. There was just enough of a clearing above them that if a helicopter went over it would see them. Luke and Denny offered to walk down the mountain and look for help but Jess told them not yet. It was safer if they stayed together.

Just when the sky darkened to the point where Jess thought they would be spending their third night on the mountain a whoop, whoop, whoop sounded above them, which Jess knew was helicopter blades. Jess lit a flare but held it in his hand, not wanting to start any new blazes. A spotlight from the chopper fell on their upturned faces. His team gleefully jumped up and down, high-fiving each other, as the chopper landed about 100 yards further up the road where there was more room to land.

The chopper took four of them at a time. Phil, Dusty Bess, and Ben were the first ordered to go. Jess told the chopper pilot to radio ahead that they needed an ambulance for Phil and Dusty. The chopper took off and forty-five minutes later returned for Jess, Denny, Jeff and Luke.

Chapter 33

Kit

Kit had stayed on her couch all-night hoping the news would interrupt the mindless shows she was staring vacantly at. The only recent news she had heard was when the breaking news anchor recited the names of the seven smoke jumpers on Jess' team that were missing. Kit listened as she heard each name and when she heard Bess' name jealousy pounded, unchecked through her system, causing her to run to the bathroom to vomit. That unwelcomed piece of news was the last thing she had heard before she had fallen asleep.

The next day Kit picked herself off the couch and made some coffee. Her stomach was still tender so she nibbled on dry toast. She needed to shower; Mr. Peterson was coming at 9:00 am so she took the world's fastest shower and didn't bother drying her hair. She didn't want to miss any news. She spent the day trying unsuccessfully to keep busy and not think anything horrible had happened to Jess and his team. Finally Kit was able to retire to her apartment.

She plopped down on her sofa her tears that she had been held at bay all day ran freely. As Kit tried in vain to clear her eyes so she could watch the news a flashing banner ran along the bottom, Missing Smoke Jumpers team found, all alive. Kit sobbed uncontrollably.

She listened to the anchor that the missing smoke jumper team had been found alive and that the most severe injuries were a broken leg and a broken wrist. Kit could see that the person with the broken leg was not Jess. She watched file footage as a man on a stretcher and Dusty were taken from an ambulance and brought into an Emergency room. The anchor sent the viewers to the on-site reporter.

The reporter standing in front of the emergency room doors relayed to the viewers that the team had escaped the out of control fire and had found refuge while the fire had raged out of control around them. They had walked to safety where a search and rescue chopper found them. The reporter commented that the team was currently receiving medical attention inside and they all credited their leader Jess Ryan with bringing them home safely.

The local stations were still interrupting the scheduled programs with updates. The fire was now thankfully contained. It had been derailed with the heavy rain that had pelted the region for hours. Kit fell asleep knowing Jess was alive, but that there was a good chance he wasn't hers to love anymore.

The news the next morning was all about Jess and his team and the efforts from everyone involved that helped battle the fire. Kit watched for any pictures of Jess and his team but the only news she heard was that they were heading home. At noon Mr. Peterson was finally picked up and Kit stood at her door watching the car pull out. She stared at the quiet street; an empty, lonely feeling settled over her so encompassing it scared her. Kit had to do something. She could not continue to sit and watch the news, to wait for a call from Jess that may not come, ever. Kit wanted to talk to Jess and it physically hurt her to think he may not want to talk to her. She pushed away the heinous thought that maybe he had even hooked up with Bess. All because she had left, pushing him too far.

Kit knew one thing and clung to it; she loved Jess, no matter what job he had, no matter how many times he'd be in danger, she loved him and any time spent with him would be a blessing that she needed to cherish. She had to tell him. He may not even give her the chance to explain, but she had to try or she'd regret it the rest of her life.

Kit ran back upstairs and got her car keys and drove to Jess' house. She didn't even know when he'd be home or even if he'd come home right away. She didn't care, he'd have to come home sometime and when he did he'd have to talk to her. He may tell her to leave but she had to see him, she had to apologize. Kit had the key and the alarm code for his house and she could have waited inside but for some reason she didn't think that was appropriate, especially if he was going to break up with her.

His car wasn't in the drive when she got there and for some reason it relieved her that he had not been home and just not calling her. Kit sat on his front porch with her back to the front door and stared down the darkening driveway. She hadn't brought her phone with her on purpose. She didn't want Jess to have the opportunity to break up with her by a call or text. She hoped he'd give her a chance to explain and she realized even her lame excuse for running still might not be enough to salvage their relationship. So Kit continued to sit at his front door, waiting and praying that he would forgive her.

Jess

The team had been exhausted after they were checked over and eventually cleared to leave the hospital. Phil had not been released and Bess had volunteered to stay with him. The fire was contained and Jess' team had been dismissed with hearty praise and the promise of commendations. The Fire Marshal asked Jess to stand in on a press briefing and Jess reluctantly agreed. He wondered if Kit would see it, if she even cared. Afterwards his crew was driven back to the motel where they had been able to shower and change before they were taken back to Denver airport. Jess and Dusty said good-bye to the men and were put on the first plane heading to Hayden.

They arrived at Hayden at a little after 5:00 pm. It had been a long day after an even longer night. Dusty's girlfriend burst into tears when they walked through the door and Dusty soaked up the attention. That boy was getting some tonight Jess though. Jess was proud of Dusty and how he had worked hard, never complaining about his wrist and how he still managed to pull his weight while he was injured. He wished he had come home to that kind of welcome. Instead he was driving home, alone.

Jess was tired as he sunk into his jeep. His thoughts were all about Kit now. He really wanted to talk to her. If she wanted to break up with him she would have to tell him to his face. He drove the forty minutes to her house and saw that her car wasn't there. His first thought was that maybe she was still at Colt's. He also thought she could be in Steamboat simply running an errand. He thought about waiting for her, forcing her to talk to him. Problem was he was exhausted and he wasn't sure where she was. For all he knew she was still with Colt. Hoping that maybe Colt had called him, Jess drove home, up the mountain to his cabin and his cell phone, praying it held information about what was going on with his woman. It was after 6:00 pm when he pulled down his dirt drive.

Chapter 34

Kit's head lifted off her knees. She heard the car engine before she saw it. Jess's jeep emerged from the aspen tunnel hugging his drive. The dirt and gravel spitting out from under his tires pinged unpredictably matching Kit's overwrought emotions. She could see his form through the windshield as he parked next to her car. Kit stood her body stiff from sitting for so long, her stomach was in knots, and her heart was pounding inside her.

Jess saw Kit's car parked near his barn. He first felt relief that quickly changed to apprehension. A movement on his porch drew his gaze. His eyes focused on a small form folded up against his front door. 'Kit,' he whispered to himself. Jess noticed how hesitantly she moved. He watched as she shakily left her sitting position to stand, her hands wiping unconsciously against her peach shorts, her body language screaming that she was ill at ease. Jess sucked in an uncomfortable breath. He knew this might not go the way he hoped. He was relieved she was at his house that she was back from Colt's, but why she was here caused his heart to thud nervously.

Kit hesitated, she was nervous waiting for Jess's reaction to her being there. If he rejected her she wasn't sure if she'd be able to forgive herself for pushing him away. She knew this was all on her. If he broke it off, it was her doing. She gulped down the emotions that clogged her throat. Her hands rubbed her crossed arms as she unconsciously hugged herself.

Jess got out of his car leaving his duffle in the back. His eyes never left her. He couldn't get a read on her; he had always been able to know what she was thinking. The fact that she was closed off to him now sent tentacles of fear rippling through him. Kit saw that he had scratches on his face and that he looked weary. Jess remained unmoving outside his car door as he stared at Kit. She was so beautiful it made his heartache. He saw how she looked like a deer caught in headlights, her large eyes searching his, her lower lip trembling and her normal cheerful smile noticeably absent. Her blue eyes were rimmed red and puffy and Jess' heart pained with the fact that she had been crying.

Kit stiffly walked down his front steps and stood staring at him, a questioning look in her misty eyes. Jess moved slowly walking towards her, his mind telling his body to grab her and never let her go. Kit couldn't wait any longer; if he pushed away she'd at least know. She ran to Jess and wrapped her arms around his neck burying her face in his shirt. She waited for him to push her off him and when he didn't she began to sob, her small shoulders shaking violently.

"I'm so sorry Jess, so, so very sorry."

He could barely understand what she was saying with his shirt muffling her words. Jess enclosed her protectively in his arms and held her tightly against him. She was sorry? She wasn't here to break up with him! The stress and emotional demons he'd been fighting washed off his body and he sagged in relief. Jess buried his face into her neck murmuring, "Baby, baby, baby." Repeatedly trying to calm her, trying to calm himself.

They clung to each other for minutes and not until Kit stopped crying and was down to a few errant sniffles did Jess finally pull back. He palmed her cheeks using thumb to wipe off a tear.

"Kit I have to sit down I'm beat." He searched her eyes for clues of what she was thinking and saw frightened pools of blue.

Kit nodded, she still didn't know how he was feeling, what he was thinking. Unchecked emotions ran through her, like butterflies with iron wings, they slammed inside of her. She felt panicky and prayed she wouldn't pass out. Jess kept his arm around her waist, holding her against his side as they walked inside. Kit puddled into him, craving the contact, recognizing it could well be the last time he touched her.

Jess unlocked his door up and looked down at Kit who stood frighteningly still next to him.

“Why didn’t you wait inside?” He asked softly.

“I didn’t want to assume...” She couldn’t finish her sentence it was too painful.

Jess disengaged the alarm and walked to the couch holding Kit's hand. He wearily plopped down pulling Kit on his lap so she straddled his hips.

“I thought you were here to break up with me.” Jess said suddenly tired. His hands were resting on her hips, and he realized just touching her calmed him.

Kit shook her head. “No. Are you going to break up with me? I deserve it if you do.” Kit whispered so softly he barely heard her.

“No.” He bit out tersely. Kit tensed on his lap frightened by his tone but relieved by his words. Her shoulders sagged in relief and tears pooled in her eyes again. Her lips were quivering. Jess took control of the conversation.

“Kit I love you. When you love someone that doesn’t go away overnight. I just don’t know why you rabbited. I'm not happy you left, again, without telling anyone where you were going. I was out of mind with worry."

"Jess, I'm so sorry. I'm a big hypocrite, I'm selfish, and I'm a terrible person." Kit was disquiet. Her confession so raw and filled with such self-loathing that Jess pressed a kiss to her forehead hoping to soothe her.

"Honey tell me what happened? What made you leave?"

Kit nodded and placed her hands on his strong shoulders giving her the courage she needed to explain what a fool she'd been, hoping he'd understand.

"Jess I thought..." She sucked in a shaky breath. "I thought that because you volunteered to go into the mine and set off that blast that you didn't care for me. It sounded so dangerous. I felt like... I thought I didn't matter to you. I was powerless, incapacitated, and I started to think that if I stayed with you, that my life would be filled with nights like that one. I was so scared for you. Jess I was scared for me too. I kept thinking how awful and empty my life would be without you. If something happened to you...I had to leave. I couldn't handle it. I had to think."

Jess listened closely to everything she was

saying her justifiable reasoning breaking his heart. He could have prevented this by talking to her way back when he got her that damn scanner. He knew she'd been concerned. He realized this was on him too. It was up to him to comfort her, to alleviate her fears that had probably been building up for months.

"Baby, you do matter, you've always mattered. Me going into the mine, it was well planned. I'd never go into something of that magnitude without a good idea of the outcome."

"Jess I know. I went to Colt." She hesitated after she said that waiting for him to lose it and when he didn't she looked at him curiously.

"Why aren't you surprised?"

"He called me. He wanted me to know you were safe. I was jealous at first, but mostly I was relieved I knew where you were and that you were safe."

"Jess I'm sorry I left. I lost faith. I should have never lost faith in you."

"Why didn't you call me?" He asked.

"I did, but not until I flew back to Denver. I was too afraid you were going to break up with me and I wanted to talk to you face-to-face. When I got home you were gone. I didn't even know about the fire."

“We, my team, got called up in the middle of the night.”

“Jess if you weren’t going to break up with me why didn’t you call me?”

“Sweetheart, I did text you once, but then I forgot my phone, it’s upstairs. I was so upset, not knowing what you were thinking. You’re text was so final sounding; I was a mess. When I got the call about the fire, I forgot to pack it. I wanted to call you when I was on the plane, that’s when I realized I’d left it home. It's upstairs.”

Jess was quiet and it made Kit nervous and she searched his eyes hoping for some insight what to he was thinking. Jess sighed exhaustion pulling at him, but he had to finish the conversation.

“Kit I love you. Believe it or not I do understand why you panicked. Baby, you lost your first husband and your financial security to gambling, then, you see him killed right in front of you. You are placed in Wit Sec away from the only life you’ve ever known. I think you have lost so much that you were afraid of losing something again.” Kit hung her head. "Oh Jess you know me; maybe even better than I know myself.”

“Sweetheart, I do know you and I am head over heels, to the moon in love with you, but I can’t go through this again. I need to know if you’re in this for the long haul. I'm not leaving my job. I love what I do. I also understand if you can't handle it, my job, my life, and you want out. There are many spouses who can't deal with the pressure. I'd rather know right now, if you want out. As it is, if you walk, I'm going to be hurting for a long time." Jess ran a hand through his hair and closed his eyes briefly before continuing.

"Kit, I need to be focused when I go on a call. You are the most important person in my life; it's critical you understand that. I can't afford to be worrying that while I'm doing my job you might be packing to leave me." Kit nodded. She placed one palm on his cheek.

"Jess I promise, I swear I'm in, I'm all in. I know you need to be focused and I won't ever give you reason to think of anything other than staying safe. Just promise me, please promise me you will always be extra, extra, come home to me, no matter what, really careful."

"I promise baby. Kit don't you know that coming home to you 'is' my incentive to be extra careful. I love you."

Kit wrapped her arms around his neck and pressed her forehead to his.

"Jess I love you so much. When I was gone I felt empty, like a piece of me was missing. Colt helped me think rationally. He knew how I was feeling before I did. He ripped me. He made me see how idiotically I was thinking. I told him I couldn't live without you, yet by leaving you I was doing exactly that. Jess, I understand now why you did what you did at the mine. Volunteering like that, for a dangerous job is a part of you. It's one of the reasons I love you. You care about others so much, you will always want to help people, and I know that, I accept that. Honest to God Jess, Colt was so exasperated with how crazy I was thinking, if I hadn't decided to come back to you on my own, when I did; I swear Colt would have flown me back to you hog-tied."

Jess smiled. Yea he was going to have to send that man a bottle or something.

Jess pulled her tight to him swallowing her tiny frame in his large possessive one. Kits arms wrapping over his shoulders, her fingers feathering through his hair. He placed a soft, sweet kiss on her lips.

"Can you spend the night?" He asked and Kit nodded.

"Jess, I missed holding you at night. I don't think I've slept since I left."

"Yea, I missed holding you too. Kit I missed everything. I missed talking to you; I missed having someone to come home to you. I missed you. I missed us."

"Oh Jess," she tenderly whispered. "So you accept my apology?"

"I do. I need to apologize you too."

Kit looked at him not understanding why he would say that.

"I knew you were concerned about my job when I bought you that scanner. I should have forced you to talk to me back then. I knew you had questions. I knew you were worried. I didn't want you thinking about me being in danger, so I avoided talking to you about it. I realize had I talked to you, we could have possibly averted this whole mess."

"I could have initiated that conversation too Jess. I have been feeling so frightened. I didn't understand how much though until that night. Jess, I want you to know I'm proud of you. I am in awe of you."

"Baby please, I just want you to love me."

"I do Jess. I do."

Jess lifted Kit off his lap so she stood in between his legs. Kit reached out both her hands to his and helped him up off the couch.

"Jess where's Lulu?"

"I called away so suddenly that my Dad came and got her."

"Why didn't he bring her to me?"

"If you and were done Kit I couldn't handle seeing you. I thought it best my parents hold on to her."

"Oh Jess I'm so sorry." Kit said remorsefully.

They walked upstairs with their arms around each other.

In the bedroom Kit turned to Jess and as she stared into his eyes. She untucked his collared shirt then slowly began to unbutton it starting at the top. Her eyes stayed on his as she felt her way from button to button. Jess let her take control. His arms were heavy, fatigued and hung at his side, his legs held him upright but just barely. His bed stood only a few short steps away from where they stood. He was bone weary, but the greater need for Kit's touch outweighed the need for sleep. Kit got to the last button and gently peeled his shirt from his shoulders looking down to his magnificent chest. She gasped and her eyes opened wide in horror. Jess' chest was covered in angry purple and blue bruises. Jess realized what she was seeing.

"Kit..."

"Jess, Oh Jess." Her whispered words were choked with concern. She pressed tender kisses to the awful marks on his chest and stomach. Jess stood still, her caresses breathed life into his weary body. Kit moved behind him to pull the shirt from his shoulders and down his arms that still hung at his sides. On his back Kit saw more bruises, large and small, splashed grotesquely against his tanned skin. He'd dropped weight since she'd seen him last and she felt helplessly guilty that she had been to blame for some of that.

"Oh Baby." She whispered as her fingers traced one of the larger angry purple areas on his side. Tears trickled down her face and Jess felt them on his back as she softly pressed her lips to his battered body.

"Kit, don't. Honey, please don't cry."

Kit continued to pay gentle attention to his back before she moved around to his front again. She reached for the snap on his jeans and cautiously peered up to his face, hoping to see reassurance in his eyes. She needed to know he was okay with her touching him. She still felt out of sync with him and it was breaking her. Kit's eyes were wet with tears and when he still hadn't touched her she broke the awkward silence as she unsnapped his jeans and then took a step back.

"Can I touch you? Do you not want me too?"

Jess cocked his head almost as if he didn't understand what she had said.

He then realized that she thought he wasn't actively participating because he didn't care if they were together or not.

"Oh Baby, no, I mean yes." He whispered quickly. He stepped to her and put his arms around her and she heard him push out a long breath. "I thought you needed to be in charge, to see that I'm physically okay."

Kit frowned looking from his face to his battered body.

"Well, mostly okay." He smiled tenderly at her. "I love you touching me. I've missed it. I am tired though and to be honest I'm nervous I won't be good for you." He told her honestly.

Kit pressed against his chest careful to not hurt him the springy hair in the center softly caressing her cheek. "We don't have to do anything Jess, I just want to hold you, I need to hold you."

"Back at you honey. Let's undress and get into bed, my legs are like Jell-O."

They quickly undressed. Kit kept her back to him as she took off her tee and shorts, for some reason she was feeling apprehensive. When they climbed into his bed, both from different sides, Kit saw him grimace in pain. She pulled the covers up past her chest and lay on her side, not touching him but facing him. Jess lay on his back, the sheet over his hips; he turned his head so that he could look at her.

"Baby please tell me you're not going to remain that far away from me? I want to touch you." He smiled so sweetly that her heart melted.

Kit's original fears started to evaporate. She scooted over to him and he stretched out his arm so she could put her head in the nook under his shoulder. Kit placed her hand on his stomach and trailed her fingers up and down his chest. Jess leaned down and kissed the top of her head.

"I just need to sleep Hun. Then your body is mine." Kit's body hummed hearing his heady words.

.

Jess watched Kit move her hand off his chest and slide it under the covers. Jess' manhood stirred just envisioning what she was touching because it was not him. When she brought her hand back up from underneath the sheet Jess could see they were glistening. She looked into his eyes mischievously and licked the juices off her two fingers. Jess' body roared to life and he croaked out. "Oh baby that's so not fair." He smiled at her sexy grin.

"Jess, I need you." Kit said as she rose onto her elbow and slowly situated her body so she was on her hands and knees above him. "I'll do all the work. I promise."

Jess groaned but his eyes twinkled as he smiled up into her beautiful face. Kit moved above him sensually, careful to keep her weight off his bruised body but excited to please him. Jess moaned and Kit's female bits responded eagerly when she realized it had been a sigh of pleasure. They detonated together, writhing against each other, their blissful joining leaving them breathless and liquid.

Kit fell off to Jess' side still cognizant of his battered body and Jess pulled her snug against his side.

"Kit I don't think I've loved you more than I do at this moment. That was perfect."

"I love you too Jess. I am so sorry I left. It's going to eat at me for a while. I probably need to apologize to Bud and Mikey D too."

"When the time's right you can. Right now I want you all to myself."

"Jess will you tell me sometime about the mine and the fire?"

Jess thought about her question for a second before answering. “I will always be honest with you love. If you want to know what happened I will tell you. I don’t want you to be afraid again. I told you I wouldn’t be able to handle you leaving a third time. I just can’t.”

“Oh Jess I won’t. I get it. I will earn back your trust, you’ll see. Part of the reason I love you so much is because of the man you are. Your job is part of you. I love all of you. I know I’m still going to worry, that’s not going to change. I know how good you are at your job. How hard you’ve trained. I won’t leave...” Her voice trailed off.

Jess peered down at Kit who was biting her lower lip.

“What?”

Kit shook her head.

“No way women, tell me.”

“I was thinking I won’t leave unless, of course, you want me too because you find someone else. I don’t think I could stay here. I couldn’t watch you be with someone else.”

“What made you say that Kit?” Jess wasn’t annoyed just surprised. He’d never given her reason to be jealous after the whole Bess thing. Then it dawned on him. She knew Bess was on his team.

Kits eyes were down focused on his chest again as she gently traced his bruises.

"Bess?"

"I know she's on your team, Jess."

"Oh honey there is nothing there you will ever have to worry about. You know she helped me find you in Vegas right?"

Kit nodded.

"The Commanding officer asked if she and her partner Phil, the guy that broke his leg, could be assigned to my team. I figured since she'd risked her job with what I asked her to do, we were even. When we met up at the airport that first day she thanked me and asked about you. She knows to keep it professional. I think she may like her partner Phil."

"Oh, okay that's good, I guess."

"When you were with Colt did you have feelings that I should know about?"

"No." She giggled. "When Iwe walked into a restaurant he had his hand was on my back. I realized how the woman in the place looked at him practically drooling. It was such a reality check. I saw how they wanted to be in my shoes and all I wanted was to be back with you. It was probably, in that instance, that I realized I would never be happy with anyone other than you Jess, ever."

"Oh babe, that's a good answer."

Kit smiled and leaned up to give his lips a delicate slow kiss. "I love you Jess."

Jess smiled down at her and tucked her against him. They were asleep within minutes.

During the night Kit and Jess had moved unconsciously in their sleep so they were spooning, which was usually how they slept. Kit was wedged firmly up against Jess's front, her head resting in his outstretched arm. Jess's other arm draped over Kit's waist holding her one hand against her stomach. Rays of light filtered in through the window landing on Jess's face. He reluctantly opened his eyes and then looked over his shoulder at the clock, which read 10:15. They had slept for over twelve hours. His body answered as he felt Kit's soft body pressed against him responding to her sexy curves, her softness, and her light lavender scent.

He was still sore but now he was rested. Kit stirred pressing back into him, soft mewling sounds escaped her puffy lips as he brought her awake with his touch. Kit extended her neck back and turned it seeking Jess' mouth with hers. Jess closed his lips over hers and stroked his tongue against hers matching the maddeningly evasive circles that had her squirming.

Kit was now fully awake and so aroused she had to stop kissing him so she could continue breathing.

“Jess, Jess.” She moaned desperately. Jess was rock hard. He had let Kit take him last night but this morning he needed her in almost a primal way. Last night was sweet; they made love because they needed to be close and gentle with each other. This morning Jess wanted rough, fast and consuming. He needed to own her.

This time they made love feverishly. They were starved for each other and their bodies reacted hungrily.

“God yes.” Kit moaned.

Kit felt like her body was being zapped with an electrical charge keyed on her most sensitive bits. She was breathless from the possessive onslaught.

Kit convulsed underneath him for the second time. Her hips bucked and her eyelids sizzled with the adrenalin surge that rocked her entire body. Not to be left behind Jess thrust forcefully into her one last time, holding his pelvis tightly against her opening as he shot into her over and over, roaring her name. He came with such force that he felt light-headed.

Jess took her legs from his shoulders and fell on top of Kit with a groan. She wrapped her arms around him holding him against her, her cheek pressed against his chest. His face wedged in her neck. They were both breathing hard, shiny with sweat and neither even attempted to speak. Jess rolled off of her and pulled her possessively against him. Kit cuddled into his strong arms leaning her head on his shoulder. They fell back to sleep lying on top of the rumpled sheets entwined in each other's arms.

Kit woke up warm, feeling safe and well rested and most importantly wrapped in Jess' arms. She peeked over Jess' shoulder to the digital clock and gasped at the hour shining back at her. Jess had woken up too. "What?" he asked sleepily when he heard her gasp.

"I have to go. It's 2:00 I have Dodger, a new dog, coming later today and Mrs. Channing is coming at 3:00." Kit started to lift from the bed and Jess pulled her back against his chest.

He eyes gleamed as he pulled her down for a slow, languid, sinfully sexy kiss that left Kit weak and needy.

"Jess..." She said breathlessly.

"I know baby. Just want you thinking of me when you leave."

"Oh Jess if you only knew how much I think about you. It's almost scary. You might run for the hills."

Jess chuckled. "I have to disagree, Hun. Nothing short of you leaving me again will ever make me run for the hills."

"Then we are probably stuck with each other because I'm not planning on ever leaving you again." She wiggled against him and he groaned.

"If you plan on being home by 3:00 we cannot start this."

Kit laughed and kissed him quickly before leaving the warmth of his arms.

Chapter 35

Kit left Jess who was still relaxing in his bed. He told her that he was going to call his team to follow up with them, run some errands, stop by the station house and then pick Lulu up from his parent's. Before she had left he had pulled her back onto the bed to sit beside him, where he was propped up against his headboard.

His hand held hers and he sweetly kissed the back of it. “We’re good right Kit?”

Kit smiled at him gently. “We’re good Jess, maybe even better, you know?”

“Yea, I’m feeling that way too. It’s like we are starting over, we’re new and... I don’t know fragile.”

“Fragile?” Kit repeated. “I don’t want fragile Jess. Fragile means it breaks easily.” Kit sounded sad.

“Then that’s the wrong word sweetheart. I feel closer to you now.”

"Me too. How bad is it that I'm already dreading walking out your front door?"

Jess smiled. "Can I come over later?" He asked her tenderly brushing a strand of hair behind her ear.

"Jess are we back to that stage of our relationship? I want you with me always. I like how we spent all our free time together before. You're my best friend." Kit hesitated. "But I never want you to feel like I suffocate you. I want you to want to be with me."

"Oh darlin', I loved spending all my free time with you. How can you suffocate me when you're my air?" Jess sighed. "Kit it's a bit unnerving to me how much I need you. How strongly I feel for you. I never thought I would love someone with the intensity that I love you."

"Jess..." Kit leaned into him kissed him with so much fervor that Jess hardened and swelled. Her delicate tongue sought his and stroked it firmly. She pulled back and licked his bottom lip before nibbling it tenderly. Kit kissed him again and started to leave.

"Are you leaving me like this?" Jess asked playfully as he looked down at the tent she had created under the sheet.

Kit laughed. "I promise to take care of you

later, at my house, deal?"

"Arrrhhhh." He moaned sending her a crooked smile.

After Kit left Jess took his cell from the nightstand. It was right where he had absentmindedly left it what seemed like ages ago. He pressed redial for Colt's number.

Colt answered on the third ring. "Jess?"

"Yea, hey."

"Kit okay, please tell me you've seen her?"

"Yea, but not until I got home last night."

"You've had a hell of a week brother."

"Under fucking statement of the year." Jess chuckled.

"Sooo, you guys okay?" Colt asked tentatively.

"Yea, we're solid. Thank you for that. She told me how you helped her."

"I just calmed her down and made her see something that she already knew."

"She told me that. When I got called into the forest fire I left my phone home, just forgot the fucker I was so out of sorts. She was coming unhinged by the time I saw her last night."

"Well, I'm glad you guys worked it out. She loves you Jess."

"I know and I love her too."

"Yea, I know man, you're a lucky guy, and except for her momentarily losing it she's very special."

"I know God I know."

"Don't sound so stressed man. She's back, you're together. You got it all."

"Yea, you're right. Thanks again Colt I owe you big time."

"No problem Jess, take care and take care of our girl."

"I will, later."

As they disconnected Jess thought about what Colt had said. Did he have it all? It started him thinking.

Next Jess called his team to check in on them. All of them we're good. Bess was still with Phil at the hospital but he was being released later that day and she was staying with him until they got home. They were all required to write a brief and

Jess told them to email it to their Commanding officer and to CC him in.

After the phone calls Jess showered and then sat down to write out his brief. After sending it off Jess set off for the firehouse.

The guys were happy to see him and he shot the breeze with them making sure he gave Dusty props. He left the firehouse after he picked up his schedule for the following week. Next he called Mikey D and Bud and asked them to meet him at the Coffee shop downtown. They were both free and so Jess headed over.

He arrived first and bought three coffees knowing how his best friends took theirs and then he found a table by the window. Mikey D arrived first and while he and Jess bro-hugged Bud came in. Jess and Bud repeated the bro-hug that Jess and Mikey D had just completed and then the three men sat down.

"What happened out there?" Bud asked referring to how had Jess and his team gone missing.

Jess ran his hand through his hair. He knew he'd be telling this story a few more times.

"We were setting a back fire and a crazy wind sent it back towards us. It jumped the ditch and clearing. One of my men broke his leg when a limb fell on it. We were surrounded, it was crazy, we climbed further up the mountain; fucking shit was flying everywhere. We had to carry Phil. We got up the mountain and moved around to the side where I knew a creek was. When we reached the creek the fire was practically on top of us. Everyone found cover along the riverbank. Then the rain started. It was coming down so hard you couldn't see your own hand in front of you. We rode out the fire and rain until morning. Then we hiked to a service road. The chopper found us before the sun set. Wild huh?"

"Wild? Shit Jess we were fucking going crazy." Jess realized his friends had been worried for him.

"I'm sorry guys I would have called but I was so...preoccupied when I got the call that I forgot my phone at home."

"Oh... Preoccupied, as in Kit, preoccupied?" Bud asked as he and Mikey D exchanged a look.

"Yea, Kit. Before I went to bed that night Colt called me. I probably should have called you. Kit was with him."

"What the fuck!" Mikey D spit out obviously pissed.

Jess held his hand up in a stop gesture. “No, guys it’s all good. He wanted me to know she was safe. He also enlightened me why she left.”

“Well, fucking enlighten us man.” Mikey D said gruffly.

“She thought I didn’t care for her because I had volunteered for the mine job.”

“Shit.” Bud said.

“Then if that wasn’t enough, she started to think about losing me and she didn’t know if she could handle it, you know if something happened to me.”

“It’s not easy. I deal with Krissy’s fears after every call.” Bud interjected.

“Yea.” Jess said. “We’re concentrating on doing our jobs, we don’t think about it. It’s important to remember if you got someone waiting for you at home, that they are a wreck…”

Bud finished his thought. “If you’re going to come home to them or not. Krissy tells me that all the time.” Bud added.

“Exactly.” Jess said.

“I guess I never thought about it.” Mikey D said. “But she could have told us, me, Bud, even

Krissy where she was going. You know, so we wouldn't worry."

"I know I told her."

"You've talked to her?" Bud sounded shocked.

"Yea, she must have sat at my cabin most of yesterday waiting for me. She apologized. Guys she was a mess. She thought I was going to break up with her and I was thinking she was there to break up with me."

"So you guys are okay?" Mikey D asked quietly.

"Yea, better than good. I know she's going to apologize to you guys too. I hope you accept it."

"She pissed us off Jess. She just can't leave when things get rough."

"Trust me she knows. She gets it. When she was with Colt she realized she should have never left. Then I was called away and because we couldn't talk all her fears became magnified. We're okay; we had a good serious talk. We had a good night." Jess said with a silly smile.

"You know Krissy and I talked about this. Krissy said that Kit has been alone for so long that she doesn't know what having a real friend is like.

She doesn't know much about her past life but it made sense. Kit is just starting to be a little friendly with Krissy, but she still hides her feelings. She knows Mikey and I care for her but she would never confide in us. You are the one Jess that's she's entrusted. No one knows her like you do. You're the first one to ever get close to her. The kid's been alone for a long time, probably even longer than we've known her."

"Wow that's pretty insightful. I didn't even think of that." Jess said quietly.

"Of course we will accept her apology but we will give her a little shit you know." Mikey D said.

"Okay, but just a little." Jess said. "Or I'll have to kick your ass." He said with a grin. Mikey D and Bud laughed and the usual, "You and what army?' and "Like you could." Comebacks were thrown. They both knew Jess could kick their asses, but they'd never admit that to him.

"So guys I need your help with something."

"Anything man."

"I'm going to ask her to marry me."

"Whoa, no way."

"Wow that's great. When?"

Jess then let them in on his plan and how he needed their help. By the time they left the coffee shop all three men were grinning ear to ear.

After leaving Bud and Mikey D. Jess went to his parent's house. They were hugging him like crazy and for the second time that day Jess wished he'd had his phone or at least used someone's to call his friends and his parents and let them know he was okay. Lulu was beside herself running little laps around his legs.

His Mom had just made his dad an early dinner so Jess sat at the table and picked at their food. He didn't want to eat without Kit. Jess told his parents all about the cave in, Kit leaving and then the fire. He then told them how Kit and he had had a great talk last night and they were solid. His parents grinned giving each other not so subtle looks.

"We like her Jess. We are kind of hoping you do too."

"I do. I love her." He said blushing.

His mother clapped her hands together. "Love, love? Like she's the one, love?"

"Yea." Jess laughed at his Mom's excitement. "She's the one. I'm going to ask her to marry me."

"Oh my gosh yea... Finally!" Before he could

question what she meant about 'finally' she flew out of the kitchen. His father just watched his wife with an amused smile and then clapped Jess on the shoulder. "I'm happy for you son, she's a great gal."

Jess's mom practically skipped back into the kitchen holding a small white box in her hand.

"Here, if you want this, it's yours. It was my grandmother's. I always meant for you to have it."

Jess opened the white puffy box and saw a gorgeous ring nestled against the white satin material. The ring was platinum and the main stone was a brilliant circle cut diamond. Around the diamond were tiny sparkling sapphires setting the diamond off perfectly. Jess thought the sapphires reminded him of her gorgeous blue eyes.

"This is perfect, Mom. Thanks. Wow I was dreading looking for a perfect ring for her. She'll love this." Jess stood and wrapped his Mom into a hearty hug before kissing her on the cheek.

"We hoped you'd get to use it someday."

"Yea, I was a little lost for a while there wasn't I?"

"You'd been at war son. Your Mom and I can't even imagine the shit you saw over there... We were just grateful you came home safe."

Jess nodded, he had never told anyone except the one doctor about what he had seen.

"Kit's the one that rescued you. We knew the day you had met her just by how you began to smile again. She brought you back to us." Jess' dad was looking a little emotional so Jess clapped him on his arm.

"So you want to hear how I'm going to propose?' He said changing the subject and the somber mood back to a festive one.

Kit practically floated through her afternoon. Mrs. Channing worked on a puzzle and Kit was able to do some laundry and clean the downstairs thoroughly. She daydreamed most of the day thinking about Jess. She went over all they had talked about and was feeling so lighthearted she was humming. She ran upstairs and grabbed her sketching pad and pencils. Kit hadn't sketched in weeks.

When Mrs. Channing's granddaughter came for her, Kit put down the sketch she was working on. Mrs. Channing waved good-bye and Kit had to promise her that no one else would work on the puzzle. Kit packed up her sketch and placed it on the stairs leading to her apartment. She wanted to clean the dog basement before her new client came.

Tim had recommended her to a lawyer who needed to board his dog when he took his client's out hunting and fishing.

Kit cleaned the downstairs room making sure it smelled cleaned as clean as it looked. She brushed hair off the ledges and swept and mopped the concrete steps leading to the outside-gated area. When Kit finished she saw that it was almost 6:00 pm. She hoped Jess would come home soon. She wanted to eat dinner with him.

The front door bell rang and Kit opened the door to an extremely handsome man in his thirties. A beautiful yellow lab sat next to him tethered on a turquoise leash.

“Hi, I’m Kit.” She said welcoming them inside.

The man hesitated for a second before extending his hand to her. “James. James Will. This is Dodger.” He said beckoning to the dog wagging her tail playfully at his side.

“Come on in and let me show you around.” Kit said as she shut the front door.

Kit showed them the side door that she asked they use in the future. She then walked them downstairs to the dog area. James was suitably impressed and even commented on how clean it looked. Kit walked them out the back steps and showed him the gated backyard. They were standing on the deck and James let Dodger off her leash and handed the leash to Kit.

Kit took the leash and opened the swinging gate that separated the adult day care back deck from the dog's back deck. James followed her after one last look at Dodger who was frolicking in the green grass. Kit opened the back door and led them inside to the downstairs kitchen.

"So I just need you to sign a waiver and we're good to go. How long will you be gone?"

"I'll be back tomorrow. I have her food in my car. I'll bring it in before I leave."

Kit nodded. "Great. I have food here but if she likes her own kind that's fine too." Kit produced a piece of paper and James read it quickly and signed it. He handed the pen and paper back to Kit.

"I didn't expect it to be this nice." He said honestly.

"Thank you." Kit smiled cheerfully at him.

James looked at her left hand, no rings. He smiled and pushed his dark hair back off his forehead. Kit was reminded of Jess and his nervous tell of pushing his own hair back. It made her smile.

“I’m a little surprised to see someone like you running this business.” James said tentatively.

“What do you mean?’ She asked genuinely curious and as naive as ever.

“You’re a beautiful woman. I just pictured a real granola type running a dog boarding business.”

Kit laughed. “Yea, sorry not granola.”

James laughed. He thought to himself how pretty and charming she was.

Jess had let himself in through the front door. He knew her new client was there and he didn’t want to interrupt her doing business. He walked towards the kitchen where he could hear laughter. Jess decided he would just introduce himself quickly. As he walked towards the kitchen doors he heard a male voice.

“So I don’t see any rings are you unattached?”

Jess had to hold himself back from crashing through the door but he wanted to hear what she would say.

“Sorry I am very much attached.”

Jess let out a pent up breath and walked

through the door.

"Hi." Jess said cheerfully entering the room.

"Jess." Kit said breathlessly walking to him. Jess put his arm possessively around her and placed a kiss to the top of her head.

"Jess Ryan." Jess said extending his hand.

"James Will. The Jess Ryan?" James said.

"Just Jess Ryan." Jess said humbly as the two men shook.

James looked at Kit. "Lucky man Jess Ryan." He said as he looked again at Kit. "So we good Kit?'

"Yup, I got Dodger, she'll be fine."

Kit and Jess followed James as he headed out, this time using the side door.

James jogged to his car and got out Dodger's dog food and then said he'd see her tomorrow.

When James had driven off Kit asked where Lulu was.

"I already let her out back. She and the other dog are running all over the place."

Jess turned so Kit was pressed to his front.

“So did I hear James ask if you had a boyfriend?” Jess already knew the answer but he played dumb.

“You did.”

“And?”

“And what?”

“What was your answer?” Kit knew now that Jess had heard everything and was teasing her.

“You...” She swatted his chest. “You heard what I said.”

“Yes, I did and it was a good answer love.”

Kit smiled up at him and he cupped the back of her head drawing her close so he could kiss her silly. Kit pressed against him fusing her mouth to his. Jess pulled away. “Upstairs, now.” Jess' low timbered dominate voice sent heat rushing to her woman parts. God her man was seriously panty melting.

They quickly climbed the stairs where Jess stopped to retrieve Kit’s sketchpad. He looked down at it and grinned. Kit had the bare bones of a sketch down on the paper. “For me?” He asked and Kit blushed.

“Let's just see how it comes out okay?”

"Okay."

Upstairs in her apartment they started up where they had left off earlier that day. Jess loved her with just his tender touches and Kit was a mass of quivering flesh. Kit was responding to him but she'd gotten quiet. He bent to kiss her and saw that her eyes were glistening and bottom lip was quivering.

"Jess..." She was tearing up and he needed to hold her. He cradled her against his chest carrying her into the bedroom then carefully placed her on the bed and climbed onto it with her holding her tightly. Tears were streaming down her face.

"Baby, what's the matter?"

"Jess, It's just, Oh God, Jess I could have lost you."

Jess crumbled thinking she was either talking about the cave in or the fire.

"Honey we talked about this. I'll always be safe.

"No. No. I mean I could have lost you because I left you. Oh God Jess I can't believe I even considered living without you."

Jess released a pensive breath and smiled down at her. "I love you Kit. You can't even begin to know how much. You know you saved me. Did you know that?"

Kit shook her head.

"My parents told me today that until you entered my life I hadn't smiled since coming back from Afghanistan. That you brought me back to life."

"That's sweet of them to say."

"It's true Kit."

"I guess we rescued each other Kit, because until I met you I was just going through the motions of existing. You made me feel again. God I never thought I'd feel again."

Kit pushed his beautiful straw colored hair back from his face and pulled him down for a kiss. They made love passionately still feeling the bloom of their relationship as it flowered.

Afterwards they remained quiet, each lost in their own thoughts, as they stroked each other contently. Kit was nestled in her favorite nook on his shoulder. Jess had his arms wrapped around her and his chin rested on her head.

"What are you thinking?" He asked after a few minutes.

Kit paused for a mere second. "Umm I'm

thinking I'm really, really hungry."

Jess started laughing and slapped her ass as he got off the bed. "Me too, let's go!"

Kit giggled and they cleaned up, dressed and Jess made her breakfast for dinner.

After they ate they took the two dogs for a long walk up the trail behind her house. Jess held Dodger's leash since they didn't know how she handled seeing wild animals but she was a well-trained dog and even when a rabbit bolted across the trail Dodger remained by their side.

After walking the dogs they sat out back on her deck while the fireflies sparkled magically illuminating pieces of the dark sky. Kit was cradled on Jess' lap neither of them wanting any distance between them.

"Do you have any dogs or adult clients tomorrow?"

"Not after Dodger leaves."

"Want to go on a picnic tomorrow evening?"

"Oh I'd love it."

"Okay I'll pick you up around 4:00 pm okay?'

"Perfect."

Kit snuggled back into Jess' warm chest.

"What should I make?" She asked as she mentally flipped through recipes in her mind.

"Nothing love this picnic is on me."

"You sure? I don't mind."

"Nope, I got this."

Jess smiled. He had this.

Chapter 36

Jess left Kit's house the next morning around 10 am. When she asked what he had planned for the day he told her that he had some errands to run and that he had to help his dad with a chore. Kit had hoped they could have spent the day together but she had things she had to do too so it wasn't a big deal. Kit left her house at the same time Jess did to attend her yoga class. After yoga she had a riding lesson and after that she went food shopping. She arrived back home and after showering she baked Jess his favorite cookies and then she went outside on her back deck to sketch. James came to collect Dodger and when they left Kit returned to the deck with her sketchbook.

Kit was so absorbed in what she was doing that she was shocked when she looked at her watch and saw she had only fifteen minutes before Jess would arrive. She ran upstairs and dressed in an outfit that she hoped would make Jess drool. She wore a thin cornflower blue V-neck tee shirt that hugged her breasts and to make it even more tantalizing she wore a sexy sheer bra. It gave the illusion that she was bra-less. The cornflower color of the shirt brought out the color of her eyes too. She donned a lightweight, Aztec print skirt that twirled sexily around her thighs, a simple pair of white sandals and she completed her little outfit with dangly silver earrings. Maybe a little much for a picnic but she wanted to look good for Jess. At 4:00 she was waiting downstairs on her front porch for him. Kit had half the cookies she had baked packed in a Tupperware and she had brought a denim jacket for later on.

Right at 4:00 Bud's car pulled up. Kit saw that Krissy was sitting in the front seat and Lulu and Maize were in the way back. Bud hopped out of the car as she walked towards him.

“Hey Kit, Jess asked us to pick you up. He’s running late.”

Kit tried not to let the disappointment show that it wouldn’t be just the two of them. She wished Jess had told her. Bud helped her into the car and Krissy turned around in the front seat to give Kit a giant smile.

“Hi!” Krissy said. “This will be so much fun. I love picnics!”

“Yes, so do I. Ummm, where are we going?’

Kit asked.

“I’m not sure. Bud where are we picnicking?” Krissy asked. The love Kit saw radiating from Krissy’s eyes as she talked to Bud was so palatable that the air in the car seemed charged. She wondered if she and Jess gave off a similar heady current.

Bud reached over and grabbed Krissy’s hand in his as he drove. “Oh sweetness you are just going to have to wait and see.” He then lifted her hand to his mouth and gave the back of her knuckles a sweet kiss. Kit turned and looked out the back window feeling very much the third wheel.

Kit wasn’t paying attention to where Bud was driving them. She was petting Lulu who had her head resting over the back seat and feeling like so selfish because she didn’t want to share Jess on their picnic. Krissy kept up a steady stream of conversation always including Kit and Kit tried to stay attentive but her mind kept wondering.

Bud pulled onto a beat-up dirt trail and Kit recognized it as the place where she and Jess had had their first picnic. Kit loved this spot. She still hadn’t shown Jess the sketch she had done of him here. It had been such a personal sketching of him. It was how she saw him, so handsome, sweet, sexy and dominant. It was where he had first made her come and Kit blushed with the memory. She smiled to herself as she thought of how wonderful a lover Jess was, talk about lucking out.

The car came to a stop and they piled out. Bud let the dogs out and they ran circles around the three humans, happy to be included. Kit didn't see Jess' car and although she knew he would not stand her up she felt awkward without him. Bud led the way up the trail, which was thankfully well maintained since Kit had her sandals on. Krissy was no better-off and had worn wedges.

They climbed the wooded trail, which wound to the right. After a twenty-minute hike they arrived at the breathtaking scenic overlook. Kit walked over to the rocky edge and drew her arms around her waist, wishing they were Jess's arms holding her. She panned the gorgeous view of the shadowed valley and lush green mountains. There was a beautiful blue-green lake sparkling in the distance and patches of snow that never melted dotted the steep rocky mountain slopes.

Kit heard a small plane drone in the distance and watched it as it buzzed across the pristine sky. The plane began to shoot white smoke out of its tail section. At first Kit was alarmed that the plane was in trouble but then she saw the plane changing direction and that the smoke was in fact white streams that formed letters. It was a skywriting plane. The plane dipped, turned, rolled, and wrote. Kit watched fascinated and read, as each letter appeared forming words.

Will you marry me?

Had been written across the blue September late afternoon sky. Kit sighed at the romantic proposal some lucky woman was receiving.

The plane turned in a large loop to head back the way it had just come from and Kit noticed a dark object fall from its side door. Kit gasped and watched as a rectangular shaped parachute opened, dangling a brave soul from its roped ends. The parachute zigged and zagged gracefully cutting through cloudless sky. Kit was hypnotized by how the parachute handler made the flight seem effortless. The parachute glided closer and closer and all of a sudden Kit gasped, taking an uneven step back; it was heading right towards where she was standing.

It took about a nanosecond later for her to realize the person parachuting towards her was her Jess. Kit placed one hand on her throat and her other fisted over her heart. She couldn't take her eyes off of him. She remembered that she was with Bud and Krissy and when she quickly turned around to look for them they were nowhere in sight.

Kit recognized Jess' large frame, as he loomed closer to where she was standing. She took another step back and surveyed the area around her. She was suddenly apprehensive. The bluff wasn't large, could he land here? What if he missed? A niggling of fear danced up her spine but she tamped it down. Her Jess did this for a living. If anyone could land on this grassy bluff her Jess could. Kit watched Jess, mesmerized as he skillfully worked the colorful ropes above him. He was just off the bluff and she clapped her hands delighted that she could now see his handsome smiling face.

Jess touched down using his knees to buffer the landing. His chute fluttered to the ground behind him. Jess took off his helmet and disengaged himself from the ropes. His eyes never left hers. His heart was hammering but not because of the jump but from the question he was about to ask his woman. He rid himself from his jumpsuit and walked the ten steps separating him from hopefully what would be his future. He saw that Kit stood still, watching him with a silly grin on her face.

When Jess got to within an arm's length of her he dropped to one knee and Kit gasped, her hands flying to her mouth. It was then she remembered what the plane had written in the sky. Oh my God she was the lucky girl! Jess was smiling as he reached into his pants pocket and produced a white square box. He smiled up at Kit and reached his free hand out towards her, which she promptly clasped with her own smaller hand.

"You saw what the plane wrote out right?" Jess asked her softly.

Kit couldn't speak she was too emotional so she just nodded.

"Kit I have loved you since the moment I saw you. You brought me back to life. You taught me what loving someone means. I thank God every day that he brought you here so I could find you. I would be the happiest man in the world if you would be my wife. Will you marry me?"

Kit's eyes were shiny with tears. Jess thought she looked taken back and it worried him. What if she said no? Maybe she didn't want to marry again? His chest suddenly felt tight.

Kit placed her one hand that Jess wasn't holding over her heart; which was threatening to pound right out of her chest. He wanted to marry her. They had never talked about marriage. Kit's face lit up and she bestowed Jess with one of the most dazzling, beautiful smiles Jess had ever seen. Kit nodded her head and sank to her knees in front of him.

"Jess I would be honored to marry you." She whispered up to him wrapping her hands around his neck.

Jess whooped and stood up bringing Kit with him. He opened the white box and Kit saw a stunning diamond and sapphire ring sparkling up at her. Kit looked at the ring and then gazed back up to Jess. Her grin was so wide that Jess couldn't help but quickly kiss her upturned lips. He took the ring out of the box and slid it on her left ring finger. He then kissed it as if to seal it there. Jess pulled her to him and gave her a sensuous, warm and very long kiss.

When he released her he said; "You are mine Kit. You are mine forever!" He whispered into her neck as he spun her around playfully. Kit squealed and clutched him tightly laughing at his antics. Jess left Kit for a minute while he gathered his chute and jumpsuit, stowing it safely in a bag someone had left by a tree.

"You had me worried." Jess said as he returned to her peppering small kisses all over her face.

"Why?" She asked.

"You took a long time to answer." He was beaming at her.

"I was a little stunned. We never discussed it and... We've been through so much. I didn't even know if you ever even had thought about marriage, I mean to anyone."

Jess wound his arm around her back and started walking them further along the trail that edged the beautiful overlook.

"Until I met you I never had thought about it." Jess confided in her.

"Oh, that's a good answer." She said leaning her head against his side. She stretched out her hand to look at the ring.

"This is an exquisite ring Jess. I adore it. It's different, it's beautiful."

"Like you, unique and beautiful."

Kit squeezed him with the arm she had around his waist as they walked.

When they rounded a small grouping of trees Kit saw Krissy, Bud, Mikey D and the dogs all waiting by a picnic table that had been elegantly set.

"Well?" Mikey D asked impatiently but with a teasing grin.

"She said yes!" Jess proudly told their friends.

"Thank God!" Mikey D and Bud said at the same time causing everyone to laugh.

"This is so festive." Kit said as she noticed the white linen tablecloth, a centerpiece of red roses, real silverware and plates, and silver domes of delicious smelling food.

"How did you do this?" Kit asked.

"Well, I had to be in the plane obviously so I asked Bud, Krissy and Mikey D to set this up."

"Thank you, thank you so much it's perfect, just perfect."

Kit looked up at Jess and then back to her three friends.

"I owe you guys an apology. I should have told you where I was going. I honestly didn't know where I was going at first." Jess squeezed her softly letting her know he had her.

"I was so upset, so worried that I wasn't thinking clearly. I acted selfishly. I was so confused. I'm really sorry if you were worried."

Mikey D walked up to her and held his arms out to her. Jess nudged her towards him and Kit went into his brotherly embrace.

"Kit, we care about you. We understand you've been through so much. We still don't know everything and maybe someday you'll confide in us, but we are your friends. Thank you for apologizing, we accept it." Mikey D paused and looked to Jess before continuing.

"Don't you EVER pull that shit again!" He said laughing as he placed a kiss on her forehead.

Mikey D stepped back and Kit was promptly pulled into a warm hug first from Bud and then Krissy. Everyone quickly hugged Jess too as heart felt congratulations were echoed by all.

"I'm starved." Bud announced causing everyone to laugh.

Epilogue

September 21 Wedding Day

The cool autumn air ruffled the treetops behind Jess' cabin. Their wedding day was a clear day; it was crisp, but not cold. There wasn't a cloud in the brilliant azure sky. It hadn't rained in a week so the grass was lush and not damp, making it easy for guests to navigate the backyard. Kit gazed out of the back window of Jess' bedroom, soon to be her bedroom too. Jess had offered his room up for her to dress in.

Kit's Mom came up behind her and placed her arms lovingly around her. Kit leaned back against her Mom. Her stomach churned as she fought down the threatening nausea. She had not been feeling well for a week. A few days ago when she confided how she felt to Krissy, she had suggested that Kit see a doctor. Kit realized she hadn't been to a doctor in years. She hadn't wanted to tell Jess because she knew he'd worry and would want to go to the doctor's with her but she honestly thought she had a bug.

“Are you okay honey? Your dad and I think he’s a wonderful man Kit.”

“I know Mom. I’m so lucky. I never thought I’d love anyone again and now I find I love him more than I thought humanly possible. I think I need to talk to Jess though.”

“Now?”

“Yes.”

Her Mom looked at Kit with concern written on her face.

“It’s okay Mom. I just need to talk to him.”

A knock came from the door and her Mom opened it allowing her dad to walk in.

“Perfect timing darling.” Her Mom said.

Her dad looked between his two beautiful women wondering what prompted the greeting.

“Dad can you go get Jess for me?”

“Are you having second thoughts, sweetie?” Her dad took her gently into his arms, embracing her.

"No, not at all. I just need to talk to Jess."

Her dad looked to his wife and she nodded so Kit's dad left the room to get him.

Mikey, Bud, Jess and his dad were in the downstairs office room waiting for the signal from the wedding planner that they should take their places for the ceremony. Jess wasn't nervous; he was ready, ready to make Kit his forever. He loved everything about her and he knew that their sex life would continue to flourish and that they would remain best friends forever. The past week had been a busy one. He'd been working his regular shift, picking up family and friends from Hayden Airport and making sure he had everything ready for the wedding. He'd only been able to spend a few hours with Kit and they had not even been able to scrape together some alone time.

Kit had seemed withdrawn, the last few days. Her smile was there but something was holding it back from lighting her eyes up the way it normally did. He was nervous that she was having second thought jitters and when he tried to sequester her so they could talk they had been constantly interrupted. So when Kit's dad came for him before the ceremony his heart slammed into his chest. He knew something was wrong and he flew out of the room to the upstairs.

Kit sat in the window seat looking down at

the backyard which was partially covered with an enormous white tent that housed linen draped tables and chairs. She pulled the satiny dressing robe around her small frame. Her hair and makeup had already been done and all she had left to do was put on her dress.

The door to the room swung open banging loudly as it smacked the doorstop behind it. Jess entered the room, his worried eyes seeking her out. He reached her in three hurried steps and Kit's parents quickly excused themselves as he knelt on his one knee in front of her. His face was even with hers as he knelt between her slender legs.

"Baby what's wrong?" Jess couldn't control the tremor in his voice. "You're okay right?"

"I'm more than okay Jess..." Her voice trailed off and he knew she wanted to say something.

"What? Kit you can tell me anything, you know that."

"I know Jess, it's just...the timing of this."

"Of what Kit? Please honey you're scaring the shit out of me."

"I went to the doctor the other day."

"Oh My God. You said you were okay?"

"I am...I am more than okay. I'm pregnant Jess." Jess remained perfectly still and pulled back to look at Kit's face. He was stunned. Had he heard her correctly?

"What?" He couldn't speak more than that one word.

"Pregnant." Kit repeated in a soft voice.

Kit let the words sink in as Jess remained still between her legs. His mouth hung open slightly and his expression went from shock, to thoughtfulness, to a tender smile.

"We're going to have a baby?"

"Yes."

"Are you okay with this?" Jess asked worried about why she seemed apprehensive.

"We never talked about it, but I've always wanted babies, a couple of them."

He rubbed his thumb tenderly over her jawline. "There's something else. What's bothering you honey?"

"I didn't want to marry you without first telling you. We never talked about kids. I never want you to feel trapped, you know, like I forced a family on you."

"Oh Baby, come here." Jess lifted Kit off the window seat and settled her on his lap. "Sweetheart I love you. I want it all, you, babies, and hopefully down the road, grandchildren. I want it all...with you, only with you Kit."

"Oh Jess."

Kit sniffed as she buried her head into his neck. Jess tensed as he felt her tears on his skin. He stroked her back concerned.

Kit spoke softly. "Jess, happy tears."

"Happy tears?" He repeated.

"Very happy tears."

They sat like that for a few minutes. "Jess I've missed you these last few days. I wanted to tell you but we kept getting interrupted."

"I had a feeling something was up. I'm happy Kit, really, really happy but I have to ask...How are you pregnant?"

Kit arched an eyebrow at him sending him a silly smirk.

"I mean you're on the pill."

"The doctor said that sometimes under stressful situations it's not as effective."

Jess was looking at her like he wasn't sure what to do with her. He then remembered how she'd been acting lately.

"Is this why you've been sort of distant?"

"Yes, I wanted to tell you but every time I tried we were interrupted."

"I love that you're pregnant Kit. This is a wonderful wedding day gift."

"Jess I love you. Thank you for loving me, for loving us."

Jess slipped his mouth over hers and swept inside her mouth seductively stroking her tongue with his. Their kiss heated up and when Jess pulled back they were both breathing hard. Jess gave her a panty-melting smile as he lifted them both so they were standing.

"I'm done waiting Kit, get your dress on, or don't, I don't care, just get your butt downstairs so I can legally make you mine." Kit giggled and gave him one last hug before he left the room.

Her parents reemerged and she gave them each a hug telling them everything was perfect. Her dad went back downstairs to wait for the signal and her Mom helped Kit put on her wedding dress. A few minutes later her dad came back upstairs.

"Oh sweetie you look beautiful." He said as he pulled her in for a hug.

Kit had already done the traditional white dress ordeal and although she told Jess she would do it again for him, since it was his first wedding, he had told her he would rather keep it low-key, which was what she had preferred as well. Kit had found a perfect dress in a boutique store in town. It was a cocktail length dress that fell above her knees. It was made of off-white lace, intricately patterned and very flattering to her curvy small figure. The neckline dipped down low but did not show any cleavage and the waist cinched her then flowed in an A-line shape. She wore pearl earrings and she was swept up with little curly tendrils escaping which gave her a whimsical princess look.

Her Dad stepped back and handed Kit a box. "This is from Jess."

Kit smiled and opened it revealing a shiny silver firefighter's shield with Jess' number embossed on the front. When she turned it over Kit saw it was engraved and she read what it said out loud.

Someone to come home to

"Oh my." Her mother said beaming. Kit smiled understanding the significance of that statement.

Kit handed the necklace to her Mom and unfastened the heart shaped one she always wore with their initials on it. She took off the heart shaped disk, adding it to the new necklace and fastened it around her neck. She knew she would never, ever take it off. Kit turned to her dad.

"Did you give Jess my present?" Jess hadn't mentioned it when he had been in the room so she didn't think he had seen it yet.

"Yes, just now, but damned if he'd let anyone see it."

Kit laughed wishing she could have seen Jess's face when he opened the framed sketch she'd wrapped for him.

"When he saw it was a picture he walked away from everyone and opened it alone. It must have been a hell of a picture because he was grinning from ear to ear." Her dad told them.

"It was." Kit told them but she did not elaborate nor did they press her to.

Kit had completed the sketch she had started over a month ago. It was of her and Jess in bed surrounded by rumpled sheets. They were looking at each other and Kit had captured how much they loved each other with their well-sated expressions. Their bodies were entwined. Jess was on top of hers as he held Kit's hands above her head with both of his. Jess' side and arm were gorgeously displayed showing the well-developed muscles he sported. Kit's one knee was bent and curved over Jess' thigh. Her hands were splayed tenderly on his back. You could see a swell of one breast but the nipple was hidden because it was pressed against Jess' chest. The sensuality flew off the picture. Every time Kit had looked at her completed work of art she felt her heart go pitty patter. She hoped Jess reacted the same way.

"Okay kiddo, it's time, let's do this." Kit's dad took her arm and then extended his other for her Mom. The three walked out of the room and down the stairs waiting to be cued by the wedding planner Jess had hired.

Kit looked through the glass doors leading out to Jess' backyard her breath hitching as she saw Jess waiting for her dressed in a black tuxedo. She hadn't known he was going to be wearing a tuxedo. He was hot! Her man was gorgeous and her tiny lacy thong dampened as she wantonly thought about the night ahead of them. At his side Lulu waited with a purple bow tied around her neck.

Krissy, Bud and Mikey D. and Jess' parents met them at the bottom of the steps. They all commented on how gorgeous Kit looked. Kit hugged each of them separately. Krissy was carrying two bouquets and she handed Kit the larger of the two.

Kit told her she looked lovely dressed in a stunning purple dress. Bud and Mikey D were also in tuxes and Kit complimented them on how dashing they both looked. Their bow ties matched Krissy's dress and also the beautiful elephant nose flowers that were present in Kit's gorgeous bouquet of Colorado wild flowers.

A soft piece of music was playing from an acoustic guitar and Kit watched as Jess' parents walked through the doors holding hands as they started the procession down the grassy isle in the middle of the tent. Next, Mikey D held his arm out to her mother. He gallantly walked Kit's Mom to her seat of honor. He then stood up next to Jess.

Next Bud and Krissy walked together down the aisle. Kit smiled to herself somehow knowing they would be following Jess and her down the marriage path next. They were so in love. They could hardly keep their hands off of each.

Finally it was Kit's turn to walk down the aisle. Her knees were shaking a little and her dad patted her hand as he placed it under his arm to rest on top of his forearm. He gave her a charming 'Dad like' smile and as the guitar began to strum the wedding March, they slowly walked down the aisle toward the makeshift altar. Kit's eyes never left Jess'. He stood waiting for her with Lulu, Mikey and Bud at his side. Jess smiled at her and his blue eyes were shiny with sentiment. Kit checked the happy tears that threatened to spill down her cheeks, not wanting to ruin her make up. She had never been happier.

Friends and family, well mostly Jess' family, surrounded them. His aunts and uncles and cousins, Jess' firehouse brothers and their spouses and dates, and even his smoke jumpers' team. Kit admitted to Jess she was a little unnerved to meet Bess, but Jess had assured her that she'd be fine, and that Phil had confided in him that they were dating officially now. Liz and her family were present and Lori who had finally come back from her month long vacation was there as well with her date.

What had originally started as a small wedding had blossomed into a wedding of seventy. Kit hadn't minded and because of the wedding planner Jess had hired she hadn't done anything but buy the dress.

Kit walked towards Jess who had a huge sappy grin on his handsome face. She watched him watch her. He drank in her lacy dress and beautiful smile and his heart melted knowing she was always going to be his. Kit smiled back at Jess and she knew that even when they were old and gray being near him would always leave her breathless. He was her happily ever after.

Kit and her dad stopped before the minister and Kit's dad kissed her on the cheek and shook

Jess' hand before sitting down next to his wife. Kit handed her wedding bouquet to Krissy who was standing at her left. She turned to Jess who gently captured both her hands within his. They held each other's gaze for a single sacred moment before turning their heads towards the minister.

The minister greeted the guests and then turned his attention to the couple before him. The ceremony was short; they had decided to forego writing their own vows, keeping the ceremony simple. When the minister announced they were husband and wife and that Jess could kiss his bride he did so with gusto and to the cheerful hooting of his firefighting brethren. Kit was breathless when he released her and he whispered in her ear that he loved his wedding presents. Kit smiled loving that he considered her surprise announcement a gift.

The wedding planner that Jess had hired had outdone herself. They hadn't wanted to wait to marry but Jess' parents insisted they needed two weeks to get the family in town, so they had relented and said two weeks they could handle. The food was perfect; the three-tiered cake was beautiful and delicious. The top of the cake was decorated with a man dressed like a firefighter, and a woman holding a leash attached to a German shepherd. The backyard had been transformed into a beautiful magical place, accented with hundreds of little lights.

The tables were decorated with white tablecloths and Colorado wild flowers graced the center of each table.

Kit relaxed in Jess' arms as he swayed them on the dance floor. Jess had missed Kit. Three days before the wedding her parents had descended and Kit had been promptly ensconced into the loving hold of her parents. Kit wouldn't let him sleep over with her patents at her house. They were sleeping in their trailer in her driveway, but he still wasn't allowed to spend the night. He had been busy with his family flying in from everywhere he had been called upon to shuttle them from Hayden to the Rabbit Ears Motel where they booked rooms.

The last few days when Jess had seen Kit she had acted almost skittish around him. He was chalking it up to nerves, but it still made him anxious. Now he knew why and his strong arms kept her tucked securely against his large frame. They were married, she was his forever and he was going to be a Dad. Jess could not have been happier.

Jess stopped dancing when a low voice asked if he could cut in. Kit knew that voice, Colt! Kit wasn't sure how Jess would react but he graciously stepped away from her, not surprised in the least that Colt was there. Kit eyed them both suspiciously. She had called Colt to invite him but he said he wasn't sure he could get away.

"I called him. He needed to be here." Jess told her shrugging his shoulders.

Jess moved away from them and Colt picked up Kit's hands placing them on his wide shoulders.

Kit smiled up at the man who had saved her life. "Thank you Colt." She said.

"What for little girl?"

"For saving my life. For giving me the chance to come here and met Jess; to start fresh."

"He's a good man, Kit. I couldn't be happier for you."

"I'm glad you're here Colt. You're my family you know?"

"I know sweetie."

"You clean up good." She teased him gently.

"Thank you, I'm not much for suit wearing but for you and Jess I made the exception."

"Well, thank you."

Jess walk back to them and he playfully told Colt he wanted his wife back. Colt laughed as he handed Kit back to Jess.

"Jess thank you for getting him here."

"I owe him. First he saved your life. He then put your head on straight remember? And he called me. He gets big time bro bonus points for that." Kit giggled.

They held each other throughout the song and Jess leaned into Kit placing his chin on her head.

Kit snuggled into Jess' arms and felt his cock against her stomach. She looked up at him and he smiled mischievously. "It's been a long couple of days Mrs. Ryan. I cannot wait until I get you alone tonight."

Jess and Kit stayed close relishing the intimate connect. Jess kissed Kit's forehead. 'What are you thinking so hard about Jess?" Kit asked gently.

"That I love you so much and you're going to be a great Mom."

"I love you too Jess and you're going to be a fantastic Dad."

"I'm going to be a Dad." He repeated is eyes betrayed his emotion.

Kit cupped his face with her hands. "Now you'll have two of us to come home to." Kit said touching her new little pendent.

Jess kissed her and smiled. “I love that baby.” He sighed contently, “Two someone’s to come home to.”

Zanne Sweeney a graduate from Kent State University is a teacher, and coach, who loves to write stories that she hopes her readers won't want to put down. "That's the ultimate compliment."

When she's not teaching, coaching, or writing Zanne loves to spend time with her family and fun loving friends. She is a novice photographer, a consummate sports fan, and is never without a book to read.

You can reach out to Zanne on Twitter @zanneweeney and on her Facebook like page: Zanne Sweeney - Author. https://www.facebook.com/zanne.sweeney.author?ref=hl

Other Zanne Sweeney books:

Neighbors

A Chance For More

www.ingramcontent.com/pod-product-compliance
Lightning Source LLC
Chambersburg PA
CBHW051928020726
47501CB00001B/27

9780692246580